Cartel Wars

Book 2

John Lenardon

Books by John Lenardon

Spy Cartel

The Russian Connection

Chasing Evil

Broken Legacy

Extinction Covenant

The Climate Syndicate

The Christ Parchments

The Severed Quill

The Black Quill Assassin

The Genius and the Assassin

The Extinction Assassin

The Crisis Makers

Harpers War

Red Robe Executions

The Existence Protocol

The Wildfire Syndicate

The Cartel Crisis

When Lies Kill

Cartel Wars – Book 1

About the Author

After a lifetime of traveling the world, I settled on an island in the Salish Sea. My writing room overlooks calm water peppered with sailboats and pontoon planes. Above them, eagles ride the winds like dragons, and hawks dart around the sky like drones.

I write thrillers filled with heroic, faulted, fighters who give us hope and never give up on saving the world.

Copyright

Evil Will Always Rationalize Its Own Existence.

Chapter 1

There were no lights inside the Mexican farmhouse. An old pickup truck drove down the driveway, spitting dust and smog from the back. Two cartel members sat in the front, ready to kill anyone who tried to stop them.

They pulled in front of the porch and climbed the steps to the front door, taking out their guns as they walked. One man kicked hard at the door and the old, wood frame shattered. The farmer dashed out of the bedroom, a rifle in his hands, confused by what was happening. The men didn't hesitate. They fired twice into his chest. Stepping over him they went into the first bedroom. A woman sat up in bed, the sheets pulled up to her neck as if they would protect her. Another shot rang out and she fell to her side.

They moved to the last bedroom door. A teenage girl was hiding under the bed, tears running down her cheeks. She kept her head down, praying they wouldn't find her. The men lifted one side of the bed and pulled her out.

"No!" she screamed, kicking and yelling. She knew the local cartel leader must have sent them to kidnap her.

Terror surged through her as they dragged her to the living room.

"Papa!" she screamed when she saw her father, lying in a pool of blood. She fought to get her arms free. One of the men turned to her and swung his fist across her face. The punch knocked her out. He threw her over his shoulder then carried her to the truck and they drove off.

The mother crawled off the bed, her hands smearing blood on the walls as she stumbled. She got to the phone and dialed.

"Sofia," she mumbled. "It's María Martínez. The cartel took my baby." She sobbed as she tried to speak. "They took Ana." She dropped the phone and collapsed.

Sofia dressed and raced to the farm. When she arrived she stepped over the shattered door and ran to Maria. She grabbed a towel and pressed it against her chest to stop the bleeding. The woman's eyes were locked open, but she saw nothing.

Sofia wiped her cheek with the back of her hand and checked the father. He was gone. She looked in the daughter's bedroom. There was no blood. They took her alive. As Sofia drove back to her home she anonymously called the police, then called Juan, her second in command. She knew if they didn't get to the girl in time she would be raped and then sold on the streets in Mexico City.

Her friend Juan was there when she arrived home. She explained what she saw.

"They must have taken her to the local cartel leaders hacienda," Sofia said.

"It's Saturday," Juan said. "That means they'll hold a party tonight.

"We have to get her back before they harm her."

"The hacienda is heavily guarded."

"I don't care. I promised the people we would protect them from the cartel, and I failed. We have to get her back no matter what."

"I'll call the rest of our team," Juan said. "I can have 20 or more here by noon.

"No. It'll turn into a firefight if we all go. Too many of our friends will be killed. So will Ana. I'm going to ask Cole for help."

"He's in Chicago. Will he come to Mexico?"

"He said he would. He keeps his promises."

****

Cole stirred from a deep sleep. He answered the phone on the first ring. It was more instinct than a conscious decision.

"Hello," he mumbled.

"Who is it?" Katie said, turning towards him.

"Sofia," Cole said, putting it on speaker. "What's the matter?"

"I need your help."

He swung his legs over the edge of the bed. "What can I do?"

"A young girl was kidnapped by the cartel. They killed her parents and took her to the local leader's hacienda."

"God. I'm sorry Sofia."

"I've seen this before. He locks them in a room until his next party, which is tonight. We don't have much time to get her back."

"I'll fly down with Katie. It's about a three-hour flight from Chicago. Meet me at the airport. I'll get Eve and Riker to come."

"Thank you, Cole. Please hurry."

Cole called Danni from the agency. "I need to fly to Piedras Negras in Mexico. Can you get the plane ready for immediate departure? And I need sat photos of the local cartel leader's hacienda. Get me all the information you can on the house and the area."

"I'll send it to you. Anything else?"

"Call Riker and Eve and ask them to meet us at the airport. Tell them time is tight. And tell Eve to bring her sniper rifle."

"Done. I'll go to Control in case you need me."

When Cole turned he saw Katie dressing.

"I'll get the go bags and call William to bring a car around," Katie said. "He can drive us to the airport."

"We get her back, no matter what it takes," he said.

"Damn right we will."

Chapter 2

Riker and Eve were sitting on the agency plane when they boarded. They nodded to each other, and Cole told the pilot to take off. Another man was sitting further back.

"Who's that?" Cole said.

"Clay," Eve said. "Clay, meet Cole and Katie."

"Why's he on board?"

"He's a retired DEA agent. On his last mission, he was part of a raiding party looking for drugs in the hacienda. He knows the place."

"The leader's hacienda?"

"That's the one," Clay said. "When we got there someone tipped him off and we were ambushed. Danni asked me to fly down with you. She thought I could give you information on the layout."

"Thanks for coming," Cole said. "I appreciate it."

"Me too," Katie said, smiling at him. He was tough and handsome.

Eve saw her looking and smiled at her. Both thought the same thing.

"What can you tell us about the hacienda, Clay?" Cole said.

"What you're facing won't be easy. Who are the people in Mexico helping you?"

"Mostly kids in their twenties who want a future for their country. Their parents took on the cartels years ago but too many of them were killed. The kids are taking over where they left off. Their leader is a girl called Sofia. We've been helping them when we can."

"Do they have any fighting experience?"

"Little to none. But they're smart and some of the bravest people I know."

"How do they get weapons?"

"The Russians were selling them to the Chicago Mafia, who planned to sell them to the cartels for a profit. The mafia boss's daughter stepped up and next thing we know we're stealing the shipments and giving them to the Mexican people to fight the cartels. We've been hiding them in farms and warehouses until we need them.

"The daughter sounds like a brave kid," Clay said.

"Thanks," Katie said. "But we're a team."

"It's you? Why are you helping fight Mexican cartels?"

"Like he said, my dad was a Chicago mafia boss," Katie said. "I think children should fix the screw-ups their parents caused."

"What more can you tell us about the hacienda?" Cole asked.

"It's about 6000 square feet. There's a four-foot fence around it. In the back, there's a pool where they hold their parties. He built six bedrooms that are more for hourly use than overnight stays. The bedroom closest to the kitchen is the master."

"So it's a whorehouse," Riker said.

"Pretty much. The guests bring escorts with them when they fly in. Except the leader. He likes them young, so he kidnaps them from the towns and farms. When he's finished with them he sends them to Mexico City to get them hooked on drugs and work the streets for him."

"He sounds pure evil."

"He is. He goes by Buitre. It means Vulture. We know of 26 murders he committed and over 56 he authorized. He's the biggest importer of weapons in the north of Mexico. Rumor is he's bringing in another shipment, but we don't have any details."

"Why hasn't the DEA arrested him?"

"He's the president's cousin. Our bureaucrats feel it would harm US-Mexico relations."

"You want to come on the mission with us?" Cole asked.

Clay leaned over and picked up a cane. "One of his guards put a bullet in my spine. That's why I agreed to help, but I'm afraid I wouldn't be much use in the field."

"Then we'll do our best to give the Vulture your regards."

"I'd appreciate that."

"What about entrances?" Eve asked.

"Doors in front and back as usual, and there's one on the side. To get access to the hallway you have to use the side door. There's only one guard at the door, but it's impossible to get across the yard without him seeing you.

You shoot him and other guards will hear it and come running.

"We could get Eve to act as a hooker to get inside," Riker said.

"Why Eve?" Katie said. "I could do it."

"Eve has years of experience," Riker said.

"Being a hooker?" Katie asked.

"Hey!" Eve said. "He means fighting."

"Sorry."

"If Eve can get inside she can open the door for us."

"It won't work," Clay said. "All the escorts will be Mexican. Don't underestimate these guys. They'll have no hesitation killing you."

****

Sofia was waiting when they landed. It was late afternoon and there was not much time left.

Sofia started talking before they said hi. "Thank you so much for helping. I don't know how to get her back. She's just a teenager."

"We'll always be here when you need us," Cole said. "Let's go to the farm and get the weapons we need and then drive to the hacienda. I want to see the property before it gets too dark."

"Do you think he's harmed the girl yet?" Katie asked.

"No," Sofia said. "He'll show her off to his friends first. Then he'll make sure everyone sees him taking her to his room."

"Damn, what a pig."

"We have to kill him if we get the chance," Sofia said. "He's destroyed so many lives and he won't stop."

Sofia drove them to a farm where some of the weapons were hidden. They took what they needed and began the drive to the hacienda.

"Fill us in on what you've been doing since we left," Cole said.

"We have the quick response teams working," Sofia said. "If the cartel shows up to collect extortion payments at the farms the farmer calls a number, and we race to the property. Four people to a team, like you suggested. We do the same in the stores. So far we've been stopping them."

"Have they found any of the hidden weapons?" Riker asked.

"Once. They snuck onto a farm at night and searched the barn. The farmer didn't know they were there."

"What happened?"

"The father woke up and saw their truck. He called for the team. Before they could arrive they dragged the parents and their two sons onto the driveway and made them kneel so they could execute them. The team got there just in time. There was a firefight. The two cartel members were killed and one of my team was seriously injured."

"I'm sorry about your team member," Katie said.

"We don't have enough members to guard every farm 24/7. I feel like it's my fault it happened."

"It's not your fault," Cole said. "This is a war and no matter how hard we try to avoid it; people will be killed."

Chapter 3

They arrived at the hacienda as the sun was setting. They could see servers on the deck setting up the bar and arranging chairs. A private jet landed on a runway near the side of the hacienda, and passengers disembarked. Men walked to the back deck laughing and yelling, girls clinging to them. The leader greeted them, and the servers quickly brought them drinks. The escorts sat beside them or got in the pool.

Music blasted through the night air as the party progressed. Cole wanted them drunk before they went in.

"I count six guards outside, and I can see at least two through the deck doors," Riker said. "Another guard is watching the plane and one on the side door."

"How do we go in?"

"Our best bet is the side door. We take the guard out and go in that way."

"If you shoot him they'll hear the gunshot," Sofia said.

Cole opened a bag in the trunk and took out a compound bow and arrows. "He's about 50 feet from the fence. After I drop him I run for the door with Riker and Sofia. Katie and Eve are back up. Everyone put their earpieces in."

"One last thing," Riker said. "If we don't come out in 15 minutes, leave. Don't come in looking for us." He looked at Sofia and Cole. "You ready?"

They ran in a crouch to the fence. Cole loaded an arrow. He stood and drew back the bow. The guard saw him. He raised his rifle to fire. Cole released the arrow and instinctively loaded another one. The arrow ran true, hitting the man in the shoulder. He fell back against the wall, but he didn't drop. He raised his rifle again. Cole released another arrow. The second one hit his heart. The man sunk to the ground, not moving. Cole dropped his bow and took out his handgun.

They jumped the fence and ran to the door. He opened it a crack and peered inside. They were at the end of a hallway with doors on either side. They moved to the one closest to the kitchen. Before they could get open the door a girl walked by the hallway. She spotted them and stopped.

Sofia put her finger to her lips asking her to stay quiet. The woman looked at her, then at the bedroom door. She had been to parties here before and knew the Vulture would have a young girl in the bedroom. She turned and walked back to the deck.

Cole looked around the corner. She was talking to a guard and pointing at the hallway. The guard waved to one of the other guards and they dashed toward them. Cole nodded toward the bedroom door and Riker and Sofia went inside. Cole aimed around the corner and fired at the guards. He hit one in the chest. The other man fired a burst at Cole. The sound of screaming could be heard over the music. More guards began running into the house.

Cole ran into the bedroom. The girl was cuffed to the bedpost. Sofia cut the cuffs and helped her off the bed, trying to calm her. Cole and Riker moved a dresser in front of the door and then dragged the bed in front of it to brace it. The guards fired through the door and then began trying to smash it open. It held for now.

"The Mexicans are running for the plane," Katie said through the earpiece. "The Vulture is with them."

"Let's get the girl out tonight. We'll get him later."

Riker looked out the only window at the back of the yard. He used his gun butt to smash the glass and clear the shards. A bullet hit the frame, splintering the wood. Riker ducked back.

"Eve. Take out the guard at the back of the house," Riker said.

Eve looked through the scope of her sniper rifle. She lined up on the man beside the wall. He was creeping closer to the window. Another man appeared on the opposite side.

She fired at the first man, the bullet piercing his neck. She aimed at the other guard. He was running back to the side of the house to find cover. As he was about to round the corner she fired again, hitting him in the back of the head.

"The yard is clear," Katie said.

Sofia and the girl climbed out the window and ran for the fence. Riker climbed out next and stood beside it, watching for guards. Cole fired bursts at the bedroom door and then dove through the window. They ran for the fence.

Katie helped the girl over and took her to the SUV. “She’s safe,” she yelled.

A guard ran around the corner of the house. He brought his rifle to his eye, aiming at Cole. Eve fired first. The bullet pierced his forehead. She kept looking for more guards. As soon as the others were in the car she ran to it, and they sped away.

As they drove toward town they heard the plane accelerating down the runway. It banked and flew low over their vehicle. Ana held Sofia’s hand. She couldn’t stop crying. Her parents were dead. Her life will never be the same. Sofia knew at some point her sorrow would turn to anger. She would be there to help her.

They dropped Ana off at her aunt’s and continued to the airport.

“I want to thank you guys for coming,” Sofia said.

“We’re not done yet,” Cole said. “The Vulture will seek revenge when he gets back to his hacienda. We killed some of his guards and made a fool out of him. He’ll kill as many people as he can to make his cartel believe he’s still strong.”

“He won’t return for a couple of days,” Sofia said. “He’ll wait until they remove the bodies and clean the blood. He’s terrified of germs. And he’ll want the bullet holes repaired. I was told he believes he’s invincible and this sort of thing makes him feel he’s not.”

“Then we have two days to stop him before he starts his killing spree.”

"I saw this happen when the DEA tried to arrest him. He's going to bring in as many cartel members as he can. My team can't take on experienced cartels in a firefight."

"I agree, and I'd like to avoid people getting killed. I have an idea."

"What?" Sofia asked.

"I'm going back to Chicago to talk to the agency. I'd like it if you came with me. You should see what we do, and I'd like you to meet someone."

"Are you sure, Cole?" Riker said. "I respect Sofia, but she's not cleared to see Control."

"Would you trust her to protect you at all costs if it came down to it?"

Riker looked at her and nodded. "From what I've seen, yeah."

"Then she's cleared. We have two days to get back here. Let's go."

Chapter 4

William was waiting by the car when the plane landed at Chicago Midway.

"I'm glad none of you were hurt, sir," he said.

"Thanks William. We'll stop at the Museum before we go to control. This lady is Sofia. Sofia, William is our support at the museum."

He held the door for her. "I've heard many good things about you, Sofia. Welcome to Chicago."

"Thank you."

The drive was short, and Riker and Eve stayed in the car. After Sofia got out she looked up at the building. "You live in a real museum. I thought it was American slang for an old house."

"I bought it from the last Director of Control," Katie said. "Cole and I live here. You can stay with us until we return to Mexico."

"When Sofia walked into the main lobby she stopped near the door. She ran her eyes over the giant T-Rex skeleton."

"Is that a real skeleton?"

"Most of it," Katie said. "They added a few missing bones."

Sofia kept her eyes on the bones as they walked under it. They took her to an elevator at the back of the room and went to the apartment on the top floor. The doors opened to a luxurious apartment filled with antiquities and art.

"Wow. Americans live strange lives."

"If Americans knew we lived here they'd also think we live strange lives," Katie said.

Katie showed her a bedroom she could use, and they dropped off their bags. William drove them to a downtown high-rise building.

"William. I'm going to need your help on this mission," Cole said. "Can you come in with us so we can update you?"

"Of course, sir."

The elevator doors opened to a floor of desks with people working on computers. Large monitors shared a wall with clocks showing the times in major cities throughout the world. Offices ran along the far end and all the windows were covered.

"This is the agency command center, Sofia," Cole said. "One floor above is the apartment where Eve and Riker are staying."

"We'll drop off our bags," Eve said. "Come up when you're finished. I'll have drinks ready."

"William, you already know about the agency," Riker said. "Want to come up for a drink with us while we wait?"

"Certainly."

"The agency we work for is called Control," Katie said. "It was created by a wealthy man who lost his daughter in a kidnapping. His guilt at not being there for her hit him hard, so he talked to his equally wealthy friends. They set up the agency and hired contractors like us to help people who need it."

"Are you part of the government?" Sofia asked.

"No," Katie said. "We accept missions from them, but we are independent. If we get caught they want to deny knowing us."

They took her to an office at the far end of the room and walked in. A mid-twenties blonde with straight hair and brown eyes was staring at one of her three monitors. She turned her chair and stood, extending her hand to shake.

"Hi, Sofia. I'm Danni. I've followed all the problems you've faced. I have to say I have a lot of respect for what you're doing in Mexico."

"Thank you."

"Danni is our…" Katie looked at Cole and then at Danni. "What are you?"

"Call me the librarian. I acquire the information and feed it to the people who need it."

"Is the Director in?" Cole asked.

"She's in Washington talking to the bureaucrats."

"The Director is new," Katie said. "You can meet her another time."

"What happened to the old one," Sofia asked.

"We killed her," Cole said. "Danni. The last director told me about a chemist who contracts for Control. Could you have him come here tomorrow? We need his help."

Danni sent a text. “Done.”

“Thanks, and could you come upstairs with us? I’m involving William more and he might have questions.”

The apartment was modern and could have been in an architectural magazine. Windows covered two walls revealing the lake and streets of Chicago.

“What would you like to drink, Sofia?” Eve asked.

“Tequila, please.”

She filled the glasses and handed them out, then they sat.

“We’ll make this brief, William,” Cole said.

“I’ll start,” Katie said. “My dad was the Chicago mafia boss of the Benetti crime family until his second in command killed him.”

“Do Americans always kill their bosses?” Sofia asked.

“Not as often as we should,” Riker said.

“It sounds like America is much like Mexico.”

“People are the same everywhere,” Riker said.

“I found out the Russians were selling my dad American weapons,” Katie said. “He was reselling them at a huge markup to the cartels. We decided instead of destroying them we would steal them and give them to the Mexican people to fight the cartels.”

“Where would the Russians get American guns?” William asked.

“The U.S. is the biggest arms dealer in the world. The Russians could buy weapons from countries that bought them from us. They used American weapons so the U.S. would take the blame.”

“What’s in it for the Russians?”

"They cut a deal with the Mexican president," Eve said. "He wants the Russians to wipe out the cartels in the north to help with his re-election. Russia agreed to do it if they could set up missile bases along the border."

"Why missile bases?"

"They could launch their missiles at us, and we wouldn't have time to retaliate," Riker said.

"It would be another Cuban Missile Crisis," William said.

"Yes."

"Russians and American Mafia," William said. "I never dreamed so many were involved. I assume Washington is also involved. Why don't they stop it?"

"They fear a war with Russia. They're using us because we're expendable. They can deny knowing anything about us if we're caught."

Sofia sat back and sipped her drink. She felt a massive weight of responsibility. "So all the great powers are relying on the Mexican people to fix their mess."

"It usually is the people that fix the greed and stupidity of our politicians," Eve said.

"What about our immediate problem?" Sofia asked. "The Vulture."

"We need to question him," Riker said. "He knows when the next gun shipment will be delivered."

"That's where the chemist comes in," Cole said. "He's a weapons specialist who developed a knockout gas we can use on his guards."

"We're going to fight the cartels by making them sleepy," Riker said. "This should be good."

Chapter 5

The next morning Cole took Katie and Sofia to Control. They met a man with greying hair, slouched shoulders, and eyeglasses pushed up on his head. Riker and Eve joined them moments later.

"Why was I called here?" he asked before anyone could talk.

"Could you tell us your name first?" Katie asked.

"Call me Chemist. That's all you need to know. I don't need to know your names."

"Okay, then," Cole said. "Now that we're friends I want to know about a knockout gas you developed."

The chemist looked at the faces in the room before answering. "I did create something for the military."

"Has it been tested?"

"The military tested it on prisoners. Once we were able to get it right they stopped dying. I made it as a mist, so it clings to a person's face and clothes. The victim tends to rub their eyes so they can see, which makes it worse. They'll be unconscious in 30 seconds, and it'll last for 3 hours depending on the size of the person. If they're outside it still works."

"What's the delivery system?" Riker asked.

"We use riot guns to shoot canisters. Same as the tear gas guns used by the police."

"We need to take out a house with about 20 guards. Some inside and some outside."

He nodded. "The canister will cover a large area inside a house. Outside it'll be effective for a 10-foot radius depending on the wind. I do have a gas that can kill a man in seconds. Maybe you'd prefer that."

"I wouldn't. When can we get the canisters?"

"I have some in weapons storage in Control's lab."

"I need at least 20," Cole said.

"There are 200 available."

"Why so many?"

"The Director asked for them. It's classified tech so I'm not sure what she was planning."

"I'm betting on a trip to Russia," Katie said.

"I heard she was a double agent." Chemist said. "I surmised that was why you killed her.

"How many of the riot guns do we have?"

"Ten."

"Is there anything else I need to know about the gas?"

"Not really."

"Tell me and let me decide."

"It's lethal to children under 10 years old. Their lungs react badly."

"I don't want to know how you found that out," Eve said.

He shrugged again. “Anything else?”

“Do we have any colorless and odorless poisons in weapons storage? The kind you slip into a drink or food.”

“Yes. I’m very proud of those. I made them undetectable during an autopsy. There’s always a big demand for that sort of thing. Saves spending a lot of money on divorce lawyers.”

“I want you to work with someone in Mexico teaching them how to make them.”

“No way. I’m not going to a narco-state and putting my life in danger, but I can have my assistant go with you. He can arrange it with Danni. I’m sure Control will sign a contract for his services at the usual fee.” He stood. “Is that all?”

“For now.”

“Good. I’ll invoice Control tonight.” They waited until he left. No one said anything for a full minute.

“Can I shoot him?” Katie finally said.

“No. We need him. Do you have someone the assistant can train, Sofia?”

“Yes. One of my team is studying chemical engineering at university.”

“Then we’re ready to go back to Mexico. We’ll leave in the morning.”

****

When they arrived at Midway airport that morning, they saw a man standing at the foot of the plane’s stairs. He was tall and athletic, and closer to 30 than 20.

"Who are you?" Cole asked.

"My name is Henry. The chemist sent me to help you. I put the gas canisters and the riot guns in the hold with my bags, and I brought a dozen gas masks."

Katie looked at her phone. Danni gave her a picture of the assistant. She nodded to Cole it was him.

"Do you know what this mission is about, Henry?"

"You want to capture a Mexican drug lord."

"Close enough. Hop on board."

After they climbed to altitude Cole called a meeting. The business jet had a couch and chairs so they could face each other. He introduced everyone.

"Did the chemist tell you that you might be in Mexico for a few days?"

"Yes. I'll help you until he tells me to return. And he mentioned I needed to train someone."

"A student who is studying chemical engineering in university," Sofia said.

"Will you be available if we have questions after?"

"We can't communicate over the phone. The information is classified. I'm surprised they're letting me tell you anything."

"The local college in Piedras Negras has a lab you can use at night."

"That's fine."

"I want you at the cartel's hacienda during the mission in case something you brought doesn't work," Cole said.

"I wasn't told I had to be there."

"I just told you."

"Will it be dangerous?" he said, his voice going higher.

“They’re a cartel. What do you think?”

When the plane hit turbulence Henry tightened his seatbelt, then pulled the window shade down. He put on headphones and attached his phone.

“He could be a problem,” Cole said. “Eve, can you keep an eye on him?”

“Sure. I’ll babysit him.”

“How are we going to use the gas?” Riker asked.

“We’ll use the riot guns to shoot it through windows. All we need to do is get close enough without getting shot.”

“That sounds easy,” Riker said.

“I got a text from one of my team,” Sofia said. “The Vulture is home.”

“Then we go tonight.”

Chapter 6

They parked far enough away from the hacienda that the blackness of the night concealed them. They went over the plan one last time. Eve and Katie would draw the guards to the pool deck by firing at the back of the house. Sofia's team would fire the gas canisters through windows. Cole and Riker would go inside to find the Vulture.

"I'll wait by the SUV," Henry said.

"You'll go with Eve and Katie. You'll die with the rest of us if these canisters don't work."

"I can't shoot a gun."

"It's easy," Riker said. "Point and shoot. Keep it in that order and you'll be fine."

Katie handed Henry a handgun. "Pull this thing and the bullet comes out this end," she said, pointing as she spoke. "And don't aim at anyone you're not planning to kill."

Katie and Cole walked ahead of the others.

"Why are you telling Henry to join us?"

"The guy that makes the weapons should be in the battle."

When they were closer, they ran in a crouch to the fence. Some of Sofia's team concealed themselves around the house, each picking a window they could fire through. Two others hid on either side of the deck. They would fire the canisters at the guards outside.

"Give us 60 seconds," Cole said to Katie. "Then begin shooting."

He and Riker ran to the front and put on their gas masks. A guard stood beside the door. They waited, hearts racing. They heard Katie and Eve begin shooting over the fence, not trying to hit anyone but wanting the rest of the guards to come to the back.

As soon as the front guard ran inside, they went in the front door. Canisters came through the deck doors, and windows shattered as they were blasted through the glass. A guard in the living room raised his gun to fire at Riker. Cole fired as they ran, and the man fell.

The firing slowed as the guards inhaled the gas. They ran to the master bedroom and Riker kicked in the door. A canister was on the floor spewing fumes. The Vulture was on the bed unconscious.

Riker lifted him over his shoulder fireman style. Cole walked in front in case anyone was still able to fight. They looked at the deck. Two cartel members were still actively firing. Riker picked up a canister emitting gas and threw it near them. One man saw them and began shooting. Eve stood and put two shots in him.

Some of Sopia's team ran for their vehicles. They drove them closer and the rest piled in. Riker threw the Vulture in the back of one of the cars and climbed in beside him.

"I'm going to check for anyone left behind," Cole said. He ran to the house. Katie followed him as a backup. At the far side of the house, a girl was lying on the ground. Cole rolled her over to see if she was shot, but there were no wounds.

"She got too close to the gas," Katie said.

Cole picked her up and they continued circling the house looking for others. She was the only one. Running to the trucks he put her inside one. They sped toward one of the farms.

Katie was sitting beside Henry in the car. She took his gun and checked the magazine.

"Only one bullet has been fired. You were supposed to shoot."

"I did once. It went off by accident."

"It's okay," Eve said from the front seat. "Men do that a lot."

"I didn't know what it was like to be in a battle."

"Think how bad it is when they use your poison gas."

He never said anything as they drove.

The rest of the team went to their homes. Sofia drove to a burned-out farmhouse. She parked behind the barn. A man was waiting in a front-end loader. Riker pulled the Vulture out of the back of the truck. He dropped him against the side of the barn. In front of him was a hole in the shape of a grave.

"Is there any way to wake him up sooner," Cole asked.

"Smelling salts," Henry mumbled. He was still visibly upset with what he saw. "I brought some in case one of you got hit." He removed a container from his pocket and handed it to Cole. Riker cuffed the Vulture's hands and ankles.

"Are you going to torture him?" Henry asked.

"Sort of," Riker said.

Cole put the smelling salts under his nose. The Vulture jerked his head away. He was disoriented when he came to but quickly saw the situation he was in. His eyes stopped on the grave.

"You know how this works," Cole said. "I'm sure you tortured a lot of people to get information."

"You're going to kill me anyway," he said. "Go to hell."

"You won't be dead when we put you in the grave."

He locked eyes with Cole. His anger turned to fear. He began swearing at him and fighting to free his hands. Riker grabbed him by his collar and dragged him to the hole.

"I told you I won't answer any of your questions," he yelled.

"Then you're no use to me." Cole nodded to Riker, and he rolled him into the hole. Riker and Cole took the shovels leaning on the house. One shovel at a time they began filling in the hole. Some of the dirt hit his face and he raised his head to clear it off. He tried standing but couldn't get up.

They covered his body. Only his face was clear. "I get to do the last bit," Riker said.

"I say we toss a coin."

They were stalling to increase the Vulture's fear. Riker took a coin from his pocket and flipped it.

"Heads," Riker said. "I win."

"Okay. Do it fast. I could use a drink."

Riker loaded his shovel.

"Wait!" the Vulture yelled. "Wait."

The Vulture looked up at them standing with shovels over his grave. He knew it would be the last thing he would see, and he knew it would take a long time to die. "I'll answer your questions."

"What do you know about more guns coming into your country?"

"The mafia is sending a new shipment."

"How many and when?" Riker said.

"It's the biggest shipment we have ever seen. It'll cross the border at Piedras Negras in two or three days from now. I told you everything I know. Get me out of here."

"How are they arriving?" Katie asked.

"Trailers will be loaded on a train and taken to San Antonio. Then semis will drive them across the border. I'm not saying anything else unless you get me out."

Cole knew this was the point where a prisoner got his bravery back. He threw a shovel full of dirt on his face. The man twisted his head back and forth and spit out the dirt.

"Where are they taking the guns in Mexico?" Katie asked again.

"I don't know," he said, beginning to sob. "I was told they would call me and tell me where they stored them and how to distribute them. They wouldn't tell me anything else. They said too many were stolen."

"Do you think he's lying"? Katie said.

"He's too scared to lie," Cole said.

"I answered your questions. Now let me out" he whined.

"Anyone got any more questions?" Riker asked.

"I do," Sofia said. "Why did you take Ana and kill her mother and father?"

He stayed silent.

"Why did you kill the Hernández family when they couldn't pay you?" Sofia asked. "Why do you kidnap kids from a college and kill them when the parents couldn't afford the ransom? I have lots of questions, but you don't have time to answer them." She pulled her handgun and fired into his forehead.

Sofia waved at the man in the front-end loader. He nodded and began pushing the rest of the dirt pile into the hole. She watched, motionless, until he was done.

"Are you okay?" Katie asked her as they drove.

"Better than before I shot him. What are you going to do now?"

"Riker and Eve will stay here to help you. We'll go back to Chicago and see if we can trace the weapons shipment. Maybe we can stop the train before it leaves."

"Or let it come here so we can steal them," Sofia said.

"It's risky. We could lose them to the cartel."

"The weapons are our only chance of survival against the cartels."

Cole nodded. "She's right. We have to take the risk."

Chapter 7

Whenever Katie walked into the museum, she gave a little wave and a hello to the T-Rex.

"It can't see you or hear you," Cole said, taking her hand in his as they stood in front of him.

"Are you saying it's deaf and blind?"

"Pretty sure it is."

"Did you think every time you came home you would walk under a T-Rex that lived over 66 million years ago?"

"No. And I never thought I'd be dating a Chicago mob boss's daughter."

"Life is full of surprises."

"How about we go upstairs, and I surprise you."

"I like that idea."

When they entered the apartment Danni was sitting on the couch. "Hi, guys."

"Why are you here?" Cole asked.

"We need to talk."

"How did you get in?"

"I work for a covert agency and control missions worldwide. The museum lock was made by a guy in Colorado."

"Can it wait until tomorrow?" Katie asked.

"You guys want your playtime. I get that. Treat this as foreplay." She smiled at them. "Three-way foreplay."

Cole sighed, then poured drinks. He knew she wouldn't leave until she said her piece.

"I found the Russian gun dealers. The next shipment is huge. Twenty containers going by train."

"We know," Katie said.

"How? The Vulture's the only one in Mexico that would know the details."

"He was helpful. Sadly, he fell into a hole."

"I'm guessing he's still in it," Danni said.

"Pretty sure."

"Are the Russians in Chicago?" Cole asked.

"Two of them are handling the sale. I'll text you the hotel and room number along with their pictures. It's a man and a woman. Both are high-ranking military types. It looks like they sent their best."

"Anything else?" Katie asked.

"Nope. Foreplay with you guys is not as exciting as I thought it would be."

"Stop thinking about foreplay with us," Katie said. "It's weird."

"You talk to a dinosaur. That's weirder."

Katie shrugged. "That's true."

"See you guys tomorrow. Have fun." She gulped the rest of her drink and left.

"I don't get it," Cole said. "The Vulture told us the Chicago Mafia is bringing in the next shipment, but we broke up your Mafia family."

"Maybe they reformed with new leadership."

"Who's left to rebuild the family?"

"I was the boss when my dad died, so not me. The lieutenants were next in line, and they were all arrested. Under them are the captains. It has to be one of them. They would have been promoted to lieutenants and one was appointed the new boss."

"A whole new generation of evil," Cole said.

"True. If we want to know about the shipments, I need to take my mafia family back. When I'm boss again I'll have the inside track."

"Who do you think is running it for now?"

"Maggie Morton. We call her Mags. She was always trying to take over. When I lived with my dad, I'd see her walking out in the morning in an evening dress and carrying her shoes. She figured by banging him she would be made the Underboss if I turned it down.

"Did it work?"

"Nope. I guess she wasn't that good in the sack."

"Let's talk to her tomorrow."

"That should be fun."

****

The next morning Katie called the detective she worked with when they arrested her Mafia family. She put it on speaker.

"Hi, Detective. It's Katie."

"Why are you calling me?"

"I need your help?"

"I'm a cop. Why would I help the previous head of an organized crime family?"

"I helped you arrest the top leaders of my dad's mafia. They must have given you extra donuts for that bust."

"Somehow you got my boss to authorize you to control a police operation. I wasn't happy about that."

"I don't care if you're happy. Are you still working in Organized Crime? I want to know if my old crime family is operating again."

There was a long pause on the line, the detective refusing to talk.

"Remember how my agency told your boss what to do," Katie said. "I still have that power."

Katie heard her sigh. "Fine. Yes. They formed again under Maggie Morton. They're slowly rebuilding the organization."

"Where do they meet?"

"At the courier service where your dad used to launder his money."

"I know it. They delivered his drugs as well as parcels."

"They meet on Fridays at 1 pm."

"I gather you run surveillance on them. Is the office bugged?"

"Not yet, and I don't want you causing me any problems. I don't need more people in the morgue."

"I'll be nice," Katie said. "I'll bring them ice cream and cookies." She disconnected.

"What happens when you say you want the family business back?" Cole said.

"Mags will put a hit on me."

"You know some great people."

"I know, right? It must be because I grew up Catholic."

"What are you going to say?"

"I'm back and I want what's mine."

"I should go with you."

"If I bring anyone to the meeting they'll see it as cowardice. I have to do this on my own."

"Bring a gun."

"I'm bringing two."

Chapter 8

Katie and Cole parked outside the building. It was an old single-story close to the river. Bicycle and truck couriers were taking goods to the city and the suburbs. Sedans and SUV's pulled into the parking lot just before the meeting time.

"I know those guys. They all worked for my dad. I guess they're the new lieutenants."

"Meaning what in the Mafia?"

"Lieutenants are in charge of a department. Loan sharking, gambling, prostitution, extortion, or drugs. They report to the Underboss, who reports to the Boss. It keeps the Boss separated from the crime."

"Are you sure you don't want me to come in with you?"

"I have to do this alone." She leaned over and kissed him on the cheek, then checked her handgun, returning it to the back of her pants and covering it with her shirt. She went into the office. Inside was a receptionist. She froze when she saw her.

"Katie? I thought you were dead."

"I'm not," she said. "Is the gang all here?"

"It's the regular meeting. Are you sure you want to go in there? Mags is in charge now."

"My dad left me the business. It's time I took it back."

She opened the meeting room door and walked in. Everyone stared at her, no one speaking.

"You're dead," a man finally said. "They saw your body in the lake."

Mags was sitting at the head of the table. She stood, still in shock.

"Hi, Mags," Katie said. "You're in my chair." Mags looked at her, not moving. Katie pulled her gun and placed it on the table, keeping her hand on it.

"I won't ask again, Mags."

Mags slowly sat in another chair. "How are you alive?" she asked.

"I'm hard to kill. The details aren't important. I'm here and that's what matters." She looked at the others. "My dad built this family. He made me his Underboss. Since he's dead that makes me the Boss. Mags will be my Underboss for now."

"Where were you?" Mags asked. Her eyes never blinked as she waited for an answer.

"Working on the gun shipments to Mexico."

"I was handling that."

"Not very well. Who was your contact there?"

"The Vulture."

"You should have known he's dead. If you shipped the guns they would have gone missing, and the Russians would have killed everyone in this room."

"Who killed him?" Mags asked.

"Again. Something you should have known. Luckily, I'm back. When's the next meeting with the Russians?"

Mags looked at her, not speaking. She was desperately looking for a way to get back in control.

"Mags. You have two strikes against you. Are you trying for three?"

"They said they'd call me."

"That leaves them in charge. Never give your power away. I'll contact them. Now I want each of you to give me an update."

For the next 30 minutes, they discussed the business. Instead of corporate product and marketing information, it revolved around drugs and killings, but it was still business. Not much had changed. If anything, mistakes were being made her dad wouldn't have made. She told them how to fix things.

"We're done for today," Katie said. "You can go. Mags, hold back." She waited until they left.

"I'm the Boss now. Do you understand that?"

"You were gone. I took over."

"And I appreciate your help."

Mags looked at her for a long time without speaking. Then she glanced at the gun still on the table. "I'll be the Underboss. Unless you leave again."

"If you try anything against me I won't hesitate to kill you."

"Understood."

"Good."

"What if the Russians contact me?" Mags asked.

"They won't. I know where they are and who they are. I'll take care of them."

Mags left without another word. Katie forced air out of her lungs in relief. Seconds later Cole came into the office.

"Were you standing outside the whole time?"

"Just in case you needed coffee or something."

She touched his hand. "Thanks."

"Now what?"

"We need to talk to the Russians."

Chapter 9

Katie called the Russian's hotel room and a woman answered.

"My name is Katie. I'm the boss of the family again. We need to talk about the deal you made with Mags."

"Katie is dead, like her father," she said.

"You're wrong. I'm back in charge of the family. Meet me in Lakefront Park in an hour. Just you. Your man can hide in the bushes the way mine will. The deals off if you don't come."

She heard her talking in Russian and a man replying. She agreed after a brief conversation.

"I guess they don't know we're the ones stealing their guns," Katie said after she disconnected.

"Or they do and it's a chance to kill us."

"I like my idea better."

"Let's go. We can walk there."

When they arrived Cole stayed back. The Russian was sitting on a park bench and Katie joined her.

"I'm Katie," she said.

The woman looked at a picture on her phone to confirm it was her. "I'm Sasha. I was told you were dead."

"I faked my death to escape some problems I was having, but I'm back in charge now and I don't want this shipment to screw up. Give me an update on your discussions with Mags."

"We're loading 20 semi-trailers on a train to get them into Mexico. My men will be in a passenger car at the end of the train until the border, then they will return here."

"Why is the shipment so big?"

"We've been ordered to speed things up." She handed Katie a sheet of paper. "This is the inventory."

"This is a lot of weapons," Katie said, glancing over it.

"The train leaves on Friday at midnight. You'll meet it in San Antonio and take it across the border."

"We could travel there with you."

"No. I don't trust you." She stood and walked away.

Katie sat thinking about what she said. Cole walked over and sat beside her. "The Russians are going to travel with the train."

"That's going to be a problem."

"We still have a decision to make. Do we destroy the guns or steal them?"

"Did you get an inventory of what they're shipping?"

Katie handed him the paper the Russian gave her.

"Wow," he said reading it. "They included six Jeeps with .30 caliber machine guns. And there are some Stinger missiles and C4. I don't know how we could destroy them all."

"It's scary as hell if the cartels get a hold of this many weapons. If we can't destroy them we have to steal them."

"It'll be hard to get the train across the border," Cole said. "Control doesn't have people in the rail system we can bribe."

"What if we hijack the train before it gets to San Antonio? We could hide the weapons in Texas and truck them across as they're needed."

Cole thought about it. "That's not a bad idea."

"The cartels won't look for them in Texas. They'll be safer. That's if we can find a hiding spot. It's hard to hide a 20 semis."

"And how do we get the trailers off the train cars? That takes heavy lifting equipment."

"Maybe Danni can find a way."

"I'll talk to her."

"While you do that I'm going to meet with Mags and our accountant," Katie said. I want to see how much money she stole from the family."

"You think she stole money?"

"She's mafia. I know she stole money."

"Do you need help?"

"No. I'm the boss. She'll respect that until she gets a chance to kill me."

"It might be time for you to find a new job."

"Not until this is over."

****

When the elevator doors opened Danni walked in. Cole was having a drink on the couch.

"You could warn me when you're coming," he said.

"Men should be able to tell when a girl's coming."

She poured herself a drink and sat beside him. "You sent me a text. What do you want to ask me, big guy?"

"About trains."

"I thought it might be something about us since Katie isn't here?"

"I need to know…"

"You want to know how to get a semi-trailer off a train car when you don't have access to a heavy lifter?"

"How do you know that? Is this room bugged?"

"I researched choo-choo trains and there's a way which I thought was totally cool. A train engine backs up the cars onto rail tracks in a yard. They slightly raise the cars, which unjoins them. Then the cars turn 45 degrees. A tractor backs up, hooks up, and drives away. The total time is under three minutes. The woman who designed that was a genius."

"It doesn't seem possible."

"I'll show you," she said, moving closer to him than she had to. She opened her phone and loaded a web page. A video showed the procedure. It worked exactly as she said. "Your next question is who owns such a system? Well. The Director is business friends with someone that does."

"Where is it?"

She gulped the rest of her drink and held the glass out for Cole to fill. He refilled both.

"I'm going to give you a happy ending. There's one in San Antonio, Texas."

"That's perfect. Will he let us use it?"

"The Director is playing slap and tickle with the company owner on the weekends, so I'm sure he will."

"Then all I need to do is hijack a train from Russian soldiers, replace the crew, take the train to San Antonio, have 20 semi-drivers waiting, and then hide the trailers."

"Yup. Your part is simple. I did all the hard work."

"I admire what you do, Danni. I'm not sure how you know so much, but I admire it."

"I have access to an infinite pool of knowledge and I'm a good swimmer."

Cole smiled. "Are you driving tonight?"

"Not now. Fill me up."

They continued drinking until the bottle was almost gone. Danni took a big sigh and tilted her head back. "I think I'm drunk."

Cole laughed. "I think you're drunk too."

"You need to carry me to bed." She kissed him on the cheek.

"You know I'm with Katie."

"I know, but if you ever want a hot drunk chick I'll be there for you." She closed her eyes and fell asleep.

Cole smiled, picked her up, and carried her to the bedroom, pulling a comforter over her. It was an hour later when Katie came home. She saw two glasses on the table and Cole was on the couch looking at a tablet.

"Who was here?" Katie asked.

"Danni. I put her to bed."

"Did she come on to you?"

"I got a kiss on the cheek."

"On purpose or did she miss your lips."

"You don't trust me?"

"You, I trust. Her, not so much."

"When you have the best you don't need the rest. And I have the best."

"Good answer. She can have the cheek. The lips are mine."

"How was your meeting?"

"Good. Mags is going to return the family's money tomorrow."

"Then we have a train to catch."

Chapter 10

Katie was sipping coffee at the table when Danni wandered in with her hair messed up and her eyes half open. She stopped when she saw Katie.

"Oh," she said, holding her forehead. "Am I in any sort of trouble?"

"If you were, you would have woken up on the sidewalk."

She poured herself a coffee and sat across from her. "I kissed Cole on the cheek. Although it was more of a falling action than a direct movement in his direction."

"We've all been drunk and did things. Just stay off his lips. New topic. He told me about the train thing. You've helped us a lot."

"About that. I want to be there when you steal the train."

"You don't work in the field."

"That's the problem. To find useful information I have to know what you guys go through. I need way more real-life experience. I've been at the practice range and I'm getting pretty good. And I learned to drive a semi. Sort of. I can't back up very well yet."

"Do you think you could shoot someone if you had to?"

"I'm sure I could shoot a couple of my old boyfriends."

"Can you fight?"

"My body is in great shape."

Cole walked in. "Why are we talking about Danni's body?" He poured himself coffee.

"It's in great shape, isn't it, Cole?" Danni said.

"Terrific shape. Why?"

"Danni wants to go on the mission with us."

"We need you for research."

"I can do that anywhere. I want more field experience, Cole."

"Okay. We can use as many people as we can get," he said.

"Katie?" Danni asked. "What do you think?"

"I don't want to see you get hurt, but if it's what you want, then yes."

"Excellent."

"I need you to do a few things today," Cole said. "Contact the truckers union and have 20 drivers waiting for us. Offer a large bonus. Then call Riker and Eve. Ask them to find 20 different locations where we can hide the trucks."

"And we'll need a conductor and a train engineer from Control," Katie said. "They'll drive the train when we capture it."

"Speaking of which," Danni said. "How exactly do you take over a train?"

"No idea," Cole said.

"I might have an idea," Katie said. "Trains have to pull into those side bits to let another one pass. Can you find out if the train pulls onto any of them near San Antonio?"

"Sure, but how can you change the crew to ours?" Danni asked.

"Train crews can only work for 12 hours," Cole said. "We could plan something for when they change crews. Our crew can take it into San Antonio."

"This should be fun," Danni said.

"I'm guessing you've never been shot at," Cole said.

****

It was late afternoon when Danni called. Cole put it on speaker.

"I have good news and bad news. And bad news that I turned into good news."

"Tell us," Katie said.

"I couldn't get 20 truckers on short notice."

"Damn it, we need them."

"I'm not finished yet. I called Sofia. She knows people who know people that immigrated to San Antonio. Some of them are truck drivers, so we have enough. And Riker and Eve are on their way there now. I gave them hiding places to check out."

"I knew you could do it."

"I'm getting the Director to contact the head of the railway and find us stop points. I'll let you know what she says."

"We need the plane ready. We'll fly to San Antonio to meet the train," Cole said.

"It's ready now. I'll meet you guys at the airport."

"Thanks, Danni," he said and disconnected.

"Do you think we should let Danni come with us?" Katie asked.

"She's one of the smartest people I know. If she wants more field work we should give it to her. I'll watch her back."

"So will I. I don't want her getting hurt."

Cole and Katie grabbed a go-bag and drove to the airport. Danni was on board drinking a coffee when they boarded. She gave them a wave with her fingers.

"Hi, guys."

"I see you meant it about coming with us."

"Yuppers. I want to see my man in action."

"He's not your man," Katie said.

"I brought donuts." She took a box off the seat and placed it on the table.

"Good call," Katie said.

They sat across from her and Katie took a jelly donut. "No napkins?"

"I like to take risks," Danni said.

"You look worried, Danni," Cole said.

"I am. Do you guys get nervous?"

"Always. We're going up against Russians who have orders to kill anyone interfering."

"Thanks. Nervous just turned into scared."

"Fear can keep you alive," Katie said. "Embrace it."

Chapter 11

When they got to the San Antonio hotel Cole checked them in.

"Your suite is on the 34th floor," the receptionist said, handing him the keys.

"We need two suites," Cole said.

"The booking was for one two-bedroom suite."

Cole looked at Danni.

"Teams should stick together," she said, smiling.

"Don't get too sticky," Katie said.

When they were in the room Cole called Riker.

"Where are you guys?"

"We're checking out the last couple of hiding spots. When we're done we'll come to the room."

Danni looked at her phone. "I got a text from the Director. She found a siding where the train stays for 15 minutes while it waits for another one to pass, and they do a crew change there. It's about an hour north of here and it's a heavily treed area in case we need cover."

"Is it in a deserted area?"

"Yes. No one will hear anything."

Danni looked at another text. "Control is saying the train will be there at 10:05 pm."

"We'll be waiting for them."

****

Cole and Katie were in the woods with Danni, sitting beside the train siding. Riker and Eve were a train car length ahead of them.

No one spoke. They wondered if this was going to go as planned. Cole kept checking his watch. The train should arrive in three minutes. He looked down the track.

"It'll be here on time," Danni said. "They have to keep to a schedule."

"Listen," Katie said.

They heard the sound of the engines and then saw the train. It was moving slow enough it could pull off the main track. They kneeled for better concealment.

"You guys see it?" Cole said.

"We have a visual," Eve replied. "And the crew van is approaching from the south."

They waited until the train stopped.

"That's our crew in the van," Danni said. "The driver will take the real crew back to San Antonio."

They watched the old crew drive away. "Now," Cole said as calmly as the could.

Eve and Riker moved to the front door of the passenger car. Katie, Danni, and Cole moved to the back entrance, crouching so they wouldn't be seen.

Cole placed a small C4 charge on the door and then tapped his earpiece. Riker did the same. They moved away from the charges and mentally counted down from three, then detonated them. The front and back doors blew inward at the same time.

Riker and Eve ran in, guns in both hands aiming for anyone trying to shoot at them. Cole began shouting for the Russians to show their hands. Riker and Eve did the same.

The Russians raised their hands, snapping their heads back and forth to see both of them. A look of shock stayed on their faces.

"Guns in the aisle!" Riker shouted. "Now!"

"Do it," Eve yelled as she and Riker moved closer.

"We are unarmed," one said.

Katie looked at Cole. "What the hell's going on here?"

"We're following orders," the man said.

"Oh hell," Katie said. She ran to the closest trailer and climbed on the train car. She shot off the lock. When she opened the doors she stood frozen, staring inside.

Cole was on the ground behind her. "Oh hell."

The trailer was empty.

"We've been had," Katie said.

"And we have no idea where the guns are," Katie said.

They checked the other trailers. They were all empty.

They went back inside the passenger car. The Russians were sitting and looking out the window. Riker and Eve kept their guns on them.

"The trailers are empty," Cole said. "Where the hell are the weapons?"

They looked at him, obviously confused.

"What are you talking about?" a man said.

"I'm going to kill you one at a time until someone talks," Cole said.

"Wait," one of the men said. "We don't know. Our orders were to ride the train to San Antonio and then return by plane to Chicago."

"Cole," Riker said, nodding to a place where they could talk without the Russians hearing. "Whoever set this up wouldn't tell them the location of the weapons."

"God damn it," Cole mumbled. "How did we screw this up so bad."

Cole called the others over. "Does anyone think these guys know anything?"

"I think they don't have a clue," Eve said.

"Have to agree," Katie said.

"This was a wild goose chase to keep us busy while they took the weapons to Mexico."

"Danni," Cole said. "Pay the truck drivers and send them home. Then you have to fly back to Control and use every resource you have to find the guns. The rest of us need to go to Mexico and talk to Sofia."

"You should come with me, Katie," Danni said. "If your mafia family knew about this you're the only one that can find out."

"I agree. It looks like me and Mags are going to have a serious talk."

Chapter 12

It was early morning when Katie and Danni arrived in Chicago. They slept on the plane, so Danni went directly to Control and Katie went to the museum. When she walked in she looked up at her T-Rex and stopped.

"I screwed up bad. I may have let a ton of weapons into Mexico." She paced and told him what happened. When she was done she took a deep breath. "I know. I need to get off my ass and fix this." She looked up once more and sighed. "Good talk. I'm on it."

Katie put a silencer on her gun and carried it in a gym bag. She knew where Mags lived. She'd been there once to find her dad, which was one of the most awkward moments in her life. She smiled at a guy going into the high rise and he let her in, then he tried to pick her up in the elevator.

When she got to her apartment door she picked the lock and walked in. Mags was on the couch watching TV. She jumped up so fast she spilled her coffee on the table.

"Katie!" she said.

Katie took her gun from the bag. "Sit down, Mags."

Mags slowly sat, putting the coffee cup down. Katie sat across from her and stared at her for a couple of minutes before speaking. She saw Mags getting more and more nervous.

“Tell me everything you know about the gun shipment. If you lie, or you leave anything out, I’ll put a bullet in your eye.”

Mags looked at the door. She knew she could never make it. She brought her eyes back to Katie. “The Russians called me about sending more guns to Mexico. I agreed because I could charge the cartels four times as much as I paid. They said they’d put the guns in trailers and transport them by train to the border, but I had to take them into Mexico.”

“How were you going to get them across the border?”

“I had a crew of drivers that would drive them across. We had border guards bribed to let them through in the middle of the night.”

“Did you ever see the weapons?”

“The Russians told me I didn’t need to.”

“You’re either lying to me or the stupidest bitch I ever met.”

“I’m not lying,” she said. “Wait. I’m not stupid either.”

“Debatable. Did you do a face-to-face with them?”

“Yes. Once. A guy and a girl.”

Katie looked at her, not knowing if she was lying. She put the gun on the table and leaned back. “You were duped.”

“How? I did what they said.”

“It doesn’t matter anymore.”

As she picked up her gun she used her other hand to stick a listening device under the coffee table. She began to appreciate the skills her dad taught her.

"We'll talk about this again later, Mags. I have to go to work." She left without saying anything else. In the hallway, she stopped and put in an earpiece, then connected it to her phone.

"Hello," she heard Mags say. "She fell for it."

There was a pause as Mags listened. "Katie was too stupid to see it was a scam. Now I want the other half of my money. Bring it to my apartment now. I want to leave town before anyone figures it out."

Another pause.

"You bring it, or I go to the cops. You got one hour."

Katie pulled out the earpiece and went downstairs. She sat in a corner waiting for the Russians. It wasn't long before a man and the woman she talked to in the park appeared. She took the next elevator to the apartment and walked in, her gun raised and ready.

"Katie!" Mags said, seeing her. "These guys are here to kill me."

"Shut up, Mags. You're starting to piss me off." She turned to the Russians. "Drop your guns on the floor."

They did as she said. She handed Mags plastic cuffs from her bag. Mags cuffed their hands behind their backs and made them sit on the floor.

She walked over to the man and held the gun barrel on his temple "You're wearing a wedding ring. Probably have kids. I'm going to put out the word you defected. Russia is not going to be happy. What do you think they'll do to your family?" He tried getting up and she slammed the barrel across his head hard enough to hurt him but not knock him out.

He glared at her, shaking in anger. "The guns are in Piedras Negras. That's all I know. They didn't give me the details."

The woman looked at him. "Keep talking and I'll kill you myself."

"How do I recognize the trailers?"

"There's a sticker on the back."

"What sticker?"

"A yellow happy face."

"You put a happy face sticker on trailers with enough weapons to kill hundreds of Mexican children. You sick bastard."

She stood and stepped back.

"Let me go," Mags said. "I'll leave the country."

"Gag them and cuff their ankles, Mags. Then you can go."

She cuffed them and used tea towels to gag them. Then she picked up the bag of money.

"Not happening. You don't get paid for what you did. But I would race to the airport because the cops are going to wonder why you have two Russians tied up in your apartment."

Katie dialed. "It's Katie, Detective. There are two Russian agents in an apartment downtown. They were running guns to Mexico. If you talk to them nicely I'm sure they'll confess, but hurry." She told her the address and disconnected. "They should be about 10 minutes, Mags.

Want to walk out with me?" Katie picked up the bag of money and Mags followed her, staring at the bag. She watched her get into a cab and then returned to the museum.

"I can't talk now," she said to the T-Rex as she walked past. "I promise I'll fill you in later."

She called Cole to update him. Then she called the detective. "Did the Russians say anything?"

"They were gone when we arrived," she said. "They left the plastic cuffs and gag on the floor. We're investigating."

"How long did it take you to get there?"

"About an hour. We have procedures to follow."

"Are you kidding me? No wonder they escaped. They could have made a snack first."

"I need you to come to the station. I need a statement."

"I have two Russian agents trying to kill me. Sure, I'll wander down to your place." She disconnected before the detective could answer.

She called Danni next. "We need to talk. Come to the museum. I'll be in the lobby."

Chapter 13

Katie took a bottle of wine and two glasses from the apartment and went to the museum lobby. She sat cross-legged on the floor in front of the T-Rex. Filling a glass she looked up at the bones, sipping her wine and telling him what happened.

When Danni came in she stood near the door and listened. She waited until the story was over, then she walked in and sat next to her.

"You actually talk to the T-Rex. I wasn't positive."

"He's a better listener than the men I dated."

"You have a point," Danni said, filling her glass. "I heard your story. So you have two Russian agents trying to kill you and you called me. Am I the bullet blocker while you run?"

"Nope. We need to work together to stay alive."

"At least we found the weapons."

"Again. Nope. Cole called me. They can't find the semis in Mexico."

"It hasn't been a good day."

"Certainly hasn't. How about we go to the apartment where we can eat and drink? Eventually, we'll forget about everything."

They went upstairs and Danni grabbed the tablet and began searching. "I need to figure out where the weapons are. If I calculate the size of the semis I could figure out how much building space they would take. Then maybe I can find comparable hiding spots. Assuming they stored them together."

"Do you ever stop thinking?"

"Yes. That's how I lasted with my last boyfriend for so long, but then I realized I like good thinking more than bad sex."

"Most girls do."

"I have a sat image of the town. I plugged in the space needed for the weapons. If they stored the 20 semis together it has to be big."

"Skip anything downtown. They would be noticed."

"It needs large doors to fit a semi. And the semi has to back in so it can't be a narrow street." She kept typing. "It identified four possible buildings. I texted them to Cole."

"Let me see the tablet. I want to check our security cameras." Katie looked at the cameras in front of the museum. Danni sat beside her on the couch.

"Look at the black SUV on the corner," Danni said.

Katie rewound the footage. "It's been there for an hour. They must know where I live."

"Maybe it's one of your mafia family?" Danni said. "Or it could be the cartel. Or the Russians. Or Mags. Or maybe…"

"I get it. Everyone wants to kill me."

"Pretty much." Danni started giggling. Then Katie did. Before long they were laughing and trying not to spill their drinks.

"Screw it. This place is like Fort Knox. We're good until we leave."

"Can I stay here tonight?"

"Sure."

"Then we're buds?"

"Unless you sleep with my boyfriend. Then I'll have to kill you."

"I had a girl say that to me in high school once."

"Bet she wasn't a mafia boss."

"True. You're scarier."

"I'll get more wine."

"Does it feel weird to you when you say it?"

"I'll get more wine?"

"No. That you're a mafia boss."

"I always wanted a normal family. Not TV sitcom normal with a mother that always has a glass of wine in her hand and a fat dad that thinks being stupid is funny." Katie paused and thought about what she said. "Actually. Maybe my life wasn't so bad."

"There should be a list online where you can pick the types of parents you want."

"I wouldn't have picked a Chicago mob boss."

"My dad and mom were teachers."

"That sounds normal."

"He was screwing one of my school friends and she was doing the school principal out of revenge. I guess that's normal for the suburbs."

"Thank God for wine."

"I think this is becoming a scotch night."

"Good idea. I'll get the bottle."

****

Katie rolled over in bed and blinked, trying to focus. She saw Danni beside her, her hair falling over her face.

"Oh god," Katie said. She looked under the covers. They were both dressed. "Thank god."

Danni stirred and pressed her hand against her forehead. "Oh god."

"I know. Everything hurts."

"Why are you in my bed?" Danni asked.

"You're in my bed."

"Oh. Still."

"I'll ask William to make us breakfast. We have to figure out who is following us and make them stop."

Katie got up and slowly moved to the kitchen. Wine bottles and crumpled potato chip bags covered the table. She groaned and began cleaning up. When Danni came in they went to the museum café for breakfast.

"What do we do about the bad guys outside?" Danni asked.

"We need to know who they are. We can't approach them on the street in case they start shooting. Innocents could be hurt."

"Then where?"

Katie went through different scenarios in her head. There were no mountains or forests nearby. A shootout in the city was off the table. That left one possibility.

"There are 16 miles of tunnels under Chicago."

"I..."

"Let me explain. They were used for transporting goods by a small railway at the turn of the century. The government closed them off years ago."

"I was saying I know about them. It's where your dad hid his guns and drugs."

"Sorry. My brain still isn't working. My dad ripped a hole in a garage floor. We can use that one."

"We need flashlights and guns."

"I have everything. We'll drive by the car outside, so they see us."

"We take armed men who want to kill us into a dark tunnel under the city. Makes sense."

"At least we'll have something to tell our kids when we're older."

"If we get older."

Chapter 14

When Katie drove out of the garage she slowly passed by the car with the two men watching the museum. They pulled out behind her. Katie followed all the traffic rules, making sure she never lost them. Danni held her gun on her lap.

"Take your finger off the trigger," Katie said.

"Sorry. I'm scared."

"The best time to follow gun safety rules is when you're scared."

Danni looked in her mirror. "I don't see them."

"That's because they know what they're doing. There's the garage. The city still has the yellow safety tape surrounding it. There's a ramp inside that takes us into the tunnels. It'll be dark as hell so don't drop your flashlight."

"In every movie I've seen the batteries go out at the wrong time and then the pretty girl gets killed."

"I'll be fine. I put in new batteries."

"I meant me."

"I know you did."

They parked and went into the old garage. Most of it was burned out from when she blew up her dad's SUV with a grenade launcher, but the ramp was still in good shape.

"At the bottom of the ramp at the side is a storage area like a small cave. We'll wait there."

"Is that where he stored his drugs?"

"And his guns. There's another one on the other side where he stored coffins."

"He buried people?"

"No one looks for bodies in a graveyard."

They walked down the ramp, flashlights on. It was a brick tunnel, curved at the top. On the ground were small rail tracks. Broken bricks and rock pieces littered the tracks.

"Is there anything living down here?" Danni asked.

"You don't want to know."

They moved into the side area and turned off their lights. Minutes later they heard footsteps on the ramp. Flashlight beams bounced off the floor as the men walked toward them.

As soon as they reached the bottom of the ramp Katie and Danni stepped out. They aimed their flashlights and guns in their faces.

"Drop your guns!" Katie yelled.

The men raised their guns toward them. Katie fired first. One of the men fired a shot at the ground as he fell. The other man aimed but couldn't see because of the light in his eyes. Danni swung her gun across his head. He never fell. Danni kicked hard between his legs. Then he fell.

"Pistol whipping works in movies," Danni said.

"Everything works in movies."

Katie collected their guns and felt for a pulse on the man she shot. There was none. Danni kept her gun on the other man.

"Who are you?" Katie said, waiting for the adrenaline to leave her.

"Go to hell," the man said.

"One chance. Then I shoot."

"No, you won't."

Katie aimed at the man she killed and fired into his chest. The other man didn't know he was already dead.

"Yes, I will."

"Wait," the man said. "It's just a contract. Nothing personal."

"You're a hitman? Who's paying you?"

"We didn't exchange names."

"What did he look like?"

"Looked military. Russian accent."

"Damn it," Katie said.

"What do we do with him?" Danni said.

"I want you to swear you'll never come after us again."

"What?"

"You heard me. Raise your left hand and swear. Then you can go."

The man stood, staring at Katie, thinking she was an amateur. He raised his left hand. Katie put a bullet through it. He grabbed it and she slammed her gun across his head. He dropped, not moving.

"What the hell was that"? Danni asked.

"He held his gun in his left hand. Now he won't be able to accurately fire one for a few weeks. Let's get out of here. You drive."

Katie was limping as they walked up the ramp. As Danni drove Katie pulled up her pant leg.

"You're bleeding," Danni said.

"It was rock pieces from when the first guy pulled the trigger.

"You okay?"

"There's no better pain killer than adrenaline, but it doesn't last long. I'll bandage it at home."

"You killed someone and shot another one in the hand. Doesn't that bother you?"

"It's better to survive and feel bad than die and feel nothing."

"Why did the Russians put a hit on you?"

"They must know we're the ones stealing their guns. They set up a fake shipment and put a hit on us. Everything has changed. We've become the hunted."

"What do we do?"

"Stay alive."

She called Cole and told him what happened.

"The hit would be on all of us, Cole. You need to watch your back."

"Were either of you hurt?"

"Katie was," Danni shouted out.

Katie glared at Danni for telling him. "It was just rock frags from a stray bullet. It's nothing."

"I should come back."

"No. Danni and I can handle it. She took one of the bad guys down by herself."

"Call me if you need me. Take care of each other," he said, and they disconnected.

"What do we do now?" Danni asked.

"We go after the Russians."

"And the Mafia?"

"Yes. Them too."

"And the cartel? They could have people here."

"Yes. And the Cartel."

"It's going to be a long day."

Chapter 15

Riker heard a knock at the hotel door. He drew his gun and peered out the peephole. “It’s Sofia,” he told everyone.

“I have news,” Sofia said.

“Come in.”

“One of my team saw a long line of semis on the road. Normally they don’t form a road train like that, so he followed them. They eventually turned off at a dirt road. I asked if he saw happy face stickers on the back and he said yes.”

“What dirt road?” Riker asked.

“He said it was a right turn about 60 miles from Palau on Highway 53. There was a Private Property sign with the Los Zetas Cartel symbol on it.”

“I need to take a look,” Cole said.

“The mountains are dark, and the roads are not maintained,” Sofia said. “It’ll be dangerous.”

“The night will give us cover. I need to confirm that’s where the weapons are stored.”

"There are no wireless signals, so no navigation systems work," Sofia said. "You won't know where to turn and what road to follow. I'll go with you."

The roads were almost empty as Cole drove. It was a long way from the city. Sofia talked about growing up in Mexico. She'd had a hard life and it felt good to talk to someone about it. The night blanketed everything except their headlights. She began concentrating on the road, glancing at the mileage indicator, and looking for the turnoff.

"Stop," she said. "We passed it."

He backed up and they took the dirt road. They saw a private property sign and another one saying authorized personnel only.

"That's the Los Zetas logo on the sign," she said.

He stopped before rounding a corner. Light from a building filtered through the trees. They got out and walked closer. Ahead of them was a guardhouse and a metal swing arm blocking the road. Two armed guards were talking, and one was smoking.

"Let's go," Cole whispered. They moved to the right of the guardhouse far enough they couldn't be heard. "There's no fence."

"Maybe it's not that important."

"Or maybe it's too big of an area to fence," Cole said.

They continued moving forward until they saw a building distorting the landscape.

"Jesus," Cole said.

It was an aluminum prefabricated structure with a rounded roof. Large swing doors were on the front, and they could see a door halfway down the side. Both had small lights above them. The faint sound of an engine could be heard at the far end. He thought it was a generator.

“That thing is huge,” Sofia said.

“I don’t see any markings or logos.”

“Or windows. We need to get inside.”

They dashed to the door on the side of the building. Sofia watched for guards as he picked the lock. He opened the door slowly, peering inside before going in. A long line of semis was backed in. The building was lit by a single row of lights along the ceiling, leaving most areas in the dark. People could be heard talking at the front. They moved slowly along the side of the trucks until they could see the guards. On one side rifles were leaning on a wall beside army bunks. He counted eight men.

They slowly moved to the back of the semis. There were 10 in a row and another 10 beside them. Both of them stopped when they saw what else was in the back of the warehouse. Hundreds of crates and metal containers were piled three or four high. Farther back he saw five trucks with mounted machine guns. He pried open some crates and saw every type of weapon there was, along with explosives and launchers. As he was about to open another one Sofia touched his hand. He stopped and listened. They heard two men talking as they walked toward them.

Quickly moving behind other crates they kneeled and waited. The men walked by them, continuing to the back.

“We have to get out of here,” he whispered.

They moved quietly to the wall and then ran alongside it to the door. When they exited he locked it again. Minutes later they were driving back to town.

"That was our 20 semis," he said,

"I've never seen so many weapons in one place," she said. "How did they get so many?"

"I thought we were stealing all the weapons before they got to the cartels. The Russians must have been using someone else to ship them as well. Maybe another mafia family."

"The Mexican people won't stand a chance if that many weapons get distributed."

"The first thing we have to do is stop whoever is shipping them. I'll call Katie in the morning. Then we have to destroy the weapons already here," he said.

"How? A lot of Los Zetas Cartel are ex-military. They're trained, experienced fighters. My team members work on farms and in shops. They would be slaughtered."

"I don't know how. I do know there are enough weapons to start a war and we don't have much time."

Chapter 16

Katie's phone woke her. She reached over and grabbed it. "Hello."

"Hi," Cole said.

"Cole. Are you okay?"

"Everyone is fine. But we have a problem."

"We always do," she said rolling on her back.

"We found a massive warehouse full of weapons. The 20 semis are in it along with hundreds of crates. There must be another mafia group shipping the other crates and gun trucks."

"Who?"

"I need you to find out. And I need to know how many they shipped in case more are hidden in Mexico."

"I'll get on it today. Danni can help me. Since we're on a hit list she's staying here for safety."

"Only do inquiries. I don't want you to take on another mafia family until we all get back. We'll do it as a team."

"I love how you worry about me."

"One more thing. Ask the chemist if he can build a bomb that can take down a building filled with weapons."

"What type of bomb?"

"The largest non-military explosions I know contain ammonium nitrate."

"The chemical fertilizer?"

"Yes. It needs to fit in the back of a truck. I'll send you the location by text. Danni can bring it up on sat photos and get the dimensions."

"How are you going to drive it into a building filled with cartel members and get out alive?"

"I'm hoping I'll think of a way. Keep me updated on what you find out about the mafia."

"I will. I hope you can come home soon. T-Rex told me he misses you."

"I'll be there as soon as I can."

Katie got up and went to the other bedroom. She opened the door and saw Danni sleeping on her stomach, her head buried in her pillow.

"Time to get up, soldier. We have work to do."

Danni never stirred. Katie shuffled to the bed and pushed on her shoulder a few times.

"Cole?" Danni mumbled.

"Seriously?"

Danni smiled. "I was just kidding."

"Get up, idiot."

They bought donuts and coffee on the way to Control. Katie updated Danni. In the office, she brought up photos of the warehouse.

"That's huge," she said. "It's a long way from town. No wonder I never found it."

"Can you get the exact size?"

"Yes."

"Call the chemist guy. Tell him we need a nitrate bomb to wipe a giant building out of existence."

"I bet Riker will want to watch. He loves explosions."

"I'm going to contact some of my mafia friends and find out who's shipping guns. Then we are going to stop them."

"How are the two of us going to stop a mafia family?"

"I'm going to get my favorite cop involved. I know she likes me."

"Pretty sure she wants to shoot you."

"Other than that she likes me. I'll be back later."

Katie went to her car. She knew there was only one mafia group big enough to transport that many weapons. The Chicago Outfit. The original boss, John Torrio, helped build organized crime in the 1920s. Al Capone was his protégé.

She knew one of their lieutenants. Tony was ambitious and smart. Mostly he was handsome. They had a one-night stand before they realized the Romeo and Juliet scenario between crime families would get them killed.

She sent him a text asking for a meeting in an hour at the aquarium. He loved that place. She sat on a bench in front of the shark tank. They'd met there before and knew he'd remember it. He was on time. He stood in front of the glass, and she stood beside him.

"I have to assume this isn't because of our emotional ties," he said. "You want something."

"I want to join our families. I still have a lot of contacts and the business is making money."

"We don't need you."

"More profit and no extra expense. Seems like good business."

"No. The weak always weaken the strong."

"We're shipping guns to Mexico. It's extremely lucrative."

"Lots of people are shipping guns to Mexico." He turned to look at her. "Is that what this is about?"

"Since we're both doing it we can make more if we join up."

"I didn't say we were doing it."

"Yeah, you did. I know you."

"Maybe we are. I don't discuss family business with outsiders."

"I have a shipment ready to go and not enough people to handle it. We do it together and we split the profits."

She took his hand and stood in front of him. "Think about it, Tony. We can work together. I'd like that."

He stared at her for a long time, not moving. Not wanting to move. "I'll talk to my people. Where's the shipment?"

"The tunnels."

"Where in the tunnels?"

"After the agreement is made," she said. "Then I'll show you. Where's yours?"

"After the agreement is made." He smiled and sighed. "I missed you, Katie. We could have had something."

"We still can."

"Let's have dinner tonight. The same hotel."

"I'd like that. I'll see you there at 7."

Katie went back to Control. Danni was looking at a map of the warehouse area.

"Did you find out who was shipping the guns?"

"The Chicago Outfit."

"Did they tell you that?"

"I had a one-nighter with a lieutenant a while back. He told me."

"You must have been good."

"I met him at the shark tank. Nothing happened."

"Yet," Danni said. "What did you tell him?"

"I offered to work with them on a shipment of guns I have."

"You have a shipment of guns?"

"I lied."

"So you're going to use invisible weapons and a happy ending to manipulate him. Good for you."

"We're only having dinner tonight. No happy endings. I have to find out if they have another shipment ready to go and if they do where they're hiding it."

Danni stared at her.

"I'm not going to sleep with him for information," Katie said.

"Do you think he'll settle for a kiss on the cheek? Men don't work that way."

"I'll figure it out as I go. What did the chemist say?"

"He'll see me this afternoon," Danni said. "But I don't know how we can get the bomb into the middle of the warehouse."

"We have to get the semis out to get the truck bomb far enough in. Could you update Cole for me?"

"Do I mention your one-nighter date?"

"He'll understand."

"You're having dinner at a hotel with an ex-lover and you're going to seduce him for information. I'm not sure he'll understand."

Katie looked at Danni and paused to think about it. "Never mind. I'll tell him later."

"Good idea."

Chapter 17

Tony was at the restaurant when Katie arrived. He kissed her on the cheek and held her chair. He was the perfect gentleman during the dinner. She had to remind herself he was a mafia lieutenant.

She talked about her dad dying and what happened to the crime family. He listened so intently that she knew he was either trying to impress her or sleep with her. After a bottle of wine, he suggested they go to his place for a nightcap. It was a short walk to his apartment. They sat on the couch and worked on a second bottle. She thought it was time to ask questions.

"What about our families joining, Tony? Did you ask your Boss?"

"Not yet. I will."

"How long have you been shipping weapons to Mexico?"

"We've done a few shipments. The Russians sold us a hell of a lot of guns."

"Why don't they sell them to the Mexicans?"

“The Russians said they didn’t want anyone seeing their planes in Mexico. We didn’t ask why.”

“How did you ship them?”

“The Russians flew them into Chicago, and we loaded them on our plane. Turnaround was a few hours.

“You have a plane? Impressive.”

“Yeah.” He put his hand on her thigh and moved closer. “We leased a Boeing 747 and painted it like a water bomber. It loads by the nose tilting up. No one questions us when we land in Mexico.”

“That’s a brilliant idea.”

“Enough about work. You’re here because we want the same thing.” He moved his hand behind her neck and pulled her closer, kissing her for a long time.

“Wait,” she said, putting his hand on his chest. “I don’t want another one-night stand.”

“Me either.”

“We need to build trust first.”

“Ask me anything,” he said, kissing her neck.

“Are you selling to Los Zetas or the Gulf?”

“Both,” he said. “Want some more wine?”

“Not yet.”

“I think Los Zetas will destroy the Gulf Cartel,” he said, rubbing his hand up and down her leg. “They’re sadistic bastards. A few of them came up here to see the weapons and pay us. The leader saw one of his people take a single bundle of cash from the bag. They shot him in the stomach and watched him bleed out. They’re sick people.”

“Where did that happen?”

"Tunnels." He leaned closer to her. "That's enough trust." He leaned in to kiss her again.

She moved away from him. "Not yet, Tony. We have time. I should go."

"Not happening. You can't lead me on and leave." He grabbed her wrist and pulled her closer.

"This isn't the movies, Tony. I'm not a helpless girl."

He put his hand behind her neck and began kissing her and running his hands over her body. She pulled free and stood, stepping back, anger overtaking her. He stood to grab her. She swung hard and fast. He fell back on the couch. She hit him again. He never moved.

"You'd think a mob lieutenant would be a nicer person. Who'd have guessed?" She finished the wine in her glass and left.

Danni was still up when she got home.

"Well. Happy ending?"

"I don't cheat."

"I got his picture. He's cute. I'd do him."

"He's yours. I did find out how they got the guns to Mexico. A plane painted like a water bomber. And the guns were never stored here. They were moved from the Russian plane to theirs. It's a good plan."

"Tomorrow I'll do a search for the plane. I should be able to tell when it comes in next."

"Does Control have pilots that can fly a 747?"

"We have two. Both retired and looking for action."

"Then we have the beginning of a plan," Katie said. "I'm going to call Cole and tell him what happened tonight."

"Don't. An honest relationship never works. We need little lies."

"Little lies grow into big ones."

She dialed and put it on speaker. "Danni is here and it's on speaker."

"No phone sex, then?" Cole said.

"I don't mind," Danni said. "But work stuff first. I talked to the chemist. He's coming here tomorrow. He says he can make the bomb when he gets to Mexico."

"Good."

"And I wrote a program to search for other buildings that fit the same size and type."

"I hope you didn't find any."

"Sorry to dash your hopes. I found another one near Nuevo Laredo. It's on someone's ranch. I should be able to find out who owns it tomorrow."

There was silence on the line.

"Cole?" Katie said. "You still there?"

"We're looking at a massive amount of kill power. It's starting to worry me."

"Can you destroy the weapons?" Katie asked.

"I don't know if we can without some of Sofia's team getting killed. I need to find a way to get the semis out and a truck bomb halfway inside the building. Whoever drives it in will be on a suicide mission."

"We'll figure it out. I want to see if the Russians are bringing in any more weapons, then I'll come to Mexico to help."

"Both of us will," Danni said.

"In the meantime, I want to tell you about tonight. I'll call you back from the bedroom."

"Spoil sport," Danni said.

She closed the bedroom door and explained what happened with Tony, not leaving out any details, including when she hit him.

"Are you seeing him again?"

"No. There's no reason. You jealous?"

"About you making out with an ex-boyfriend? What do you think?"

"You don't have to be. Not ever."

"I guess I should be glad you didn't hit me the first time we kissed."

"I had to make the first move with you. Three times before you figured it out."

"You were annoying when I met you."

"What about now?"

"You're responding well to training."

"It's lucky you're not here."

"I miss you," he said.

"Me too. Stay safe."

"I'm not sure I can."

Chapter 18

Sofia called Cole in a panic. “Two of my team just told me trucks filled with cartel members took weapons from the warehouse. And they took two of the gun trucks.”

“Why?”

“They’ve done this before. They’ll go through a town in Gulf territory shooting or kidnapping people. It’s to tell the Gulf Cartel they’re taking over their territory and to instill terror in the people. I’m getting my team together to intercept them.”

“We need to stop them on the road before they get to a town. We’re on our way.”

Minutes later they were speeding down the highway. He called Sofia. “Where are they now?”

“They’re on Highway 57 coming towards us. We should meet them about 50 miles from town. We’ll wait for you on the side of the road.”

They raced down the highway, watching for Sofia and her team.

“There,” Eve said, pointing.

They saw trucks parked on the side of the road. Sofia was standing in front of the vehicles holding a rifle. She waved to them as they approached.

"They should be here soon," she said.

"Face your trucks south and angle them like an arrowhead," Cole said. "It'll be harder to smash through them."

Cole parked his car sideways across the highway in front of everyone. They got out and stood behind it.

"I'm going to find a sniper position," Eve said. "Our greatest threat is the machine guns on the trucks. I'll take out the shooters if it comes to it." She ran down the road and took cover.

"Sofia. Station three of your team on each side of the road. Tell them to stay concealed." Cole watched to make sure they couldn't be seen. "Tell the rest to stand behind their truck engines."

They stared down the road like they were watching for a train about to hit them and there was nothing they could do about it.

"Here they come," Sofia yelled to her team. "Do not shoot unless they do."

"I count five pickup trucks and two trucks with machine guns," Cole said.

"All filled with experienced fighters," Riker said. "Odds are not in our favor."

The approaching vehicles slowed, then stopped a short distance away. A man got out of the first one.

"Do you think you can fight my soldiers?" he yelled at Cole, followed by a laugh. "We do not have a problem killing your children."

"No one has to die today. If you want to challenge the Gulf Cartel attack them. Not innocent people."

"People need to fear us. Today is their lesson day." He turned and waved to his men. The cartel members got out of their trucks and stood beside him. They raised their rifles to their eyes. "You have one last chance."

"You don't." Cole raised his rifle and fired from the hip. The bullet hit the leader in the middle of the forehead. He fell back. The cartel froze, not believing what happened. No one ever shot the leader. Seconds later they began firing.

Cole and Riker ducked behind their vehicle. Sofia's team returned fire. Eve aimed at the last gun truck and put a bullet in the shooter's temple. The shooter in front began firing. Eve aimed again; this time the bullet struck his neck. At the same time, the team positioned along the sides of the road began firing.

Three of the cartel members were killed in the first volley. Some started shooting at them. The rest kept firing at Cole and the others. Bullets tore through the cartel. Some tried to get back to their trucks but didn't make it. Others were shot where they stood. Minutes later the firing slowed.

"Cease fire!" Cole yelled. He yelled it again, and then Sofia did.

The smell of gunpowder swept over them like a heavy rain. The sounds of the people in pain cut through the air. Sofia shouted orders to help the wounded. Eve checked on the team on the sides of the road. One was dead. Two were injured.

Cole and Riker walked to the cartel trucks with their rifles ready. They kicked the guns away from the wounded and confirmed the dead. Sofia approached them.

"Five of the cartel are wounded," Cole said. "The rest are confirmed kills."

"Cuff them," she said to one of her team.

"We can bandage them," Riker said.

"So they can do this again? Do you honestly think they'll stop?"

"Why cuff them?"

"To let them bleed out."

"This one is not that bad," Riker said. "We can save him."

Sofia fired a bullet into his head and then went to help Eve on the side of the road.

"She's getting crueler," Riker said.

"She has to tell the parents their children died," Cole said. "Maybe she has a reason."

They put the bodies in their trucks and drove them onto a side road to clear the highway. People stared as they drove by them. They didn't care about the cartel dying. No one in Mexico did. The team kept the gun trucks and cartel weapons so they couldn't be used against them again. Cole asked Sofia to meet him after she dealt with her wounded and dead.

It was about four hours later when she came to the hotel. They poured her a drink. She gulped the first one, then sipped the second one.

"You wanted to talk to me," she said.

"What you're going through affects a person," Cole said.

"It sure as hell does."

"Cole is saying we're here if you ever want to talk," Eve said.

She smiled. "Are Cole and Riker good at talking about feelings? Katie implied they weren't."

"Katie is right. They're terrible at it. But they still care."

"I appreciate that."

"You're good at what you do, Sofia," Riker said. "We respect you for it, and we care about you. Sometimes talking helps."

"I have to take wounded kids back to their parents. Or worse, their children's bodies. I have no idea what words we can say that will make that better."

"You also save lives," Cole said.

Sofia looked at him and smiled.

"I'm sorry. I do suck at this stuff," Cole said. "We just want to help."

They stayed quiet for a time, not sure what to say.

"Keeping your feelings inside makes the coffin heavier," Eve said.

They all stopped and looked at Eve, mentally repeating what she said.

"What?" Eve said, watching them stare at her. "It's a saying."

Riker shook his head no.

Chapter 19

Danni and Katie were in her office looking for other warehouses. At the same time, they were dreading finding any more than the two they knew about.

The chemist walked in and sat in front of the desk. “Danni told me you wanted something blown up,” he said.

“Danni, could you bring up the warehouse Cole found?” Katie said.

She put it on the screen.

“See that dot. “That’s a person.”

He leaned forward. “Damn, that place is big. What’s in it?”

“Twenty semi-trailers filled with weapons along with dozens of crates and gun trucks.

“I love a challenge, but this is crazy.”

“We’re thinking you could use chemical fertilizer.”

“Not unless I positioned it exactly. And if the place is full I couldn’t do that.”

“Where would you place it?”

“I’d have to see the place first. Maybe I could detonate some of the explosives stored in the building, but you would have to get the trucks out. Do you know how many explosive devices are in there?"

"I suspect there's C4, land mines, grenades, and some stinger missiles. That type of thing. The back half is crates of weapons."

"Not all of those would detonate. No idea how many would survive."

"That's not what I was hoping for."

"It's hard to destroy weapons. Can you steal them?"

"They're heavily guarded. And I don't know where we'd hide them. There's so many."

"Then you're screwed," he said. He stood and left without another word.

"There's a whole lot of problems inside that man," Katie said.

"Now what?" Danni asked.

"I'm going for a walk."

"Why?"

"I think better when I walk. I'll come back when I figure out what to do."

Katie strolled along the river. Nothing was coming to her. As she was heading back she saw two children on the grass fighting over a toy. The mother watched them and let them fight. It seemed she was wishing she made better choices in life. Then it hit her. Katie smiled. She knew what to do. After dashing back to Control, she burst into Danni's office then called Cole and put it on speaker.

"Hi, Cole. I have an idea about the guns."

"Good, because I don't."

"We tell the Gulf Cartel where they are."

There was a pause before Cole spoke. "That's a great idea. If we can't steal them, we can use them."

"What's a great idea?" Danni said. "I don't get it."

"If we leak to the Gulf where the warehouse is and how many weapons it contains..."

"They'll go running over there to steal them," Danni said, interrupting her. "And if we tell Los Zetas the Gulf Cartel is coming, they'll lay down an ambush. It'll turn into a major battle."

"After they fight it out we can cuff the ones that are left and take the weapons," he said. "We'll figure out a hiding spot later."

"It's like in Chicago," Katie said. "The gangs kill each other faster than the cops can arrest them. It's the only thing that gets any of them off the street."

"Sofia will know someone that can leak it to the Cartels," Cole said. "Danni, you need to work your magic and find a place where we can hide the weapons."

"I'm going to stay here in case the Russians land another plane," Katie said.

"That was a great idea," Cole said.

"Some kids helped me."

"I'll tell Sofia to get her team ready. They're going to have to take on both cartels."

****

It was midnight when Katie lay in bed watching a movie. Her mind wandered to the guns. When she looked at the screen she saw it was a romance movie about a city girl on a ranch who falls for the ranch hand. He turns out to be the owner. And she's a writer. It had to be the thousandth time she'd seen the plot. Her breathing stopped when she looked at the ranch. That's it. She knocked on Danni's door and then went in.

"Hey!" Danni said pulling the covers up to her neck. "I could have been doing stuff in here."

"You already finished. I heard you turn off the vibrator."

"I was brushing my teeth."

"Sure you were."

"What do you want?"

"I know where we can hide the weapons."

"Twenty semis. Where?

"The Directors ranch in Texas."

"Wow. That makes sense. They wouldn't look in Texas."

"Bingo," Katie said.

"Bingo?"

"Never mind. It's something Cole says.

"During sex?"

"No. Tomorrow we'll tell the Director."

Katie began leaving.

"When does he say bingo?" Danni asked. "Is it at the end?"

"Go charge your batteries. We'll talk in the morning."

Chapter 20

Danni and Katie knocked and waited until the Director asked them into her office.

“What’s up?” she asked as they sat.

“We’d like to store 20 semis at your ranch,” Katie said.

“I assume it’s the 20 semis filled with weapons,” the Director said.

“Yes,” Katie said. “Your ranch is too far from the road for anyone to see. It’s a perfect spot to hide them.”

“And the ranch is in Texas but close to the Mexican border so we can distribute them later to the other towns along the border,” Danni said.

“Can you guarantee the cartel won’t attack my ranch? I have innocent people working there.”

“They’ll never find the weapons,” Katie said. “But I can’t guarantee anything.”

“I’ll call my ranch manager.” The Director dialed her cell and put it on speaker. “Casey. Katie and Danni want to hide 20 semis filled with weapons on the property. Can we do it?”

There was a pause. “We have room to store them, but I don’t know how we’ll hide them. Our barn’s not big enough.”

“What about using hay?” Katie said.

“Is that you Katie? Hi, again.”

“Hi, Casey.”

“Our hay production is bad because of the drought. I don’t think we have enough to spare.”

“Remember when we had to replace the barn roof last year,” the Director said.

“Yes,” Casey said. There was a pause. “That might work.”

“What?” Katie asked.

“We needed to cover the barn when it started raining, so we bought huge tarps. We would have enough to cover the trailers. If anyone asks we can say we are covering machinery.”

“Great idea,” Katie said. “If we can steal them from the cartel we can drive them up in a few days.”

“Do you need drivers?” Casey asked.

“Yes. One’s that won’t ask what the load is.”

“There’s a strike at the biggest transportation company in town because the office staff want to form a union,” Casey said. “I bet the drivers could use the money.”

“It would work if they didn’t need to know what they're transporting.”

“They know not to ask if it’s coming from Mexico. But they won’t cross the border. They’ll only drive from the US side.

"Sofia can arrange for drivers on the Mexican side. They'll take them to a transport company just across the river. Your drivers can drive them to the ranch."

"I'll make the arrangements for this side."

"Thanks, Casey," the Director said and disconnected.

"Director. Can you arrange the border for us?"

"I know someone in Washington that can do it. Let me know the date."

They went back to Danni's office to call Cole.

"The Director said we could store the semis at her ranch," Katie said.

"Can we get them across the border?" he asked.

"She's arranging that too. And Casey said she could get us drivers for the American side."

"When do you want to do this? The Director has to make sure the right border guards are in place."

"I'll get Sofia to call her contacts. With luck, we can set it up in two days."

"This is going to be a major battle. I should come down and help."

"Me too," Danni said. She heard a notification and looked at her screen. "Oh damn. It's here."

"What's here?"

"The plane. The 747 that takes the guns to Mexico." She activated another screen. On it were images of the Midway airport. A 747 painted as a waterbomber sat at one of the hangers.

"They'll have a fast turnaround when the Russian plane lands. Can you find out the destination?"

Danni began searching. “It’s Nuevo Leon, about 120 miles south of the border.”

“Can you fly down ahead of it and wait for it at the airport?” Cole asked. “You need to follow the trucks, so we know where they’re hiding them.”

“This isn’t getting any less dangerous,” Danni said.

“It can’t get any more dangerous,” Katie said. “We’ll meet up with you later.”

“Sounds good.”

“Cole. You’re going to be in the middle of a battle between the cartels. Don’t get killed.”

“Not my intent,” Cole said. “See you soon.”

Chapter 21

Sofia's team gathered a mile from the warehouse. Cole and Sofia stood on the back of a pickup facing them. Mixed in with the fighters were the drivers.

"Los Zetas are mostly ex-military and more experienced than the Gulf, but both will kill without hesitation," Sofia said. "You have to fight from cover. Don't take chances."

"Drivers," Cole said. "You'll stay in hiding until the shooting stops. When I give the order you'll go in and take a semi. One of Sofia's team will hand you directions on where to drop off your truck. We'll pull the wounded off the road, but there'll be abandoned vehicles everywhere. If you can't drive around them, push them out of the way. Just get out of here as soon as you can. Any questions?"

"I'm a driver," one of the men said. "Will we have any problems crossing the border?"

"No. We have an arrangement with the border guards. Travel as a road train. American drivers will take over on the other side of the border. Someone there will pay you and bus you back to Mexico."

The drivers left for their vehicles. Sofia's team stayed.

"Protect each other," Sofia said. "I don't want to have conversations with your families." She scanned their faces, her heart breaking. They were not soldiers. They were kids trying to survive. "Let's go," she mumbled.

****

Sofia's team parked on a side road behind the trees. They couldn't be seen by anyone on the highway. Cole, Sofia, Riker, and Eve hid close to the warehouse. The waiting was the hardest part.

They're here," Riker whispered as he watched vehicles come up the driveway and park. At the same time, men came out of the warehouse. They all gathered in front of the doors. A man shouted instructions.

"It's Los Zetas," Sofia said.

Some hid along the sides of the building and others inside. They all watched the driveway.

"This will be a bloodbath when the Gulf arrives," Eve said.

"Maybe not," Riker said. He nodded at the back of the building. Gulf members were walking in a crouch as they slowly came up behind the Zetas. Without warning they opened fire. Four of the Zetas dropped instantly. The others returned fire and ran to the front. One of the Gulf was hit in the leg.

The Zetas ran to the front of the warehouse for cover and the firefight began. Without warning Gulf gun trucks and vehicles raced down the driveway. They slammed on the brakes and jumped out. They began firing. The exposed Zetas were being fired on from both sides.

Soon the area was littered with bodies and wounded. One of the Zetas grabbed a grenade launcher and fired at a truck. It was too close to him. It exploded into the air and then came down on top of him and one of his team.

The Zetas closest to the entrance ran inside the warehouse. The Gulf continued firing as the rest of the Zetas ran for the door. None made it.

The firing became sporadic, then stopped. Two of the Gulf walked through the bodies, firing headshots before checking if they were alive or dead. A group stood outside the door, talking.

"Do we go in?" Riker said.

"Not yet. There are too many alive," Cole said.

"It could be a problem if they start a firefight inside a warehouse filled with explosives," Riker said.

"A big problem."

"Is there a back door?" Eve asked.

"Yes," Cole said. "I'm thinking the Zetas will use it. They lost a lot of men."

"We know what we would do if we were inside the place," Riker said.

"What?" Sofia said.

"Plant explosives among the crates."

"Jesus," she said. "Will they do that?"

"Most are ex-military, so I think they will," Eve said. "They want to cause the most damage to the enemy if they lose."

"What do we do?"

"Tell your team to find cover at the back. When the Zetas run out we engage them."

Sofia told them and they all ran to the back of the warehouse. "Now what happens?"

"The Zetas will get them into a firefight to draw them closer to the back of the warehouse. When the Gulf members are surrounded by the explosives they planted they'll run out the door and detonate. It'll take out the back half of the warehouse."

The air was still. Cole controlled his breathing, hoping no one on his team fired too soon. Sofia touched his shoulder. He nodded at her it was okay. As he turned his head back to the door he heard the first shot.

Bursts of gunfire exploded inside the warehouse. They heard yelling and screams. The back door was pushed open, and men began running out. Two of the men stayed beside the door and sprayed bullets inside to keep the Gulf from coming out. One man stopped and turned, and then they all stopped.

The men beside the door fired a final burst before running to join the others. The man flipped the switch. The back wall blew out, the concussive force knocking the men over. Pieces of the ceiling mixed with wood from the crates and parts of guns rose in the air surrounded by a fireball. The men lay there, staring. No one expected an explosion that big. As the pieces rained down on them Sofia's team began firing.

The cartel kneeled and looked around to see where the shooters were. It was too late. The barrage of bullets hit them hard. They fell before they could get a shot off.

Seconds later the burning crates were the only sound. The smell of gunpowder and smoke entered their lungs. Not one of Sofia's team moved. They kept their guns raised, trying to absorb what they were seeing.

Sofia stood first. She waved to her team, and they stood, guns still ready. They checked the bodies. No one lived through it. Cole moved to the hole that used to be the back door and looked inside. A fire consumed the crates and the bodies.

It was over. No one cheered. No one felt relieved. They just stood there, scanning the destruction.

"Check for wounded," Riker yelled. "Take their weapons. Do not kill them."

"Call in the drivers, Sofia," Cole said. "Have some of your team move the vehicles to make a path. If a cartel truck can't be started have the first semi plow through it."

"The crates took the force of the blast," Eve said. "I think the semis are okay. I'll help them move the pickups that work and pull the bodies to the side."

"I'll make sure none of our team is hurt," Riker said.

They snapped around when they heard a shot. A girl was standing over a wounded cartel member. She fired again. Then fired again, and again. "I'll take care of her," Riker said. He gently took her rifle. She stood looking down at the body, remembering what he did to her when she was younger. Riker waved over another girl. She hugged her. She put her hand on her back and walked her to the cars.

"It's over," Cole said to a person standing beside him.

"It'll never be over for us," she said.

Chapter 22

The drivers appeared as they were moving the bodies and clearing the vehicles. One of the Gulf Cartel pickups wouldn't start.

"Can one of you push the truck out of the way?" Sofia asked.

"I can," a man said.

"Then you take the first truck."

Sofia looked at her team. "One person will ride with each driver." She confirmed each of them wore a sidearm. "Do you remember what I told you?"

They all said yes, knowing they would shoot the driver if he tried to steal the truck.

"Drivers of the last two trucks," Cole yelled. "Check them for damage from the explosion before you leave."

As the trucks began pulling out he walked to the back with the last two drivers and their guards. They looked at the back of the trailer and verified the damage was light.

Sofia joined Cole and the others while they were inspecting the remaining weapons.

"Not much survived," Riker said.

"Looks like the gas tanks on the gun trucks exploded," Eve said. "They're destroyed."

"There's some ammo boxes and a few gun crates untouched," Cole said.

"I'll have my team put them in their pickups. I don't want to leave anything for the cartel to use against us."

"We need to move fast. I'm sure they heard us 100 miles away. Cops will be here soon."

"Eve and I will head for the ranch to help Casie get ready," Riker said.

They made sure they didn't leave anything that could identify them and drove toward Piedras Negras. Sofia made sure all her team left. She and Cole stood looking at the carnage.

"I don't understand how this happens," Cole said.

"My people have an expression," Sofia said. "Too far from God and too close to America. This ends when they stop selling their guns and buying the drugs."

She was right. Cole didn't know what to say so he stayed quiet. They began the drive to the border. As they drove they saw a semi parked on the side of the road. He pulled in behind it.

"It has the happy face sticker. It's one of ours."

Pulling their weapons they approached the cab. It was empty.

"Listen," Sofia said.

They heard a girl's voice. It sounded like she was pleading. Cole ran full speed toward it, Sofia following.

They saw a man with his hand around his female guard's neck, pushing her against a tree and trying to kiss her. She was fighting but wasn't strong enough to stop him.

Cole grabbed the man's arm and pulled him away from the girl. He slammed his fist across his face. The man's head snapped back, and he fell. Sofia took his gun. The girl began kicking him in the chest and head. Cole and Sofia let her. When she stopped she let out a loud scream of rage that blasted through the desert.

"He pulled over because he said he had to pee. I got out to stretch my legs, then he grabbed me and dragged me here. He took my gun. He told me he was Gulf Cartel and either I did what he wanted, or he would kill me."

"You're okay now," Sofia said.

"No, I'm not. I'm tired of being abused. I'm tired of these bastards doing what they want to us."

She kicked him again. Then she took his gun from Sofia. The man sat up, putting his hands in front of him.

"No," he said. "Don't shoot me."

She aimed at his thigh and fired. The man yelled and rolled over, grabbing the wound. Cole gently took the gun from her.

"They'll kill him for not getting the truck," Sofia said.

"I'll drive the semi to the border," Cole said.

"I want to go with you," she said.

"What's your name?"

"Carla."

"Maybe you should go home and talk to your friends or parents."

"I'm 20, not 10. I don't want a pajama party. I want to stop being angry."

"Cole," Sofia said, taking him out of hearing range. "I know what she's going through. She's scared and wants to feel safe. Would you let her ride with you?"

"Could you follow us? We can all stay at the ranch tonight."

"Of course."

On the drive, Carla never said anything for a long time. Then she turned to him. "I'm sorry. Others have gone through a lot worse than me. I should have acted better."

"You have no reason to be sorry. I can't imagine the hell you go through every day wondering if the cartel will show up at your home."

"It felt good to shoot him. Is that wrong?"

"It's human."

"I'm glad you and your friends are helping us."

"Sofia is doing most of the work." He paused. "You're going to be okay. Eventually, this will end."

"No, it won't. There'll always be evil people in the world."

"You'll always be strong enough to defeat them."

They never spoke much on the trip. Cole could feel her sadness.

Sofia pulled up beside the semi when they pulled into the transport company. An American driver approached.

"It's all yours," Cole said.

"Thanks." He got in and pulled onto the highway, heading to the ranch.

As they drove to the ranch Sofia stared straight ahead, her mind miles away. Carla sat in the back, looking out the window.

"What are you thinking?" he asked.

"It's time we attacked Los Zetas. They had their asses kicked tonight and they're weakened."

"Where did you want to attack?"

"They have a camp west of here in the hills."

"Near the border?"

"It's in Texas."

"Why would they have a camp in Texas?"

"They have a secret crossing they use to bring drugs into the U.S. They store them there for distribution. Trucks pick up the drugs and drive them across the country, and the cash is stored there until they take it to Mexico."

"If we take their money they can't buy the guns. How big is the camp?" Cole said.

"I was told 20 to 30 people. It's heavily guarded because of the drugs and money.

"That's too many. You can maybe get 10 of your team across the border without drawing suspicion."

"I might have a way," Sofia said. "During the Vietnam War, a lot of the American kids didn't want to fight. They knew it was a political war and America couldn't win. They were right. Thousands died for no reason."

"I know about the protests at the time."

"Many of them fled to Canada. I read a book that said some moved to an island off the coast of BC. They formed their own community and still live there with their families."

"Are you saying the Mexicans did something similar?"

"Some did. They left Mexico to save their children from the cartels, but they didn't want to face the racism in the American cities. They found water in the mountains and built homes, eventually becoming a community of self-sufficient farmers and tradespeople. There's nothing around them so people leave them alone."

"It's called Santuario. Sanctuary," Carla said. "My grandfather and grandmother live there. I visit them when I can."

"You think they'll help us, Carla?"

"They're Mexican. They want to make their country safe enough to go home. I know they'll help."

"Tomorrow we'll go see them."

Chapter 23

The drive from the ranch to Sanctuary was slow and hot. Most of it was on dirt roads far from the highways. As they got closer they entered forested land.

"I can see why they chose this place," Cole said.

"My grandad says they don't get any visitors," Carla said. "Even hikers don't come this far."

"They must be happy when you visit."

"Yes. They're the only family I have left. My parents refused to go with them and were killed by the cartel."

"How do they get supplies in?"

"They use donkeys and horses. This is the way in," Carla said.

"There's nothing here."

"Only for a short distance."

They walked into the bush. A few yards in they found a path that wound its way through the trees.

"We have to walk about a mile."

When they came to a clearing they stopped and stared. People were walking in and out of stores and horses were tied up on the street waiting for them. It was a beautiful town.

"Carla!" an old woman said. Everyone nearby stopped and stared.

"Hi, Yaya," she said as they hugged.

The rest of the people went back to what they were doing.

"I'm so glad you're here."

"This is Sofia and Cole."

She nodded to them.

"They're friends, Yaya. Good friends."

"Then welcome. Come. I'll make coffee."

She took them to her home. Her grandfather hugged Carla, a grin spreading across his face.

"Are you okay?" he asked.

"We need your help."

The grandparents looked at each other, then back at her. "Anything."

"Hear me first. Then decide."

She told them about their plans to attack the cartel. They listened quietly until she finished.

"We left Mexico to get away from the cartels," he said. "We don't want to fight them."

"You can never leave Mexico. It's part of who you are," Carla said. "It's part of all of us."

He placed his hand on his wife's and looked at her. She nodded.

"We need to get the townspeople together and ask them," he said. "We owe Carla that."

"Let's go to the church," she said.

They walked until they came to a small church that held about 80 people. He rang the church bell and people came and sat in the pews, some still carrying their groceries, others holding babies or the hands of their children. They knew the church bell meant to gather for something important.

Carla stood at the front with the priest. She explained what she wanted. A man stood.

"We came here to avoid the cartel. Why would we fight them?"

"You have people you love in Mexico. Friends and relatives. You're fighting for them."

They began talking to others near them, some angry they were being asked, others in agreement. Carla waited. After a time they became quiet. The same man stood. "I'll help." Others stood with him. Cole counted 18 people.

"Thank you," Cole said. "We'll bring weapons to town in two days. The cartel is in a camp not far from here."

"We know it," a man said.

"We are not going to go in shooting," Sofia said. "We have a plan to avoid anyone getting hurt."

They waited until everyone left.

"I want to see the camp," Cole said.

"There's a road that can take us close to it," Sofia said.

"Then let's take a look."

They walked back to the car and drove to the cartel site, hiding the car off the road. It was in a valley. The road ran through the middle of it and then continued north, linking up with the highways.

They lay on a cliff, staring through binoculars. There was a large, enclosed building on one side of the road and tents for sleeping and eating on the other side. Men were mulling around and talking. Vehicles were parked behind the tents.

"Look," Carla said, pointing.

"It's a cave," Sofia said.

"I think it's guarded because that's where they keep the money and drugs," she said.

"I count 22 people," Sofia said. "But we don't know how many are inside."

"They're all carrying sidearms," Carla said.

"There are a dozen tents," Cole said. "One must be for meals. The rest look like they're for sleeping. The main building might be for preparing the drugs."

They all turned their heads when they heard an engine coming from the south.

"It's a Cessna," Sofia said.

"The drug smugglers plane of choice," Cole said.

The plane landed on the road and stopped outside the building. Men began loading drug packages on the plane.

"That's a lot of drugs for a small plane," Sofia said.

"They'll know the weight capacity. It can land at any ranch in Texas, then they can drive them to the cities."

"Any ideas how to stop these guys, Cole?"

Cole looked at the area for a long time before speaking. "We need to get inside the camp before they can start shooting at us. I might know a way." Cole dialed Danni.

"Where are you?" she asked.

"Looking at a cartel drug distribution center in Texas. You?"

"Watching trucks unloading rifles into a big barn in Nuevo Leon. Your stuff sounds more exciting. I'll put you on speaker. Your last girlfriend is with me."

"Last girlfriend?" Katie said. "Seriously?"

"Hi, Katie."

"Hi, Cole."

"Danni, I need you to contact the Director."

"Why?"

"Ask her if she knows someone with 50 head of cattle I can borrow."

There was silence on the line.

"Say again?"

"I need 50 head of cattle and some real cowboys that know how to herd them. Take my location from my phone. I need them tomorrow."

"You're getting weirder, Cole. I like that. I'll call you after I talk to her."

"Wait," Katie said. "What are you planning?"

"Something I saw in a western movie. I'll explain later." He disconnected.

"It's going to drive Katie and Danni nuts until you tell them why," Sofia said, smiling.

"I know. It's fun, right."

Chapter 24

It was morning when Danni called Cole. Everyone was in the kitchen eating breakfast at the ranch. Cole put it on speaker.

"The Director knows someone that owns longhorns, and his ranch is close to the cartel drug site. She said the guy would have them at your location by noon. The rancher said he hates drug dealers and will do anything to stop them.

"Thanks, Danni. How are you guys doing?"

"We know where they stored the weapons. When you come here with Sofia we can figure out what to do."

"What about the moo cows?" Katie said. "What are they for?"

"I'll tell you about it when I see you. Talk soon." He disconnected.

"Is she your girlfriend?" Carla asked.

"Yes. I'm a lucky guy."

After breakfast, they drove to Sanctuary. The townspeople rode horses to the camp with them. The ride was long and hot, but they made it before the longhorns were due to arrive. Cole rode south to meet up with the owner.

When he found them he explained what they were going to do, telling them it could be dangerous. They all said they were looking forward to screwing with the drug dealers. By the time he finished, the cattle were close to the site. Riker and Eve were perched on top of the hills their rifles ready. The townspeople were on their horses waiting out of sight.

"Let's do this!" he yelled.

The ranch hands started whistling and yelling and the longhorns began charging toward the camp. Dust covered everything and everyone. As they approached the camp the guards on the road stood, staring, not believing what they were seeing. They never knew how to react, so they ran back to the center of the camp.

The townspeople pulled in behind the cattle and rode with them. The guards stood watching the approaching stampede, moving to the sides of the road to let them through. Everyone came out of the tents and buildings to see what was happening. Two came from the cave entrance.

The cattle reached town and kept running. The smell of the herd and the dust cloud increased as they raced through the town. As the cattle kept going, Cole and the rest pulled their horses to a stop in the middle of the cartel members.

"Drop your weapons! Hands in the air!" they yelled and aimed their guns. The cartel was confused. The townspeople moved their horses through the cartel, aiming at them while they yelled and adding to the confusion. Some used the horses to knock them over.

A cartel member pulled his sidearm. Eve fired, hitting him in the chest. Another tried it on the other side of the street. Riker put one in his neck. The rest of them saw the men drop. The people on horses were shouting for them to drop their weapons. The horses continued banging into them.

They dropped their guns. First, it was one at a time. Then in groups. Townspeople got off their horses and took the guns. They forced them to lie face down in the dirt. One man tried to run back inside the building. Eve didn't give him a chance.

The dust and smell of the cattle slowly melted into the ground. The cartel lay face down, hands behind their heads. The cattlemen turned their horses and rode after the longhorns. It wasn't long before they saw the cattle being walked back the way they came. The cattlemen looked at the cartel on the ground and smiled.

"Best fun we've had in a long time," the ranch owner said as he shook Cole's hand. "Me and my boys thank you." They continued on their way home.

Inside the building, Cole saw packages of drugs ready to be picked up. There were too many to count. It horrified him to think of how many lives it would have destroyed.

The cartel captives were brought into the building and searched. They cuffed them and made them sit along a wall.

Cole thanked the people who helped, glad none were injured. They said it felt good to pay back the cartel and offered their help anytime he needed it. Riker and Eve came down and stood with Cole, Sofia, and Carla.

“How did you think of doing this?” Carla asked.

“I watch old cowboy movies,” Cole said.

“Cole always wanted to be John Wayne,” Riker said. “Today he finally got his chance.”

“You’re a strange man,” Carla said to Cole. “I wish there were more like you in the world.”

“Let’s go see what’s in the cave.”

They walked over to it and went in. Stacks of bills were piled on pallets.

“That is a lot of money,” Sofia said.

“What are you doing with it?” Carla asked.

“We’ll distribute it to people along the border,” Sofia said. “And some will go to help the cause.”

“It’s not enough to make up for what the people lost over the years, but it can help,” Cole said. “Could you guys load it in the cartel SUVs? I need to call Danni.”

“I’ll help,” Eve said.

“Danni. We have the money and the bad guys. Can you call the DEA and give them the location? They can destroy the drugs and arrest these guys. We’re finishing up and will be gone shortly. Then could you arrange with the border guards to let us pass to Piedras Negras? We have some cash with us. I’ll call you when we’re close to the crossing.”

“On it. Are you okay?”

“Everyone is fine. I wish all of our operations could have gone so smoothly.”

“I’ll make the calls. I’m glad you’re safe.” She disconnected.

“What do we do with the cartel?” Carla asked. “They’ll escape if we leave before the DEA arrives.”

"I saw a panel van in the back. Could you drive it to the cave entrance?"

"Why? Actually, never mind. I just saw cattle used to capture the cartel. I know you have a plan."

Cole moved the captives inside the cave. When Carla brought the van he had her park it across the opening, the sliding door on the opposite side.

"Cute plan," Riker said. "You made a prison."

"They can't climb over the top, but they could crawl under," Eve said.

"I wasn't done yet." Cole shot the tires, so it was too low to get under it.

"Carla. Could you bring another vehicle and park it next to this one? I don't want them to push the van over to escape."

"On it."

"It'll hold them until the DEA arrives," Eve said.

Carla stood beside him, staring at the prison he made. "Yes. A very strange man. I can see why Sofia calls you a friend."

"I take that as an honor."

Chapter 25

Katie and Danni met them at the hotel in Piedras Negras that night. Cole told them about the camp and how relieved he was none of the team or the townspeople were hurt. They asked him to repeat the part about the longhorns being stampeded through the camp.

"I have to start watching Western movies," Katie said.

"They're like romantic comedies except people get shot and there are cows," Riker said.

"I'm worried what Los Zetas might do," Cole said. "They must think the Gulf Cartel took their money and drugs."

"At some point, the Russians are going to get more involved," Katie said.

"The Director called me back to Chicago," Danni said. "She has to report to Washington, and she wants me there to give them the perspective of someone in the middle of it. It should be one of you guys going."

"We're not good with bureaucrats," Cole said.

Sofia answered her phone. It was one of her team. Her hand shook slightly as she listened.

"What is it?" Cole asked.

"The Zetas attacked a small village near here," she said. "It's in Gulf Territory. Maybe they thought the Gulf Cartel hit their camp."

"What happened?"

"It's really bad. They gathered everyone in the town square and then dragged the three local police officers out of the station. They made them kneel and executed them in front of the people. Same with the mayor. I have friends in the town. I don't know if they're alive."

Sofia picked up her drink, but her hand was still shaking.

"Take your time, Sofia," Katie said.

"They collected extortion money and said they want regular payments. As they left they shot up the stores. I don't know yet how many were killed. I know the Gulf Cartel will retaliate."

No one talked. No one knew what to say.

Cole finally spoke. "This is what we were trying to stop."

"I'm sorry, Sofia," Katie said.

"Danni," Cole said. "When you go back to Control could you call us with an update on what the Director knows?"

"I'm going with her," Katie said. "I want to find out if the Russians are shipping more guns."

"If you find them you can't go up against them alone. Riker, will you and Eve go with them?"

"That leaves you here alone."

"I have Sofia to help me."

"And Carla," Sofia said. "She knows the people in the village and wants to stick with me to help get revenge for them."

"Do you know who the cartel leader was?"

"Yes. He's a well-known local leader. He works out of a small ranch about 90 miles northwest of here. Why?"

"We have to send a message that what they did is not going to be allowed."

"He has eight or nine cartel members around him all the time. He won't be easy to kill."

"I could stay and use my sniper rifle," Eve said.

"No. I want his cartel to know they can be attacked at any time in any place."

"Be careful," Katie said. "I know I don't have to say it, but it makes me feel better."

"I will. Sofia can show me where he lives."

"Carla's been there. She can take us."

"Why?" Riker asked.

Sofia paused before answering. "I'd rather not say. She told me what happened in confidence."

"Of course."

"We should get some sleep," Eve said. "The plane leaves early tomorrow."

"I'll let you guys know what happens," Cole said.

****

Night had fallen as Cole sat in the car with Sofia and Carla. They could see the hacienda in the distance. Lights were on over the front door and one in the backyard.

"They don't have any guards outside," Cole said.

"They don't believe anyone would attack them, and they're right," Carla said. "They have one guard in the living room. Two others sleep in bedrooms in the main house. The other members and the ranch hands sleep in the building in the back."

"Carla, do you know the layout of the rooms?" Cole asked, wishing there was another way to ask it.

"Yes," Carla said. "You enter through the living room. The kitchen is on the right and the hallway is on the left. The bedrooms and bathrooms are down the hallway." She paused. "The master bedroom is the last one on the right." Carla swallowed hard and kept her eyes down.

"I won't ask what happened to you, Carla. But I'm sorry it did."

"Thank you."

"Sofia, here's an earpiece. If you see anyone outside let me know. I should be back shortly."

He ran to the house and glanced in the window. A man was in a chair watching TV. The sound was low so the others could sleep. Cole tried the door, but it was locked. He kneeled and picked the lock, then slowly opened it, his other hand taking out his knife.

He moved slowly inside and closed the door, then walked behind the man. Cole looked at the TV and realized his reflection was on the screen. Before the man could reach his handgun. Cole put his hand over his mouth and jammed his blade into the side of the man's neck. He twisted it to open the wound, then pulled it out. The man grabbed his neck and fell.

Cole moved toward the master bedroom. He listened at the door. All he heard was snoring. Opening the door, he went in. He was standing over the leader when the man opened his eyes. By the time he realized what was happening, Cole swung his fist hard across his face and then hit him again.

The man was small compared to Cole. He threw him over his shoulder firemen style and moved outside, then ran with him back to the car. He put the man in the back and got in beside him, then cuffed and gagged him.

"Why did you bring him?" Carla asked.

"A man like him should never die in his sleep."

"Where do we take him?"

"To the village he terrorized."

Carla kept staring at the leader. She dialed and spoke to a woman in Spanish. "They'll be waiting for us."

When they arrived people had already gathered in the town center. A truck with a rope tied to the back was beside them. They hauled the leader out of the car. He woke and began screaming threats against them, his voice cracking from fear.

They cut his cuffs and tied his wrists to the end of the rope. A man got into the truck. Everyone was silent. The man knew what was going to happen and began pleading with them. The driver started the truck and sped down the dirt road, the sound of screams disappearing into the night.

"If he's still alive when he returns they'll keep doing it until there's little left of him," Carla said. "Then they'll dump his body outside his ranch, so the others know.

"Why this way?" Cole asked

"He did it to their priest," Carla said.

Cole nodded. "Let's go home."

"Cole," Carla said, touching his arm. "Thank you for this."

Cole nodded. This was not something he wanted to be thanked for.

Chapter 26

The Director was already at Control when Katie and Danni arrived. She saw them on the monitors and called them into her office.

"You two have been through a lot," she said. "I want you to know your work has been noticed by me and by Washington."

"If Washington knows what's happening they should do something about it," Katie said.

"You know the problem. They don't want trouble with Russia."

"Doing nothing never solves a problem."

"You're right," the Director said. She leaned back in her chair. "Things have escalated."

"How?" Danni asked.

"The attack on the village was what the Mexican government was hoping for. It was a reason to ask Russia for help."

"It was a small village. What good is the Russian military?" Danni asked.

"Russia has formed an organization called the Russian International Assistance Team. Its members are all military."

"It sounds like a fake search and rescue group," Katie said.

"It is. Their real purpose is to set up military bases in the country and pretend they're there to help the people. They'll do the odd helicopter rescue or find someone who is lost to make it appear like they're assisting."

"Where and when are they arriving?" Katie said.

"I don't know. They won't use a commercial airport or file a flight plan. I need you to work your magic, Danni. Find out where and when they land."

"I already know where. I did a huge amount of research when this all started."

"Where?"

"In 2018 the president decided to build an airport 90 miles west of Piedras Negras. It would be a shipping airport between the US and Mexico. The plan was to build a manufacturing mega center beside the airport. They could fly from there all over the US so it would speed up delivery."

"There's no airport there," the Director said.

"There's a runway big enough for 747s and an airport terminal. It's probably covered in dirt and weeds so it's not visible in sat photos, but it could easily be restored."

"Why didn't they finish it?" Katie said.

"A new president was elected. He halted construction because of massive corruption. The cost had tripled and there was no end in sight. Same as every American government project."

"You think they'll set up a base there?" Katie said.

"No reason why not," Danni said. "They could land missiles on us before our guys could put their cigarettes down. No more MAD

"What's MAD?" Katie asked.

"Mutually Assured Destruction. If the Russians launched we had time to see it and launch on them. It ensured everyone on earth died. It was the only thing that kept us alive during the Cold War."

"Damn it, politicians are stupid," Katie said. "They have the intelligence of kids on a playground."

"You have to get me proof so I can take it to Washington," the Director said.

"Why? So our politicians can form committees and yell at each other to get on TV?" Danni said.

"We're five people and some brave Mexican kids," Katie said. "What the hell can we do?"

"Stop them any way you can. Money will be unlimited, and I'll give you every resource you want. Just stop them."

Katie sat back in her seat, staring at Danni.

"We should go back to Mexico," Danni said.

"There are no Russians in Mexico yet. That means They're in Chicago directing the mission. We need to find them."

"Then what?"

"We can find out when the first planes are due to land in Mexico. If they have troops on them? Will they bring weapons and what type? How many men? When will the missiles arrive?"

"So just the basics."

"Pretty much."

"Will the Russians in Chicago tell us if we ask nicely?" Danni said.

"No. But the Detective might know someone. We'll start with her.

****

Danni was at Control researching as Katie walked into the police station. She went to the front desk and asked for Detective Jane Wilks with the Bureau of Organized Crime. The officer said to wait a moment and called her. The detective paused in the doorway when she saw Katie. She grimaced and took her to an office and closed the door. She stood behind the table and put her hands on the desk, leaning towards her.

"My boss told me you were coming and assigned me to work with you. I have a pile of cases on my desk that he gave to the other detectives. Now, they're all pissed at me. Who the friggin hell are you that you can tell the police what to do?"

"I thought we became buddies when I helped you take down my mafia family, but I'm just not feeling the love."

The Detective sat and glared at Katie.

"Okay then," Katie said. "If you're finished complaining we have a lot of work to do.

"What do you want?"

"What I'm about to tell you is classified. If you tell anyone you will be fired and face a lengthy jail term. Do you understand?"

"Got it."

"The Russians are planning on putting nuclear missiles in Mexico aimed at the US. If they're successful they'll be able to destroy us before we can retaliate."

The detective leaned back in her chair, her mouth slightly opening. "I work organized crime. Not international warfare."

"There are Russians in Chicago that are fronting the operation. They have sent thousands of weapons to Mexico to cause a war between the cartels. When enough Mexicans are killed in the crossfire the Mexican government will ask the Russians to send in their military to help. We think they have already made the request."

The detective laughed. "Is this a joke?"

Katie sat stone-faced across from her. "No. Now I want you to get your mind around it and do your job."

She leaned forward. "What job?"

"The Russians were using the Mafia to send the guns. We stole most of them, but some made it through. You must have confidential informants inside the mafia. One of them will have information on where we can find the Russians in Chicago."

"You were a Mafia boss. Why do you need my CIs?"

"Your snitches are in every crime family."

"Jesus," she said. She stood and began pacing the room. She stopped and stared at Katie. "I'll talk to my CIs. If they know anything I'll tell you."

"Not good enough. I'm your new partner."

"What do you know about police work?"

"I've been on the other side of the law all my life. I know how you operate as well as you do."

"I need to talk to the captain," she said and left. Minutes later she returned. Katie could see the anger on her face. "Fine."

"Who do we talk to first?"

The Detective paused.

"You're thinking of someone. Who?"

"An informant in one of the families. He may know something."

"Let's go."

"You don't say a word if we find him. You don't even gesture. Got it?"

They drove to a cheap bar, ignoring the smell of stale beer when they walked in. The detective saw some men at a table and went over. She slammed one of the men's heads against the table and handcuffed him.

"What the hell are you doing?" he said.

"I'm bringing you in for questioning."

She pushed him outside. Katie grabbed his arm and pulled him into an ally.

"Are you nuts? Those guys will never trust me again. You just got me killed."

"Don't look at her," Katie said. "Only me. Answer my questions and this will be painless. Don't, and I'll take you back to your friends and thank you for helping us."

"Who is this bitch?"

"Do you know any Russians that are doing gun deals?"

"I'm not talking to you."

Katie put her hand on his neck and slammed him against the wall. "Remember Rico Benetti?"

"What about him?'

"See a resemblance?"

He looked at her, then his eyes widened. "You're his kid. Your old man was a crazy son of a bitch."

"He was. And I inherited his genes. Only I'm more on the sadistic side." She pulled out a knife and put it on the top of his ear, pressing down.

"You can't do that," the Detective said.

"Russians," she said to the man.

He began yelling as blood dripped down the side of his neck. "Alright! Stop! All I know is Russians are looking for buyers to take the guns to Mexico."

"Where are they?"

"They're Russians. They'll be in Russian Town."

"I believe him," the Detective said. "Let him go."

Katie hesitated, then stepped back from him. The Detective removed his cuffs.

"Keep that bitch away from me," he said as he held his ear and walked away.

They went back to the car.

"I'm a cop. You can't be cutting people in front of me."

"Understood. Next time you can do it."

"Next time neither of us do it."

"Are you saying a Chicago cop has ever mistreated a suspect for information?"

She paused. "It happens," she mumbled.

"See. I'm already one of the team."

Chapter 27

"So now we go to Russian Town?" the detective asked.

"Yes. They're middle-aged men in America for a few weeks. What will they miss?"

"Russian food."

"Seriously? No one misses Russian food. They've been away from their wives and girlfriends for weeks. We hit the strip joints."

"Then turn left here. I know the most likely place."

They sat outside a strip club, watching people going in. Katie called Danni. "I need the security cameras for the strip club on the corner of Fifth and Carlisle. Can you send a feed to my phone?"

"Give me five."

Danni did it in four. They looked at the people in the club.

"What good is this? We don't know what they look like."

"They'll look like Russian G.I. Joe's. Perfect posture and no necks. They'll keep looking around because they'll wonder if they're in danger. They won't attract attention to themselves. No yelling or slapping the server's ass."

"Like those four guys," the detective said pointing at the phone.

"Just like those four guys."

"We should go in."

"Not you. You look like a cop."

She looked at her clothes, then in the rearview mirror. "I do?"

She called Danni again. "Danni, do you have any digital resumes for a stripper?"

"It's a job I never applied for, but I can pull one from the net."

"Send it to me."

"Are you doing it for the money or the excitement?" Danni asked.

"I need to go undercover."

"Hang on. Okay. Sent."

Katie read it, then opened a couple of buttons on her shirt, changed her hair as much as she could with her hands, and applied lipstick. "What do you think?"

"You'd make a good stripper."

"Thanks." She went inside the club and sat at the bar. She waited until the server approached the Russian's table and followed her. As she put the drinks down Katie told her she was looking for a job and asked where the manager was. The server told her he only did interviews during lunch and to come back.

“Can I send him my resume?” she said showing the server her phone. She made sure the Russians overheard her.

“I don’t care what you do,” the server said.

They looked at her and smiled. She put her hands on the edge of the table and leaned over, showing her cleavage. “You boys would hire me, wouldn’t you?” she said smiling back at them. With her fingers, she pressed a listening device under the table. She winked at them and left.

“Any luck?”

“Maybe. I planted a bug under the table.” Katie called Danni. “Can you get the signal?”

“I got it,” Danni said. “I’m running translation software.”

“You guys have the best tech I’ve ever seen,” the detective said.

“What are they saying?”

“One said he wants to screw your brains out. Another one talked about flipping you over and…”

“Not what I want to hear. Are these the guys?”

“Yes. I ran facial rec on a Russian military database. It's definitely them.”

“Good. We need to know when they’ll leave for Mexico.”

“So far it’s all sex talk, and not the good kind. Men are pigs.”

“Women are a lot worse when they watch male strippers.”

“True.”

They continued listening.

"Then there's another rude comment. Ew. Gross. One said he wondered what Mexican strippers are like. Another one just said they'll find out in a couple of days."

"We have our answer," Katie said. "Two days. Can you find their hotel?"

"Give me some time and I will. And they'll probably fly commercial, so I'll find their flights."

"Thanks, Danni. I'll see you soon."

"I want your systems," the detective said. "And Danni. Why do you have such great access to information?"

Katie looked at her, not answering.

"Right. Covert agency."

"I'll drop you off. We'll talk later."

"If we're partners you need to keep me up to date."

"I'll tell you what I can when I can," she said, dropping her at the station.

When Katie got home Danni was lying on the floor in front of the fireplace on her stomach. Her tablet and a drink were in front of her. Katie poured a drink and sat beside her, resting her back on the couch.

"You're wearing shorts and a T-shirt. If you're hot why is the fireplace on?"

"Are you flirting with me?"

"No."

"I like to dress this way. I look cute."

"If Cole was here I'd make you change."

"You are flirting with me, but I don't mind.

"What have you found out?"

"I identified the Russians and found the hotel. But they're not booked on any commercial flights out of either airport."

"If they aren't flying commercial they must be flying on a Russian plane."

"Yup. There's a Russian transport plane scheduled to land tomorrow at Midway Airport. Then it's continuing to Mexico."

"They wouldn't fly it here just to pick up four Russians."

"That's what I thought. I think they're stopping to transfer the final shipment of weapons to the water bomber."

Danni finished her drink. "Why didn't you bring the bottle?"

Katie brought it and refilled their glasses. "We have to intercept that flight. We have enough weapons in Mexico."

"Why not get the detective to bring her Boy Scouts to the party?"

"Good idea. We could let the cops handle this one. I'll talk to her in the morning."

"I want to be there."

"I'm fine with that. Just wear something else."

"I have a towel I like."

"I'm going to bed to call Cole."

"I wish I had a boy for sex talk. Can I borrow Cole when you're finished?"

"I'll ask him, but he'll say no."

"Why?"

"Because I'll tell him to."

****

When Katie and Danni showed up at the police station they were put in the interview room to wait for the detective.

"I hoped we were done," she said when she walked in and sat down. "You must be Danni. I need to know people like you."

"Thanks. I think."

"I come bearing gifts," Katie said.

"What gifts?"

"A major bust. Four Russians, a mafia group, cartel members, and hundreds of illegal weapons."

She sat in front of them, staring at Katie and then Danni. "Explain."

"The Russians are flying a plane load of weapons into Midway this afternoon. If it's the same as the others it'll be rifles, handguns, grenade launchers, stinger missiles, and gun trucks. Plus C4 and maybe some more landmines."

"Why?"

"They'll transfer it to fake a water bomber and the mafia will fly it to Mexico," Danni said. "Then they'll sell it to the cartels to kill each other and the Mexican people."

"Damn, you guys are bizarre."

"I want you to get some of your buddies together so we can stop them."

"Tell them to wear extra body armor," Danni said. "These guys will fire everything they have at us."

"There's no such thing as extra body armor."

"I'm talking about Level IV Body Armor. It protects against armor-piercing rifle fire with bullets made of a steel core. It's used by combat soldiers."

"Yeah. I'll check the broom closet and see if we have any."

She looked at her tablet. "The Russian plane ETA is 3:05 pm."

"I need to talk to my captain."

As she said it the door opened, and the captain poked his head in. "The briefing is in 10 minutes, detective. Let's go." He closed the door and left.

"I gather your agency already talked to him."

Katie nodded. "Let's go."

They met in a room with a large screen TV on the wall. Danni connected to it. When everyone involved was there they closed the door and the blinds.

Danni walked to the front of the room and brought up a sat photo of the airport. She zoomed in on one section. "The Russian plane is an Antonov An-12. This is the hanger assigned to it. The Mafia plane is a Boeing 747-400ERF. It's painted like a waterbomber. As you can see it's already there."

"About a dozen mafia members and some cartel members will transfer the weapons between the planes," Katie said. "There will also be four Russian military guys. Everyone will be armed. Everyone will try to kill you."

The meeting continued as the police discussed how to do the takedown. Katie kept looking at her watch. The plane must have landed by now. Danni checked her laptop and confirmed it did. It was taxiing to the hangar. Minutes later they left for the airport.

"This is getting real," Danni said. "Sometimes I don't like reality."

"Stay in cover and let the professionals take care of them," Katie said.

"I could hide behind you."

"You could. But don't. The Russians will make me a target."

"So will the mafia. And the cartel."

Katie puffed her cheeks out and slowly exhaled. "I have to make better life choices."

Chapter 28

Sirens were blasting and lights flashing as they sped towards the hanger. Katie followed the police onto the tarmac.

The men were transferring the weapons when they saw them. They dropped what they were doing and grabbed their guns, taking cover behind the cars and their SUVs. They began firing before the police could stop.

Bullets pierced their windshields and their doors as they slammed on the brakes and got out. One officer went down but his vest saved him and one of his team dragged him behind the car.

The mafia and cartel never let up, firing at anyone they could see. The police spread out, seeking cover. One of the police yelled over a bullhorn, trying to get them to stop shooting. A bullet hit him in the shoulder, and he crawled to cover.

One of the gang members fell. Then another and another. The police were better trained and better equipped. Katie looked for the Russians but couldn't see them. Danni stayed behind the car, leaning out and firing. She hit one man in the leg.

Two of the mafia tried to get into one of the SUV’s. Both were wounded before they could make it. Another officer got on the bullhorn to tell them they had no place to go. To drop their weapons.

Katie saw a man with a rifle aiming at the detective. The detective glanced at him and realized what was about to happen. Katie fired twice at him, both shots hitting his chest. The detective looked at her and mouthed the word thanks.

Slowly the shooting eased. The police began moving forward through the cars, firing on the remaining shooters. Katie noticed the Russians getting into their SUV. She ran to the detective's car, Danni following in a low crouch. The Russians sped by them.

“Let’s go,” Katie yelled. As the detective was moving toward the car Katie jumped in the driver’s seat and Danni got the back. The detective stopped on the driver’s side expecting Katie to move over.

“Get in or stay here!” Katie yelled.

She got in the passenger seat and Katie sped away in pursuit. She put on the lights and siren as she drove.

“You can’t drive a police car.”

“Seems I can.” She hit the gas and followed the Russians. The detective checked her weapon and loaded a new mag.

“They turned left,” Danni said from the back. She still had her tablet and was checking the roads. “They could be trying to get on Highway 55.”

The car ran a red light, clipping the back of another car. The driver regained control without slowing.

"It's okay," Danni said. "It was just a Lexus."

"Red light ahead," the detective said, putting one hand on the dashboard.

"I have my police lights on," Katie said.

"You overestimate the intelligence of the public."

"Not really." She never slowed. A box truck started entering the intersection.

"Truck!"

Katie swerved around the front of it, tires screeching but she kept control of the car. The detective looked at her.

"My dad taught me to drive. Ironically to escape police cars." Katie smiled and accelerated.

"Highway entrance in one block," Danni said.

The SUV drove around two cars on the entranceway, horns blasting at them as they passed. The cars heard the siren and moved over as Katie went by them.

"I have to get one of these cars," she said.

"They're heading south out of the city," Danni said. "I checked traffic ahead. It's light."

"We have to cease pursuit," the detective said.

"You can get out anytime you like, but I'm not stopping."

"We do not pursue speeding vehicles if we feel the public could be injured. Stop the vehicle." She pointed her gun at Katie.

"You shoot me, and you'll spend the rest of your life in a black site that's far worse than any prison you can imagine."

Katie concentrated on her driving. The detective lowered her weapon.

"Good decision," Katie said.

"They're pulling off the highway," Danni said. "This road leads to the Glen Forest Waterfall Preserve. There won't be many cars there."

The Russian car slammed on the brakes, then began reversing towards Katie.

"No you don't," Kate said. She cut around the car and spun her car around, so it faced the Russians. Without hesitating she hit the gas again. "I'm glad you have a ramming bar on the front of this thing."

"No!" the detective yelled.

Katie slammed into the front of the Russian car. Their hood buckled and smoke came from the engine. Katie saw them getting out of the car, some clinging to the door for support. Katie and the detective got out; guns aimed.

"On the ground!" she shouted.

The Russians raised their guns and were about to fire. Katie shot the two on her side of the car. The detective shot the driver, but the other man ran behind the car for cover.

"Drop it! Show me your hands!" the detective yelled.

Without warning Katie moved toward the back of the car. The man was kneeling, waiting for the detective to come around the corner, his gun ready. Katie approached him from behind. "Drop it, bitch."

The man looked at her, then put the gun on the ground. The detective cuffed him.

"I can't get out!" Danni yelled. "Open the damn door."

Katie did and they walked back to the Russian.

"I'll call for a car," the detective said.

"No need. I had a chopper follow us," Danni said. "Should be here…," she looked up when she heard the blades, "…about now."

The chopper landed on the road.

"He's my prisoner," the detective said.

"You can have the dead ones. We have questions for this one."

"That's not how this works."

Danni typed on her tablet. Minutes later the detective got a call from her captain telling her to let them have the man. She glared at Katie.

"Sorry about your car," Katie said. "And everything else."

Katie cuffed the Russian and pushed him to the chopper. The detective leaned against her car as she stared at the helicopter flying away.

The chopper landed next to a Control detention center. Two armed guards were waiting by the entrance, watching the chopper land. It was a plain concrete building surrounded by dead grass and a wire fence. Katie had been here with Cole once when he wanted somebody questioned.

Katie and Danni took the Russian inside. The walls were concrete, and the doors were steel. There were no windows or pictures on the walls. Katie put the man in one of the rooms and cuffed him to a railing attached to the back wall. It was high enough that he couldn't sit. There was no furniture or windows in the room.

They left him and went to an office at the end of the hall. A man inside walked from behind his desk and hugged Katie and Danni. He was in his 50s and looked like a drill sergeant with kind eyes.

"Hi, Wes," Katie said.

"It's good to see you guys," he said. "It's been a while."

"I love what you've done with the place," Danni joked.

"I do love decorating." He pointed at a picture of his wife and children. It was the only thing on the desk.

"We brought a present."

"I heard. Russian military guy. Control filled me in on the situation. We'll question him and I'll send you the results."

"Thanks. We don't have much time."

"I'll put Nadia on it."

"That'll do it. We have to go."

As they were leaving Katie stopped and looked at the Russian, not speaking. He tried to look defiant, but the fear leaked from his body. That was what she wanted. They left for the chopper.

"Will they torture him?" Danni asked.

"No, torture doesn't work. A person will say anything to stop the pain. Nadia is a psychiatrist. She'll do a complete background on him first and find his greatest fear, then use it to get him to talk. After that, we'll send him back to Russia and let his bosses deal with his failure.

They climbed in the chopper. Katie asked the pilot to land at the airport to get her car. The entire area was a crime scene. Investigators had covered the bodies and were gathering evidence. The detective's captain saw them land and walked over to them.

"This is a good bust," she said.

"I imagine there were a lot of weapons we kept off the streets," Katie said.

"More than weapons. We found replacement parts for Russian attack helicopters and missile parts for short-range tactical nukes."

"Then I'll leave you with the mess we made," Katie said.

"This was a good bust," the Captain said. "Thanks."

"I couldn't have done it without the detective. She's a good cop."

"I'll tell her what you said."

Chapter 29

Cole and Sofia were waiting at the airport when the plane landed in Pietras Negas. Danni was told she was needed at Control and stayed back. They had dinner with Riker and Eve at a quiet table in the hotel restaurant, then went to the room and shared the latest updates.

"On the way down here I found out things have escalated," Katie said. "Washington told Mexico they know about the Russian plans. The Mexicans told them to stay out of their business. There were threats of trade sanctions and closing the border, but nothing worked."

"Where does it stand now?"

"They're still talking, but the Director said she doubts it'll do any good. The Mexicans say the Russians are only there to help get rid of the cartels."

"I'm guessing they don't care what Washington thinks," Eve said. "And the Director told us the feds have taken over the investigation at the airport."

"That's going to piss off the detective," Katie said.

"Did Control tell you what they want us to do next?" Riker said.

"Keep the cartels from killing Mexican people," Katie said.

"We need a way to calm the cartels down," Cole said. "The Mexican government has to rationalize bringing in the Russians. They won't be able to do that if the people are no longer being threatened."

"I'm not sure we can calm down sadistic killers," Eve said. "And I don't think we can scare them."

"Maybe we can distract them," Katie said. "Their goal is to get money by making and selling drugs. What if we interfere with it so much they come after us?"

"Then they might stop killing the people in villages," Sofia said. "It's a good idea. But how?"

"First we need a better base of operations than the hotel room," Cole said.

"The hotel has conference rooms on the second floor," Eve said. "One is a media room we could rent. Danni can bring down all the tech equipment she needs, and the Wi-Fi here is good."

"Sounds a lot better than some of the other places we used," Riker said.

"And it's one floor above the pool, Riker," Eve said. "You can watch the bikini babes when you get bored."

"Only because I have lifeguard training."

"Yeah. That's why," Eve said.

"We should celebrate the wins for once instead of mourning the losses," Cole said. He got two bottles of tequila from the cupboard and glasses for everyone.

"I like the way you think, buddy," Riker said.

****

The knock on the door the next morning was hangover loud. Cole got up, wrapped a towel around himself, and answered, his eyes still half closed.

"Danni?"

“Hi, Cole. You look happy to see me.” She smiled and looked at his towel.

“It happens in the morning.”

“Get dressed, big guy. I have a bunch of stuff in the lobby that you need to bring up. Reception is watching it for me.”

“Tell them to put it in the media room. We booked it.” He handed her a room key. “Here’s a key. Don’t knock. I need another hour's sleep.”

“I’ll make coffee when I get back. Katie here?”

“I don’t remember.”

“I miss all the good parties.”

After the staff helped her put the equipment in the room she returned and ordered breakfast for the room. She knocked on the bedroom door and yelled for Cole to get up. When she heard the shower she walked into the bathroom to tell Katie breakfast was coming. Cole had his head tilted back and his hands in his hair as he rinsed it. He saw her when he finished. “I’ll be there in a minute.”

“Sorry, I thought you were Katie.”

“Now that you know, close the door.”

She paused, smiled, and winked at him before leaving.

Breakfast had arrived by the time Cole walked into the kitchen.

“Sorry, Cole,” she said.

“What for?” Katie asked.

“I walked into his shower.”

Katie looked at her. “I’m too hungover to even glare at you.” They ate in silence. Danni kept smiling at Cole.

It was an hour before they met Riker and Eve in the media room. Danni set up her computer and connected it to the monitor on the wall.

"I brought listening devices, tiny security cameras, earpieces, trackers, and a bunch of other stuff we might be able to use. So what did you want to do with it all?"

"We want to have the cartels turn their attention to us. I'm hoping they'll leave the people alone and the Russians won't be needed. We have one chance to get this right.

"I thought the Russians were already approved for entry," Danni said.

"The government still has to convince the people."

"Short of wearing a towel, how do we distract them?" Danni said.

"What towel?" Katie asked.

"Not important," Cole said. "I'll brief Sofia."

"Now that I'm here I need to tell you the latest update."

"I gather it's not good news."

"Of course not," Danni said. "I told the Director about an abandoned runway northwest of here. The Mexican government built it to fly freight to the States, but the corruption was so bad the president stopped construction. I was able to confirm Mexico gave the Russians a 99-year lease on it."

"How bad of a shape is it in?"

"It can be restored pretty easily. The government approved Mexican contractors to repair the runway and the terminal. They haven't got all the paperwork in place yet so I'm not sure when they'll start."

"How big is the runway?" Riker asked.

"Big enough for 747s."

"They could fly all their military equipment in," Riker said.

"And their missiles," Eve said.

"I need to see it," Cole said.

"So do I," Danni said. "I need to find some weaknesses so we can slow repairs to the runway."

"Let's go, Danni," Cole said.

"There could be people watching the airport," Riker said. "Keep both eyes open."

"Will do."

Traffic was heavy and slow as they drove toward the airport. Danni kept one arm outside, letting the wind cool her. "Do you have any idea how you can destroy a runway?" she asked.

"I'd use an anti-runway penetration bomb," Cole said. "Maybe a Matra Durandal from the Gulf War. It's a 450-pound bomb with parachute braking, a rocket booster, and two warheads. The plane comes in at a low level and drops it. A parachute slows it, then it fires a rocket to hit the runway. It creates a crater, and then a smaller charge penetrates the crater to destroy concrete slabs around it. Takes a long time to repair the mess."

Danni turned toward him and stared.

"What?" he said.

"I swear you get excited when you talk about this stuff."

"Then it's lucky I'm not wearing a towel."

She laughed and put her arm out the window again.

They stopped when they saw the turnoff to the airport. The area was fenced and gated. Cole scanned the airport with binoculars. "I don't see anyone."

He took the wheel wrench from the trunk and broke the lock. They slowly drove in, stopping by the runway. They got out and walked down it.

"It's in pretty good shape," Danni said.

"No cracks or waves. The dirt probably protected it from the heat. Let's check out the building."

They drove closer and went in. Everything inside was covered in a layer of dust, and some windows were broken, but the floors and walls were in good shape.

"They can clean this up in a few days," Danni said.

"The Russians could house a lot of people in here. And there's plenty of land for maintenance shops and weapons storage."

"And they have a helicopter pad on the side."

"Sadly, it's perfect for them."

"Let's go back to the hotel. We've seen enough."

"Oh hell," Danni said, glancing out the window. Two SUVs were speeding down the road toward them. When they reached the terminal they exited the trucks.

"Russians," Danni said. "We're so screwed."

Chapter 30

"This way," Cole said, and they ran to a door marked Maintenance. He kicked it in, and they ran inside. There were metal work desks scattered around the open floor. Cole pointed at a metal cabinet, and they hid behind it. It was the only thing that could stop high-powered rounds. They waited with their guns in their hands.

"They must have surveillance cameras we missed," Danni whispered. "What do we do?"

"We stay alive until help comes."

The door opened and two men came in, rifles at their eyes, ready to shoot. They moved slowly to opposite ends of the room. "Stay here," Cole whispered.

He jumped up and began running for the back door, firing as he ran. Both men returned fire. Cole hit one, wounding him. The other man ducked, then aimed. Danni stood and fired three shots into his chest. Then she fired twice into the wounded man.

Cole ran back to cover. "I was leading them away from you. All you had to do was stay down."

"Katie would be mad as hell at me if I let you get killed."

The door flew open, and four men ran in and took cover behind the desks. They saw where their men were lying and figured out where the shots came from, then lay down bursts of fire at Cole and Danni.

"Come out!" one yelled. "We won't shoot you."

"I don't believe them," Danni said.

Two more men entered. Cole fired and hit one of them. More bursts of fire hit around them. Two men entered from the back door. Cole checked his mag. "I'm out."

Danni checked hers. "Two left."

"We might have a chance if we surrender."

Danni nodded. "Sure. We could tell them it's just a misunderstanding."

Cole sent Riker a 911 text. He knew Riker would come after them. "Hold your fire," he yelled. He threw his gun to the side. Danni threw hers beside it.

"Stand up. Hands raised."

They stood, hands in the air. A Russian officer entered the room. "Bring them!" the Russian yelled. "I need to question them."

They were cuffed and pushed to the vehicles. One vehicle stayed behind to collect the bodies.

"They didn't cover our eyes," Danni said. "We're not getting out of this alive, are we?"

"There's always a chance," Cole said.

They continued back to the highway, eventually turning into a driveway. The hacienda was large and new.

The Russians pushed them through the house to a deck by a pool. A Mexican in a suit sat at a table with two Russians.

"They were in the airport," a Russian said.

"I don't want any blood on the deck," one of the sitting Russians said. "Take them to the spare room."

Cole and Danni were taken down a hallway and thrown into a room. The only furniture was two chairs. They pushed them into the chairs leaving their hands cuffed behind their backs.

One of the Russians from the deck came in. "Get out," he said to his men as he put on leather gloves.

He smiled at Cole and Danni. He stood over Cole and swung his fist across Cole's face. His head snapped back. Blood ran from his mouth.

"This is going to be a long process," the Russian said.

"Let her go. She's a clerk. She doesn't know anything."

"A clerk?" Danni said.

"We have plans for her."

"What plans?" Danni asked.

He touched her cheek and smiled at her. Cole began to stand and stop him. He was hit twice, almost blacking out.

"Stop it, you jerk!" Danni yelled.

The door opened and another Russian came in. He whispered to him, and they left.

"Are you alright?" Danni said.

"Don't look him in the eyes. Don't talk to him unless he asks you a question, then answer the shortest way you know how. And don't call him names."

"Why is the Mexican here?"

"He might be sent here by the Mexican President to help them out."

"How do we get out of here, Cole?"

"I don't know."

****

Riker stared at his phone when he got the 911.

"What is it?" Eve said.

"Cole sent a 911."

"Jesus," Katie said. "He has to be in a lot of trouble to do that."

They ran out and sped to the airport. When they arrived they took out their weapons and rushed into the building. They were searching when they heard Eve shouting. They ran into the maintenance room. Blood covered the floor in numerous locations.

"They were dragging bodies out the back," Riker said.

Katie looked around the room, spotting where Cole and Danni might have taken cover. She searched the floor, then picked something up.

"What is it?" Riker asked.

"A bracelet. Danni showed it to me once. Her dad gave it to her. She must have left it for us to find."

"Then she's still alive," Eve said. "And so is Cole."

"Over here," Katie said.

They walked to a spot near the door and examined a footprint in the blood. "That's a military boot," Riker said. "The Russians would take them for questioning."

"Where?"

Cole called Sofia. “Are there any haciendas near the airport the Russians could rent?”

“Yes,” she said, nodding. “We know where they’re staying. I’ll text you the directions.”

“Riker. I’ll follow you in Cole’s car in case we need it,” Eve said. “He always has weapons in it.”

Riker increased his speed. When they could see the hacienda he stopped. Katie began to get out of the car.

“Wait,” Riker said. “Cole knows how to stay alive. And he knows how to protect Danni. We have to think this through. We don’t know how many men are in the house.”

They all ran to a small hill on the east side of the house and scanned the area.

“They’re Russians,” Riker said. “I count five men on the deck. No idea how many are inside.”

“How do we get in?” Katie asked.

“There is no way we can get across the yard without being seen. They’ll kill Danni and Cole before we can reach them.”

“Riker’s right,” Eve said. “We have to wait until dark.”

“No. They could be torturing him.”

“I’m sorry, Katie,” Riker said. “We have to wait.”

She kept her binoculars on the area hoping for a glimpse of them.

Chapter 31

Cole and Danni looked at each other when the Russian returned. She sat up straight, her leg bouncing slightly, thinking this was the end.

The Russian took out his gun and chambered a round. He placed it on Danni's temple.

"I will kill her if you don't answer my questions."

"You kill her, and I have nothing left to live for."

"Really?" she said, staring at him. "I feel the same about you."

The Russian looked at them. "Idiots."

"I'll answer your questions," Cole said. "You won't be alive by morning, so it won't matter what I tell you."

"You talk brave. Let's hope you die just as brave."

"We know about you shipping guns to the cartels, so they'll kill more Mexican people. We know the President is part of it. We know you're setting up a missile base to take out the U.S. There is nothing we don't know."

He stood in front of Cole, staring down at him. He paused before speaking. "Then I have no reason to keep you alive."

"Sure, you do. You need to know what we have planned. How we're going to stop you."

The man holstered his gun and swung at Cole again. Then again. He returned his gun to Danni's temple again.

"I told you she doesn't know anything."

"Then I have no reason to keep her alive," the Russian said.

"Our government is sending troops here to blow up the airfield," Danni said, rapidly firing the words. "They're going to drop anti-runway penetration bombs. If you repair the runway they'll do it again. You can't win."

The Russian backhanded her hard enough she fell out of her chair. He smiled, then walked over to pick her up. She rolled on her back and kicked with all her strength into his crotch. He doubled over. She kicked again, this time hitting his face. He dropped to the ground on his side. Before Cole could help she stood and dropped with her full weight, her knee hitting his neck. Cole heard the crack when it broke. The Russian never moved. She slowly stood; her eyes locked on him.

"Jesus," Cole whispered. "We have to talk later."

He twisted his hands around and took a knife from the man's belt. After cutting his cuffs he did Danni's.

Taking his gun he held one finger to his lips so Danni wouldn't talk. They waited. No one heard anything. They moved to the farthest corner.

"Where did you learn to do that?"

"I've been taking fighting lessons at Control. I didn't think it would work. I'll never get that sound out of my head."

"You saved our asses," he said. He wiped the blood from his mouth and kissed her cheek. "Thanks."

She took his face in her hands and kissed him on the lips.

"Ow," he said, hurting from where he was hit.

"Sorry."

He grunted, trying to hide his awkwardness.

"What do we do now?" she asked.

"I have a girlfriend."

"I meant about getting out of here."

"Oh. We wait until we hear gunfire."

"What gunfire?"

"My friends are the best at what they do. I know they're outside this place somewhere. They'll wait for dark and then come in."

"We've got some time and nothing to do," Danni said and touched his arm.

"We're surrounded by Russians, and you want to make out. Did they teach that in your fighting classes?"

"In lesson four. It was my favorite lesson."

They turned when the door opened. Cole fired before the guard could.

****

Katie moved to the bottom of the hill out of sight of the hacienda. She paced back and forth trying to control her urge to run to the house.

When dusk settled she looked at Riker. He shook his head. He knew what she was going through and was amazed by her discipline. When it was dark she walked up the hill.

"I'm going in," she said. "You can decide if you want to come with me."

"We do it properly. We don't know how many there are in the house."

"What's properly mean?"

"We need to find out what room they're in. Eve and I can take out the two guards outside the front door. Then we need to draw the rest of the guards out. At the same time, you guys go in the back door." He stopped talking when he heard gunfire.

"Screw that," Katie said and began running to the house, the rest chasing after her. The two guards in front were moving inside the house. They turned when they heard the footsteps. Riker and Eve fired as they ran, and both men dropped. They stood at the side of the open door and looked in. Bullets poured through the opening.

Katie ran to the back of the house. The glass doors were open. She saw three guards behind cover, firing at the front door. She moved inside and began firing at the guards. They turned. Eve and Riker fired at them. The guards were in a crossfire from the front and back. The first two were killed. One more was hiding behind a wall. Riker fired four times through the wall. The man dropped and Riker loaded a new mag.

Katie saw two guards in the hallway just outside a bedroom door. She fired. A guard was about to return fire when Cole opened the bedroom door and fired at the man's head. The man dropped. The last guard fired at Katie. The bullet grazed her side, and she doubled over from the shock and pain. Cole stepped in front of the man, grabbed his gun barrel, and pushed it to the side. He locked eyes with him and fired twice, point-blank into his chest.

He turned and ran to Katie, helping her lie down. Eve and Riker appeared. Cole pulled up her shirt and looked at it. The bullet cut a ravine into her flesh.

"Would you get the car?" he said to Eve as he helped Katie stand.

Eve ran to bring the car closer.

"I'm alright," Katie said, holding her side. "Except for the pain. That part sucks."

"There's a medic kit in the car. We'll fix you on the way home."

"Guys," Danni said loudly from the living room. They went to the room. Danni was standing beside a wounded guard. He had his arm around her neck and his gun aimed at her temple. She had both hands on his arm.

Cole held up his hand as he walked closer. "There's been enough killing. Just leave."

"You shoot and she dies."

"No one's going to shoot," Cole said. "Let her go."

They saw Eve appear behind the man. She pressed her gun against the back of his head. "Let her go," she said.

The man hesitated. Eve pressed the gun harder. Slowly he lowered his hand and dropped the gun. He released Danni. Eve kicked the back of his knee and he dropped. He raised his hands to shoulder height, looking Cole in the eyes, expecting to be shot.

"Leave," Cole said, not wanting any more killing.

The man struggled to stand and then hobbled into the darkness. Danni ran to Cole and hugged him. “Thank you. Thank you,” she repeated, kissing him on the cheek over and over.

“Oh, come on,” Katie said. “Eve took him down. Climb off Cole before I shoot you.”

Danni released him. “The guy came in behind me.”

“I’m sure he’s not the first one,” Katie said, still angry.

“Hey! Not nice.”

“Let’s go,” Cole said. “We need to fix Katie.”

Chapter 32

Katie spent the next two days recuperating. One afternoon Danni came from the media room in the hotel with her tablet. She sat at the table with Cole and Katie.

"The Mexican doctor was good," Katie said. "How do you find these guys?"

"Whenever we're in a location Control makes a list of doctors nearby and runs background checks on them. It's standard procedure."

"I'm glad they do."

"I rented a hacienda," Danni said as she read from her tablet. "Modern and spacious, has wireless, four bedrooms, and a pool. And it comes with a caretaker family. She cooks and cleans, and the husband takes care of the grounds. They come in when we need them. Plus there's a landing strip for small planes."

"Then it's a cartel house?" Katie said.

"Yup. The owner died in a shootout with the Zetas six weeks ago and the family are too scared to live in it anymore."

"Why do we need it?"

"It's dumb living in a hotel, and I'm tired of hearing you guys banging like bunnies. Plus it's close to the Russian airport. That's our main goal now."

"Never say banging like bunnies again," Katie said.

"At least it's taking less time."

"No, it's not," Katie said, throwing a napkin at her, and grabbing her wound. "Ouch."

"I'll tell Eve and Riker," Danni said.

Danni looked at her phone. "It's a text from the Director. I needed her permission to rent the house, so she knows all about it."

"What does she want?"

"She said Washington wants us to do a flyover and take pictures, then send them. The sat photos don't capture everything."

"Can you rent a plane?" Cole said. "I have a pilot's license."

"There's already one at the hacienda. I suspect they used it for drug deliveries. We could use it if we don't tell anyone."

"I'll tell Riker and Eve to get ready. You'll have to pack up the media room. We'll leave as soon as we can."

****

It was a modern hacienda with a fence surrounding it. The gates were open, and an older man and woman were standing in the doorway.

"They said the caretakers would be here to show us the place," Danni said. "That must be them."

After choosing bedrooms and putting clothes away they had lunch on the deck by the pool.

"I feel like a normal person for the first time in a long time," Katie said. She leaned her head back on the chair and closed her eyes, letting the sun wash away every care she had.

Riker came out of the house with binoculars. "We can see the airport," he said, staring at it.

"Anything happening?" Cole asked.

"They have equipment on the runway. Looks like they're repairing it. Nothing in the building yet."

Danni walked out in a bikini and a towel around her waist and sat at the table. She put her phone down and ate some fruit. "The Director called me."

"Tell her we're on vacation," Eve said.

"I wish. She wanted security cams set up around the airport so they could see what's happening."

"It's clear land all around it. There's no place to put them."

"I told her that. She said to buy a telescope and watch it that way. I'll get one tomorrow. She also said to do the flyover today. Washington wants to see the pics."

She put more fruit on the plate and kept eating, glancing at Katie. "Katie."

"What?"

"Why are you staring at me?"

"As long as I have a giant bandage on my side no one should be allowed to wear bikinis. It's not fair."

"Sorry, babe. I live in Chicago. Here I have sun and a pool. I'm taking advantage while I can."

The caretaker woman came to the table. "The police are here to see you," she said.

"Bring them in," Cole said.

"What's going on?" Eve said.

"No idea."

Two officers came onto the deck. One stared at Danni too long.

"How can we help you?" Cole said.

They introduced themselves as local police officers.

"Mexico has some of the best resorts in the world," one said. "Why are you staying here?"

"We don't like crowds," Riker said.

"I'd hate to come to this house if there is any trouble. You could sit in jail for a long time before we finished investigating."

"I can assure you we're peaceful people."

"We'll see."

"What's happening at the airport?" Riker asked.

"You can see it from here. Is that why you're renting this hacienda?"

"No. We didn't know until we got here."

"I will warn you to stay away from the site. The Russian International Assistance Team will be occupying it. They're in Mexico to train our people on air and sea rescue and save those in trouble. The airspace above it is restricted."

"Restricted, how?" Riker said.

"They have permission to shoot down any planes flying into their airspace."

"So they can practice rescuing survivors?" Danni said, smiling at them.

"There won't be any survivors. Hopefully, we'll never meet again." They turned and left.

"They seem nice," Danni said.

"I bet they were sent by the local cartel to welcome us," Katie said.

"Then we should consider ourselves thoroughly welcomed."

"You heard him say planes will be shot down, right," Katie said.

"I'm sure they don't mean us," Cole said.

"Pretty sure they do."

"I don't think they have any surface-to-air missiles in place yet."

"I bet they have stingers," Katie said.

"Stingers are good to 11,000 feet. I can take the plane to 14,000 for a short time. It'll give us enough clearance to be sure it doesn't reach us."

"Why a short time?"

"Not much oxygen. A pilot gets hypoxia and might think he can fly without the plane."

"Or we just die from numerous medical problems," Riker said.

"It's nice to have choices," Cole said.

Chapter 33

Cole checked the plane thoroughly. Then he checked it again. It seemed to be well maintained, and it was fueled and ready. The dirt runway was not long enough to allow for even small problems. He sat in the pilot's seat with Riker beside him.

"You okay with this thing?" Riker asked.

"I'd prefer to rip it apart and check it, but I've done everything I can."

He brought it to takeoff speed and climbed, watching the gauges. He banked in both directions, then ascended and descended.

"Everything looks okay. Is your camera ready?"

"I tested it on Eve last night," Riker said. "Works great."

"Stay weird, Riker."

"I have no choice, buddy."

"I'm going to climb to 14,000 feet. I'll fly over at an angle so you can get good footage. I should be able to descend before we run into problems."

When he hit altitude he banked to fly over the airport. He saw people stop working and staring up at them. A guard ran into the building and then ran back onto the runway.

Riker videoed as they approached. “Someone has a stinger aimed at us,” Riker said, staring through the video camera.

“I hope the stats are right about it only working to 11,000. We’re at 14,000.”

“It's supersonic. We’ll know pretty fast.”

Cole maintained his flight path.

“They fired!” Riker yelled. “Incoming!”

Cole kept the plane steady. “Where is it?” He tried looking around.

“Behind and below.”

“Keep recording.”

Cole knew they didn’t have much time.

“We’re past the runway. Keep your altitude until I can find the missile.” Riker snapped his head around, unable to see it.

“If it travels supersonic it should have hit us by now.”

“Stay high,” Riker said. “They may launch another one.”

“I have to turn and fly over again to make sure we get it all.”

“We’ll be too high for too long.”

“No choice. I’m not doing this again.” Cole said and flew back over the runway.

“No more missiles,” Riker said. “They must have figured out they can’t reach us.”

"I'm heading down to find some air." He slowly leveled the plane and began to descend.

"What are you doing?" Riker said.

"I need to descend."

"You're climbing. Down is the other way."

Cole knew he needed oxygen. He dropped the nose and his speed increased.

"Ease off the power," Riker said. "We're picking up too much speed."

Cole fought to pull the nose up. Slowly he leveled off at 5,000 feet. "You okay?"

"How would I know?"

They saw the hacienda runway in the distance. Both felt the tension leaving them.

"Cole, am I still affected, or did our engine stop?"

"I was hoping it was just me that noticed it. Why can't cartel guys take care of their planes."

"Start it."

"I've been trying."

"Can you do a dead stick landing?"

"Looks like we'll find out."

"Can we make the runway?"

"I don't know."

The plane glided towards the landing. The only sound was the wind rushing by them. Riker had his hand on the dash as if it would protect him.

"Everyone is beside the runway, watching," Riker said.

"And wondering why we don't have an engine. We're at 3,000. 2500. 2000."

"We're going to land short."

Cole fought the controls, doing everything he could to maintain his height, but gravity always wins. The plane hit hard and one of the wheel struts broke off. Cole and Riker were snapped forward. The plane twisted, dust exploding from under it. All they could do was hang on. Slowly it came to a stop.

Riker looked at Cole through a dust cloud. "You injured?"

"Just a sprained wrist. Nothing serious."

"Good flying."

"We crashed."

"We crashed and lived."

Everyone ran to the plane and opened the doors.

"Are you alright?" Katie said as Cole got out. He held onto the plane until his dizziness stopped. Danni and Eve were helping Riker.

"What happened?" Katie asked.

"The propellor thingy stopped going around," Riker said.

They all turned to look north when they heard a helicopter.

"It could be the Russians," Cole said, unable to run. They watched the helicopter land and a woman got out.

"It's the Director," Danni said. "What the hell is she doing here?"

The Director approached them, staring at the wreckage. "You crashed the plane," she said.

"Cole did it," Riker said.

"Thanks, buddy."

"We need to talk," she said.

"Do want a coffee or juice?" Danni said as they walked inside the house.

"Orange juice. Add tequila."

After they poured drinks they sat in the living room. The Director took a sip, looked at the glass, and put it down.

"Did you get the footage?"

"Yes," Riker said.

"Show me the video." Riker handed her the camera and she looked at the footage before putting the camera down.

"I see they launched a stinger," she asked.

"Yup," Riker said. "They're nasty people."

"You got your thumb in the shot. It's blue. I'm guessing you were flying over 11,000 feet at low oxygen."

"A little over," Cole said.

She looked at him.

"Fine. 14,000. We had to be sure the stinger didn't reach us."

"You're no good to me dead."

"I can feel the love," Riker said.

"Danni," the Director said. "Put the footage on a USB for me, but first delete Riker and Eve's sex shoot."

"You didn't delete it?" Eve said, grabbing the camera.

"I was going to later," Riker said.

"Idiot."

Danni took the camera to her computer in the bedroom to edit it. She returned in a few minutes with two USB's. She handed the second one to Riker. "This is the sex footage in case you want to work on your technique."

"I give good technique," Riker said. "Tell her Eve."

"We'll watch it later," Eve said.

"I'm here to update you," the Director said. She took another drink and put her glass down. "Washington discussed blowing up the airport but determined it would cause the problems we're trying to avoid. A conflict with Russia would be disastrous."

"Then what do we do?" Cole asked.

"We know Russia is bribing the Mexican president and contributing to his re-election. We're supplying money to the guy running against him.

"Same corruption, new corrupter," Katie said.

"Do you think you can get him elected?" Riker asked.

"We have done it in other countries for decades."

"Which is why there are so many screwed-up countries in the world," Katie said.

"Point taken."

What do we do?"

"The president is running on stopping the cartels from killing people," the Director said. "So far the skirmishes have been relatively small."

"Maybe in your mind," Katie said. "The people don't feel the same way."

"I'm not being flippant. I know what they face every day. You need to stop the cartels and stall the Russians."

"Is that it?" Katie asked.

"For now, she picked up her glass, looked at it, then put it down again. "There's still part of the committee that wants to send a bomber to destroy the airport. We have to prevent that from happening." She stood. "Don't fail. And for god's sake buy better tequila," she said as she left.

"I wonder if she has any friends?" Danni said.

Chapter 34

When Cole answered his phone it was Sofia. She spoke quickly like she was panicking.

"One of my team just saw six Gulf Cartel vehicles on the highway. She said they turned up a road that leads to a small village in Los Zetas territory.

"What are they doing?"

"They want revenge on the Zetas for when they attacked the Gulf village. It could be a massacre."

"Can we beat them there?" Cole asked.

"It'll be close. I'm on my way to meet with my team. They're bringing a gun truck. Get to Highway 16. We'll text directions when you're on the road."

"We're leaving now."

They ran to the car and drove to the highway.

"Six trucks, maybe two or three per truck," Riker said. "That's a lot of cartel members."

"I know. We'll have to play it smart." He dialed Sofia. "Don't drive into town until we get there. We have to do this as a team."

"Hurry."

Cole increased speed. The directions said to turn onto 16 then take the third right turn onto a dirt road. The village was five miles in. When he hit the road he kept it at top speed. Coming around a corner he saw Sofia and her team standing by her car, rifles in their hands. A gun truck was behind the cars. He pulled in front of them.

"The village is just around the corner," Sofia said. "They can't see us from here."

"I don't want anyone getting killed, so listen carefully."

Cole explained his plan and they left for their positions. Eve and Riker left in the gun truck and he and Katie ran to the south side of the town square. He gave the others time to get ready. In the square the cartel had corralled about 50 people, some were children and babies. The villagers were kneeling, the youngest kids clinging to their parents. The cartel was in front of them, the leader shouting orders to his men. They were about to kill them.

Cole looked at Katie. She nodded. They stood behind part of a wall and fired. Two men went down. The others started returning fire and people started screaming and lying face down. Mothers covered their children with their bodies. Pieces of the wall exploded into the air when the bullets hit. They had no chance to fire back.

Sofia and the others ran behind the cartel and kept yelling at them to drop their guns. At the same time, Riker and Eve sped into the square in the gun truck, slamming on the brakes. Riker had the machine gun aimed at them.

The men turned toward Riker, then toward the others circling them. Cole and Katie ran into the square and yelled the same thing. They looked at Cole, the people behind them, and at the gun truck. You could see the confusion on their faces. They knew there was no way to survive.

Some started dropping their guns. One raised his at Cole. A shot rang out and the cartel member dropped from a back shot. Cole nodded a thanks to Sofia. The rest put their guns down. Some of the villagers moved to the side and watched as the villagers grabbed their weapons and made them kneel. They stood over them and aimed.

"Don't shoot," Cole yelled. "It's over. It's over."

He couldn't stop them. The cartel was going to murder their children. They knew they would return if they let them go free. Shots blasted through the air. Some of the cartel members tried to run but never made it. Cole kept yelling at the townspeople to stop. In 30 seconds it was over. The only man alive was on his knees, bent over so his head was on the ground and his arms covering it. They let him live. He was the leader. He looked up, pleading.

Cole looked at the bodies. He'd never seen anything like this. His heart pounded. The villagers wanted to send the message that no one kills their kids. No one. Katie and Danni stood frozen, staring at the bodies and the blood. One of the villagers approached Cole.

"Thank you," he said. "You saved us."

Cole didn't know what to say. He looked at the cartel leader. Two of the men dragged him backward out of the square. He was still pleading and threatening.

"We'll take care of this," the villager said, nodding at the bodies.

Sofia approached him. “Keep the weapons. Learn how to use them. We’ll bring more tomorrow.” She touched his hand and then waved at her team to return to their cars.

Riker and Eve got out of the gun truck to talk to Cole. “I’ve seen some bad things in my life, but this is the worst,” Riker said.

“Think what it would have been like if we never arrived,” Eve said. “There were mothers holding babies for god's sake.”

“I didn’t want this to end this way,” Cole said.

“If you let them go did you think they would never terrorize anyone again?” Riker said. “They would have been back tomorrow with double the men.”

“I know. Evil never quits.” Cole took a picture of the bodies. “I want the Director to fully understand what’s happening here.”

“The Gulf Cartel is going to look for revenge for this,” Riker said. “We need to be ready for the next attack.”

Chapter 35

When they got back to the hacienda Cole sent the photo to the Director. She called two minutes later.

"Is the team alright?"

"There were no serious injuries."

"I'm sorry you went through that. I can't imagine what it must have been like."

"I want you to imagine it."

"I understand that you're angry."

"I don't give a damn if you understand my anger. I want you to tell Washington to get off their ass and start doing something.

"It's Mexico's problem."

"We sell them the guns and we buy their drugs. We are the problem."

"I promise you I'm doing everything I can. Would you like me to send agents to help you?"

"No. No one trusts Americans."

"They're talking about sanctions on Mexico, but I don't see it being approved. They're one of our biggest trading partners and they think sanctions will push Mexico closer to Russia."

"Sanctions have never worked."

"If it's any help I talked to Director Abramson."

"Jimmy?"

"He's willing to help. He'll keep his chopper fueled and ready in case you need it. I'll keep you updated," she disconnected.

Cole went to the living room, trying to control his anger. Sofia was there with the others. "The Director said Jimmy will bring his chopper anytime we call him."

"That's fantastic," Eve said. "I love Jimmy."

"Who's Jimmy?" Sofia said.

"He's one of the Directors," Eve said. "He used to fly a Huey helicopter in Vietnam. He still has some and keeps them in perfect working order. His real name is William, but they call him Jimmy because he played Jimmy Hendrix when he flew in Nam. He helped me get rid of a cartel leader once."

"He must be 80," Sofia said.

"Almost. I'd trust him with my life."

"What's next, Cole?" Katie asked.

"Maybe I can answer that," Danni said. "I pulled a new satellite photo of the airport. There are a lot more trucks there now. Some are workers' trucks, and some are carrying lumber. The sides of the trucks say they're Mexican builders, electricians, and plumbers. They're getting the building ready for the military to live and work in it."

"Can you get the plan approvals?" Riker asked.

"I'll search the planning department, but this is happening so fast I'm guessing the president said to let them do what they want and don't ask questions."

"Can he do that?" Sofia asked.

"He can if he declared that piece of land Russian, like an embassy."

"Then we'll never know what they're doing in the building."

"Not unless we break in," Riker said.

"Do you know any of the workers, Sofia?" Cole asked.

"Send me the names of the companies on the trucks. I know many of the people in the city. I'll ask them what they're doing."

"We need to tell the people what's happening. Danni, can you do a social media blast in Mexico?"

"What do you need me to do?"

"I want you to say what the Russians are doing. You need to tell the people the Americans will aim nukes at Mexico if they succeed in building the military bases. Use anonymous accounts and a VPN that shows you live in Mexico."

"One of the guys at Control wrote an AI program that can create hundreds of fake accounts. "He'll be ecstatic to finally use it."

"That's perfect."

"I'll head back to Chicago in the morning, but I have a problem," Danni said. "My Spanish sucks. I know the words, but followers would know it's my second language."

"I could ask Carla to go with you," Sofia said.

"That would be great."

"Guys," Katie yelled, standing on the deck.

They walked out to join her. Heads tilted up as they heard a plane overhead.

"That's the Russian transport plane," Riker said.

"That thing is huge," Katie said.

"They must be bringing in military personnel."

"And equipment."

"I need to get closer so I can see what they're unloading," Cole said.

"I'll go with you," Riker said.

The plane had stopped by the time they got to a secure hill with their binoculars. The nose of the plane was raised, and a ramp was extended to allow unloading. They watched as men and women came off the plane. They lined up on the tarmac and an officer gave them instructions before they took their gear into the building.

"They're in uniform," Cole said. "Can you read the logo on their jackets?"

Riker took a camera with a telephoto lens and took a picture of one of the men. Then he zoomed in on the camera's viewer. "It says Russian International Assistance Team."

They kept watching as they began unloading. A military jeep drove down the ramp, then a small forklift unloaded pallets.

"Those are tents. I guess they'll set up outside while they build living quarters inside," Cole said. "And I see computer equipment."

"These guys are settling in for the long haul."

"I count about 30 soldiers."

"And I suspect more are on the way."

"We're never going to dislodge them," Cole said.

"We got their missiles out of Cuba in the 60s."

"Because Kennedy gave up our missile sites in Egypt. We have nothing left to give up."

"That's true," Riker said.

"I need to set up a camera inside. We have to see what's happening."

"How?"

"I could go in as one of the contractors. Maybe Sofia can get someone to hire me for the day."

"You look as Mexican as I do.

"Then I'll ask Sofia if she's ever done any construction work."

Chapter 36

Sofia got out of the truck and went into the airport building with all the other contractors. The Russians wanted the counters ripped out and were using the space to build sleeping areas. Everything indicated they were staying for a long time.

Sofia's job was to carry the debris out of the building to a truck. She kept watching the Russians as she worked. They talked to the Mexican workers like they were servants. She heard them speaking Russian when she walked by them. The way they laughed and watched her she knew what they were saying. She smiled and kept working.

At one point they told her to work on the counters at the other end of the building. The Russians were setting up a kitchen area. She saw some of them carry crates through a door not far from her. She mentally recorded the time it took for them to go to the plane and back. She'd have six minutes to get inside.

Waiting until they left, she saw no one was watching. She slipped inside the door. It was a large storage room originally meant for lost luggage. Crates of various sizes were piled along the walls, leaving room for more to arrive. She opened one. Inside were security cameras packed in foam cutouts. She took a photo, storing it in a hidden folder on her phone in case she was caught. Another crate was filled with metal parts, but she didn't know what they were for. As she opened each one she photographed the contents until it was time to get out.

Before she could leave a man and a woman walked in carrying another crate. They put it down and began yelling at her in Russian. She replied in Spanish, not wanting them to know she spoke English. The man pushed her arms up and searched her, taking her phone. They began asking her questions.

"I don't speak Russian," she kept saying in Spanish.

"What are you doing in here?" the woman asked in broken Spanish, using a loud, aggressive voice.

"I thought it was a bathroom," Sofia said. "Stop yelling at me."

They spoke to each other in Russian. The woman looked at Sofia's phone but didn't see anything suspicious.

"Strip," she said in Spanish.

"What? No."

The woman took out her gun. "Strip," she yelled.

Sofia had no choice. Her anger overpowered her humiliation. She pulled off her shirt and the man grabbed it from her. He examined it, looking under the collar and at each button. When he was sure there were no cameras he threw it on the floor.

"Pants," the woman said in Russian, pointing at them.

Sofia took them off, standing in her underwear. She stood with her arms at her sides in defiance. The man looked in the pockets and along the top of them. He turned them inside out but again couldn't find anything.

He looked at Sofia, then spoke to the woman in Russian. She got mad and shook her head. It was obvious he wanted her to take everything off and the woman said no. She told her to dress. Sofia did, then began to walk to the door. The man grabbed her by the arm and held her. She ignored the pain and glared at him. It seemed the man wanted her questioned, but the woman didn't. He won. They dragged her to an office. The desk and chairs were still in it. He kicked a chair into the center of the room and pushed her into it. Her anger turned to fear.

The questions came fast. Sofia kept saying she didn't understand his broken Spanish. After a time the man called for security. The Russian gave them instructions and they took her to a car, throwing her in.

On the top of the hill Cole and Riker peered through their binoculars.

"It's Sofia," Cole said.

"We need stop that car."

They ran for their car and raced to the road. As they pulled onto it they saw the security car in front of them.

"We can't do anything until they stop," Riker said.

They kept their distance. When the guards reached a dirt road they turned off.

"What is this place?" Cole asked.

"Looks like an abandoned mine."

They took her into a tin shack that was once used as an office.

"I'm guessing they'll interrogate her and then kill her. No one would find her body here."

They ran to the shack and looked in a broken glass window. Sofia was standing on a chair. A noose was around her neck, the other end attached to a rafter. Her hands were cuffed behind her. One of the men began putting on gloves. He spoke to her in fluent Spanish.

"Who are you?" he yelled.

"I'm Sofia. I'm just a construction worker. Why are you doing this?"

The man brought his arm back to hit her in the stomach. Cole and Riker burst into the room. Cole slammed his fist into the man's kidneys, then kicked him in the back of the knee. Sofia tried desperately to stop from falling off the chair.

Riker hit the other Russian in the face. The man turned his head back and smiled at him.

"Oh, hell," Riker said.

The man took out a knife. Riker took out his. When he slashed at the man's face he snapped his head back. It was the brief second he needed. Riker slashed his blade at an angle across his chest. Without stopping he continued slashing up and across and down. His final slash was across his throat. The Russian fell to his knees, then onto his face.

The man Cole was fighting swung at him, knocking him to the ground. As Cole got up the Russian kicked the chair from under Sofia. She hung from the noose, her feet kicking under her, trying to find a solid surface. Riker grabbed her and held her high enough to release the tension.

The Russian tried to kick Riker's legs from under him. Cole slammed his forehead into his nose. Before the man could recover he jammed his knife under his chin as far as it would go. The man collapsed. Cole pulled his knife out of the body and cut the rope where it was tied to a post, then cut her cuffs.

Riker lowered her to the ground. She gasped for breath as they took the off noose. She held one hand on her neck. As she began to breathe normally she looked at Cole and Riker.

"It's over," Cole said, touching her arm.

She nodded, staring down at the man, then at the other one.

"Let's get out of here," Cole said.

"What about the bodies?" Riker said.

"There's too much blood to clean up. We leave them."

Sofia never spoke as they were driving back to the house. Cole looked at her. Tears ran down her cheeks. She took his hand and held it, never looking at him.

"When I was a kid I had nightmares about dying that way," she said.

"You're a strong woman, Sofia. One of the strongest I ever met. You'll be okay."

She nodded and wiped away the tears. She kept holding Cole's hand. Sofia hugged Cole after he got out of the car. Then she hugged Riker.

"I do love a hug from a beautiful woman," Riker said, trying to lighten the moment.

"Anytime," Sofia said.

"Let's get a drink," Cole said.

They went to the deck where everyone was waiting to learn what happened. Cole was making a drink when he called Danni inside.

"What's up?" she said.

"I need a favor."

"Are handcuffs involved, because I'm okay with that."

"Not that kind of favor," he said. "I always thought Sofia was invincible. She never expressed anything except strength to me, but we found her with a rope around her neck and I think it terrified her."

"I can see why it would."

"I'm not good with talking about things. Could you talk to her? Just tell her if she needs someone you'll be there. Tell her we all will be there for her."

"Yes. Of course. I'll do it tonight. But why me?"

"She respects you and likes you. We all do."

"Thank you for that. I'll ask if she wants to talk to me."

"Thanks," Cole said and kissed her on the forehead.

"My lips are lower," she said pointing a finger at them.

"I'll remember for next time."

They returned to the deck.

"I took photos of the crates they were storing," Sofia said, showing them on her phone. "These are the security cameras." She swiped to another one. "I have no idea what these are."

"Can I see that?" Riker said. He zoomed in. "These are weapon parts."

"In the back of the room I saw large computers still wrapped in plastic, and there were at least ten racks of servers. Why would they need so many?"

"We used to initiate wars by sending the air force to weaken the enemy, then send in ground troops," Riker said. "Now we hack the infrastructure first. Our country has very weak security on our electrical grids and our water supplies. The Russians will bring them down before they launch. It adds to the chaos and eventually results in people fighting each other to survive."

"I know the Russians have been testing our systems for years," Danni said. "Mostly small pokes and prods to see how fast we can recover."

"Whatever it takes, we have to stop the airbase from activating," Cole said.

Chapter 37

Earlier in the morning Danni returned to Chicago with Carla to work on the social media blast. The others were on the deck having lunch. Katie kept peering through the telescope at the airport.

"Leave it," Cole said. "We'll find a way."

"It's frustrating just standing here and doing nothing."

"Then sit and have lunch."

Eve heard a knock on the door and let Sofia in.

"Danni called me and told me to come here," Sofia said.

"She called you directly?" Katie said. "Why?"

"She said I'll find out when she calls you."

Cole's phone rang. He answered it and put it on speaker.

"Hi, guys, It's Danni. The Director is here with me. We didn't want to call until Sofia arrived."

"How do you know when she arrived?" Katie asked. "Never mind. I should expect it by now."

"Any chance this is good news?" Riker said.

"I wish," Danni said.

"What's up?" Katie asked.

"You've damaged the Gulf Cartel more than we thought," the Director said.

"That's good, isn't it?" Eve asked.

"Yes and no. We've seen the weakness you caused, but so has the Los Zetas Cartel. They have decided to take advantage of the situation."

"How?" Sofia asked.

"There was a party last night. Zetas Cartel leaders gathered from everywhere. Fortunately, our escort informants were there. Los Zetas is going to attack the Gulf Cartel."

"They do that all the time," Cole said.

"This time it's going to be a war to the end. As far as we can tell the Gulf Cartel doesn't know it's coming."

"Can they beat them?" Riker asked.

"The original Zetas were Mexican Special Forces deserters," Sofia said. "They're known for beheading police to instill fear in people, and they showed no mercy to anyone who betrayed them. I think they could win."

"Do you think they'll kill civilians, Sofia?" the Director asked.

"Many will become, as America says, collateral damage. Women and children included. If Los Zetas can control the northeast border of Mexico they'll have exclusive access to the drug and immigration land routes. Even places like Colombia and Venezuela will have to go through them."

"If Los Zetas succeeds how will it affect the Russian situation?" Cole asked.

"The Mexican President will use this as an excuse to give the Russians complete access to the northeast of Mexico. I can see them setting up more bases."

"Anyone have suggestions on how we can stop this?" the Director said. "It's out of control and getting worse."

"We need to distribute weapons to the people as fast as possible," Cole said. "Sofia, can you use your team to do a road trip."

"Yes. Where to?"

"All along the border. That's the area Los Zetas wants to control. You'll have to contact people to tell them you're coming. They can help you with the weapons."

"I can work with Sofia," Katie said.

"How's your Spanish, and can you drive a semi?" Riker said.

"Good point."

"I'll go," Eve said. "You guys can tackle the Russians."

"Speaking of the Russians, I want Danni back here," Cole said.

"Why?" the Director asked.

"Sofia saw computer systems in the airport. Danni might be able to give us an idea of how powerful they are and maybe she can hack into them."

"I might be able to plant a virus if I get access to them," Danni said.

"You and Carla can go back to Mexico tomorrow, Danni," the Director said.

"Director," Cole said. "This is getting out of hand. At what point is Washington going to get involved?"

"You know what they're like. Every decision takes multiple committee meetings and approvals. To physically do something takes a lot longer. The best I can do for now is give you everything you ask for. Keep me informed." She disconnected.

"Being a mafia boss was easier than this," Katie said.

"You live in a cartel leader's hacienda across from a Russian missile base," Riker said with a smile. "You should take photos. Your grandkids will never believe your stories."

Chapter 38

Sofia went to the living room and called people she knew in other towns along the border. If she didn't know anyone she called the priests. A little at a time she established contacts.

"Some of the guns need a special skill set to use properly," Eve said, walking into the room and sitting with her.

"There are ex-military people in most places," Sofia said. "They originally joined to fight for their country. Now we're going to give them another chance."

"Can you drive a semi?" Eve asked.

"I'll bring someone with me that can. I know drivers who lost their jobs and trucks to the cartels. You should have a driver as well. An American woman driving alone across Mexico is suspicious."

"I'll take Riker. He's pretty useless without me."

Sofia smiled. "You have a nice relationship. You are always teasing each other."

"I spent a long time training him. It's been slow progress but he's better than when we first met."

"You're lucky to have each other. My boyfriend left because he thought my life was too dangerous and he could get hurt."

"I'm sorry. Sounds like you were lucky to get rid of him."

"I guess. When are you and Riker leaving?"

"We'll travel at night. We should be able to fit in with the other trucks on the road."

They walked to the deck.

"Let's go Riker. It's you and me against the world."

"Stay in contact," Cole said. "And put a tracker on the trucks.

"Someone in the town will drive you to the next town if need it," Sofia said. "Just ask."

"I'll bring cash to pay them."

"They aren't doing it for the money."

"I know. It just shows we respect what they're doing, and I know they have families to take care of."

"Now it looks like it's you and me against the world," Cole said to Katie after they left.

"Don't worry. I'll take care of you."

They turned when Danni walked onto the deck. "Hi, guys. I left early to get down here. Carla went home. I passed Eve outside and she gave me an update on the weapons distribution. Anything new with the Russians?"

"Hi, Danni," Katie said. "Sofia talked to one of the contractors He told her they set up the computer systems and they brought in portable air conditioning units."

"I have to get access."

"You remember what happened to Sofia when they caught her?" Cole said.

"Missiles are going to be aimed at my country. What do you suggest we do?"

"If I went instead of you, could I add a virus?" Cole asked.

"You'll have to understand the systems. How to hack a server and which server to plant it on. You could do it after a ton of training, but the world may be unlivable by then."

"Point taken. We'll do surveillance tonight. Count the guards and watch the patrols. If it's too secure you'll have to go in as a Russian during the day. Any chance you speak their language."

"It was never on my bucket list," she said, staring at the pool. "I want to do some laps. I haven't had much of a chance to exercise."

"Cole will like that."

"You like swimming, Cole?"

"He likes watching you swim."

"I'm okay with that."

"Everyone needs to stop talking about me."

****

Riker and Eve pulled the semi out of the barn. They drove toward a collection of villages two hours south. Sofia had talked to people about them coming with the weapons. There was only one road, but it was two lanes in both directions and traffic was light. They never saw any police cars. Eve checked her navigation system.

"Take the next right," she said.

After turning they drove down a dirt driveway to a farmhouse. A man sat on the porch, a shotgun lying across his lap. He waited until Riker stopped and they got out. He continued to cradle it in his arms as he walked toward them.

"Are you Santiago?" Eve asked.

"Si. Sofia told me about you. She also told me Los Zetas was coming."

Riker looked around but didn't see anyone. "Are the people coming to pick up the weapons?"

The man put his fingers in the corners of his mouth and let out an ear-piercing whistle. People of all ages came from behind the house and from inside the barn. They formed a semi-circle around Eve and Riker.

Riker smiled at Eve. "Looks like we have help unloading."

"These people are from the other villages as well." He waved his arm in a circle above his head. Some of them went behind the barn and drove out in trucks. They stopped behind the semi.

"You know the people," Eve said. "It would be best if you distribute the weapons. We thought we would give the heavy weapons to ex-military."

The man nodded. "I thought the same."

Riker opened the back doors and the man climbed in. He helped another man up and they opened the crates. He looked at the faces below him. He pointed to one of the truck owners, then gave him rifles and ammunition boxes. He continued pointing, then handing them out.

No one joked or smiled. The process continued until all the weapons were gone from the truck.

Riker closed the back doors and turned. The people were still facing him and Eve. Riker didn't know what they wanted.

The man they met first shook his hand, then Eve's. "Thank you," he said looking into their eyes.

One at a time the people passed in front of them. Each one shook their hands and thanked them. Some of the women hugged them. After they did they drove off in their trucks. When the last one left the owner of the farm went inside without another word.

"These people are going to go through hell when the cartel shows up," she said.

"They've been going through hell for a long time."

Chapter 39

Eve and Riker began driving the empty semi away from the farm.

"I thought we would be going to multiple villages. We may as well go back to the hacienda for tonight. Tomorrow we go west."

When they were close to home Riker slowed. He saw a vehicle partially concealed on the side of the road. "See the truck?"

"Keep driving past it like we don't."

They pulled into the driveway and parked. Using the truck as cover they dashed back to the road. The darkness covered them as they slipped through the bushes, approaching the truck from behind it. Eve crouched and went along the passenger's side. Cole took the driver's side.

The driver was watching the house through the open passenger window. Eve moved between him and the hacienda and aimed her gun at him. He instinctively reached for his. Riker pressed his gun against the man's head and took his weapon. He opened the door and pulled him from the truck, dumping him on the ground. They stood over him.

"Open your shirt," Riker said.

"Riker?" Eve said. "Is there something we need to talk about?"

"Open it," Riker repeated.

The man pulled his shirt open.

"Look at the tats," he said. "He's Los Zetas."

"Oh. I get it now," Eve said. "Why are you watching us?"

He glared at her, staying quiet. Riker pulled him to his feet.

"What do we do with him?" Eve asked.

"He's useless if he doesn't talk to us. I guess we put a bullet in his stomach and tie him to a tree until he bleeds out."

"Sounds good." Eve aimed at his stomach. The fear spread across his face, and he held his hands in front of him "Wait," he said. "I was only told to watch the hacienda. Nothing else."

Eve lowered her gun. "Why?"

"I don't know."

"I'm bored and need a drink." She raised it again.

"Wait. Please."

"Give me your phone," Eve said. "She went through the photos. "He's been here all day. He took photos of the house from all directions."

"Is Los Zetas going to attack us?" Riker asked.

Eve's head was down looking at the phone. Without warning the man pulled a knife from his belt and quickly moved behind her, pressing the blade against her neck. Riker stepped back and aimed at him. His head was behind Eve's, and he couldn't get a shot.

"Drop your gun," the man said. He pressed the knife harder against her neck. Eve froze. Riker slowly put his gun on the ground and stepped closer.

"Stay back or I'll kill her." The man moved the knife a couple of inches away from Eve's throat as he watched Riker.

Without warning Riker grabbed the knife blade, putting his fingers between the blade and Eve's throat. The man drew his knife across his fingers. Eve saw her chance and grabbed the man's hand. She moved to the side and jammed the knife into his thigh, then pulled it out. The man rolled on the ground, grabbing the wound. He looked up at them, expecting to be shot.

Riker picked up his gun with his good hand and aimed it at him. "Go tell your boss we'll be waiting for him."

The man got up and hobbled to his truck, then drove away.

"That was a crazy thing to do," she said. She took a handkerchief from his back pocket and wrapped his fingers.

"It was my fingers or your neck."

"Let's get you home so I can bandage your hand."

"We could have one-handed sex tonight."

"You saved my life. You can do anything you want to me tonight."

"Then this was worth it."

The others were on the deck having a drink.

"What happened to your hand?" Cole asked.

“We found a cartel guy watching the house.”

“I’ll get bandages if someone pours us a drink,” Eve said.

“On it,” Danni said.

“Did he say anything?”

“No, but we know he was Los Zetas, and he was taking photos of the house. Which means they’re planning to attack us.”

“It's never boring around you guys,” Danni said.

“I wish it was,” Katie said. “What do we do?”

“I’ll see if Sofia can find out if they are going to attack us.”

“In the morning Eve and I will take out another semi to distribute more weapons,” Riker said.

“Guess I’m driving,” Eve said, cleaning and wrapping his hand.

“You always are, no matter who’s behind the wheel.”

****

Sofia and her driver Carlos were approaching a town. She’d contacted the priest, and he told her to bring the weapons to the church.

“You alright?” Carlos asked as he downshifted to slow down.

“It’s weird the priest told me to bring them to the church. There are too many to store in a small building.”

“Maybe he’ll have the people waiting and they’ll take them to their homes,” Carlos said.

"That many people around a church at night is suspicious. Park two blocks away. We'll walk in and check it out first."

They ran along the back of the buildings to the church. No one was there. Moving to the front she opened the door slightly and looked in. Cartel members were standing in groups, fully armed. She gently closed the door, and they started walking back to the truck.

"We need to get out of here."

As they approached their semi they saw people gathered around it. A woman came forward to talk to them.

"We heard you were coming and have been watching for the truck. The priest is paid by the cartel. He told them you were coming."

"We saw the cartel in the church waiting for us. I'm glad you're here."

Carlos opened the back of the truck and handed out rifles and handguns until everyone had one. Five of the men were ex-military and took rifles, extra ammunition, and grenades.

"What are you going to do?" Sofia asked one of the military men.

"We are going to fight back. We're tired of losing everything we work so hard for."

"You know the cartel will come back with more men?"

"We know. We'll be ready."

They walked toward the church in a group, the military men in front. Sofia looked at Carlos. He handed her a rifle and took one for himself, then caught up to them.

Two men ran around the back and the rest stood to the side of the church steps.

One of the men held the church door open. Two others pulled the pins on the grenades and tossed them inside. They jumped down the side of the steps and took cover.

The explosions shook the church walls and blasted the ears of the people outside. They all ran inside, Sofia and Carlos with them. Shots came at them from the remaining cartel. Two of them were hit as they returned fire. The two men at the back of the church entered and moved to the corners of the church and began firing. The cartel was surrounded. The few remaining ones raised their guns over the pews without looking and sprayed bullets in every direction.

The townspeople fired as a group, not stopping until they were nearly out of ammunition. The pews could never stop the bullets. In minutes it was over. The cartel lay dead on the floor and slumped over pews. Two of the military men were wounded, and one was dead. They all turned when the office door opened. The priest came out. He looked at the bodies and crossed himself. "God will forgive you, my children," he said.

"He won't forgive you," a man said, then shot him in the chest.

The people moved through the bodies, checking for the cartel wounded and removing the guns. Others helped their own wounded. A woman walked over to Sofia. "The church will be burned, and we'll build a new one. It will be a house of God, not a house of evil."

Sofia hugged her. “I’m sorry for what you are going through.”

She touched her hand. “With your guns, we can fight for our children. We want them to have a Mexico without the cartel. Thank you.” She turned to help her friends.

Chapter 40

Cole lay on the couch with his laptop, enjoying the time he had to write. Katie went to bed to give him some space. He looked up when Danni came out wrapped in a towel.

"If you're going swimming you should put on the pool lights."

"How?"

"Switch is on the left side of the door."

"Thanks. Want to be my lifeguard?"

"I get so few chances to write anymore. I'd like to stay with it."

"I understand. I won't be long."

He heard her dive into the water and swim lengths. His mind drifted. He forced it back to his story. After a time he didn't hear Danni and wondered if she was okay. He got up and walked to the pool. She was floating on her back, gently moving her arms to stay afloat. She looked ethereally backlit by the pool lights.

"Hi," she said. "Coming in?"

"You should wear a swimsuit. And maybe water wings if you're swimming alone."

She giggled. "I'm a good swimmer."

"I shouldn't disturb you."

"Yet you're still looking at me. It feels nice to be noticed."

"I'm sure you couldn't go anywhere without being noticed. I'm going back to my writing."

She came in a few minutes later, leaned over the back of the couch, and kissed him on the cheek. "Thanks for worrying about me."

"We're a team. We watch out for each other."

"Night, Cole."

"Night, Danni."

He looked blankly at the monitor. His concentration was gone. He leaned his head back and slowly fell asleep.

It was morning when he woke by a lover's kiss. He sighed, keeping his eyes closed. "Morning, Danni," he whispered.

"You better be joking, mister," Katie said.

"Hi, guys," Danni said, walking into the kitchen.

"You're lucky," Katie said to Cole.

"Why is Cole lucky?" Danni asked.

"He can live another day," Katie said. "I'll help you make breakfast."

Cole got up and walked to the deck, stretching, and letting the sun hit his face. The cool morning air washed over him, and he took a deep breath. He looked at the airport and then moved quickly to the telescope.

"Guys," he said.

They went over to him.

"What is it?"

"About 30 cartel members are at the airport."

"Why?"

"I wish I knew. The leader is talking to a couple of the Russians. Okay, now I'm confused. A dozen Russians came out and are aiming rifles at the cartel. The cartel just raised their weapons at the Russians."

"None of it makes sense," Katie said.

"The cartel is leaving," Cole said.

"I have a theory," Danni said. "This is Los Zetas territory. I bet they're asking for extortion payments from the Russians."

"They can't be that crazy," Katie said.

"If you're asking me if the cartels are a bunch of crazies I have to say yes."

"I gather the Russians told them to piss off."

"Everyone they ask the first time tells them that. It doesn't mean they will."

"It would be great if the cartel went after the Russians."

"The cartel outnumbers them. It could happen."

They ate breakfast and spent time discussing how they could secure the hacienda if the cartel attacked them. After an hour Cole went back to the telescope.

"Anything new?" Katie asked, walking out with her coffee. Danni came with her.

"They put a machine gun post on the roof, and they positioned one of the jeeps and two guards near the start of the road. They're securing the place like a missile base should be secured."

"They should have done that to begin with," Danni said.

"They're still outnumbered by the cartel," Cole said.

"Maybe not for long," Danni said, staring at a Mexican military helicopter approaching It landed in front of the building and soldiers jumped out, taking positions around the building.

"That's the end of the cartel threat," Katie said.

"Not really," Danni said. "A lot of the Mexican military have supported cartels in battles. We don't know who those guys will shoot at in a firefight."

"This is a weird country," Katie said.

"Now I can't get physical access to the computers. I have to find another way to hack them. Cole, can you drive me into town? I need to buy a server and some other computer stuff."

"What are you going to do with it?"

"I'm going to try to trick the computer security team into thinking I'm their tech department in Moscow and ask them to do some maintenance procedures. It should give me a back door, but it's going to take some time."

"You don't speak Russian."

"We have someone at Control that was born in Moscow. Eli is a tech guy who can help me with the language issue. If he'll talk to me. He might still be mad about me leaving him naked on the elevator."

"I want to hear that story," Katie said.

"Later. Cole, get ready for a call from Control. They're going to think the credit card was stolen when they see the charges I'm about to rack up."

Chapter 41

Eve and Riker picked up another semi full of weapons and drove toward the next town. They were in the middle of Los Zetas territory and worried about everyone they passed.

"We're going to stop in the center of a small cluster of villages," Eve said, looking at a map on her phone. "Sofia said the people will drive to meet us."

When they were 20 miles from the location a truck began following them. Then more vehicles pulled off the side roads and joined them. Before long the semi was at the front of a long line of cars and trucks.

"What are they doing?" Riker said.

"Maybe Sofia set this up."

"If this many people know where we are, then so does the cartel."

"If they know the route we planned they could ambush us."

"We don't have much choice now. We'll have to see how this plays out," Riker said, checking his handgun.

One of the pickups passed them and pulled in front, matching their speed. A girl was sitting in the back. She waved to indicate they were to follow her.

"She doesn't look cartel. Neither does the driver."

"That doesn't mean much. But we have a dozen vehicles behind us, so we have to keep going."

As they drove they saw a car racing towards them. It was flashing its lights, and a man was half out the window waving for them to stop. Everyone pulled in behind the semi. The people left their vehicles and walked to the front.

"The cartel set up a roadblock about two miles ahead," the man in the car said.

"We'll be massacred if we charge the cartel," Eve said.

"There's no traffic coming from behind us," Riker said. "They must have blocked the road there too."

"If we turn around they'll come after us," Eve said. "We have to take them on. It's always better to be the aggressor."

Riker looked at the trailer, lost in thought.

"What's going on in your brain?" Eve asked.

"I have a plan. It's messy, but it might save some lives."

Riker and Eve handed out the weapons until the trailer was empty, then closed the doors. He stood at the back of the trailer and told them what he was going to do. They went back to their cars, mumbling about the crazy American.

"This the best plan you got?" Eve said after they got in the cab.

"It's the only plan I got. If you have a better one tell me now."

"I have nothing. Let's do this." She took out her handgun and held it in her lap. Cole started the truck and began driving.

"You sure you can do this?"

"We're about to find out."

He picked up speed. The cars followed, driving two abreast and only a few feet behind each other.

Riker drove around a corner and saw the cartel down the road. "This is it."

"You kill me, and I'll haunt you forever," Eve said.

"If this goes wrong we can haunt each other."

He accelerated toward the roadblock. The cartel members aimed at the semi. When they were closer they began firing, hitting the cab with bullets. Riker never slowed.

A short distance from the cars he slammed on the front brakes and turned the wheel. The cab began stopping but the trailer didn't. The semi jackknifed and slid sideways down the highway.

The cartel froze at first, not believing what they were seeing. As the trailer came closer they ran for the side of the road. The trailer slammed into the cars, knocking them out of the way. Some of them hit the cartel members and slid over them.

When it stopped Eve and Riker looked at each other. Riker exhaled slowly and Eve let her head fall forward, wondering how she ended up doing these things.

The people in the vehicles behind the semi jumped out and ran around the trailer. They began firing before the cartel could react. The cartel tried to return fire, but they were overwhelmed. Some tried running but never made it. Others dropped their guns and held their hands high. Nothing did any good. The people had a chance to do what the cartel did to them.

In minutes the shooting stopped. The people walked through the bodies, taking guns away. The townspeople who were injured were being helped by the others.

The truck never tilted over because of the cars it hit. The bullet damage to the cab seemed to be the worst thing but it was driveable. Riker put his arms on the steering wheel and his head down. “I wish people would stop killing people.”

“The only way to stop evil is by being evil,” Eve said.

Two of the men approached the cab and they got out to talk to them. The men shook their hands and thanked them for giving them a chance to fight back. They said they would make sure other villages hear how the cartel was defeated.

“There are cars behind us waiting to ambush us,” Riker said to them. “Have four of your vehicles follow me.”

There were no ditches, and the ground was baked hard by the sun so he could turn the semi around. When he was on the highway he took it to speed. Turning a curve he saw two cars parked across the road. He never slowed. The truck slammed into the cars and spun them into the ditch. They heard gunfire behind them. Neither of them looked in the side mirrors.

Chapter 42

Cole was up before the others. He sat on the deck with his laptop, working on his latest chapter. Occasionally he would look up, wondering what to do with one of his characters. He hated killing them off.

Katie came onto the deck. "Morning."

"Morning," he said.

"How long have you been here?"

"Not sure."

"Want a coffee?"

"Love it."

"You seem quiet. What's the matter?"

"I'm trying to decide if I should kill one of my characters. It's hard when you get to know them."

"I don't like it when a character I like is killed. It either makes me sad or I think it was long overdue. Either way, it makes me mad at the writer."

"So I shouldn't?"

"I expect emotion in a book. Anger's an emotion."

"But she's young, perky, and beautiful."

"Do it. No one likes that kind of person."

"Then I'll make it quick."

"Good man."

"Have you seen Danni?"

"She set up her computer stuff in the spare bedroom. She's in there working."

Cole went to see her. The server was active, and she was sitting in front of a laptop typing.

"How's it going?"

"I'm connecting to Control's network to get more power. Then we should be good to go."

"What's the plan?"

"The Russian computer system will be very secure and take a long time to break into, so I'm going to hack the wetware. I'll get Eli to translate."

"Wetware? Should I ask?"

"Hardware is anything you can pick up and throw out a window. Software is the program. Wetware is the person using the computer. People are always the weakest entry point. The computer jockeys will be young, away from their girlfriends, and horny. They can't use government computers for porn, so they'll use their phones. I'll hack one and use it to get into the servers."

"How."

"I'll bump into one of them online and let them talk me into sending them photos and a video. Inside the video will be a program that lets me into his phone.

"You're going to put on a sex show?"

"No. Katie is. You need to get me all the sexy photos and videos you took of Katie. I'll pick the best one."

"I never took photos of her."

"Seriously?" she said. "Then you have until lunch. Get on it."

"I'm not doing that."

"Tell Katie she's doing it for her country."

"What good is hacking their phones?"

"Their phone will be on the desk where they work. I can turn on their mics and record ambient sounds like keystrokes. Then I put that through a program that will work out the keys they press. If I get enough keystrokes it looks at the pauses, key pressures, sounds, and other stats to tell me what they typed. When they log on to the server during the day I have the password."

"What if the Russians type differently from the Americans?"

"Then we have to break into the airport. That's going to be far more dangerous."

"I was hoping we didn't need to do that."

"Sorry. Like I said, their systems have good security. It's a missile base. Now. About Katie's pics."

"I'm not doing that."

"Fine. Take my phone."

Why?"

Danni undid her shirt buttons and leaned her back against a wall, putting her hands in her pockets.

"Let's do this, big boy. It's for your country."

"I do love my country." Cole took some photos and a video.

"I'll send copies to you. Keep the ones you like," Danni said.

Cole went back to the deck. Riker and Eve were finishing their coffee.

"We're going to pick up another truck and keep distributing the weapons," Eve said. "The next town is too far to return here tonight."

"Be careful," Katie said.

"We will," Riker said. "People are getting to know about us. That means the cartel is also getting to know about us."

"What are you guys going to do?" Eve asked.

"Danni is going to send sexy photos of herself to a Russian on the base," Cole said.

"What?" Katie said.

"I'll explain later."

"I don't get it, but I want to see the photos when I get back," Riker said.

"Me too," Eve said, smiling.

"Who took the photos?" Katie said, staring at Cole.

"Oh, buddy," Riker said as he and Eve were leaving. "I hope you're still alive when we get back."

Katie glared at Cole. "I could have done it."

"Next time."

"Next time use me."

"To send to a Russian?"

"No, dummy. You're not sending pictures of me to a Russian soldier. It's for us."

"I have the password to a phone," Danni said as she came out of her room.

"Let me see the video and the photos," Katie said, holding her hand out.

"I can't," Danni said. "They're classified."

"You showed Cole."

"He took them."

"Can you access their systems?" Cole asked.

"No. After I sent them he told me personal phones are not allowed in the computer room. I still need physical access."

"How are you going to get inside?" Katie asked. "There are military guards now?"

"The Russian I sent the video to is going to meet me outside the building at the back."

"Wow," Cole said. "You are good."

"He thinks I'm a horny American tourist that wants to check off sex with a Russian."

"Do you?" Katie asked.

"I set my sights higher than a military jock," Danni said. "Let's go, Cole."

They drove to the hill and looked through night vision binoculars.

"What time are you going to have sex with this guy?"

"Seriously?"

"I was kidding."

"I'm meeting him in 12 minutes. He said there's an emergency side door in case of fires. He'll turn off the alarm and come out there. You have to be close so you can hit him on the head."

"I can do that."

They moved through the bushes until they were close to the door. When they got there a man in a uniform was leaning on the wall scanning the area. The door was open a crack.

"Ready?" Cole asked.

"No. I normally don't make out with someone I don't know. It feels awkward."

"Turn him so his back is facing out."

"I know what to do."

She walked toward him. When he saw her he smiled and stood upright. She leaned her back on the wall and he stood in front of her. She grabbed his shirt and pulled him towards her before kissing him.

Cole ran up behind them and swung his gun butt across his head. Before he could fall he put him over his shoulder and carried him into the bushes to conceal him.

"Take his clothes off," Cole said, undoing his shirt.

"What? Why?"

"I'm putting on his uniform."

"I want you to know I normally don't undress a guy I don't know."

"Good for you."

Cole exchanged clothes and they ran to the door, slipping inside and closing it. They moved down the hallway to another door and opened it slightly. A guard was at the far end of the building. Two others were talking in the corner.

They walked to the computer lab door, fighting the urge to run. Inside were the servers. No one was in the room that late at night.

Danni sat at a computer and entered the password. It worked. She put a USB into the side of it, waited a short time, then took it out.

"The virus is loaded. Let's get out of here."

They went to the door and peered out. The men were still in the same place. One of them began walking towards the door.

"Someone's coming," Cole said.

Their eyes darted around the room.

"There's no place to hide," he said.

She took his hand and dragged him into the darkest corner. She pushed his back against the wall and pressed against him. "Kiss me."

Cole looked at the door and it began to open. The man called out someone's name and spoke in Russian. Danni put her hand on the back of Cole's neck and began kissing him. With her other hand, she put his hand on her breast and held it there.

When the Russian saw them he laughed and spoke again. Cole kept kissing Danni as he waved his other hand to tell the man should leave. He laughed and walked out.

"That was close," Cole said.

"Yeah. We were close." She said, taking a deep breath.

He walked back to the door and looked out. No one was watching. They walked to the exit and ran into the woods.

"Now what?" Danni said.

"Put his clothes back on him," Cole said undoing the shirt and removing the pants. He put his own clothes on.

"Why are we doing this?"

"Take his wallet and everything in his pockets. Don't take his ID card."

"You want him to think I was here to rob him."

"Yes."

Cole carried him back to the building and then ran back to the car.

"Sorry for being so aggressive back there," Danni said as they drove. "I guess me putting your hand on my boob wasn't necessary."

"You thought of a way to get us out of a bad situation."

"Sure. That's what it was."

Chapter 43

Cole never slept much. He kept going over in his mind what happened at the airport, and he wasn't sure why he was thinking about it. He'd been in worse situations.

As he sat on the deck the heat eased his muscles and took his tension away. A slight breeze brushed by him, barely able to stir the water in the pool. He reached for his phone when it rang.

"Cole," Sofia said. "I tried calling before but the connection was bad."

"Are you okay?"

"The cartel knows which towns have not received weapons yet. They went to one and kidnapped one of the high school classes in Arandas. They killed the teacher and stole the school bus to transport them."

"Why would they take kids?"

"They told the principal it was to warn them never to accept weapons or they would kill their children. They said to tell the other towns."

"Do you think they would?"

"They kidnapped some college kids a year ago and they were found in a mass grave two weeks later. This is bad. I have my team searching for them but it's a large area."

Cole put his laptop down and started pacing. "Do you know where they took them?"

"No."

"What are the parents doing?"

"They're helping search, but the cartel could be in the mountains, in a camp, or on a farm. Maybe they took them to a city. We don't know."

"I'll get Control to search for them. As soon as I find anything I'll call you."

"Cole. They will kill them at some point. They are only keeping them alive to terrorize the parents and warn other towns."

"I'll get my team together. I'll call you when we find something."

Cole walked into Danni's bedroom. He gently shook her shoulder. She looked up at him. "This is a nice way to wake up."

"We have a major problem. I need you to connect to the Control servers."

"I'll meet you in the computer room."

Cole went to the room and turned on the computers. Danni came in moments later.

"They kidnapped a high school class from a town called Arandas. They took them in a stolen school bus."

"Jesus," Danni said. "I'll have the system search for school busses in weird locations. Maybe I'll get a hit."

"I'm going to wake the others and start driving to the area," Cole said. "Call me as soon as you see anything."

"On it."

They were in the car speeding to the area when Sofia called. "Did Danni see anything?"

"She's scanning the satellite images. If anyone can find them, she can."

"The parents are terrified, Cole."

"Danni is on the other line. I'll call you back… Danni. What have you got?"

"There's a ranch at the base of the mountains southwest of here. It's four buildings surrounded by trees. I don't see any kids, but I see a school bus. It's got the name of the town on the side."

"Good work, Danni. Text Katie the directions."

"Already did. I'll call Sofia and tell her how to get there."

"Tell her not to say anything to the townspeople. If they all show up there will be a lot of people killed."

"Got it. Come home safe."

Katie guided them to the location. "Danni said it should be around the next curve in the road."

They took their rifles and slowly approached the back of the buildings.

"Eve and I will check the two buildings on the east side," Riker said.

"We'll take these ones. Meet back here," Cole said.

Cole and Katie ran in a crouch to a back window of the largest building and peered in a window. Eight men and women were inside at a table eating. They ran to the other building. It contained old cars and a workshop.

When Eve and Riker returned they all moved farther away to talk.

“I counted at least a dozen men and women, but no kids,” Cole said.

“The farthest building is a riding area. Two people working with horses. The other one is a large shed. There are no windows.”

“The school bus is here so that must be where they are holding the kids,” Katie said. “Can we break the door down?”

“If we do the two working the horses will hear us warn the others,” Eve said.

“Here’s how we play this,” Cole said. “Riker and I will put some bullets in the house. They’re going to come out shooting. You guys take the kids up the mountain while we distract them. There’s a road on the other side.”

“You’ll be killed,” Katie said. “There are too many of them.”

“Riker and I will survive long enough for you to get the kids to safety, then we’ll get away in our car.”

“I don’t like that idea,” Katie said.

“I don’t either, but it’s all I got,” Cole said.

Katie looked at him, knowing he was right. She wrapped her arms around him and kissed him. “Don’t die.”

“Same to you.”

Eve touched Riker’s hand. He locked eyes with her. They both knew what each was thinking. Eve nodded and she and Katie ran for the shed. Riker and Cole moved behind a pickup truck parked sideways to the house.

"You ready to piss off some cartel killers, buddy?" Riker said.

"Hell, no."

Chapter 44

Riker and Cole checked the mags in their weapons and leaned over the hood aiming at the house. They put four shots into the living room window. There was a pause. Suddenly people came pouring out of the house firing at the vehicles, not knowing which one they were behind.

Riker and Cole returned fire as the men ran for cover. One dropped and the rest hid behind the trucks, but now they knew where Cole and Riker were firing from and blasted the truck.

It was too far to run to another vehicle. They popped up, fired, and ducked again. Riker shot another man, wounding him. The men were moving closer and spreading out. Nothing was stopping them. Cole looked at Riker. They realized this was a dumb idea, but they hoped Katie and Eve got the kids to safety. They both knew there was no way out.

"This plan sucks," Cole said.

"Sure does." They fired randomly at the cartel.

"You're a good man, Riker."

"You too, buddy."

Their rifles were empty. They checked their handguns.

"I have two left."

"I have one."

They heard a car speeding towards them. It slammed into a man running across the driveway and then stopped behind the truck where Riker and Cole kneeled.

"Get in!" Sofia yelled as the bullets peppered the car. They jumped in the back seat and Sofia hit the gas. The car spun around, kicking dust and dirt, then raced down the driveway. In her mirror, she saw men getting in their cars and chasing them.

"I count three cars in pursuit," Riker said.

Sofia handed him her handgun. "My rifles on the floor. Stop them."

Cole used the rifle butt to smash out the back window. He aimed at the closest car. The driver tried to swerve to make him miss but it didn't work. Cole put two bullets into him. The car swerved off the road and began to roll when it hit the ditch. The next car sped ahead, closing the distance.

"Hang on!" Sofia yelled. She slammed on the brakes. The car chasing them hit the back of her car. Both vehicles stopped. The driver looked wide-eyed at Cole and Riker. Both fired before he could duck. Sofia sped away. The last car couldn't get around the damaged car. The cartel jumped out and fired but they were too late.

"Where are the kids?" Sofia said, still driving.

"Katie and Eve took them east up the mountain," Cole said. He called Danni and told her where they were. "I need a road that takes us to the other side of it."

"Two miles from the building there's a road on your left that loops around. It'll take you to the base of the mountain. I'll keep watching to see if more cartel members show up."

"Thanks," he said and disconnected. Sofia followed Danni's directions.

"This is where we get out," Sofia said. She stopped and opened the trunk. It contained rifles and ammunition.

"I was going to hand these out to farms I passed."

They each grabbed more magazines and guns and began moving up the mountain.

"Katie should hit the top directly above us," Riker said. "We'll move to the left and climb so we can come up behind the cartel. We have to stop them before they catch those kids."

****

Katie led the kids up the mountain. Eve ran behind them to cover their backs. When they were near a treed area she saw some of the students slowing and gasping for breath.

"We'll rest here," she said.

The kids sat in a group, anxiously talking to each other. One of them approached Kate and Eve. "Thank you for rescuing us."

"We're not out of this yet," Eve said.

"What do we do now?"

"We have others searching for us. Hopefully, they'll find us before the cartel does. Plus we have a satellite watching us."

"Satellite? Are you spies?"

"No, but we have a good friend that operates one."

Katie walked to the center of the group while Eve watched the area.

"My name is Katie. Her's is Eve. We are going to get you home. I promise. But if we see the cartel you must do exactly what we tell you."

One girl was shaking and looking at the ground. Katie touched her shoulder and kneeled beside her. "What's your name?"

"Maria," she stuttered.

"We're going to be fine, Maria. You'll be home soon."

"I saw the cartel kill my father." Maria looked up at her. "I'm really scared."

Katie waved over the girl that talked to her first. "Stay with her. Protect her."

"I will," the girl said.

"One more minute," Katie said to the group, then went to talk to Eve.

"Look," Eve said, nodding to the base of the hill.

A group of cartels were beginning to climb. They were too far away to make out how many.

"It gets worse." Eve pointed to another area. Two men on All Terrain Vehicles were speeding up the hill.

"Can you hit them from here?"

"This isn't a sniper rifle. And the bush cover is sporadic. Maybe when they get closer."

"We need to get going,' Katie said to the group.

"I'll stay here and wait for them," Eve said.

"You have to come with us. I need you to watch our six."

Eve looked down the mountain again. They were coming fast. “Okay. Let’s go.”

Katie and Eve kept pushing the kids as they neared the peak of the mountain. When they reached the top the kids sat to catch their breath.

“We fight them from here,” Eve said. “I don’t want them above us if we’re running down the other side.”

“The ATVs are close. Can you hit them?”

“Maybe.” Eve kneeled and aimed at the closest one. The trees kept her from getting a shot. She looked ahead of the rider and saw a clearing. She would only get one chance. She waited, following the rider, watching the kill zone. As the rider entered the area she fired. The ATV shot out from under him, and he hit the ground. The vehicle hit a tree and stopped.

Eve ran to position herself over the other rider. There were no clearings. The man was getting closer. She kneeled again, watching the bushes as he drove through them. She waited. He was getting too close.

Eve estimated where he would be and aimed. She squeezed the trigger, but the bullet hit a tree. Katie aimed her rifle and fired a burst at him. He kept coming. She fired another and another. The man fell.

Eve looked at Katie. “Did I mention we should conserve ammo?”

“Sorry. Men should learn when to stop,” Katie said.

The men kept climbing through the bush. They began firing. Katie and Eve ducked.

“They’re too spread out to get them all,” Katie said.

“Do we run?” Eve asked.

“We don’t. The kids do.” She went to the group. “I want you guys to run down the mountain. I can see a road at the bottom. We’ll stay here and delay them.”

“What if there are too many?” a girl asked.

“We’re trained in warfare,” Eve said. “Run now or you will die.”

They got up and began going down the hill as fast as they could.

“We’re trained in warfare?” Katie said. “Who says that?”

“I know. It’s all I could think of.”

“We’re in trouble.”

“Yes we are. So let's create some chaos.”

Katie smiled at her. They moved to the edge above the cartel and began firing at any target they could see. The men returned fire as they climbed, but they never stopped climbing. As they approached the top they fired enough that Katie and Eve couldn’t stand and return fire without being hit.

They moved back and kneeled, waiting for the cartel to come over the edge. They heard them climbing. The cartel was close.

Without warning rifle fire came from the left side of the cartel. Katie and Eve ran to the cliff and fired down on them. Cole, Riker, and Sofia kept shooting from the side.

Some of the cartel members were hit. The fire from the top and the side was too much. The remaining ones ran down the mountain to get away.

In minutes it was over. Katie and Eve waited as the others walked to the top.

"It's good to see you guys," Eve said.

"So good," Katie said.

"Anyone injured?" Sofia asked.

"Just the bad guys."

"Where are the kids?" Riker asked.

They walked to the other side of the mountain and looked down. The students were lying near the top. Some had rocks, and some had large sticks and branches. Their eyes were wide when they looked up.

"I told you guys to run," Eve said.

"We thought we could help," one said.

"Is anyone hurt?"

"I twisted my ankle," a boy said.

"Can you walk?"

"Not very well."

"I fell on my back," another one said. "It really hurts."

"Riker and I will get the ATVs to take the injured kids down," Cole said.

"Eve and I can check for any wounded," Katie said. "Sofia, if you have a signal can you call the parents to get their kids? We'll meet them where you parked."

Katie and Eve began walking the mountain looking for survivors. Three of the cartel members were wounded and raised their hands in surrender. They took their guns away and left them to find their way home. Parents were arriving by the time they got the kids off the mountain. They were crying and hugging their children. Some hugged Sofia and the others.

"I'll deliver weapons to your town tomorrow," Sofia said to the mayor. "You need to protect your kids."

"We know nothing about guns," he replied.

"I'll send someone to train you."

The man looked at the others. They nodded. "We'll do whatever it takes."

The girl that was so scared walked toward Katie.

"Thank you," she said, tears in her eyes. She hugged Katie and Eve before one of the other parents took her home.

Chapter 45

Danni was in the computer room when everyone arrived at the hacienda. She met them on the deck, and they told her what happened.

"That's so great," Danni said.

"How's it going with the Russian computers?" Cole said.

"I'm in," Danni said. "I found their programs for missile launches but they're too complex for me to understand. The Director is getting someone in Washington to look at it. I also learned there is another plane landing at 1 am tonight. It doesn't list what it's carrying."

"Anything else?"

"I freaked out the Director."

"How? She's the calmest person I know." Cole said.

"I found a long-term plan to build a military seaport on the west coast of Mexico. I haven't found the details yet but it's not far from San Diego."

"I can see why she freaked," Eve said.

"I've never seen her so agitated. She said she was flying to Washington immediately."

"We have to find something we can use to stall the Russians," Cole said.

"Can you bring down their computers?" Katie asked.

"That would only stall them for a while."

"Can you hack their emails?" Cole said.

"I did. I sent a fake email to the commander that appeared like it came from the president. It had a video I downloaded of him making a speech about how great it is the Russians sent a search and rescue team. A virus was inside it. Once I had his email I sent a video of the big plane they're using to the president and cracked his. Now I own both."

"Sneaky," Riker said. "Did you learn anything?"

"I looked through the president's secure emails. He's protecting the Los Zetas Cartel."

"What do you mean by protecting," Cole asked.

"He keeps the military and police away from them. In turn, the cartel pays him a percentage of profits. It's one way he pays for his campaigns. I haven't confirmed it, but I think he has the same arrangement with the Gulf Cartel."

"Corruption at the highest levels," Eve said.

"Here's the kicker," Danni said. "He asked the cartel to terrorize one of the villages and kill the mayor. The mayor has been bad-mouthing him online."

"And they're going to do it?"

"Yes. But it's a trick. He never told the cartel he's sending in the Russians to kill them and save the village."

"If the Russians save the town it'll hit all the news channels and social media," Katie said. "The president can say Mexico needs the Russians to help with the cartels. It justifies him allowing Russian military bases."

"Meanwhile a village full of innocent people may get killed."

"We can't let that happen," Katie said.

"I thought of a way we can turn this to our advantage," Danni said. "I can fake an email from the president and send the Russians to the wrong town. When the cartel goes to kill the mayor we can help the people ambush them. We video it and blast it across social media as proof the people can defeat the cartels."

"It sends the message the Mexicans don't need the Russians," Katie said. "I love it. You're a smart puppy, Danni."

"A smart puppy that needs a drink. I'll pour."

The evening turned into a party. Katie sat on Cole's lap and wrapped her arms around his neck. "We saved some kids today. That felt good."

"I don't know how anyone could do what the cartel does."

"I'm glad I got you." She put her head on his shoulder and let the alcohol shut down her mind. Minutes later she fell asleep.

Cole carried her to bed and then went out to talk to Riker. The rest had retired, and he was on the deck sipping a drink.

"What are you thinking about?" Cole asked, sitting beside him.

"This is bigger than I imagined. Russians will be aiming missiles at the U.S. and building seaports across from San Diego. We better not screw this up."

"Washington can't tell Mexico to kick out the Russians. There are American military bases in at least 80 countries. We have no moral high ground."

"And our allies surround Russia with nukes," Riker said. "I can see why they want bases in Mexico."

"We still have to try to stop them."

"I know. Failure is not an option."

"I know you're worried when you start quoting movies."

"We can't let anyone get killed at the village. If our plan fails Mexicans will think the cartels can do what they want and they need the Russians."

"We can do this."

"We have to do this."

Chapter 46

A mid-afternoon sun carpeted the soccer field. School kids were standing in a group near Cole and the others. The visitor's stands were partially filled with parents and friends.

“It’s been a lot of years since I played soccer,” Riker said.

“I used to play with my dad,” Katie said. “It was one of the few normal times I had growing up.”

“We’re playing against teenage boys and girls,” Eve said. “We can beat them.”

“We’re playing against teenage boys and girls who play soccer all the time,” Sofia said. “Let's try not to embarrass ourselves.”

“Don’t forget the real reason we’re here, guys,” Danni said. “The cartel should arrive any minute.”

“Did you take care of the Russians?” Cole asked.

“I sent them in the opposite direction.”

“Then let’s start playing. Keep your eyes open.”

The Mexican kids were good. Very good. Sofia was the best on their side, but it wasn’t enough.

"I never thought I'd say this, but I wish the cartel would show," Riker said. "It's embarrassing how bad we're losing."

"You got your wish," Katie said, nodding to the road.

A line of trucks was approaching. They drove onto the field and the men exited, forming a half circle in front of everyone.

The men and women on the bleachers watched, not moving. A man from the cartel stepped forward. He was overly muscular and had a mustache he carefully trimmed. He scanned the people, stopping at Cole.

"Who are you?"

"I'm your worst nightmare," Cole said.

He laughed. "Take those two girls," he said to his friends. "And bring me the mayor."

"No, please!" one of the girls yelled as a man grabbed her and began pulling her to a truck. Riker stepped in front of him. The man let go of the girl and grabbed his handgun. The rest of the cartel raised their weapons.

The people in the stands reached down and picked up rifles. They stood and aimed at the cartel. The cartel members turned their guns toward them. The people walked off the stands and stood beside Cole and the others, guns still aimed. Two of them handed weapons to Cole and his team. Seconds later vehicles came from around a building and parked behind the cartel. Sofia's team got out and stood behind the group, rifles ready. The cartel leader looked at all the weapons aimed at them.

"Leave," Katie said to the teen soccer players. They ran behind the bleachers and watched from there. Except for one girl. She stood defiantly beside Katie, glaring at the cartel leader. Katie felt it was something personal. She handed her a handgun. The girl held it in both hands and aimed it at the leader.

"You're outnumbered three-to-one," Cole said. "Drop your weapons and you'll get to live for another day."

The leader looked at the people surrounding him, then back at Cole.

"We don't run from farmers and shop owners."

"Then you die by our hands," one of the townspeople said.

The cartel leader looked around again. His eyes stopped on the girl holding the handgun in both hands aimed at his chest. He knew her. Her hands didn't shake. Her eyes never left his face. He recognized the hatred. He looked at the others and saw the same anger and determination.

"We'll be back with many more people," he said. "I'll have more fun with you." He winked at the girl.

The girl fired twice. Both bullets hit him in the heart. The man collapsed facedown. Two of the cartel members panicked and began firing. In seconds multiple bullets hit them. The rest of the cartel dropped their weapons, knowing they didn't stand a chance.

"On your knees, hands above your heads!" Cole yelled.

The people gathered their weapons and surrounded them. Some wanted to shoot them, others wanted them gone from the field.

The mayor moved in front of the cartel. "We'll kill you if you return," he said. "We are armed and prepared to defend our children. Take your dead and leave."

The men never moved, scared it was a trick.

"Now!" the mayor yelled.

They grabbed the bodies and went to their vehicles, speeding off.

The girl handed Katie's gun back, her face expressionless.

"Do you need to talk?" Katie asked.

"Not anymore," she said and left.

"Did you get the video?" Cole asked Sofia as they walked back to their vehicles.

"Two of my team did it with their cell phones. I'll send the footage to you."

"We'll delete who did the killings, and the rest will be anonymously broadcast over social media. The news will pick it up by tonight."

"I hope this will encourage other towns to stand up and fight," Sofia said. "They'll see the cartels can be defeated."

"And that Mexico doesn't need the Russians."

"The president is going to be mad as hell," Danni said.

"So will the Russians."

Danni looked at her phone. "The Director said you did a good job."

"How do they know everything so fast?" Katie asked.

Danni smiled. "That's classified."

"I'm part of the team now. I get to know the super secret stuff. Make her tell me, Cole."

"When your dad ran the mafia did he tell you everything?"

"No."

"No one knows everything. Not even the Director. Secrets keep us safe."

"Then I guess I'll never tell you the kinkiest thing I love to do in bed," she said walking ahead.

"Oh, buddy," Riker said. "You screwed that up."

Chapter 47

The next night the Director called the hacienda. She asked Sofia to be there. Danni connected her phone to the TV so they could all watch her.

"I'm guessing there's more bad news," Cole said.

"Good and bad," the Director said. "You've been doing a good job in getting the towns to protect themselves. They have weapons, and they've seen how other towns have resisted the cartels."

"That's a good thing, right?" Danni said.

"Not for you. Thc cartels jointly decided to put a hit on you. We know because our government was watching the hit team, and your names came up."

"That's not good," Katie said.

"How will they kill us?" Cole asked.

"You mean try to kill us," Katie said.

"The hit team is from Mexico City. They're not subtle or classy. They use lots of firepower."

"We could go back to Chicago until this is over," Danni said.

"They'll go anywhere in the world to find you. The hit will be worth at least a million US. Last year they took out a cartel leader who was in witness protection, and they killed a man who was at a high-security US military base. They don't care about collateral damage. Don't underestimate them."

"What do we do?" Danni asked.

"We need to meet them in a place where we have the advantage," Riker said. "Somewhere we know, and they don't."

"What about the hacienda?" Danni said.

"Too easy to blow it up with us inside," Riker said.

"You're right, Riker," Katie said. "We use what we know, and we know the Chicago tunnels. There are miles of intersections and branches where we can hide. It's perfect for an ambush."

Riker nodded. "That's a good idea. It's black as hell down there and all the buildings above were abandoned a long time ago."

"And it'll make them overconfident if they think we ran away to hide," Katie said.

"Then the tunnels are where we take them," Riker said. "Hopefully, the cartel won't send any more hitmen after us if we defeat them."

"We won't give them a chance," Cole said. "When we return to Mexico we'll go after whoever hired them."

"There's more," the Director said. "After they kill you they're going after Sofia."

"How?" Sofia asked.

"We don't know yet."

"I always knew that was a possibility, but I'm not going to wait around," Sofia said. "I'll keep distributing the weapons.

"I can stay and help her," Danni said. "Unless one of us has to drive a semi because I don't know how yet."

"We've changed to using box trucks with company logos. No one is noticing us that way."

"Then I'll arrange for the plane for you guys," Danni said.

They stayed quiet and looked at each other, realizing how much danger they were in.

"We have to stop a Mexican hit squad," Katie mumbled. "Words I never thought I'd say."

Chapter 48

When they arrived in Chicago they went to the museum. Katie stopped to talk to the T-Rex while the rest went upstairs. They were having coffee when she walked in.

"Everything okay with T-Rex?" Cole asked.

"He's been lonely without me. I need to spend more time with him."

"You could take him for a walk," Riker said.

"I can't find a leash that long."

"When we finish our coffee we'll go to the Control weapons center," Cole said.

"You mean we get to play with tanks and fighter jets?" Katie said.

"No, but we can train you on archery there. You need to know how to use a bow."

"Then we should go now."

"You haven't had your coffee yet," Cole said.

"We're going to fight killers in dark tunnels under the city. I feel like I don't need caffeine."

Cole drove them to the weapons center. Eve and Riker went to a storage area while Katie followed Cole.

"We have a gun range next door. This room is for archery. You have targets at different distances, and you can choose your bow type. I'm going to show you how to use a crossbow," he said taking one off the wall.

"I tried one once. It took too long to reload."

"These have unique design features."

They moved to an area in front of the closest target. He handed her the bow.

"It's got a scope on it like a rifle," she said. "That's cool. Why are there four arrows underneath it?"

"The bow was designed by Control for combat. After each shot, it'll automatically retract the string and load another arrow. And you can use a cartridge to load four more.

Katie examined the weapon. "Why are the arrows different?"

"They're designed for different purposes." He took the crossbow from her and manually loaded an arrow with a device on the tip. He aimed at the farthest target and fired. When the arrow hit the target it exploded, shredding it.

"If the target is wearing a vest it'll take his head off."

"That's mean."

"We also have other types of arrows, and you can change the shooting order."

"Are these what you're going to use?"

"No. I prefer a recurve bow. It gives me pinpoint accuracy and more power."

"Is yours designed by Control?"

"Yes. Now, let's get you shooting."

They spent most of the day at the range. Riker and Eve came in later carrying large bags and said it was time to leave.

“What’s in the bags?”

“Things for the fight,” Eve said. “We need to stop at the tunnels and prepare the battleground.

****

It was after dinner when the Director walked into the apartment. “Someone needs to offer me a drink. It’s been a long day.”

“Hi, Director,” Cole said. “Want a drink?” He never got up.

She stood looking at him then poured her own and sat in a chair. “Your friends have arrived in town.”

“The Mexican hitmen?” Katie asked.

“Your assassins are four men and one woman. I did a background check on them. They have worked as a team for six years and never failed an assignment. Talented with guns, knives, and hand-to-hand combat.”

“Did you come here just to give us a pep talk,” Riker said.

“Know your enemy, Riker.”

“We know what we’re facing.”

“I came to offer you help. I can put 20 men in the tunnels. They can work with you.”

“There are 16 miles of tunnels with no lights,” Cole said. “We’d end up killing each other.”

“I had to offer. Is there anything I can do?”

"Not for now," Cole said. "Have you heard from Danni?"

"She and Sofia are distributing weapons. I sent out a warning to them. Two Russian trucks left the airport with armed soldiers. I don't know if they're looking for them."

"Can you send them 20 of our guys?" Katie asked.

"Not in time. I'm watching the situation. You concentrate on your problems. I know the hotel the hitmen are staying at. You'll have to lead them to the tunnels."

The Director picked up the bottle of tequila and looked at the label. "This is good."

"We brought it back from Mexico," Eve said. "It's the best we found."

"Thanks," the Director said as she left with the bottle.

"She took the bottle," Katie said. "That's just cruel."

"Nature of the beast," Riker said. "How are we going to get the Mexicans to follow us to the tunnels?"

"I can have one of my mafia guys sell them the information on our location," Katie said. "He can tell them where we're hiding in the tunnels until they leave town."

"Then we'll do this tonight," Cole said.

"None of them can leave the tunnels," Riker said. "If they do they'll never stop coming after us until we're dead."

Chapter 49

They lowered their weapons through the hole in the dilapidated bar floor and then climbed down the ropes into the tunnels, leaving them in place. Cole insisted they wear bulletproof vests, and everyone agreed. Moving away from the opening they waited at a side tunnel. No one spoke. The darkness surrounded them. A brief spot of light could be seen through the hole where they came in.

It was a short wait before they heard something. They glanced around the corner. Looking toward the entrance they saw people climbing down the rope. Cole and the others put on their night goggles and hid behind the corner. The hit team was wearing the same goggles. They moved in a V shape as they slowly walked down the tunnel, rifles raised.

When they were closer Cole tapped Riker on the shoulder. On the other side of the tunnel was a powerful spotlight on a stand. Riker flipped a switch, and it blasted the light down the tunnel. The attackers grabbed their goggles and ripped them off. Before they could fire Katie and Cole stepped out. The hit team couldn't see them. Cole fired first, his arrow piercing the neck of the man in front of the group. He fell. Katie fired her crossbow. The arrow hit a man in his shoulder and detonated. The explosion killed him instantly. They ducked back into the side tunnel.

Bullets began blasting down the tunnel towards them. When some hit the light they were smothered in darkness again. Without their goggles on the attackers were firing blind. They stopped. Cole and the team began running down the tunnel to the next side entrance and ducked inside. Cole watched the hit team.

He saw them put their goggles on as they moved to a side tunnel. They scanned the area for more lights or traps. Then the team moved forward, hugging the wall, ready to fire at anything that moved.

One of them raised a fist and they all stopped. He grabbed a grenade and pulled the pin, then tossed it underhand close to the opening. Katie saw him throw it. Katie ran toward it in a crouch. She grabbed it before it hit the ground and without straightening up or stopping, she threw it underhanded back down the tunnel toward the men. She fell where she was and covered her head. It exploded mid-air near them. The man who threw it was hit by shrapnel.

Katie lay on the ground, not moving. Cole ran to her. Riker and Eve lay down cover fire as he dragged her into the tunnel entrance on the other side. He rolled her over. Her face was cut, and blood covered her arm.

"You alright?"

"My arm was hit."

"Your forehead and cheek are bleeding."

"It's okay. I landed on rocks."

"Don't ever do that again," Cole said.

"Okay. Your turn next time."

Eve and Riker continued to fire down the tunnel. The man who threw the grenade tried to get up. Eve didn't let him, the shots echoing through the tunnels.

Cole loaded an arrow, stepped out, and fired. The arrow pierced a man's thigh. He fell and tried to pull it out. Cole reloaded, his anger overcoming him. His second arrow hit the man's chest, and another hit his neck.

They saw the last person running down the tunnel the way they came in. Riker chased after her, both disappearing in the darkness.

Eve ran to Katie. Cole was helping her stand. They took off her coat and he wrapped a bandage around the wound. In the distance, they heard shots. There was a pause and then another shot.

"I'm going to check it out," Eve said, running toward the sounds.

When Cole and Katie caught up to them Riker was being held up by Eve.

"Where are you hurt?" Cole said.

"Fell on sharp rocks when I was chasing her," Riker said. "Nothing serious."

They stepped over the body of the last attacker as they left. When they were outside Eve brought the car alongside them and they got in.

"I called Control," Katie said. "They'll be a doctor at the museum by the time we get there."

"Do we need one?" Riker asked.

“The tunnels are infested with rats. Even a small cut can get infected. He can decide if we need a tetanus shot.”

When they were at the museum Katie touched the T-Rex as she walked by him. “Hi, honey, I’m home,” she said.

The Doctor was waiting at the elevator. “I always seem to be here. I should get a rental nearby.”

“We’re glad you came, Doc.,” Cole said.

In the apartment, they took Riker into one room and Katie into the other.

When he came out he stopped to talk to them. “No permanent damage. Riker was cut up by rocks but after seeing all his other wounds I think he’ll recover pretty quickly. You guys get tetanus shots every few years so you’re fine. I gave one to Katie just in case. Keep them both calm and let them rest.”

“So, no sex for either of them?” Cole said smiling.

“Only with each other,” the doc said, returning the smile with a wink.

“Don’t tell them that,” Eve said as the doctor was leaving.

“We heard it,” Riker yelled from the bedroom.

Katie walked down the hallway to the living room. “I’ll take one for the team.”

“That’s my girl,” Riker said as he came in next.

“I’m calling the detective to tell her there are dead Mexican assassins in the tunnel,” Katie said.

“Why?”

"She hates paperwork, and this will be days of it. And I don't want dead smelly things down there in case we have to go back in."

"I'm worried about Danni and Sofia," Cole said. "We'll fly back to Mexico tomorrow."

Chapter 50

The box truck stayed at the posted speed to avoid being stopped. On the side was the name of a popular furniture company. Danni and Sofia had made two stops and had enough arms for one more village before returning home.

Sofia drove. The windows were open, and they wore shorts to survive the heat. Danni had her feet on the dash and one arm out the window.

"When does the heat ease up?" Danni asked.

"It's Mexico. It doesn't. That's why all the tourists stay on the coast."

"I get that now."

"We're about two miles from the farm turnoff. The girl I contacted said she'd have people waiting for us."

Sofia turned into the driveway. A girl was sitting on a porch watching for them.

"No one else is here," Danni said, stopping.

"They could be in the barn to get out of the sun."

"Something doesn't feel right," Danni said, sitting up and putting on her shoes. "We should leave."

"You're right." Sofia stopped and scanned the area. She began backing up to turn when an SUV pulled in behind her. It parked touching her bumper. At the same time, Russian soldiers came running out of the barn.

"Oh hell, we're in deep trouble," Sofia said.

Sofia saw the girl on the porch go inside the house. The Russians opened the vehicle doors and pulled them out, pushing them against the truck. A man cuffed them and put them in the SUV behind their truck, and then one got in beside them. The others got in an SUV hidden in the barn and the vehicles drove back to the highway.

"We're screwed," Danni said.

"Keep quiet or I'll gag you," the man said with a thick Russian accent.

Danni looked at Sofia. They could see the fear in each other's eyes. They drove for 30 minutes before turning off the highway onto a dirt road. At the end of it was an old house with a Russian military SUV parked in front. A man sat in the back of it. He was watching a Russian soldier dragging an old man's body behind the barn.

Danni and Sofia were taken inside the house and pushed on the couch.

"What do you want?" Sofia asked.

Another man entered the house. His insignia showed he was a high-ranking officer. A long scar ran diagonally along his cheek.

"Take her outside," he said nodding at Sofia.

When they left he sat beside Danni and put his hand on her leg. "You are going to tell me why you and your American friends are here."

"I'm on vacation," Danni said, hesitantly. "It's a beautiful country."

"I was hoping you'd resist," he said, rubbing his hand along the inside of her leg. "It's so much more fun that way."

"Go to hell." Danni's voice gave away her fear.

"Your name is Danni Olivia Schofield. You work for an agency called Control, but my people can't seem to find any information about them. I know you've been stealing guns from us and handing them out to the Mexicans. You've caused a lot of problems for the cartels.

"You're nuts. None of that is true."

"I want to know about Control and what other plans they have. I want to know where you are hiding the guns. How many of you are there? We are going to have a long slow conversation."

Danni tried to stand but he stopped her.

"If you do as I say you will be free to go When we are done. If you don't I will give you to the Los Zetas Cartel. You won't like what they do to girls like you."

"Go screw yourself."

He sat back on the couch and looked at her for a few moments. Then he walked to the door and talked to his men. One of them brought Sofia back in and sat her beside Danni. Then he left with them.

"Are you okay?" Sofia whispered.

"For now." Danni tried to free her hands from the cuffs but couldn't. She stood and went to the kitchen. In a drawer was a knife. She grabbed it and cut her cuffs. As she moved toward Sofia the door opened and two men entered. One of the Russians knocked the knife from her hand and grabbed her arms.

"Take her to the barn," the officer said. "Do what you want to her but don't kill her." As he spoke he removed a container from his pocket and opened it. Inside was a syringe and a vial of fluid.

"No," Danni said and kicked, almost hitting the case. She fought against the man holding her. He backhanded her and she fell. He picked her up.

"Leave her alone," Danni yelled as she was pulled outside.

The officer looked at Sofia and smiled. "She is going to be difficult to deal with, so let's try you first." He put the syringe in the vial and drew out some of the liquid.

"What is that?" Sofia asked, her heart racing.

"A drug developed in my country. It'll make you… how should I say it? Compliant. Most people live through it. Actually, maybe not most, but some."

"Why are you doing this?"

"You are stopping the Mexicans from thinking they need us to destroy the cartels. I can't allow that. I am going to ask you questions about your team."

Sofia's eyes were fixed on the syringe. He held it in the air and ejected a small amount. "It just takes a little bit. Too much is not good."

"When we are done, we can have a little fun. You are very pretty." He smiled as he approached her, the syringe in his hand. "Would you prefer the arm or the leg?"

"Please, don't," she begged.

"Fine. The leg."

He leaned toward her and lowered the syringe to just above her thigh.

"Wait!" Without standing he looked up at her Sofia slammed her head into his. His head snapped back, and blood came from his nose. "You bitch." He raised his hand to strike her.

Sofia leaned back and kicked hard, hitting him in the knee. She heard a crack. He doubled over as he grabbed it. She stood and swept his legs out from under him. When he fell she raised her foot and smashed her heel down on his temple. She kept stomping on his temple and his neck until he stopped moving. Finding another knife she cut her cuffs. Walking back to him she saw he was still breathing. She took the syringe and filled it, then jammed it into his neck, pressing all of it into him.

Sofia stood over him trying to bring her breathing under control. She took his gun and then looked out the window. Guards were talking in the yard. Going out the back door, she ran to the barn.

Danni was pressed against a post. A guard held his hand around her neck and ran his other hand over her breasts. Danni grabbed the hand on her neck and twisted it. He was too strong. He ripped open her shirt.

Danni saw Sofia appear behind the guard. She snapped her eyes back to the guard and spat in his face to distract him. The man brought his hand back to slam his fist into her face. Sofia jammed the knife into his armpit, pulled it out, then buried it in the side of his neck. He grabbed his throat, eyes wide, then fell. Danni took his gun and kicked him out of anger.

"We're not out of this yet," Sofia said. "There are three more guards between us and the SUV."

"I'm tired of these pricks," Danni said, tying her shirt in a knot.

Danni and Sofia checked the magazines. Both were full.

"I say we go cowboy on their asses," Danni said.

"Cowboy?"

"Do what I do."

Danni held the gun in both hands, her arms extended. Sofia mimicked her. They walked out of the barn. The Russians saw them and began to take out their weapons. Danni and Sofia fired before they could. With each step, they fired again and again. When their guns were empty the guards were laying on the ground. They stood over them.

"He drove," Sofia said and took the keys from his pocket.

"Oh god," Danni said as she saw two Russians running from the back of the house toward them.

They raced to the SUV and got in. Danni struggled to get the key in the ignition.

"Hurry," Sofia said. She stuck her gun out the window and then realized it was empty. The Russians took out their handguns as they got closer. Bullets peppered the windshield before Danni got it started. She put it in gear and hit the gas. The truck spun around, kicking dirt and rocks at the Russians.

Sofia looked back and saw them getting into the other SUV. "They're coming after us."

Danni checked her mirror and saw them giving chase. Sofia searched the glove box and side panels. "No guns."

Danni couldn't get away from them. The passenger leaned out and began firing. Bullets hit the back window. She saw a curve ahead. She took it as fast as she could, the back wheels almost cutting loose before she brought it back under control. The dust trail she left was making the SUV behind them slow down so they could see the road.

"There's a stop sign where this connects to the highway," Sofia said. "If we go through it we'll be hit by traffic."

"We don't have a choice."

Danni kept hitting the horn as they approached it. Then she put on her emergency lights. "Why don't these idiots stop?"

"It's Mexico. Keep going. Maybe we can get lucky."

Danni was seconds from the speeding cars on the highway. She saw a pickup coming toward the intersection and hit the gas pedal to get ahead of him. When she reached the pavement she cranked the wheel. The pickup driver blasted his horn and cut around her without slowing. The SUV's back end cut left. She turned to correct it. She overcorrected. She corrected again and regained control. They both looked back. The Russians were gaining on them.

Chapter 51

Sofia called a friend and told her they were coming in fast, and Russians were chasing them. She told her to get ready.

"Two miles ahead is a turn-off to the right. Take it."

"Where are we going?"

"To a farm one of my team owns."

Danni kept cutting around cars.

"That's the turn," Sofia said.

Danni waited until the last minute, slammed on the brakes and turned, then hit the gas.

"They're closing on us. The farm is a mile from here."

"Then what?"

"Then we hope someone is there that can help us."

Danni kept her speed up on the way to the farm, slamming on the brakes when she was close to the barn.

"Inside," Sofia said. "Run." Danni and Sofia ran toward the barn doors. The Russians stopped behind them and got out of their truck. They were preparing to shoot.

An old man stepped onto the porch and fired at the ground in front of the Russians. They both turned to kill him. Bullets came from the darkness inside the barn. Both Russians fell. One was only injured. He began firing into the barn. The old man fired again, this time into flesh. The shotgun ended the Russian.

Danni and Sofia walked out of the barn. They took the weapons from the Russians and checked for life. A teen girl and boy walked out and stood beside them. The old man turned and went back inside.

"My papa doesn't think we should fight them or the cartel," the boy said.

"I'm glad you think differently," Sofia said.

"What do we do with them?" the girl asked.

"Call the response team," Sofia said. "Have them take care of the bodies and the damaged SUV. We'll take the one they drove. And tell them to pick up a box truck from the Morella's farm and distribute the weapons, then to get rid of the bodies at that farm."

"We'll call them," the girl said.

Thank you for your help," Sofia said and hugged them. "We needed you today."

The drive to the hacienda was quiet. They thought about how close they came to being killed. When they got home they walked to the deck, dropping into chairs.

"I feel exhausted, and I don't know why," Danni said.

"Maybe being nearly raped, drugged, and killed takes it out of you," Sofia said.

"That's true. I have to avoid those things in the future."

"The Russians are going to come after us. We need to be careful."

"Do you know the girl that ratted us out?"

"No, but I'm sure she had her reasons. Maybe they threatened her family, or maybe she needed money to feed them."

"You're very forgiving."

"No one in Mexico wants what's happening," Sofia said. "Right now, all I want is a drink."

"I need a shower first. I still have blood on me."

"I'll pour, then take my turn after you."

Danni went to the bedroom for new clothes. She wanted to burn what she was wearing. As she showered anger began to surge through her. She stood under the water and let it cascade over her. A man took her power away. She promised herself she would never let it happen again.

Sofia was in the kitchen when the others came in.

"Where's Danni?" Cole asked.

"She's taking a shower to wash the anger off. She was almost raped."

"Is she okay?"

"She will be."

"I'm so glad you guys are alright," Katie said.

"We all have stories to tell. How about drinks on the deck? I'll get out some snacks."

"I'll help," Katie said.

"I'm going to check on Danni," Cole said.

He went to the bedroom and knocked. No one answered so he went in. Danni was in a towel curled up on the bed. Cole sat beside her and touched her shoulder. Danni sat up and hugged him for a long time.

"Bad day?" Cole said.

"Real bad. I don't know how you guys do this all the time."

"We rely on each other to get through the bad parts. We're all here for you."

"Thanks, Cole," she said hugging him again.

"Get dressed and come to the deck. We have drinks and snacks and a lot to talk about."

Danni nodded and Cole left.

They sat on the deck and told their stories until day became night. The fear and anger were replaced more by the love of good friends than the drinks.

"The Russians are just as bad as the cartel," Danni said.

"We need to destroy their base," Cole said.

"They're Russian military soldiers," Katie said. "How the hell can we do that?"

"I've been thinking a lot about that. What if we get the cartel to do it?"

"Why would they?" Eve asked. "And could they?"

"We attack the cartel and make them believe it's the Russians doing it. They'll want revenge and might damage them enough the Russians will rethink staying in Mexico. We can help the cartel during the battle."

"You want to work with the cartel?"

"No. They won't know we're going to help them. I haven't figured out the details yet, and my mind is too foggy tonight. We'll talk about it tomorrow."

"On that note," Riker said. "I'm going to bed."

"Good idea," Eve said.

"I'm too drunk to drive so can I stay here tonight?" Sofia said, standing.

"Of course," Cole said, "but can I talk to you first?" Cole took her into the living room.

Katie watched as they leaned on the counter and talked. After a time Sofia nodded and went to bed.

"What was that about?" Katie asked.

"I asked her for a favor. We'll discuss it in the morning."

"I'm going to stay up for a while," Danni said.

"Coming Cole?"

"I'll talk to Danni for a bit. Be in soon."

Katie hesitated, then left.

"I'm okay," Danni said.

"I know."

They both sat staring past the deck into the night. It was a while before anyone spoke.

"Have you ever had someone able to do anything they want to you, and you can't stop them?" Danni said.

"That must be a horrible feeling. I'm sorry you went through it, but let's not forget you and Sofia took on Russian soldiers and kicked their asses."

"I guess we did."

"We're a team and you're an important part of it," he said. "I want you to stay with us."

"I will." She gently kissed him on the lips. "You and I have some unfinished business."

Cole looked at her as she walked away.

****

The next morning when Cole and Katie wandered into the living room the others were drinking coffee. Cole answered a knock on the door. Sofia answered it with him. They talked to a guy Katie recognized as one of Sofia's team, and then they brought in a canvas bag and put it on a chair.

"What is it?" Danni asked.

"I asked my team to wash the blood from the Russian uniforms and bring them here."

"Why?" Riker asked.

"We're going to wear them when we ambush the cartel," Cole said. "And since Danni and Sofia brought the Russian SUV here we can use that too. It has the military logo on the doors so it's easily recognizable."

"You want to pretend we're Russians and attack the cartel," Riker said.

"Not a bad idea," Eve said. "But where do we attack them?"

"Sofia had an idea," Cole said.

"One of my team sees the local cartel leader drive between the city and his ranch on the weekends," Sofia said. "He's paranoid because we killed some of the other leaders, so he has protection.

"What kind of protection?"

"He's in an SUV. In front of him is another SUV and behind him are two motorcycles. The bikers are from an American personal protection company and are specifically trained for motorbikes."

"Why bikers?" Danni asked.

"When they have to chase someone they can weave between traffic if the roads are busy," Riker said.

"We could do a drive-by shooting on the highway," Eve said. "Wait until there are no cars around and then hit them."

"I don't want to kill the leader, just make it look like the Russians tried. We need him alive so he can attack the missile base."

"I have a motorcycle in Chicago we can bring down," Katie said.

"Let me guess," Cole said. "Your dad had you trained on it in case the cops chased you."

"Yup."

"What kind is it?" Riker asked.

"A blacked-out BMW S1000R that was customized for extra speed and agility. And it has a heads-up display like a fighter pilot. It gives me navigation, comms, and infrared with a zoom. Plus some other toys."

"Damn, I'm in love," Riker said. "When can I ride it?"

"I'll ask the plane to bring it down here," Danni said, laughing. "Then you can date it."

"Hell ya."

"I didn't know you were a biker, Katie," Cole said.

"I wish I grew up with unicorn pictures and a best friend I could talk to about boys, but I was trained to be a survivor instead."

"Now Cole's your best friend," Riker said.

"And your unicorn," Eve said.

Katie smiled. "Yes he is."

Chapter 52

Katie walked into the living room dressed in skin-tight black leather. Under her arm was a helmet.

"Wow," Riker said. "Does that outfit come with a whip?"

"It's a special material designed to protect me from fire and road scrapes."

"You look amazing," Cole said.

"Thanks. You and Riker look good as Russian officers."

"I'm leaving the bullet holes in the uniform and keeping it," Riker said. "I can't wait until there's a costume party."

"The cartel leader will be in position in one hour," Sofia said. "We should go. I know a side road we can hide on to wait for him."

"Will it be dark enough for the attack?" Danni asked.

"It will be by the time we get there. He only travels at night."

Danni and Sofi stayed at the hacienda. Riker drove and Cole sat in the passenger seat of the Russian SUV. Katie followed them on her bike. They drove to the turnoff and parked, waiting. It wasn't long before they saw the leader's procession coming.

"I see the target," Riker said.

They waited until the two SUVs and the two motorbikes passed, then pulled in behind them.

"You're up, Katie," Cole said.

Katie cut around Cole and accelerated. When she was beside the motorcycles she nodded her head in a hello to them. They looked at her but never responded.

Katie moved beside the second SUV. She saw the outline of two men in the back and two in the front. In one movement she drew a gun from a holster embedded on the side of her bike and fired four bullets into the vehicle, making sure she missed the passengers.

The motorbikes behind cut into the lane and accelerated. Katie put her gun away and twisted the throttle. Her bike burst ahead. She looked back to make sure the bikers could keep up. She was surprised when she saw them closing the distance. Their bikes were more powerful than she thought they would be.

As she increased speed they matched her. Looking back she saw them shooting at her. She cut in front of a pickup, placing it between her and them. When they got closer she cut out again. This time she took the bike to over 130 mph, saving the top end for an emergency. Her knee almost touched the ground as she sped around a curve. Again the shots came. They were matching her speed and her abilities.

There was a turn-off ahead. She cut in front of a car and slowed just enough to make the turn without spilling the bike. They couldn't turn fast enough so they slowed and doubled back to follow her. It gave Katie some distance. She saw the lights of a farmhouse and aimed for it. The blackness of the night made her concentrate on everything in front of her.

Katie slowed enough to spin the bike around to face them. "Maximum headlight," she said, and the voice-controlled helmet put her light on its brightest setting. It was too bright for traffic, instead designed to blind an attacker. The biker in front slowed and raised his arm to block some of the light. She drew her gun and fired again and again. The shots knocked the man off his bike. He rolled and landed face up, not moving.

The other rider was still approaching. He kept his eyes down to avoid being blinded. Katie fired. The gun was empty. She turned and headed into the desert. Her bike bounced and shook from the uneven ground. Ahead she saw a dirt road. "Zoom in," she said, and the camera responded. There was a ditch along the side of the road. A normal headlight wouldn't see it until it was too late. Not at that speed.

She raced towards it. The rider chasing her was increasing speed. "Headlight out." Blackness enveloped her. A night vision camera activated. She hit the throttle and jumped the bike over the ditch.

The biker behind her never saw the ditch in the dust and darkness. The front wheel went in, and the biker flew over the handlebars, landing on the far side of the road. The biker slowly stood, picking up the gun.

"For Christ's sake," Katie said. "Give it up."

He aimed at Katie. She was racing towards him before he could shoot. When she was close she jumped off her bike and hit him hard, wrapping her arms around him and taking him to the ground.

He was momentarily stunned, then sat up, hands on the ground beside him. Katie crawled to his gun where it lay in the dirt. She kneeled and aimed at him. He held his hand up to stop her, then slowly removed the helmet.

Katie lowered her aim when she saw it was a girl close to her age.

"You win," she said. "Where the hell did you learn to ride like that?"

Katie took off her helmet. "Chicago. You?"

"Phoenix. Any chance we can end this without you shooting me?"

"I just wanted to pull you off your protection detail."

"You could have just asked. The guys a prick."

Katie chuckled. "Your bike is trashed."

The girl looked back at it and saw she was right. "I could use a ride."

"Let's go." They walked to Katie's bike. There was minimal damage. Katie pulled out a set of cuffs from a pocket on the bike.

"Cuffs? Is this a date?"

"I don't know you that well."

"I'm Blake."

"Katie," Katie said getting on her bike. "Get on,"

Blake got on behind Katie.

"Arms around my waist," Katie said.

Blake slowly slid her hands around Katie and moved closer to her. After she did Katie handcuffed her wrists.

"This is new."

"Too easy to push me off at high speed."

"I'm loving the foreplay. Maybe we could go for a drink."

"Sure. I know a place."

Chapter 53

Cole waited until the motorbikes were gone and there was a straight stretch. He pulled parallel to the leader's SUV. The man in the back saw the Russian logo on the truck and then looked at Cole. He didn't seem concerned.

Cole rolled down his window and put his arm out. He aimed the handgun and waited until the leader ducked. He fired, hitting the passenger. The lead truck pulled in front of him. The leader's vehicle sped ahead and disappeared into the night. Riker hit the brakes. The SUV did the same.

"I thought they would run," Riker said.

"Maybe we should."

"Riker put it in reverse and hit the gas. As he sped backward down the highway he hit the brakes and turned the wheel. The SUV spun around, and he hit the gas again. The SUV did the same maneuver.

They raced down the highway the wrong way, dodging oncoming cars. A man in front of the cartel SUV began shooting. Bullets penetrated the windows. Riker weaved to miss the cars and the bullets.

"What's plan B?" Cole said.

"We should have made a plan B."

"I have an idea. Head to the Russian military base."

"With a truck we stole from the Russians we killed?"

"They won't know the men are dead. They'll think it's them coming back."

"You sure?"

"No. I've never been sure about anything when people are involved. Take the next left."

They left the main highway and were pursued toward the airport.

"When we get there did you want to stop and ask for help?" Riker said.

"They have guards posted at the front of the building. We'll let them take care of the bad guys."

They continued until they saw the airport, driving through the main gate without slowing. The guards saw their uniforms and never fired. By the time the cartel went through it was too late. Riker kept driving to the building. Two men were standing outside the door with rifles ready.

"Let's hope they're good shots," Cole said.

"Let's hope they think we're Russians."

Cole rolled down his window so they would see his uniform. The men saw them coming in at high speed. When they saw the logo they changed their aim to the cartel SUV.

The cartel driver was close behind Riker. Without warning Riker slammed on the brakes. The cartel did the same. Riker positioned them so the cartel truck was in front of the guards. The guards opened fire. The cartel returned fire. Riker sped away. Behind them, the sound of the shooting had stopped.

"Pretty sure the Russians ended them."

"Lucky us."

"Want a drink?"

"I want a bottle."

When they arrived at the hacienda they went to the deck. Katie, Danni, and Sofia were sitting with drinks and a bowl of chips and salsa. With them was a girl they didn't know.

"Cole," Katie said and jumped up, hugging him.

"What about me?" Riker said.

"You're Eve's huggy buddy."

"I only like to hug naked," Eve said, sipping her drink.

"I can wait," Riker said.

"This is Blake," Katie said. "She was one of the bikers trying to kill me."

"I guess you two made up."

"It wasn't personal," Blake said. "We're all friends now."

"Is that why there are handcuffs on the table?"

"It was a trust-building exercise," Katie said.

"Or as Riker says, only enemies and lovers should wear cuffs," Eve said, laughing.

"Too much information," Cole said.

"It was nice meeting you guys, but I have to go," Blake said.

"Where to?"

"I'll tell the cartel leader I killed the biker that shot at him then found the SUV guys and killed them too. It should be a good bonus."

"Take the Russian truck," Cole said. "It makes your story more believable."

"Thanks. I appreciate it."

"No problem."

"We have to get together again, Katie," Blake said.

Katie stood to hug her goodbye. Halfway through the hug, Blake placed her hands on Katie's face and kissed her on the lips. Katie froze, staring at Blake as she left.

"I didn't expect that."

"I bet I liked it more than you," Riker said, pouring another drink and smiling.

"Maybe not," Katie said.

"Should I be worried?" Cole said.

"You should be enthusiastic," Riker said.

"I should go too," Sofia said. "I want to see my family and sleep in my own bed tonight. I'll let you guys figure out the kissing."

"Thanks for your help today, Sofia," Cole said. "We couldn't do this without you."

"You're saving my country. I owe you. Night."

"It's been a good night," Riker said. "The cartel thinks the Russians attacked them and the Russians think the cartel was doing a drive-by shooting at them."

Katie saw Danni staring at her phone. "What's up," Danni?"

"The Director sent me a text. She says the Russians are sending gunship helicopters into Mexico. They'll be training the Mexican military on how to fly them. Something called an Mi-24. They're attack helicopters."

"Did she say where they'll be stationed?"

"At the airport near us. And she said they're sending more troops. Some are for training the Mexican military, others for guarding the airport."

"One step forward and two back," Katie said.

"The Mexican president still needs to get re-elected in the fall," Eve said. "All this goes away if he fails."

"Control is already blasting social media with information about his real plans, but it's not working," Danni said.

"Why so quiet, Cole?" Katie asked.

"If the Russians are training the Mexicans it can only mean one thing. The president could order the Mexican military to attack the States. With Russia backing them they could win."

"What reason would Mexico have to attack the States?" Katie asked.

"We stole half a million square miles of their country. That's a pretty good reason."

"What the hell do we do?" Riker said.

"I don't know, but we better figure it out fast," Cole said.

Chapter 54

There was a loud knock at the door that night. Katie stumbled out of bed to answer it. “Who is it?”

“It’s Blake. I left my medicine here.”

Katie was still half-asleep when she opened the door. “What medicine?”

“The cartel members pushed past Blake and dashed into the room. One put his hand over Katie’s mouth and aimed a gun at her head. Two others opened Eve and Riker's room and went in, guns ready, yelling for them to get up. At the samc timc two went into Cole’s room. They pushed them all into the living room and cuffed them. One of the men saw one more bedroom door and burst in. The bed was made, and no one was in the room or the bathroom.

“Blake, you bitch,” Katie said.

“I got a big bonus for this one,” she said.

“You’ll die for this.”

“Look around. There’s no one to rescue you.”

Katie looked at Cole. They both wondered where Danni was.

A man came into the room. They recognized him as the cartel leader. “Stand them up.”

He stood in front of Cole. “This one pretended to be a Russian officer,” he said to his members. “He tried to kill me.” The man hit him hard in the stomach, doubling him over. Two men pulled him upright again.

Cole gasped to get his breath back.

“Why did you shoot at me?” the cartel leader asked.

“The Russians paid me. They gave me the uniform and the truck. Ask them why they want you dead.”

He looked at Cole, trying to understand.

“They killed two of your men at the airport tonight,” Riker said. “Didn’t give them a chance to surrender. They just shot them.”

“You don’t get it,” Katie said. “Your president brought the Russians here to kill the cartel. More men are coming in two days. Then they’re setting up more military bases. You won’t stand a chance against trained military.”

“Don’t underestimate us.”

“I don’t underestimate their weapons,” Katie said. “Or the hundreds of soldiers they’re bringing here.”

“Why are they doing this?”

“The president was paid off. He’ll get elected if he says he got rid of you guys. And the Russians will use Mexican land to aim missiles at the US. Everybody wins except you. You die.”

The man looked at their faces. It was apparent this was too much for him to understand very quickly. Cole was worried when he did get it their lives would be useless.

****

Danni crouched and peered in the living room window. She got out of the window before they got her, but now what? She was unarmed and ran out so fast she left her phone and her shoes. All she had was the T-shirt she slept in.

She needed a weapon. She went around to the garage and entered the back door. On a workbench, she found a utility knife with a curved blade and two oily rags. She kept searching until she found a box of matches.

She needed one more thing. Living so far from town these guys always had gas stored. She looked on the floor and in cupboards before she found a full jerry can.

Going outside, she poured a pool of gas under one of the cartel's SUVs then soaked the two rags. Then she opened the gas tank and hung one of them out of it. She looked at the house. So far no one noticed her.

Danni spilled a line of gas in the opposite direction from the house. The SUV would conceal the line of flames if anyone came out. She put the jerry can on the ground at the end of the line and put the rag part way in. Taking out a match she lit it, then ran with all the speed she could muster to the deck.

The gas in the jerry can exploded, lighting the line of gas on the ground. Some of the men in the house ran to the SUV, guns ready. Moving around the vehicle they saw the line of fuel reaching the gas tank. They turned to run. It was too late. The vehicle exploded. A ball of flame engulfed them. Screams cut through the night air as the explosion lit them on fire.

The men inside the house dashed to the window to look out. Danni crouched and went inside, using Cole's body for cover. She cut his cuffs and then pressed the knife into his palm. She turned to leave. The leader glanced back and saw her as she was running across the deck.

"Get her!" the leader yelled.

"I got this," Blake said as she bolted after Danni.

As Blake was running past Cole he stuck his leg out and tripped her. She got up and glared at him then ran after her.

Cole saw the anger in the leader's face. There was only him and one of his men left. Cole squeezed the utility knife, getting ready. The leader grabbed his man's rifle and stomped over to Cole. He swung his rifle butt to hit him in the face. Cole ducked. When he straightened up he slashed the knife across the leader's throat. The other man took out his handgun. Riker ran at him, hitting him hard with his shoulder. Before the man could get up Eve dropped with her full body weight driving her knee into his throat. He never moved. Cole cut everyone's cuffs.

"I'm going after Danni." He put on his shoes and took the rifle.

"This is my fault," Katie said, doing the same. "I'm coming with you.

Danni was running across the fields, her bare feet hurting more with each step. She stopped and put her hands on her knees gasping for breath. She knew someone had to be chasing her. She glanced back at the house and saw an outline of someone running full speed towards her.

"God damn her," she said, recognizing Blake. She took a deep breath and started to run again. But she was slowing. She saw bushes to her right and headed for them. Glancing back she saw Blake had closed the distance.

Danni stopped. "Screw this." She turned and ran straight at her. Blake didn't expect it. Danni knocked her over and straddled her chest, pounding her fists into her.

Blake brought one leg over Danni's head and twisted, bringing her to the ground beside her. She got on her chest and held her wrists down.

"What's your problem, bitch?" Blake yelled.

"You are!" Danni yelled back, trying to free her arms.

"I'm on your side. I work for Control."

Danni stopped. She looked at her for any sign of truth.

"You done?"

Danni nodded, still not believing her. Blake rolled off her and sat on the ground, holding her cheek.

"Why did you have to hit me so hard?"

"You were trying to kill me."

"No, I wasn't. I was trying to stop you so we could talk."

Blake stood and brushed her clothes off. When she was about to help Danni up she was hit hard from the side. Seconds later Katie was on top of her hitting her until Cole pulled her off.

"Everybody has to stop hitting me in the face!" she yelled.

Cole looked at Danni. "What's going on?"

"She said she works for Control."

"You could have told Katie to stop," Blake said, sitting on the ground.

"I could have," Danni said.

"If you work for Control why did you bring the cartel to our home?" Cole said.

"I didn't. They knew where you lived. I asked to come with them so I could help you guys. I chased Danni so one of them didn't go after her."

They all looked at each other, no one knowing if they should believe her.

"The Director sent me. They built a fake background file for me, and I got a job with the cartel as a personal bodyguard."

"Tell me why the Director didn't tell us about you."

"You guys might have told Sofia, and she doesn't trust her."

"She's wrong," Cole said. "Sofia would give her life for us."

"The Director trusts no one. I'm sure she worries about every one of you."

"That's true," Katie said, getting up. She held her hand out to help Blake up.

"Are we friends now?" Blake said.

"You lied to us. You have a long way to go."

"We could kiss and make up."

"I'm not gay," Katie said and began walking back.

"Not yet," she heard Blake say.

My feet are bleeding," Danni said. "Can I have a horsey ride, Cole?"

"Sure." She jumped on his back, and he grabbed her legs.

They walked back in silence, each of them trying to figure out what was happening with Blake. By the time they got back Riker and Eve had put the bodies and the blood-soaked rug in the cartel's other SUV.

"We can get rid of them later," Eve said.

Cole dialed the Director and put it on speaker. "Want to tell us about Blake?"

"I'm guessing you figured out she's one of mine."

"Hi, Director," Blake said.

"Hi, Blake. Why did you blow your cover?"

"The cartel was going to kill the team. I thought it was a good time."

"Everyone alright?"

"We are," Danni said, looking at the bottom of her foot. "The cartel, not so much."

"Since your cover is blown come back to Control before the cartel kill you."

"Send the plane."

"I need it. Fly commercial."

The call disconnected.

"You guys ever feel the love from her?" Blake said.

"Never," Katie said.

"Yeah. Me either."

"I'm going to go bandage my feet," Danni said.

"I'll help," Katie said.

Chapter 55

It was early morning when Katie answered the door. She took Sofia to the living room.

"Why is there a burned-out SUV and another one full of bodies in your front yard?" Sofia asked. "And why is one of them the local cartel leader?"

"It's what we do to uninvited guests," Katie said.

"I'll call ahead from now on," Sofia said. "I'll have some of my team come by to get rid of them."

"Thanks," Cole said.

"I have news," Sofia said. "The Gulf and Los Zetas cartels are holding a meeting tomorrow. They want to merge under dual leadership."

"Why?" Riker asked.

"Because the Russians scare the hell out of them. They can bring heavy weapons down on their heads. Attack helicopters, missiles, and gun trucks. They know they won't survive."

Do you know where the meeting is?"

"No."

"I still have access to their emails," Danni said. "I can find the time and location, but if I can, so can the Russians."

"Riker and I will go there," Cole said. "It's a surveillance mission only. I want to see if they can come to an agreement."

Danni did a search and returned to the living room. "I found the texts between the cartels. The meeting is tomorrow at 1 pm. It's at an abandoned camp in the mountains where they used to prepare drugs for shipment. It's basically a roof on posts."

"Good work."

"There's more. Control told me the Russians are landing a transport plane later today. It'll have two attack helicopters on it. They're the Mi-24 gunships we talked about."

"That's not good."

"I checked the presidents email, and he told the Russians about the cartel meeting. They are going to send the attack helicopters to kill them."

Danni put her hand on Cole's. "Anyone in the area will be in extreme danger. You have to be careful."

"I know, but we're here for a reason. Things are getting worse, and we have to know what the Russians will do."

"He needs his hand back, Danni," Katie said.

"Why don't you ever do that to me?" Riker asked Eve.

"Danni. Do Riker next, will ya?"

****

Cole and Riker lay in the bushes on a hill. In a valley below them was the building Danni showed him. They didn't expect the cartel for another 30 minutes.

"Eve told me you and Danni are becoming a thing," Riker said.

"A thing? Are you in grade ten?"

"It's obvious she likes you."

"Everyone likes me."

"The only reason I'm mentioning this is we have to keep our team cohesive. You know that."

Cole turned and stared at him. "Aren't we too old for a conversation about who likes who?"

"I'm just saying you should talk to Katie about it."

"About what?"

"You don't tune into people very well."

"Did Eve say that too?"

"She didn't need to."

"We're expecting a fight between a Russian gunship and the cartels, and you want to talk about who likes who. Pull up your panties, dude. There's a war on."

They both went silent.

"Hear it?" Riker said.

"Trucks."

They aimed their binoculars east along the road.

"It's an SUV. There's another one about a half mile behind it. Looks like our cartel buddies are here."

"I don't hear any choppers."

The SUVs stopped in front of the building and the men went inside. They sat on benches across the table from each other. Their bodyguards stood beside the trucks scanning the area.

The conversation was animated with raised voices and hands slamming on the table. It was ten minutes later when Riker touched Cole's shoulder and pointed west. Far in the distance, they saw the chopper. Their binoculars confirmed it was the Russians.

"Danni was right," Riker said. "It's a gunship." He pointed his cell phone camera at it. "A video may come in handy."

As the chopper flew closer the cartel guards began watching it. One of them opened the back of the SUV and took out a surface-to-air missile.

They concentrated on the chopper coming at them. The leaders came out of the building and looked up at it. One of the men yelled at his guard to start the SUV as he moved toward it.

They watched the gunship so intently they didn't notice the one behind them. It fired a missile. Before the men could turn it hit the ground in the middle of them. The explosion blasted a shockwave, bending trees and blowing the roof off the building. The vehicles rose in the air surrounded by fire and smoke, parts blasted off them. Bodies were blown in every direction.

"Jesus," Cole said.

The first helicopter sprayed the ground with gunfire, ensuring there were no survivors. They began circling the area to make sure no one else was nearby.

"We have to get out of here," Riker said.

They began running down the other side of the mountain. The helicopters could be heard nearby. Partway down Cole saw a large rock outcropping.

“Riker!” he yelled and pointed.

They jumped under the rock and pressed themselves as close inside as they could. One of the choppers flew directly over them. They held their breath hoping it wouldn’t see them.

The chopper slowed and turned, then reduced its altitude until the pilot could see under the rock. He fired a missile.

Cole and Riker were already running in opposite directions when the missile hit. They were picked up by the blast and tossed through the air. Riker was slammed into a tree and dropped to the ground. Cole was thrown through the air and hit the ground hard. He rolled downhill until he hit a log. Neither moved.

Chapter 56

A torrent of pain surged through Cole when he woke. Moving his head slowly he tested his neck, then raised himself on his elbows. The choppers had left.

He had to find Riker. Fighting to stay conscious he pulled himself up, using one hand on the fallen tree. The dizziness took over and he stayed there for a moment.

"Riker!" he yelled. "Riker!"

Cole moved across the mountain to where he thought the blast would have tossed his friend. The rocks slipped from under his feet, but he kept going.

He heard a groan a short distance away. As he got closer he saw him lying at the bottom of a tree, face up. He kneeled beside him.

"How bad is it?"

Riker began gasping for breath. "My body really hates me right now."

"Can you move?"

"Pretty sure dancing is out of the question, but I should be able to walk. Help me up, buddy."

Cole stepped behind him and lifted him. He wanted to drop him as soon as he tried, but he kept at it.

"How are you doing?" Riker asked.

"I'm glad it's downhill to the car."

Riker tried to walk, then stopped. "I can't put pressure on my left ankle."

Cole looked at it. "It's not broken, but you're not going to be able to walk on it." He stood in front of Riker and took his wrist.

"You need both your hands to climb down. Leave me here and come back with help."

"No. We don't know if the Russians will send someone to find us. Besides, if I fall I can use you as a cushion."

"Glad to be helpful."

Cole lifted him over his shoulder and started down. They fell twice, both yelling in pain. After a long battle, they made it to the car.

"Katie was a lot lighter," Cole said.

"No man should choose a hot chick over his buddy."

"Every man should do that." He helped him get in the car and began driving to the hacienda.

When they arrived they sat in the vehicle. Both knew when they got out the pain would kick them in the ass. Katie and Eve came outside.

"Are you guys alright?" Katie asked.

"We're a bit screwed up," Riker said. When Eve saw him struggling to get out of the car she ran to help him.

"What happened?"

"Russians shot a missile at us. We didn't get far enough away in time."

Katie opened Cole's door. She put his arm over her shoulders and helped him to the house. He and Riker sat on the couch.

"Scotch," they both said at the same time.

Danni came in. "You guys look terrible." She sat beside Cole. "Where and what number, Riker?"

"I was tossed through the air and hit a tree, so everything hurts. I'd say a nine out of ten."

"Cole?"

"I rolled into a log. I'd say an eight, but I can handle pain better than Riker."

"Anything sticking out of your bodies?"

"Just my nose and my man bit," Riker said. "We only have some scrapes and bruises. Rest is muscular. We've had worse."

They gulped their drinks, and then both held their glasses out for a refill.

"What happened?" Danni asked.

"Two Russian helicopters blew the cartel guys into tiny pieces. Then they flew over the area looking for anyone nearby. We didn't get away in time and a missile hit near us."

"The worst part was being carried down the hill fireman style by Cole. All I could see was his ass."

"Why?"

"I was upside down."

"I meant why did he carry you, dumbass?" Eve said.

"My ankle doesn't work."

Eve examined it. "It's a sprain. I'll wrap it. You stay off it and let it heal."

“It's lucky I have a spare one.”

“We have a video of the choppers blowing up the cartel leaders,” Cole said.

“What do we do with it?” Danni asked.

“I want Sofia to send it to the cartels. I want them to know the Russians are coming for them. With luck, they’ll attack each other.”

“I could put it on social media.”

“No. For now, I want a fight between them.”

“The cartel has a serious problem with those choppers on site,” Riker said. “It gives the Russians the upper hand.

“Against them and us. We need to find a way to destroy them, or this ends badly for all of us.”

Chapter 57

Katie and Danni brought everyone coffee as they sat on the deck. The sun had been up for an hour, and it was already getting hot. A gentle breeze would have helped but it seemed unlikely.

"Danni sent me the video," Sofia said. "I'm glad you guys made it."

"I hope sending it to the cartel does some good," Cole said.

"People on my team are hearing rumors of cartel activity. Both the Los Zetas and the Gulf. Normally that means they're going to attack each other. But this is different."

"Different how?" Danni said.

"We've seen a large number of vehicles from both cartels driving to a hacienda. Two of my team followed one with a Los Zetas logo on the door. At the hacienda, there were close to forty vehicles, including six trucks with machine guns on the back. Then a box truck arrived, and my team saw them unloading all types of weapons."

"Is this normally what they do before a battle?" Cole asked.

"No. I've never seen that many cartel members in one place before. And the collectors never came for payments yesterday or today. They're low-level members who don't normally fight, but one of my team recognized one at the hacienda. Everyone from both cartels is involved."

"What do you think is happening?" Eve asked.

"They're going to attack someone. The only target I can think of is the Russians."

"They won't win," Riker said. "I have no idea the type of protection they set up at the airport, but it has to be multiple levels."

"The cartels look weak," Sofia said. "They have to do something. Without people fearing them they have no power."

"What happens if the cartel beats the Russians?" Katie said.

"The Russians will bring in four times as many soldiers and more attack helicopters and wipe out the cartels," Cole said.

"And if the Russians win?"

"The cartels will attempt to start over with who is left alive and then go on a recruitment drive," Sofia said. "They'll kidnap young men and girls and force them to join."

"There's something else to consider," Danni said. "If we know about the attack so will the Russians."

"They'll be waiting for them," Riker said.

"What do we do?" Sofia asked.

Riker took a deep breath and slowly let it out. "Your team saw 40 vehicles. If we estimate three men per vehicle that's 120 fighters. The Russian base has about 60. Some of the cartel are useless at fighting but will be a target distraction while the others kill the Russians. They may win this."

"On the other hand the Russians have the home ground and the tactical fighting skills," Cole said. "Plus they have two attack helicopters. If they know the cartel is coming they have the upper hand."

"At least if the Russians lose it would slow them down building the missile base," Riker said.

"Then you want to help the cartel?" Sofia said in disbelief.

"I want to even the playing field. The losses will be greater that way."

"How?" Danni said.

"The biggest threat to the cartel is the helicopters," Cole said. "We have to take them out."

"Again. How?"

"The Director with the Vietnam-era chopper," Eve said. "Jimmy."

"He can't go up against two modern attack helicopters in an ancient Huey," Riker said.

"You met him. I bet he can. We can at least ask him."

"Eve's right," Cole said. "Fly to his ranch and talk to him. Tell him all the details and ask if it's possible. We should travel in pairs so take Riker. Danni, I need you at Control in Chicago. You have to find every piece of information you can on what the Russians are doing, especially if they're flying in reinforcements. And find out if the Mexican president is going to get involved by sending in the military."

"What about me?" Sofia said.

"Ask your team to talk to everyone they know about the fight. We need details on the exact numbers and what weapons the cartel has. Most importantly we need the date and time of the attack. Katie and I will run surveillance on the airport."

"Cole. Would you walk me to my car?" Sofia said.

They left and Sofia leaned on the door.

"What's up?"

"This is our best chance to remove the cartels. It's why you came to help us. My team should help the Russians."

"If the Russians win you have a new enemy."

"They have no interest in the Mexican people. We'll be left alone."

"The Russians will have to justify why they're in the country. They can't do that if the cartel is gone. If I were the president I'd encourage the southern cartels to come here and fill the void."

"Then we accomplish nothing."

"No one wins wars. Our goal is to motivate the people to elect leaders that stop the bloodshed."

Chapter 58

When Eve and Riker arrived at Jimmy's ranch in Texas a woman opened the door. She brought them through to the backyard. Jimmy was on the patio reading a newspaper. In front of him was an expansive yard of trees. The morning sun was beginning to fight its way through the branches.

When he saw them he stood, his smile morphing into a grin. "Eve. It's so good to see you." He hugged her and then held his hand out to Riker. "I see you brought deadweight."

She laughed. "I did. We need to talk."

"Sit." He turned to his assistant. "Could you bring us coffee and those croissants you make that I love so much?"

She left and they sat around a table.

"I know you're having trouble in Mexico. The Director has been keeping me up to date."

"Then you know the Russians are setting up a missile base."

"Yeah. It's a dangerous situation. When they did it in Cuba our president took us 90 minutes from launch. It was a terrifying time."

"We could use your helicopter skills," Riker said.

"Control told me the cartel is going to attack the Russian base," Jimmy said. "Is that what this is about?"

"Fraid so," Eve said. "The cartel outnumbers them two to one. There's a chance they could win, but the Russians have the better weapons and are trained fighters."

"Who do you want to win?"

"We want them to wipe each other out. It'll give us more time for the people to vote in a new president."

"I heard the Russians have advanced attack helicopters."

"Two Mi-24 gunships," Riker said.

"My Huey wouldn't last 10 seconds."

"Then you can't help us?"

"I didn't say that."

The coffee and croissants came, and they waited until everything was served. Riker took a big bite. "Wow. She's a damn good baker."

"She bakes because her mother taught her, and she loves it. I'm lucky to have her around."

"Can you help us?" Eve said.

Jimmy leaned back in his chair and stared over his yard. He never said anything for a long time.

"Jimmy?" Eve said.

He sat forward. "I'm going to show you something that's classified at the highest level. Do you understand?"

"Yes," Eve said. "We know how to treat classified information."

"Let's take a ride," he said, standing.

Riker took another croissant before they walked to the side of the house. The ride was in a four-passenger golf cart. He took them to the tree line, then through it. On the other side was a large metal warehouse.

They went into a reception area. “Good morning, sir,” a woman said. “Are you having a good day?”

“I am,” he said.

She pressed a button under the desk and a door behind her opened. Inside was a small room with another locked door.

“This is a man trap,” Eve said, staring at a security camera. “She won’t open that door until the one behind us closes, which turns this into a prison cell. And she was asking you if we were forcing you to take us inside. What the hell is in this place?”

The door clicked open. Inside the building was a combat helicopter surrounded by men working on it. Riker stared at it. “That’s vicious looking. The missile systems are different than anything I’ve seen, and the blades are a strange design.”

“This is the most advanced helicopter on earth.”

Riker began walking around it.

“He loves weapons,” Eve said. “He’ll do that for hours if we let him.”

“There’s a lot to stare at.”

Riker dashed back. “Why are the rotors that way? And what are the weapons systems?”

“I’ve spent 10 years designing and testing it. It responds to voice control. We can fly it remotely. In a fight, it can take over from the pilot. There are a ton of features. None of which I’ll explain in detail.”

“Why the rotors?”

“It produces half the decibel level of the newest stealth chopper.”

“Why does the tail rotor look so weird?”

“The rotor can turn in any direction. It gives the chopper flight capabilities never imagined before.”

Riker went back to examine it in detail.

Jimmy put his hands behind him and took a deep breath. “I’ve never tested it in battle. Your situation is a good opportunity. I’ll have it pulled to the landing pad.”

“What do you call it?” Eve said.

“Viper 1. It has no American markings and is not part of the military. Washington has deniability if we are shot down.”

“Is it ready for battle?”

“She has to lose her virginity to someone. Who better than the Russian army?”

Chapter 59

Cole rolled over in bed and looked at Katie.

"Danni is in Chicago and Eve and Riker are at Jimmy's. We have the place to ourselves."

"What are you suggesting?"

"A naked swim, then breakfast by the pool."

"What kind of girl do you think I am, sir?" she said in a Southern accent.

"The best kind."

"Yes, I am." She laughed and jumped out of bed, pulling her pajamas off as she raced for the pool. Cole did the same, chasing after her. They both dove in without stopping. Cole pulled her closer and began kissing her. Then he stopped.

"What's the matter?" she said.

He nodded to the deck chairs. Katie turned to look.

"Danni?" Katie said. "Why the hell are you here?"

"I came for the sex show," Danni said, smiling. "Don't stop."

Katie spoke, pausing between each word. "Why are you here?"

"I convinced the Director I have access to everything from here. I didn't know you guys were going to play sea horsey."

Katie swam to the edge and got out, ignoring Danni as she walked by her naked.

"Your turn, Cole," Katie said, holding up her phone to take a video.

"You can be weird sometimes, Danni," he said.

"That's why you like me. Sorry about the aqua interruptus."

"Me too."

"I could help."

"Stop it. Go get me a towel."

"No need," Katie said bringing him one. "Meet me in the shower. And lock the door."

"On it." He got out and wrapped the towel around his waist.

"She's bossy," Danni said as he walked by.

When Katie and Cole came back to the deck Sofia was there talking to Danni.

"Danni was filling me in on your playing sea horsey, as she calls it," Sofia said.

"Of course she was," Katie said.

"On a more serious note, a man is going to be here in a few minutes. He called me and asked me to meet him here."

"Who is he?"

"All I know is he's a representative of the Mexican government."

"It sounds serious," Cole said.

"I think it is."

They heard a knock.

"That must be him," Sofia said.

"Don't let him in until I get my gun," Cole said.

When he was sitting at the table again Sofia opened the door. A man in an expensive business suit came in with two other men.

"Don't sit," Cole said. "You won't be here that long."

The two men stood behind him, their hands at their sides, watching.

"I represent the presidential office of the Mexican Government. My name is not important. My reason for being here is."

"What reason?" Sofia asked.

"We know you have been stealing guns and killing the cartel. And we know about your team and the Americans helping you."

"What do you want?" Cole said.

"As you're aware, there is going to be a battle between the cartels and the Russians."

"If you know about it, why not stop it?" Katie said.

"We have a signed agreement with the Russians. They paid a stipend to the president, and he agreed to let them control the airport land. That includes defending it anyway they deem necessary."

"You mean they bribed the president, and he told them they can do what they want. That must have been a hell of a big bribe."

"We don't have the legal right to interfere with what happens at the military base. It's classed as Russian territory."

"Why are you here?" Sofia asked.

The president wants you to help the Russians. You're already fighting the cartels."

"You want the Russians to win," Cole said.

"If they do, our financial arrangements will continue. Plus, we are willing to offer a substantial monetary reward if you work for the government."

"You let the Mexican people die and now you want us to work with you?" Sofia said, standing in front of him.

"We want to be fair."

Sofia looked at him for a moment. He thought she was considering it. She was wondering where to hit him. When she chose a spot she swung hard and fast, connecting with his chin. As he was falling the two men behind him reached for their guns. Cole already had his out and aimed.

"Don't," he said. "Pick up your garbage and take it with you."

The man she hit held his hand up to stop them. "That was a big mistake." The guards helped him up and they walked out. Sofia was rubbing her hand.

"I wanted to kill him," she said.

"They would have replaced him in a day. Good swing though."

She nodded, shaking her hand to ease the pain. "Thanks."

"They must be worried the Russians might lose," Katie said. "It means their bribe money disappears."

"They probably get bribes from the cartels as well, but the Russians would pay more," Cole said.

"What do we do?" Danni asked.

"We get involved in the fight. I want to damage both sides as much as we can."

"If we do we could use the battle to destroy their computer systems," Danni said.

"How?"

"If they're fighting we won't be noticed. We can plant C4 and make a big boom." She expressed it with her arms going up in the air and blowing out her cheeks.

"In the middle of a battle you want to break into the computer room, plant C4, then try to escape?" Cole said.

"Yes. Killing 20 soldiers is not as effective as killing 20 servers. It'll take longer to replace the servers, install the software, and get things running again. Whether the Russians win or lose we'll slow them down."

"I hate to say it, but she's right," Katie said.

Cole nodded. "Big boom it is then."

Chapter 60

Jimmy was doing a last check before he started the helicopter. Eve was watching him from the copilot's seat. In the back was seating for four passengers and Riker was in one of them.

"Don't we need headsets?" Riker asked.

"Wait for it, deadweight."

When Jimmy started it Riker understood how quiet it was. The noise level inside was the same as a car on a highway.

"I get it now," Riker said.

"We also have a stealth exterior. We don't show up on radar."

"This is an amazing invention," Eve said.

"It took the best engineers and scientists available. Let's hope they did a good job or it's going to be the most expensive scrap heap in history."

He climbed and headed toward the hacienda.

"Is it bulletproof?" Riker asked.

"Sorry, Jimmy. He's like a kid in a toy store."

"Nothing is bulletproof. It's bullet resistant."

"What's the payload?"

"That's classified. I can tell you it has a nose cannon that turns 360 and can punch a hole in a tank."

"How fast are we going?" Eve asked.

"We're hitting 380 mph, but I've had it faster."

"What's the fastest?"

"Classified."

"It's great the data displays on the windshield," Eve said. "Everything is right in front of you. You don't need a helmet."

"Nova. Go to autopilot."

"Okay, Jimmy," a girl's voice said. "I have the controls."

"Nova?"

"The brains of the chopper. It's the most advanced system in any aircraft in the world."

"What do the initials mean?" Riker asked.

"Nothing. I hate acronyms."

"Did you name her after an ex-girlfriend, Jimmy?"

"Not an ex. Nova. Gimme some Jimmy."

Hendrix played over the speaker system. They flew low to the ground and Eve had trouble adjusting to the speed. She had to concentrate on something in the distance to keep her eyes steady. Jimmy watched the Heads Up Display and the area around him. After a time Eve began to relax.

"We're five minutes from landing," Nova said.

"Thanks, Nova. I'll take over."

"Can Nova land it?" Riker asked.

"Yes, but she knows I like to."

Jimmy touched down at the hacienda and shut off the chopper. They went inside.

Cole looked up when they walked in. “Why didn’t I hear a chopper?”

“That’s classified,” Riker said.

“He’s learning,” Jimmy said. “Any word on when the party starts?”

“One of my team is dating a cartel member,” Sofia said. “He told her the Russians have a shift change at 4 pm. They’re going to attack then.”

“Why is one of your team dating a cartel member?” Danni asked.

“I use the word dating to be polite. She’s sleeping with him so she can get information.”

“That must be difficult for her.”

“She says he’s good in bed, so she doesn’t mind.”

“That seems like a fair trade,” Danni said. “Would you put out for information, Cole?”

“I’d be willing to sacrifice my body for my country,” Riker said.

“That’s because you’re a slut,” Eve said. “It's one of the things I like about you.”

“Jimmy, you know the Russians have two attack helicopters,” Cole said. “Are you sure your Huey will defeat them?”

“I brought my own attack helicopter.”

“That’s great. We should destroy them before the battle starts. I don’t want the scenario where one is engaged in a fight with you and the other one slaughters the cartels.”

"I'll go before the fight and tap on their windshields. I can get them to chase me out of the area."

"I'm going with you," Eve said.

"You're needed in a sniper position," Cole said.

"If Jimmy doesn't take out the choppers in an hour you won't need a sniper. If he does, he can drop me on the hill."

Cole looked at Jimmy, realizing how much he was asking from him. "Don't take too many risks, Jimmy. We can always fight another day."

"There's no time to calculate risk when a missile is coming up your ass, but I hear what you're saying.

"Everyone knows the plan," Cole said. Your number one goal is to stay alive."

Jimmy looked at Katie. "He's not good with the pep talks is he?"

"No, but we still love him," Katie said.

"I thought I was getting better at it," Cole said.

Katie shook her head and touched his hand.

Chapter 61

Jimmy ran checks on his helicopter, then paused before starting it.

"What's the matter?" Eve asked.

"You don't have to come with me."

"An extra set of eyes can be helpful."

He hesitated and looked at her.

"I love that you care about me, Jimmy, but I dragged you into this. I'm coming."

Jimmy nodded, knowing he couldn't win an argument with her. He started it, then pointed at a screen. "Keep your eyes on here. Nova has 360 cameras that will show you where the targets are. If I'm busy with one of the choppers tell me if the other one is going to shoot me in the back."

"I can do that. Nova. Play Foxy Lady for me."

They lifted off. Minutes later they were over the airport.

"Can't you destroy them on the ground?" she asked.

"I could, but Nova likes foreplay."

Eve laughed as Jimmy fired the nose canon into the tarmac beside the choppers. They waited until the pilots ran out and the choppers were starting before he led them away.

"They're coming fast," Eve said as she watched the screen.

"Two Russian Mi-24 gunships following us, Jimmy," Nova said.

"Roger that, Nova."

"Would you like me to remove them?"

"Not yet Nova. We're over a village."

"They're closing in," Eve said.

"I'm letting them."

"Incoming radar-guided missile," Nova said.

"Deploy chaff."

"Deploying."

Jimmy banked hard left and accelerated to get away from the area. The missile hit the chaff and exploded. Jimmy turned the chopper toward the helicopters. One of them fired a nose cannon, the bullets bouncing off the windshield.

He watched the display until he had a lock on the chopper and then fired. The bullets penetrated their cockpit, hitting the pilot. Seconds later the chopper exploded. The Russian pilot beside the explosion banked to get away from it.

Jimmy burst forward after him. Eve was shocked a helicopter could accelerate so fast. They pulled in behind him. The chopper pilot tried to bank and descend to lose him. Jimmy stayed on him.

They twisted and turned. Jimmy closed the distance. In one last attempt, the Russian pilot descended at high speed.

When he was close to the ground he banked right and turned.

"Incoming missile," Nova said.

"Deploy chaff," Jimmy said and banked and accelerated. The missile wasn't tricked.

"Chaff failure," Nova said.

Jimmy turned away from the missile. "Nova. Take it out."

Nova snapped the nose cannon around to face backward and then fired. The missile exploded near them, knocking the chopper around. Jimmy gained control and climbed, then leveled.

It was Jimmy's turn. He turned toward the Russian helicopter and locked on. He fired a missile. The Russian pilot banked and deployed chaff. The missile ignored it and hit his chopper, the explosion filling the air with flame and debris.

"Why did your missile ignore the chaff?" Eve asked.

"We created an intelligent missile that can analyze the target shape before detonating.

"This is a hell of a fighter you built."

"She did good today. Nova kept track of the data and sent it to our home computers. I can analyze it when I get there."

As they flew back they saw cartel trucks parked in front of the airport. The cartel was behind their vehicles exchanging gunfire with the Russians.

"It looks like the battle started. Put me on the hill, Jimmy."

"You got it."

"Wait. There's a machine gun on the roof. It'll destroy the cartel."

Jimmy flew behind the building and hovered level with the machine gun nest. The men felt the rotor wash and looked back at the chopper. They froze. There was nothing they could do.

"Run!" Jimmy yelled over the broadcast system.

The two men ran for the stairs. As they opened the door and were entering the stairwell Jimmy launched a missile. When the smoke cleared all that was left was a large hole in the roof where the machine gun used to be.

"Eve. Can you hear me?" the voice came over the speakers.

"Cole. Where are you?"

"There are four guards at the back protecting the computer room. Can Jimmy help us?"

"On the way," Jimmy said. "Give me your location so you're not collateral damage."

"We're at the tree line. About 100 yards from the building."

"Stay there," Jimmy said. "I'll take care of them."

Jimmy moved to the back of the building and descended to just above the ground. The guards fired at them. As he fired the nose cannon he turned the chopper, sweeping across the building. The four guards fell from the onslaught.

"That should do it," Jimmy said.

"Since you're here can you punch a hole in the wall?" Danni asked.

"Hang on." Jimmy kept the cannon on one spot. The wall exploded. When he stopped there was a large opening with smoke pouring out.

"You do know how to open a door for a girl, Jimmy," Danni said.

"Pleasures all mine."

Danni and Cole ran for the opening and stood just outside of it. Cole held his rifle as he looked for anyone in the room. Some of the servers were destroyed, but not all of them. They ran inside and attached C4 to the remaining ones. "Let's get out of here," Danni said.

As they were about to leave two guards burst through the door. Cole and Danni ducked behind a wall as the bullets came at them. Cole returned fire. Danni kneeled and fired with him. More bullets blasted the walls around them.

Cole took one of the C4 packages and cut some off. He inserted a detonator and a timer, setting it for three seconds, then threw it. The explosion blew out the door and the men disappeared in smoke and fire. Danni and Cole ran out of the hole and back to the hill.

"Now what?" Danni said.

"Sofia, can you hear me?"

"Loud and clear."

"It's time. Position your team."

Chapter 62

The Russians were returning fire from behind cover. Some men lay on the ground, bleeding out. No one stepped out to help them.

Sofia and her team sped down the driveway and skidded to a stop behind the cartel. They jumped out and used their trucks as cover. The cartel members turned and saw them, then looked at the Russians. They had no place to run. Two men got into a vehicle and raced down the road to escape. One of Sofia's gun trucks stopped them.

The cartel looked at the Russians, then at Sofia's team. They had no cover but fired at anyone they could see. The team returned fire. The cartel couldn't escape. They stopped firing and raised their hands in surrender. Sofia's team ran in a crouch to the few remaining ones and took their guns, then made them lay face down.

The Russians stopped firing. They thought Sofia's team was there to help them. Then her team began firing at them. Some Russians fell because they left cover. Some because they couldn't run back to it in time. The firing kept coming. Sofia saw one of her team get hit in the shoulder. "Medic!"

she yelled and pointed. Then another one was shot in the hand and one in the chest. The Russians were better shots.

"Fire from cover!" Sofia yelled.

From the right, they saw a helicopter coming towards them. Jimmy flew at the Russians, lowered the nose cannon, and kept firing as he flew over them. The Russians never had a chance. Some aimed their rifles at the chopper and fired. Bullets hit the outside and the windshield, but none got through.

Jimmy turned and hovered, aiming at the ones that survived. They knew it was hopeless, but they were soldiers. They never lowered their weapons. They were waiting for him to come closer.

"Leave them, Jimmy," Eve said. "We did enough damage."

Jimmy hovered in case he was needed. Sofia's team left the cartel on the ground and drove off. As soon as they did the cartel got in their trucks, taking their dead and wounded. The Russians stood and watched, humiliated by the defeat. All except one of them. He fired a missile.

"Warning," Nova said. "A stinger missile is approaching on our six," Nova said.

"Jimmy looked at the display. The back camera showed it approaching fast. Eve waited for Jimmy to do something. As the missile was getting closer Jimmy waited. At the last second, he accelerated to full speed and pulled up. The missile flew under the chopper, missing it by a few feet. It looped and headed straight up at them. Jimmy lowered the nose, so he was facing it.

"Take out the missile, Nova."

Nova lined up on the missile and fired the nose cannon. As the missile exploded she banked the chopper and descended.

"I thought you could do it, Nova. Goddamn good job."

"You didn't know if that would work?"

"Not until now. I didn't know if we did the calculations right."

"Jesus, Jimmy," Eve said.

"I was pretty sure it would work," he said and grinned. "Turn up the music, Nova."

Eve looked at him as they raced across the countryside with Hendrix blasting in the cockpit.

"I love this guy," she mumbled through a laugh.

****

After they landed, the others began to show. Sofia stayed to help the wounded on her team, then took them home. Soon they were on the deck, drinks in hand. No one was cheerful. The mission was successful, but people died. No one wanted that.

"We needed you today, Jimmy," Cole said raising his glass. "To Jimmy, everyone."

They all raised their glasses and toasted him.

"Thank you. I had the best co-pilot a man could ask for."

Eve laughed and sat in his lap then kissed him on the cheek. He laughed with her.

"On that note Nova and I are going home. We need to discuss the day." He left and took his chopper home to analyze the data and start repairs.

Food was brought out and bottles were emptied. Slowly they became numb to what they experienced earlier. Danni pulled her chair next to Cole.

"Did we win anything today, Cole?"

"We stayed alive. And we damaged the cartel and the Russians."

"But they'll be back."

"Yes."

"So it was a temporary win."

"It was a step forward. If the Russians might leave if they think the hassles in Mexico are not worth it."

"What about the cartel?"

"Sofia is starting a revolution. More and more people are seeing her success and want to mimic it. We're going to distribute more weapons along the border to help them."

"Where are we getting more weapons?" Riker asked.

"I may as well tell everyone. The Director called me yesterday, I didn't mention before it because we were busy. But the US government is going to covertly supply us with unlimited weapons. They'll give them to Control, and Control will help us get them into Mexico."

Everyone raised their glasses. "To the Mexican people," Katie said.

Riker was standing by the pool, staring at the water. Cole walked over to talk to him.

"We pissed off a lot of bad people today," Riker said.

"I know."

"They're going to come after us like we never seen before. Do you want to talk to our team about it?"

"Not now. Tomorrow. We'll have to move to a more secure location. And we'll have to be armed at all times. We're going to be hunted."

Chapter 63

The next morning Cole was on the deck typing on his laptop. Eve brought a coffee and sat with him.

"Jimmy sent me the video of the fight," Eve said.

"Good. I need to see the damage."

"I'll send it to you. The building was hit hard. The back is blown out, and part of the roof has a hole. The destruction along the front is the worst."

"Looks like we stopped them for a while."

"I estimated 22 dead and more than that wounded."

Cole looked at her but never responded. There was nothing he could say about that type of tragedy.

"He didn't get the cartel in the video, but they were hit just as bad."

Danni dashed onto the deck with her tablet in her hands. "Guys. I got an urgent message from the Director. She said the president is sending the military to arrest Sofia as a gesture to appease the Russians."

"When?" Cole asked.

"Today. I tried calling her, but her phone is off."

"I'm going to get her. I'll contact you guys when we're safe."

"I should go with you," Eve said.

"I need you and Riker here to protect the others. If the president is going after Sofia he may come after us at the same time. You need to get everyone into the States. Go to the Director's ranch and I'll meet you there."

Cole got his gun and a rifle and ran to the car. As he sped down the road he called Katie and explained what he was doing.

"I can meet you," she said. "You'll need help."

"There's no time. Get across the border as fast as you can."

Sofia lived about 20 minutes away. Cole cut in and out of traffic, breaking every speed limit they had. When he reached her farm he looked for military trucks. The place looked empty. He ran inside without knocking.

Sofia was still in bed. When she heard him outside her door she grabbed her gun off the bedside table. It was aimed at the door when he opened it.

"Cole? What's the matter?"

"The president is going to arrest you. Get dressed. We have to go." Cole went into the living room to watch for trucks.

Then he heard it. A helicopter. He turned and saw Sofia behind him. They looked out the back window and saw it approaching.

"We need to run for your truck," she said.

"It won't work. The chopper can follow us anywhere we go. We need to stay and fight."

"How?"

Cole looked around the room. There was nothing that would stop bullets.

"Get in bed with me."

"What? Why?"

"We need them off guard. Go."

They ran into the bedroom and removed their shirts. Sofia lay behind Cole, pressing against him. The sheet was pulled up far enough to cover their arms. In their hands they held their guns. They heard the men on the porch, and then the front door opening. The hardest part was keeping their eyes closed to pretend they were sleeping.

The footsteps in the hallway got closer. The door burst open. Cole and Sofia opened their eyes and saw two soldiers with their rifles aimed at the bed. "Get up or we shoot!" one yelled. They lowered their rifles thinking they were safe.

Cole and Sofia fired from under the covers. One man grabbed his chest and dropped. The other man jerked back when he was hit in the shoulder. He ran into the kitchen. Cole made sure the fallen man was dead. He glanced around the corner of the door frame and a burst of bullets hit the frame. Sofia stood beside him with her gun raised.

The soldier was behind a wall. He poked his rifle around the corner and fired without looking. Cole stepped into the hallway. Sofia stood beside him. They fired through the wall where the soldier was standing. The wooden walls could never stop a bullet. The man fell into the hallway and Cole fired again to make sure he was dead.

He picked up the rifle and turned to Sofia. "We need to get the pilot before he radios for help. If I go outside he'll take off before I can stop him." Cole dashed to the bedroom and put on the soldier's uniform. "You're going to be my prisoner. It'll give me time to get clos enough to shoot him." He looked at her, waiting.

"What?" she said.

"You need a shirt," Cole said.

"Oh yeah. Sorry." She put on her T-shirt.

He pulled his hat low and walked out behind her, the rifle aimed at her back. The pilot watched them. As they got closer he saw the soldier wasn't a Mexican. He began climbing. Cole stepped out from behind Sofia and began firing into the cockpit. Sofia pulled a gun from the back of her pants and fired with Cole. The chopper was 20 feet off the ground. The pilot slumped over, and the chopper spun around and crashed sideways. Cole pushed Sofia to the ground and covered her to protect her from the pieces of the blades.

When the noise of the crash stopped he turned and looked back. The pilot wasn't moving. He looked down at Sofia. "Are you alright?"

She nodded. "Yes."

"We have to get out of here."

"I'll grab my go bag and meet you at the car."

Minutes later they were on the road heading to the highway.

"Where are we going?"

"We'll go to the ranch in Texas. We'll be safe there."

"What if they're waiting for me at the border?"

"We'll figure it out."

"Thank you for coming. It terrifies me to think what the military would have done to me."

"We're friends. We help each other."

"I know, but I owe you."

"You should text your team and tell them to lay low for a few days."

"I will. Where do we cross?"

"Not Piedras Negras. They'll have someone waiting for us there."

"They'll have pictures of us at every border crossing."

"Maybe we can fly over. The Texas ranch has a runway."

"There's an airport an hour's drive from here. It's only for small planes."

"Is it cartel?"

"Mostly, but some locals use it for hobby flying."

"Then we can steal a plane."

"It won't be that easy. The cartels guard the planes. Some of them are used for drug smuggling."

"We don't have a choice. We'll wait until tonight."

Chapter 64

The rain came with the night. At first, it was a drizzle but quickly turned into a hard rain pushed by the wind. Small planes were lined up on the side of the runway. On the other side was a warehouse with two guards sitting in chairs just inside the open doors. Sofia and Cole stood at the side of a storage shed, looking at the planes. They kept wiping their faces to remove the rain. Cole looked at the clouds getting darker and moving faster.

"Which one do we take?" Sofia asked.

"The twin-engine Cessna. It's designed for freight. The cartel must be transporting drugs in it."

"Where do we get the keys?"

"They usually leave them in the plane. Follow me."

They ran in a crouch to the planes, then used them as cover to get to the twin. They got in and watched the guards. So far they weren't paying attention.

"If this is a drug carrier the cartel is going to be pissed," she said.

"Good. With luck, they won't shoot at it. Put on your harness and headset." Cole kept watching them. "You ready?"

"No. I'm terrified."

"Me too."

Cole started the engine. As soon as he did the guards stood and began running towards the plane, yelling at them. The rain made it hard for them to see.

"They seem mad," Sofia said.

"If they're mad now wait until we take off."

Cole pulled out and took the plane to takeoff speed as fast as he could. The guards began firing as he taxied, bullets piercing the skin of the plane. He began to climb. There was a loud warning in the cockpit. He looked at the gauges, and then at the right engine. Smoke was pouring out of it.

"We're on fire!" Sofia yelled.

Cole shut the engine down.

"Don't turn it off. We need engines." She pulled her harness tighter.

"We can fly on one engine."

"What if he shoots the other one?"

"We're out of range. We're going to be okay."

The plane bounced like they were driving too fast on a dirt road full of potholes.

"You ever flown on one engine?"

"Not in a two-engine plane."

"Oh good."

"Here's my phone. Call Casey. She's in my contacts. Then put it on speaker."

Sofia called. It didn't connect. She tried again and it worked.

"Hi Cole. Everything alright?"

"I stole a plane from the cartel, and they shot out an engine on take off. Now I'm in the middle of a storm. I've had better days."

"What can I do?"

"We're 50 minutes out. Does the runway have landing lights?"

"No. But I have highway flares. They last about 20 minutes. Call me when you're closer and I'll lay them out beside the runway. It's the best I can do."

"Thanks, Casey."

"Say again. You're cutting out."

The connection failed. He concentrated on his controls. Sofia looked out the window, both hands clinging to her harness.

"I'm sorry I sounded like such a coward before," she said.

"You are one of the bravest people I know. I'm proud to work with you."

"Sometimes in high-stress situations, I get super focused on survival at all costs. I forget about the things around me."

"Like a shirt?"

She laughed. "Sorry about that. I didn't mean to embarrass you."

"Embarrassment was the last thing I felt," he said, smiling as he looked out the window.

"Is that a compliment?"

"Absolutely."

She knew Cole was trying to keep her distracted, so she didn't feel as scared. Without warning the plane dropped, then leveled.

"I get panicky when I'm not in control, and I have no way to control what happens to me in a plane."

"I get that. I'm the same."

"Cole?"

"Yeah?"

"Why is there a helicopter flying next to us?"

Cole looked over. He saw a chopper off his wingtip. As it pulled ahead slightly he saw the machine gunner in the open doorway.

"You see that, right?" Sofia asked.

The machine gunner aimed at the cockpit. Cole dropped the nose of the plane and went into a steep dive. He banked hard to get on the opposite side of the chopper and then climbed, pushing the remaining engine to the max. The storm tossed them around inside the cockpit.

"Oh God," Sofia said and crossed herself.

"I'm trying to get inside the clouds so he can't find us."

Cole fought the controls, his climb speed slowing. He kept going, hoping the engine would hold out. He knew he was pushing it too hard. "Can you see the chopper?"

Sofia snapped her head around. "No. Why don't these things have a sunroof?"

He descended, leveling off at 2000 feet.

Sofia looked everywhere she could. The rain covered her window in a sheet of water. "Cole! He's back."

Cole saw him and banked to the left. The machine gunner fired. They felt bullets hitting the plane. Cole straightened out and dove again, leveling at 1000 feet.

"I don't see him," she said, her voice shaking.

"We just crossed the Rio. We're in Texas now. He won't follow us."

Sofia nodded, unable to speak.

Cole kept adjusting his speed and altitude.

"What the matter?"

"I have a warning light on the right wheel. He must have damaged it. Call Casey and tell her I need the flares."

The storm stopped him from seeing the flares until he was almost over them. He descended, lining up on them.

"Do you remember the brace position they show you on commercial flights?" he asked.

"I've seen it on TV. Why?"

"Do it."

Sofia touched his arm and then assumed the position. The plane rocked and bounced. The side winds pushed him off course and he fought to get it back.

When he was a few feet from the ground he raised the nose of the plane. They hit hard. Cole kept it on two wheels to burn off speed. The wing touched the ground and the plane slid down the runway. Sofia yelled and Cole covered his head with his arms as it spun around before stopping.

When he looked up he saw the windshield covered in a wall of water All he heard was the rain and wind. He looked at Sofia. She wasn't moving. He saw blood on her face. Jumping from the cockpit he ran to her side and pulled her out. The rain washed the blood away and he saw an open wound on her forehead. By then Casey pulled up in her truck. Cole carried Sofia to it. Before they got to the house Sofia groaned and opened her eyes. “Am I dead?”

“No. We made it.”

She touched her forehead. “Ow.”

Cole pulled her hand away. “Don’t touch.”

“You landed a shot-up plane at night in a rainstorm,” Casey said. “Damn good flying.”

“I would have done better but gravity’s a bitch.”

Cole helped her to the couch and Casey got the medic kit.

“It’s a cut. Head wounds bleed a lot, but you’ll be fine.” She cleaned and bandaged her wound.

“You hurt anywhere else?”

“My chest.”

“Probably from the harness. Let’s get your t-shirt off,” Casey said. “Cole. Give us a minute.”

“It’s okay,” Sofia said. “He’s already seen me.”

Casey looked at Cole. “Are there any boobs you haven’t seen?”

“You have a patient, Casey. Concentrate.”

Casey helped her remove her shirt. “There’s a lot of bruising. You’re the one with the emergency medical training, Cole. I only work on horses. Cole gently examined her ribs.

“You’re bruised but nothing broken or cracked,” he said. “Could you get her some dry clothes, Casey?”

“How about some painkillers for both of you?”

“Tequila for me, please,” Sofia said.

“Same for me,” Cole said.

"I meant Advil."

"I'm the one with medical training," Cole said. "Tequila is better."

"Are you hurt anywhere?"

"Nothing a drink and dry clothes won't fix. Any word on Katie and the others?"

"Not yet."

Cole looked at the front door. "Bring a bottle. It's going to be a long night."

Chapter 65

There was a light rain, but the clouds were moving faster and getting darker. Riker and Eve were putting their bags on the hacienda's deck.

"What's keeping Danni?" Riker asked.

"I'll get her," Katie said and ran into the house. "Danni!"

"In here."

Katie went to the computer room. Danni was sitting at the desk typing. "We're leaving. Let's go."

"I sent the data to Control. Now I'm packing up the computer."

"How long?"

"Two more minutes, if you stop talking."

"You have one minute."

"You're still talking."

Danni kept typing as she stood. "There. Done. I wiped the drive."

They ran to the deck. Riker and Eve were scanning the skies.

"There!" Katie said. "That has to be the chopper the Director sent."

They felt relieved at first. Then the helicopter got closer.

"Oh hell. It's a Mexican military chopper," Riker said.

"Do we run?" Danni said.

"We can't outrun a chopper."

"What do we do?"

"Looks like we go to jail," Eve said.

The chopper began descending, its nose gun aiming at the deck. The chopper wash hit the group and they brought their arms up to protect their faces. It landed facing the deck, the engine still running.

From the corner of their eyes, they saw another chopper appear hovering just off the ground on the side of the deck. The nose cannon was at eye level with the Mexican pilot.

"It's Jimmy and Nova," Eve whispered to herself, a grin growing on her face.

The pilot and troops looked at Jimmy's helicopter. They had never seen weapons or a design like it. It wasn't hard to figure out they were outgunned.

"Piss off," Jimmy said over his broadcast system. "Now."

They saw the pilot and co-pilot talking and staring at the helicopter in front of them. Jimmy fired his nose cannon into the ground in front of them. The military chopper climbed and banked to head back in the direction it came from. Jimmy landed the helicopter next to the deck.

"Let's go. They could be back with friends."

They grabbed their bags and ran for the door. In minutes Jimmy was climbing and heading north to the States.

Eve was in the co-pilot's seat. She looked at Jimmy. “The Director?”

“Yup, she called me.”

“Thanks, Jimmy.”

“I got your back.”

He flew them to the ranch. By the time they arrived, the sky was clear, and the only remanence of the storm was a slight breeze.

“Why is there a crashed plane on the side of the runway?” Katie asked.

“Probably Cole trying to fly again,” Riker said.

“Are you coming in, Jimmy?”

“Not this time. Nova still needs a little TLC.”

They thanked Jimmy and went inside. Hugs were exchanged and questions were answered about the plane.

“The director will be here shortly,” Casey said. “She wants to brief you personally on the latest news. We can have breakfast while we wait. She never eats breakfast.”

They were just finishing when the plane landed. The Director came and sat at the table, pouring herself a coffee.

“You did a great job in Mexico. The cartel is in disarray and the Russians are back to square one with their missile base.”

“I suspect your next word is but,” Cole said.

The Director shrugged. “But the Russians are already sending more weapons and personnel. Two days after that they’re sending the missiles.”

“We can’t keep doing this,” Katie said. “We’ve been almost killed too many times.”

“If we quit it was all for nothing,” Sofia said.

“We’re not going to quit,” the Director said. “We’re building a military base across the border from the Russians. If they build more bases so will we.”

“What good does that do?”

“We’re going to do news interviews and tell the Mexican people if they vote for the same president they’ll be in the middle of a nuclear war and will not survive. It’ll put pressure on the president to back down.”

“Will it work?” Katie said.

“It’ll help. But there is one other thing you have to do. The top military advisor in Mexico is a longtime friend of the president. He’s the one who started this mess. He doesn’t want to be a politician. He wants a war.”

“Why?”

“He wants on the world stage. He’ll be the one who says what Russia is allowed to do in Mexico. He’ll use that to demand the US follows certain rules.”

“Ramirez?” Sofia said.

“Yes. That’s him.”

“We all know him,” she said. “He’s a monster that works with the southern cartels. He just built a mansion that he seldom leaves. If we remove him most of this will end. The president is not strong enough to keep going on his own.”

“Why didn’t we go after him in the beginning?” Cole asked.

“Many have tried,” the Director said. “The last one that did was forced to watch his family killed, and then he was locked up in solitary confinement for life.”

“Are you asking us to kill him?” Riker said.

"You know we can't send in American troops. It's up to you guys."

Danni was searching on her tablet as the Director spoke. She summarized what she found. "Guards surround the mansion. He has multiple security levels and lives on top of a mountain with no road access. And his bedroom is a steel safe room. It's no wonder no one can hurt him."

"I didn't say it would be easy."

Katie took Danni's tablet and did a search. "You said you'll give us anything we want."

"I will."

She turned the tablet toward the Director and showed her a picture. "I want a Super Puma AS332 helicopter with the same design and logos as the Mexican president."

They all looked at her. Cole smiled. "You're brilliant."

"I know," she said, returning his smile.

"Seems I'm not," Riker said. "Who wants to fill me in?"

"Katie wants to mimic a visit from the president to get the target onto the helicopter pad," Cole said. "Then we can kill him."

"Bingo," Katie said.

"Then we only have to deal with 20 guards, a machine gun, and Stinger missiles on the roof," Danni said. "Seems easy enough."

Chapter 66

Rameriz's hacienda lay northwest of Tampico. It was built in the mountains at the top of the tallest ridge. There are no roads connecting to it. All supplies are flown in by helicopter.

The mansion is 20 rooms of luxury. Behind it are living quarters for guards and house staff. In the front is a helicopter landing pad. At the side is a new pool. Rameriz pulled helicopters off a burning wildfire and forced them to redirect the water to fill it.

Security cameras surrounded the area, some in trees in the forest, some on the fence surrounding the property. Two men were stationed on the roof with a machine gun and stinger missiles to take down attacking aircraft. The house was higher than the surrounding area so there was no place for a sniper position. It was the safest house in Mexico, or at least Santiago Ramirez thought it was. That wasn't his real name. No one knew what that was. On his way to becoming wealthy he spared no one that got in his way. Instead, he killed them, instilling fear in others.

At the ranch in Texas, the group sat at the kitchen table looking at a laptop with a satellite photo of the hacienda. The Director returned to Control.

“We can’t break in,” Riker said. “We could never make it out alive. There are no roads. He has a large generator in the back of the house and there are solar panels on the worker’s quarters. The storage batteries are in a concrete building so we can’t shut down the power. No matter how we attack it they have the upper hand.”

“Does control have a nuke, Danni?” Riker asked.

“If they do they never let me play with it.”

“That sounds so unfair,” Katie said.

“I know, right?”

“Katie’s idea about mimicking the president is our only chance,” Cole said. “But we could never land, shoot him, then escape before the guards blasted the chopper full of holes.”

“And using a stinger missile on us.”

“Danni,” Cole said. “Can you use AI to fake the president's voice?”

“Control has software that makes a person sound like anyone they want. As the person speaks it converts the sound. We just need a large sample of the voice.”

“Would presidential speeches work? They always go on forever.”

“Sofia would have to be the speaker on our end. We’re not fluent enough in Spanish.”

“Can you make her sound like a man?”

“Yes.”

“That’s cool,” Eve said. “Can you do it for Riker too?”

"Hey. My voice is manly."

"It gets kind of high at the end."

"Of sex?"

"Of sentences."

"Eve," Cole said. "Would Jimmy be willing to help us again?"

"I'm sure of it. Where else can he test out his new toy? I'll have him pick me up here when it's time."

"Danni, can you get the appointment calendar for the president?"

"I could hack in."

"How long will it take the Director to get us the chopper?"

"Two days. She's leasing one in Dallas and telling the company it's for a movie shoot."

"Tell her we need our best pilot from Control. And say it's a high-risk situation so make it a volunteer."

"Why?"

"I might have a way we can do this, but our timing has to be perfect," Cole said. "Danni. Can we go to your bedroom?"

"Anytime."

"What?" Katie said.

"Her computer is in there. I need her to create a simulation of the attack."

"I was talking to Danni," Katie said, glaring at her.

"You can come and watch if you like," Danni said, then left for the bedroom. Cole followed her.

"Can a person die if they fall out of a helicopter?" Katie said.

"Depends how high you are when you push them out," Riker said.

"Stop it," Eve said. "Both of you."

Danni started her computer and Cole sat beside her.

"Why do you like pushing Katie's buttons?" Cole asked.

"You asked me a question and I answered truthfully. Now let's talk about your stimulation."

"I said simulation."

"Not what I heard."

They kept talking and designing it for the next hour. When it was working they went back to the deck. Danni leaned over and kissed Katie on the cheek.

"Cole says I push your buttons. I want to say I'm sorry. I'm just flirty. I can't stop. I tried, but nope. No luck. Forgive me?"

"I'll forgive you if you forgive me."

"Forgive you for what?"

"You'll know when it happens."

Chapter 67

When the fake presidential helicopter landed in the front yard of the ranch Cole and the others came out to see it. The pilot shut off the engine and opened the side door for them. Inside were leather seats and redwood panels.

"Wow. This must be worth a fortune," Katie said.

"A few million," the pilot said, extending his hand. "I'm TJ, your pilot."

Katie introduced the others. "Where did you learn to fly choppers?"

"I've been a contract pilot for a lot of years. I fly choppers and fixed wing."

"Did Control explain the mission?" Cole asked.

"I've been briefed. You ready to depart?"

"Two secs," Cole said and went inside with Katie. He retrieved a bow and a dozen arrows. Katie retrieved her rifle. Moments later Riker appeared with his rifle.

"Why the bow?" TJ asked.

"If I use a bow they won't understand what happened. It'll slow their reaction time before they fire back. Every second will matter when we escape."

Danni looked at her cell. "Eve just texted that her and Jimmy are on their way to the location."

"Tell them so are we. Did you send the message to Ramirez that the president is coming?"

"Yes. He said he would have his favorite girls waiting for him. Some men are pigs."

"Not all of us."

"I know you're not. I wish I was going with you."

"We need you here in case someone calls out the military. You'll have to monitor the airwaves and tell us where they're coming from. It's a long way to the border. Speaking of which. Did you verify with Control about refueling"?

"Yes. I texted you the location of an oil rig off of Matamoros. The Director called in a favor and they're expecting you. Jimmy will refuel there as well."

"Then we're set," Cole said. "Let's mount up."

Danni grabbed him and hugged him. Then she did the same to Katie and Riker.

"I love a hug from a beautiful girl," Riker said, patting her back.

"They're free all week," Danni said.

Minutes later they were airborne. Their fuel would last until the oil rig. After refueling it would take them to the mountain and back to the rig.

When you are on edge about an upcoming fight it makes a trip seem longer. Riker talked to Katie about his past experiences. She loved the stories. Cole sat quietly going over the plan in his head, worried he missed a tiny detail. That's what gets you killed.

The rig had two men waiting on the landing pad. They refueled them and said Jimmy had come and gone. Then they began the last leg of their journey. Their anxiety increased as they got closer.

"We're 10 minutes out," TJ said.

"I'll call Jimmy to see if he's in position," Cole said.

Jimmy told him everything was ready. Katie and Riker checked their rifles and Cole put his bow and arrows near the door.

"I'm going to have enough time for two arrows before they realize what happened and start firing. You guys have to take out the shooters so we can get away. You ready?"

They both nodded.

"Let's do this," Cole said.

They saw the hacienda out the window. Ramirez was on the edge of the landing pad and two guards were on either side of him. The machine gunner on the roof was aiming at the chopper as it landed. The other man had the launcher on his shoulder with a stinger loaded.

Katie put her hand on the door. Riker kneeled and had his rifle ready.

"Five seconds to touchdown," TJ said.

Cole loaded and arrow and nodded at Katie. She pulled open the door. He drew back his bow and fired his first arrow, fighting the rotor wash to stay accurate. It pierced Ramirez's shoulder. Cole had already loaded another arrow. His guards looked at him, then at the chopper, not sure what happened. Cole fired again. This time hitting him in the side. The guards now responded and began firing. Riker and Katie returned fire as TJ climbed and banked.

From behind the house, Jimmy pulled his chopper high enough he could see the men on the roof. One had a missile ready to launch. He fired the nose cannon. Both men were hit and slammed hard enough to fly off the roof. Jimmy brought his chopper to the front of the hacienda. He kept firing as he swept the nose in a wide arc across the guards. They fell as the bullets blasted the area. Those behind cover returned fire, hitting the chopper.

"Guy with a stinger at the edge of the pool!" Eve yelled.

TJ lowered his chopper and Katie and Riker fired at him, dropping him in the water.

"They're carrying Rameriz inside the house," Eve said. "Maybe he's still alive."

"Not for long," Jimmy said. He swung the chopper around, so it faced the house. He fired a missile into the front door. It exploded. Bodies flew through the air and down the steps. Smoke poured from the house.

"Time to bug out," Jimmy said.

More guards came around from the back. TJ appeared and they began firing out the side door to give Jimmy cover fire. Jimmy turned and headed for the edge of the mountaintop. As soon as he was past it he dropped the nose and sped down the mountainside to escape the bullets. TJ followed him.

Near the bottom, they leveled out and flew just above the treetops before climbing again. Cole closed the door, and they sat in the chairs.

"How bad is your chopper hit?" TJ asked Jimmy.

"Flight controls seem to be working. What about you?"

"So far, so good."

"Riker," Eve said. "You guys okay?"

"Just bruised from being knocked around, but the interior of this thing took a beating. I hope the Director took out insurance."

"Let's head for the rig to refuel," Cole said. "I'll call Danni."

Cole called and Danni answered on the first ring.

"Are you guys in one piece?"

"All good. Let me know if you see or hear any talk about sending military choppers after us."

"I'm on it. I confirmed the guys on the rig are waiting for you."

Cole sat back, suddenly feeling a sharp pain near his ribs. He touched it. When he looked at his hand he saw the blood.

Katie watched him. "Oh hell," she said. "Cole's hit. Riker, get the medic kit."

She lifted his arm and his shirt to see the wound.

"It's just a graze," he said.

She pulled his shirt open, ripping the buttons, then moved him to the couch. Riker opened the kit and handed Katie what she needed to clean the wound.

"You're going to need stitches when we get back," Katie said.

"He needs them now," Riker said. "We have to close the wound."

"I've never done that."

"I'll do it. I took a knitting course once. Did you know there's a knitting term called a rib stitch? Wonder if that would work."

"Don't touch him."

"It's alright," Cole said. "We've all been trained in medical procedures. For example, I learned this is going to hurt like hell and I need a bottle of scotch."

"You hurt him, and I'll hurt you twice as bad," Katie said to Riker, then left to get the scotch.

"That woman does love you," Riker said.

Cole nodded. "I'm lucky. Except for getting shot. That wasn't so lucky."

"Looks like no bones were hit," Riker said looking at the wound.

Cole's phone rang and Riker answered.

"Riker? Where's Cole?" Danni said.

"He's here. I'm fixing a hole in his shirt."

"Why is there a… Oh god. Was he hit? Where was he hit?"

"Calm down. A bullet sideswiped his ribs. I'm making him pretty again."

Katie pulled the phone away. "Fix Cole. You can flirt with Danni later."

"Katie! How bad is it," she heard Danni yell.

"He'll be fine. Why are you calling?"

"The president put two choppers in the air out of Matamoros. They're heading towards you guys."

"I'll advise Jimmy," Katie said. She disconnected and called him. "Jimmy, we have a problem. Two military helicopters have been launched from Matamoros and all we have is two rifles and a bow for weapons."

"Tell TJ to refuel and head for Texas," Jimmy said. "I'll fly ahead and intercept them."

"It's two heavily armed attack helicopters, Jimmy. You need to run."

"If I do, you guys are dead. Be safe." Jimmy cut off his comms.

Chapter 68

Jimmy flew near maximum speed so he could refuel and leave before TJ got there. As he approached the rig he saw the men waiting for him. While they refueled him he checked the damage. One of the men approached.

"Are those bullet holes?" he asked.

"No. I hit a hailstorm."

"In Mexico?"

"Climate change."

Eve stood beside him, trying to hide her smile. Jimmy moved around the helicopter, checking it in detail, then went back to Eve.

"How bad is it?"

"Flyable and fixable. It's the others I'm worried about."

"If it comes down to it, can you fight the military choppers?"

"There's only been one helicopter dogfight I know of."

"Who won?"

"The best pilot."

Jimmy took Eve away from the refuelers. "I need you to wait here for TJ and fly back with him. Will you do that for me?"

"You can't get rid of me that easy. I'm coming with you."

"You know how I call your boyfriend deadweight? That's what you would be."

"I don't weigh enough to make a difference, and don't you dare argue with me about that."

Jimmy paused. She could see he was trying to think of another argument.

"Do you really not know how stubborn I am?" she said.

"I guess I do."

Jimmy saw the refueling was finished. He waved to the guys to thank them then looked at Eve. "Let's go."

"Smart man, Jimmy."

They boarded and Jimmy headed north into the path of the military choppers. He contacted TJ.

"TJ. After you refuel, fly the course we plotted. I'll meet you at the ranch."

"Jimmy. I know what you're planning. I can help you deal with them."

"How? You're in an unarmed delivery wagon and you have four souls on board, one seriously injured. Take them home."

Riker came on. "Is Eve with you?"

"I tried to leave her, but she insisted."

"I forced him, Riker. I'll see you at the ranch."

"Call me as soon as you're safe."

"I will." She disconnected.

"How long before we see them?" she asked.

"I don't know. Keep your eyes on the skies."

Eve concentrated on looking for the choppers. It wasn't long before she saw them.

"There," she said, pointing.

"That's them. I want to get closer before I turn."

"Turn where?"

"Back to Mexican land. I want them to follow me long enough they'll never get back to TJ before he crosses the border."

"We're getting close, Jimmy. Are you planning on slapping them on the ass when we pass?"

"I want to be close enough they can see my finger in the air." Jimmy got closer, then fired his nose cannon, purposefully missing them. Without warning he banked west. "I don't want to kill them. Just make them follow."

"It worked," Eve said looking at the camera screen. They're both coming after us. How long before we can lose them."

"I need to play with them for a few minutes." Jimmy turned on his Hendrix music and accelerated slightly.

"Missile inbound," Nova said. "Missile inbound."

"Eject chaff, Nova."

The chaff burst from the chopper and the missile took the bait. Jimmy sped ahead to get out of the explosive area. The choppers kept coming.

"Missile inbound," Nova said. "Missile inbound. Ejecting chaff."

Jimmy banked hard left and sped ahead again. "They're slow learners."

"I see land ahead, Jimmy."

"As soon as we cross it they'll be out of range to find TJ. Then we can lose them."

One of the choppers fired a burst. Some of the bullets hit the chopper. Jimmy climbed and the choppers followed. When he descended at high speed he was over the shore.

"Enough of this. He took it to full speed and sped away from them."

"We're losing them. Damn, it's nice to be with the fastest kid on the block."

Danni called. "Jimmy. The chopper pilots told their boss you out-flew them, so they launched a fighter jet."

"What fighter jet? I thought they didn't have any."

"They have four operational Northrop F-5 Tigers. One is in Matamoros. It's reported to carry two sidewinder missiles and two 20-mil cannons. It's old but it can still hurt you."

Jimmy paused before answering. He wondered what he could do to avoid it. "Thanks for the heads up, Danni."

"Can you fight an attack plane?" Eve asked.

"Sometimes a helicopter can win against a jet, but I haven't tested my weapons since we've been shot."

"What do we do?"

"We have no choice. We fight."

Jimmy flew inland and then headed north. The closest part of the border was at least 200 miles. Plenty of time for the fighter jet to find them since they were heading his way.

"Nova, where's the closest treed terrain?"

"There's a mountainous, forested area thirty miles northeast."

"Why there?" Eve asked.

"I can use the landscape to blend in. The advantage we have is a jet has a minimum speed and a large turning circle. I can hover and turn on a dime."

"Do you think you can beat him?"

"The only truthful answer in any battle is maybe."

"There's an F-5 Tiger aircraft approaching from two o'clock," Nova said.

Jimmy dropped the chopper to 50 feet above the canopy. A deep canyon appeared ahead of him. He flew between the two ranges and slowed.

"Target is four miles and closing," Nova said. "It has a lock on us."

Jimmy turned the chopper and aimed at the fighter jet.

"It's fired a sidewinder," Nova said.

"Nova, take it out."

The nose gun moved with perfect precision until it hit the missile. Jimmy was too close. The concussive wave hit them, rocking the chopper. Jimmy brought it under control as the plane shot over them seconds later. It climbed at a sharp angle. Jimmy was more maneuverable. He burst forward as the plane tried to loop over and descend at high speed. Jimmy was inside the loop. He raised his nose and fired a missile. The plane ejected chaff and banked. The missile ignored the chaff from the plane and hit the fighter, the explosion raining the remains of the plane into the forest. Jimmy banked and pulled away.

"We lost our hydraulics," he said.

"What does that mean?"

"It's like losing your power steering in a car. It's harder to control but it can be done. I have some serious work to do on Nova when we get back."

"You're a hell of a pilot, Jimmy."

"Nova is a hell of a helicopter."

"Thanks, Jimmy," Nova said.

"How much does she understand?"

"There are only 170,000 active words in the English language," Nova said. "Human communication is quite simple for me."

"Could you contact TJ and ask where he is?" Eve asked.

"I've been tracking him. He's 57.5 miles from the US border. He should be at the ranch in 38 minutes."

"Can you find out how Cole is?"

"I have monitored their communications. Danni called Cole to say she has a nurse's uniform and can help him recover. Katie said Danni might not be able to recover when she's done with her."

Eve began laughing. "Would you turn up the music, Nova?"

They headed home as the music blasted through the speakers.

Chapter 69

Jimmy landed at the ranch and left the chopper running.

"Aren't you coming in?" Eve said.

"Nova is beat up pretty bad. I need to take her home and give her a rest."

"I get it. We owe you so much, Jimmy. I hope someday we can repay you."

"I wouldn't have missed it, Eve. Give my best to the others and come visit me sometime."

"I will." She waited until Jimmy took off and banked, then went inside. Everyone was in the living room. Cole was lying on the couch, a glass of scotch held on his stomach and his head resting in Katie's lap.

Riker hugged her and got her a drink. They began telling each other the stories of the day.

"Where's TJ?" Eve asked.

"He took the chopper to Dallas," Katie said. "Seems he has an ex-girlfriend he wants to get reacquainted with."

"I'm so glad you guys made it," Eve said.

"Back at ya," Riker said.

Danni heard the plane landing first. "Listen."

"Who is it?" Eve said.

"It's the Director," Danni said. "She told me she would be here."

"Why didn't you tell us?" Katie asked.

"I just did."

Katie was going to stand but Cole held her back. Moments later the Director walked in.

"Looks like the gang's all here," she said. She stopped at the kitchen to get a drink and then sat with them.

"You guys did a great job. I have confirmation Rameriz is dead, although shooting down a fighter jet wasn't the best move."

"He fired a missile at us," Eve said.

"I know."

"Why are you here?" Cole asked.

"To tell you your next assignment."

"Cole is shot, and we all almost died," Katie said. "You can't give us a night off?"

"Things are happening too quickly."

"What things?"

"The Russians are mad as hell and refusing to pay any more to the government unless they get protection. The northern cartels are almost gone. That was another source of income the politicians lost. And Rameriz was supposed to replace the president because he was more competent. Now they think the president had him killed. So pretty much everyone wants the president dead."

"Isn't that a good thing?" Danni asked.

"The president disappeared. In an ironic twist, the Mexican government contacted Washington to ask them to help find him. They said it would improve relations between the countries. I need you to find him and stop him."

"Are you asking us to kill him?" Riker said.

"The vice president wants to watch him die. He said he needs confirmation."

"Do you know where he is?" Danni asked.

"Not yet. That's why you're coming back to Chicago with me."

"I'm more useful here with Cole." She looked around. "And the others."

"Cole is coming with us too."

"Why?"

"I have doctors that can get him back to health faster."

"We can do that," Katie said.

The Director walked over to him and examined him. "He has an increased heart rate and shortness of breath. He's lost blood and you're giving him scotch. Lift his shirt."

They saw blood on the bandage and knew the wound opened.

"I have a doctor on board with medical equipment. Riker. Help him on board. Danni, you have two minutes to get your things."

"I'll go with him," Katie said.

"He doesn't need you. You'll stay here."

Minutes later the plane was taxing and then climbing.

Katie poured a double and gulped it. "What a bitch."

"Sure is," Riker said.

"I wouldn't worry about Danni," Eve said. "Cole won't figure out she's flirting with him for at least two days."

"I'm worried about Cole, not Danni."

"Don't. Control's doctors are the best."

"I know. Still worried."

****

The Director dropped Cole and Danni at the museum. Danni offered to stay with him until he recovered. She lay on the bed beside him, her head resting on her hand.

"I'm okay," he mumbled.

"I'm your new nurse until you're better. I can work out of the apartment in case you need anything, and William is here to help."

"You need to find the president."

"I know where he is."

"How?"

"I left a software tracker when I broke into his system to get his text and emails. Men always take their tablets with them. It has all their porn on it."

"Why didn't you tell the Director?"

"About the porn?"

"About the tracker."

"The team needs time to recuperate. If I told her she'd make them start the attack tonight."

"Good idea. A couple of days won't matter."

"You need to get better. I'll sleep with you tonight."

"That's not a good idea. I won't sleep if you're here."

"I'll keep my clothes on and put pillows between us."

"Won't work."

"Fine. Then I'll check on you every hour."

"Not until morning."

"You're hard to take care of."

"I've heard that before."

"Then I'll go to the living room. I need a drink." She stood to leave.

"Danni," Cole said as she reached the door. "Thanks."

"People take care of the ones they love." She smiled and left.

Danni poured her drink and then sat in front of the fireplace with her tablet. She studied the area the president was in so she could offer advice to the team when they went after him. At first, she wondered why she couldn't just tell the Mexicans, but then she realized this way they would owe the Director a favor for helping. It was how this stuff worked.

She was about to close the tablet and go to bed when a hand went over her mouth and she felt a gun pressed against her temple.

Chapter 70

Danni grabbed the hand and turned to see who it was. "Blake!" she mumbled from under the hand.

"Hi, Danni."

She let Danni pull her hand away. "What the hell is the matter with you?"

"Miss me?"

"I lost half the skin off my feet the last time you chased me. No, I don't miss you. Why are you here?"

The Director wants me to work with you. It seems you're great with the brain but not so much the bod. I'm here to protect you while you're in Chicago."

"By giving me a heart attack?"

"Sorry about that." Blake took her drink from the table and drank from it.

"I don't need your protection. My bod is just fine."

"I agree. You're hot. But you had no idea what to do tonight. What if I was an assassin?" She emptied the glass and handed it back to Danni.

“I’ll get you your own glass,” Danni said, retrieving one from the kitchen and filling hers as well. “Why does the Director think I need protection?”

“She thinks you’re the only person that can find the president and I agree with her. Except I’m betting you already know his location.”

“Why?”

“She said you cracked his emails. If you did you would have put a tracker on his tablet. It’s what I would do. I’m guessing you’re stalling so you can spend some quality time with Cole. I saw how you look at him.”

“Are you going to tell the Director?”

“No, but that means you owe me a favor.”

“You’re not nice.”

“I can be,” she said and winked at her.

“Are you going to stay here?”

“Yes. Tonight you’re going to tell me where the target is and we’re going to discuss how to capture him alive.”

“Riker and the others can do that.”

“So can we. The Director offered me a bonus if I can get him to a place where his friends can find him. I’ll split it with you. If they do it there’s no bonus. Just a slam, bam, thank you, ma’am from Control.”

Danni looked at the fire. She wanted to get rid of Blake and had no idea how.

“The contract is worth fifty grand.”

“Fifty thousand dollars?”

“That’s your half.”

“Why are you paid so much?”

"I'm the best contractor they have, and there's nothing I won't do."

Danni looked at her, pausing.

"Cash," Blake said.

She picked up her tablet. "Fine. Just this once."

"Good girl. Where is he?"

"I'm going with you. I don't trust you."

"Good. Let's go."

"In two days. I'm staying to take care of Cole first."

"The target could go somewhere else in two days."

"He won't."

"He might. Why don't you tell me where he is?"

"I already told you. I don't trust you."

Blake sat back and nodded. "I wouldn't respect you if you did, but we can fix that. Ask me anything."

"Are you going to kill me tonight and take my tablet?"

"If that was my goal you'd be dead."

"Why don't you?"

"Two reasons. One is, I have long time work with Control and won't risk it."

"The other one."

"I like smart girls. Especially cute ones. And you can be very useful to me in the future."

Danni looked at her for a long time.

"Are we good?" Blake asked.

"I love it when my team gets along," they heard from behind them. They both turned.

Cole was supporting himself by holding onto a chair. He held a gun in one hand.

"Why are you out of bed?" Danni said.

"Making sure Blake and you stayed friends."

"You don't trust me either?" Blake said. "I thought the doc gave you pain killers."

"I knew you broke into the apartment, so I didn't take any."

Danni went to him and took his hand. "Let's get you back to bed. I can handle Blake."

"How? She's a killer."

"I spiked her drink."

They looked at Blake. She was lying down in front of the fireplace, asleep.

Cole started laughing and grabbed his side. "Ouch."

Danni helped him back to bed and took the gun from him. "I'll put Blake to bed and stay with you tonight. We'll lock the door. It's steel."

She went back to Blake. She lifted her up and turned away from her. Then she put Blake's arms over her shoulders and leaned over to take her weight. After dragging her into the second bedroom she tossed her on the bed and covered her with the comforter. Cole was already asleep when she returned. She lay beside him, checked the tracker to see if it moved, then went to sleep.

Chapter 71

Danni was in the living room when Blake came stumbling in.

"Did you drug me last night?" she said.

"Yup. We keep knockout pills in the kitchen. They work like a charm."

"You bitch. Why would you do that?" She fell back in a chair.

"We talked about that last night. I don't trust you and I had to protect Cole. And me."

"I'm not a threat to either of you. I told you."

"I don't trust what a person says if I don't trust the person."

William came into the room. "Is there a problem here?"

"Yes. No one trusts me," Blake said.

"I read your file. I can see why."

"How did you get my file?"

He smiled at Danni. "I'll make more coffee and perhaps we can all calm down."

"You have my file too?"

"You've done some very untrustworthy things," Danni said.

"Survival comes at a cost," Blake said.

"So does trust."

William brought Blake a coffee. "There's more brewing."

"Make lots," Blake said. "I'm still drowsy."

"I want to get this over with so I can take care of Cole," Danni said. "We're going after the president today."

"Perhaps the rest of the team can assist you," William said.

"The president's emails say he has the hacienda under surveillance. If they leave they'll be arrested or killed. They thought I wasn't worth watching. Which hurts."

"Then let's teach them a lesson," Blake said.

"I like that idea."

"Where is he?"

"The plane will be ready this afternoon. We're leaving from Midway airport."

"For where?"

"You never quit, do you?"

"I promise to earn your trust before this is over, and I never break a promise."

Danni looked at her, then at William. He shrugged. "Fine. We're going to Acapulco. When someone wanted to build a luxury hotel, the president got rid of all the environmental laws for him. The guy lives in the top suite of the hotel but he's in Europe, so he's letting the president stay there. I assume he has another hotel to build and needs him for that one too."

"What hotel?"

"I'll tell you when we get there."

"You're all tease, and no please," Blake said. "But I'll wait."

"Yes, you will. I booked a suite on the floor below his. We'll run surveillance on the place then find a way to get him out."

"We can buy new dinner dresses and bikinis when we get there. This should be fun."

****

When they arrived at the hotel Danni checked the lobby, found all the exits, and noted where the elevators were. The top floor required a special key card.

Blake waited until a cleaner was on the elevator and then stole her master access card. Danni duplicated it and they dropped it off at reception saying they found it on the floor.

"We need to see if there are guards in the hallway," Blake said. "Which means we need to buy bikinis and wraps in the gift shop."

"Why?"

"Because men are simple. Trust me."

They put them on and bought tall umbrella drinks at the bar. Stopping the elevator on the top floor Blake put her arm around Danni's shoulders and they stumbled off the elevator, acting drunk. Two guards were standing in in front of them.

"How did you get here?" One asked, stepping towards them.

"My mommy and daddy had sex," Blake said laughing. "How about you?"

She pulled Danni's head towards her and kissed her with a lover's kiss, then stumbled into the guard to stop from falling. The guard grabbed their arms and pushed them into the elevator, then pressed the lobby button.

"Don't come back."

Danni stopped the elevator on the floor below and they went to their room.

"You didn't need to kiss me," Danni said.

"You kissed me back."

"I was acting. Why did you kiss me?"

"Nothing distracts a man more than two hot chicks kissing. I took his wallet when I bumped into him." She opened it and removed a key card. "The room door needs a card. Duplicate it and I'll take his wallet back. I'll say it fell in the elevator."

Danni created a duplicate and gave the original to Blake.

"Don't be upset about the kiss," Blake said. "We're about to kidnap a president. If we get caught and sent to prison you better know how to kiss girls."

"Just warn me next time."

"Foreplay it is," she said leaving.

Danni answered her phone. "Hi, Cole."

"Hi, Danni. How's it going with Blake."

"She may not survive the fall from the balcony."

"Play nice. You guys make a good team."

"How are you?"

"Getting better. It's nice to have William's cooking again."

"I bet," she said. "I need some ideas. The president is in the top floor of a hotel. There are two armed guards in the hallway, and I don't know how many are inside. Any ideas how to get to him out of there?"

"You have a rich, lonely man in a hotel for days with nothing to do. What do you think he'll want?"

"You're thinking he'll hire hookers."

"The best escorts can make a man forget everything bad in his life."

"How do you know that?"

"I must have read it in a book once."

"Liar," she said. "I bet Blake would make a good hooker."

"If she goes in by herself, she might not be able to incapacitate the guards."

"I have to go with her?"

"She'll need backup."

"Fine. But I don't know anything about being an escort."

"Talk to Blake."

"Good idea. I bet she knows lots about it. Get better soon, Cole." After she disconnected Blake walked in.

"Cole said we should be escorts to get into the room."

"I already thought of that, but you're a weak link."

"Why?"

"How many men have you had sex with?"

"That's none of your business."

"Have you had sex with Cole yet?"

She just glared at Blake.

"See. Weak link. Stand up." Blake looked at her and sighed. She walked around her, staring at her body and her hair, then poked her boob a couple of times. Danni slapped her hand away. "I guess we could make it work."

"How do we get him to hire us?"

"We're going to be a surprise gift from his friend who owns the hotel."

"The guards will recognize us."

"By tonight there'll be a shift change."

"They'll search us. How do we get a gun inside? And how do we get him out of the hotel?"

"We'll improvise, but first we need to buy sexy dresses. And when we go in you need to follow my lead, no matter what I do."

"That scares me more than kidnapping a president."

Chapter 72

Danni stood in front of the mirror in the bedroom. She straightened her dress for the fifth time, pulling the low-cut dress higher for the sixth time.

"You look totally gorgeous," Blake said as she entered.

"I feel terrified."

"We can do this," Blake said, pushing Danni's boobs together to show more cleavage.

"Stop it," she said as she pushed her hands away.

"Let's go."

They went to the top floor and the guards stopped them in the hallway.

"The hotel owner sent us as a special gift," Blake said. "Everything is taken care of."

They looked at each other, then at the girls. One went into the room, while the other one watched them. After a few minutes, the man came out.

"Raise your arms," he said.

They raised them to shoulder level. He ran his hands over Blake, pausing at her breasts. "Your boss isn't going to like you playing with the presents," Blake said.

He moved to Danni and did much the same. She slapped his hands away. He opened the door and let them in.

The man inside was built slightly too short to reach the top cupboards in a kitchen and slightly too fat to tie his shoelaces. He sat on a chair, holding a tequila and staring at them. He moved his hand in a circle, and they slowly turned around for him. He smiled.

"You're American?"

"Miami," Danni said. "We're here on a working vacation." Her smile broadened.

"Could we refresh your drink?" Blake said.

He looked at his glass and nodded to the bar. Blake took his glass and went to fill it. Danni saw him watching her butt. Blake returned with a full glass and handed it to him.

"Do you two like each other?"

"All the time," Blake said.

"Show me."

"Can I get a drink first?" Danni said.

He glared at her for not doing what he told her.

"She's new at this," Blake said, kissing her cheek. "First timer."

Blake put her hand behind her neck and pulled her towards her, then kissed her for a long time. She kept glancing at the man, waiting for him to take a drink. When he didn't, she kept going, gently rubbing her hands over her. Danni tried not to freak, then realized she wasn't freaking.

Blake saw him take a large drink, then another. She stopped touching Danni and turned to the man.

"Why are you stopping?" Danni said.

"Wait for it."

Seconds later the man dropped his drink and his head fell on his chest.

"What happened"?

"Control has a drug that mimics a heart attack. His lips will turn blue, and his breathing will become shallow. Call the guards in."

Danni got them.

"He's having a heart attack," Blake said. "Call an ambulance." She pulled him to the floor and began CPR. She kept pretending to help him until the ambulance arrived. The paramedics put him on a gurney and took him to the ambulance. The guards tried to get in with him.

"There's no room," a paramedic said. "Follow us in your car."

The guards ran for their car. Blake and Danni got in the ambulance, and it sped away.

"What the hell is going on?" Danni said.

Blake told the driver to pull around to the back of the hotel. They parked next to a panel van. Blake opened the doors, and they threw him in, then she and Danni drove away.

"Now can you tell me what just happened?"

"The paramedics were paid by Control. You can buy anything in Mexico."

"Where are we going?"

"Away from town."

"You could have told me what you were planning."

"I said to play along with me. Although the kissing part was all you."

"Shut up."

They continued driving, turning down a dirt road until they came to a treed area. Blake parked off the road and opened the back doors. The president was groaning and trying to get up.

An SUV pulled up beside the van. Three Mexican men and a woman got out. They forced him into the SUV. The woman handed Blake a gym bag. Without a word, they drove off with the president.

"Control paid you for the mission, then you took a bonus, and the Mexicans paid you," Danni said.

"A girl has to make a living," Blake said with a smile.

"How much is in there?"

"Fifty thousand. It's your cut like I promised," she said, holding her hand out with the bag. Danni never took it, so she dropped it in front of her.

"There are things you think you will never do until you do them," Blake said. "Like kissing me. You risked your life for the money. Take it. Give it to a charity if you want."

Blake got in the van and waited. Danni got in beside her. With the bag.

Chapter 73

They heard shots on the road ahead of them as they began driving back to the city. Blake and Danni looked at each other, and then Blake hit the gas. Speeding down the dirt road they raced around a corner. The SUV was in the ditch on its side and a black sedan was parked in front of it. Blake slammed on the brakes and watched. The four people that took the President were not moving. The presidents two guards were on the road helping him get into the backseat of a black sedan. One held the door, and the other one was leaning into the car doing up the president's seatbelt.

"They must have put a tracker on him," Blake said.

"What do we do?"

"We could leave."

"You won't get your bonus if you fail."

"Good point." Blake sped toward them.

The one holding the door saw them. He began firing, bullets piercing the windshield. Blake increased speed. The other guard slammed the door to protect the president, then took out his gun. Before he could fire Blake ran into both of them. One man was thrown across the road and the other was crushed under the wheels. Danni fired out the window at the man lying on the road, putting three bullets in him. They ran to the car and pulled the President out. He was still drowsy and unable to fight. Blake cuffed his wrists and threw him in the back of the van.

They went to the SUV. The three men were dead. The woman was leaning over the wheel, blood coming from her forehead. There was no pulse. They drove back to the highway.

"Search him for a tracker," Blake said.

"Ew."

Blake stared at her.

"Fine." Danni searched his clothes and found one under his collar. She threw it out the window, then called the Director and told her the situation.

"What do we do with him?" Danni asked.

"I promised him to the vice president. Take him to Mexico City. I'll arrange a drop-off point and contact you."

"That's 200 miles," Blake said. "The president's people will know we have him and come after us."

"Everything we've done has led up to this point. You have to deliver him alive. I'll notify Riker and Eve. They can meet you along the way."

"No," Danni said. "They're under surveillance. It'll give away our location if they meet us."

"Then you're on your own. Don't fail."

"Thanks for the help," Blake said and disconnected.

"How are we going to do this?" Danni said.

"It'll be dark soon. We have to go in the morning. We need the light.

"We can't exactly get a hotel."

"You're friends with Sofia. Does she know anyone in the area?"

"Her network doesn't extend this far down."

"Then it's a motel for the night."

They found one along the highway and checked into a two-bed unit that was older than they were. They threw him on one of the beds. Blake opened her bag and took out a bottle of pills.

"What are those?"

"Knock out pills."

"You carry them with you?"

"Don't you?"

"No."

Blake opened a bottle of water and forced it down his throat. "He'll sleep until morning. Our van will be on security cameras, so they know what we're driving. I'm going to ditch it and bring back some food. We can get another car in the morning."

Danni sat on the bed, waiting. There was a TV, but the channels were too bad to watch. She lay back to rest, waking when Blake returned. She put the take-out food on the bed, and they ate.

The only thing left was sleep. Blake undressed and crawled into the empty bed. Danni looked at the two beds.

"Seriously," Blake said. "You have to choose who to sleep with?"

"No," Danni mumbled. She took off her dress and got in beside her.

"You're safe. I promise I won't make a pass."

"Good."

Danni lay staring at the ceiling until she finally fell asleep. When she woke, Blake was gone. The president wasn't. She jumped up and slowly pulled the drapes back. No one was in the parking lot. "What the hell, Blake?" she mumbled to herself.

She dressed and sat on the bed staring at the door until she returned.

"Where were you?" she said.

"I got a change of clothes for us. We can't keep wearing escort clothes. We change and then we need to leave. The guy is still out so we have to carry him to the car."

Outside was an almost new sedan. Blake opened the trunk, and they threw him in.

"Are you going to drug him again?"

"Yes. I don't want him getting noisy."

They began driving, stopping only for gas and food.

"They expect us to come in from the south. I'm going to loop around the city and come in from the north."

"Did the Director send you the drop-off location?"

"Not yet. I don't think they'd give it to her until the last minute."

They never spoke much on the drive. Both were worried about what might happen. When they were north of the city they stopped on a dirt road. Minutes later the Director texted them the drop-off address.

"Remember, we can't trust anyone," Blake said.

"Except you, right? I can trust you?"

"I got your back. You're too good a kisser to let die."

"Stop it," Danni said. Then she thought about it. "Really?"

"Time to focus."

Blake drove into the city, watching every car they passed and the ones behind her. Danni navigated to the location. It was a business tower.

"Entrance to the underground parking is around the corner," Danni said, looking at her phone. "There are five levels. We meet them on the lowest one. There shouldn't be anyone there this time of day."

Blake pulled into a street parking space. "We're going to take a walk and see who's waiting for us."

They walked down the stairs and slowly opened the door a crack. The only vehicles were two SUVs with blacked-out windows. Another vehicle was at the top, blocking anyone from going down.

They counted six armed men in suits gathered around one of the SUVs. Two of them were smoking. Blake nodded to go back up the stairs.

"What's wrong?" Danni whispered.

"If they were government agents they would be positioned differently, a man would be watching the stairway, and no one would be smoking. Plus, the car blocking the way would be turned around in a chase position."

"Who are they?"

"I think they're a hit squad."

They got back in their car and Blake drove a few blocks away. “You’re the brains in the outfit. You tell me why the Director lied to us?”

Danni called Riker and explained what happened. “Why would the director have a hit team waiting for us?”

“I have no idea,” Riker said. “We’ll come down there to help.”

“If there’s a contract on us there’s a good chance there’s one on you guys too. I bet someone is watching the hacienda. You should go back to Chicago and protect Cole.”

“What are you going to do?”

“I wish I knew. We have a president in the trunk and no idea where to take him.”

Chapter 74

Riker briefed Eve and Katie on the situation. They got their guns and go bags. Before leaving they looked out the windows.

"I don't see anyone," Riker said.

"That just means they're good at their job," Katie said. "We could make a run for it."

"They'd have the roads blocked. We'd never get by them."

Riker looked around the house. "We need them to come to the house."

"How do we do that?" Eve said.

Katie smiled. "We could blow the place up."

"Why?" Eve said.

"That's a good idea," Riker said. "If this place explodes, they'll come to investigate. They have to see the bodies to make sure we're dead and kill us if we're not."

Eve looked around. "How do we survive the explosion?"

Katie looked at the deck. “The pool. We could put the umbrella in the water and stay under it. It would block most of the debris from falling on us.”

“Your idea is crazy enough to work. I’ll get the C4.”

“Plant it at the front of the house so they have to go around the back to get in,” Eve said.

They planted it in the entranceway and kitchen at the front, then put the open umbrella in the pool and got under it with their rifles.

“Are you guys ready?” Riker asked.

“I’m in a pool under an umbrella about to blow up a hacienda,” Eve said. “How do I know if I’m ready?”

He kissed her and smiled, then flipped the remote. The explosion shook the ground, sending a shockwave in every direction. The water in the pool turned into waves, washing over them. Parts of the house showered onto the umbrella.

They peered over the edge of the pool. Pieces of the walls and ceiling were missing, and the rest of the house was burning. Riker moved the umbrella to the far side of the pool and pushed it onto the deck. Moving back to the edge of the pool they waited.

“Right now, they’re looking through their binoculars for anyone that survived. Then they’ll come to the house to confirm we’re dead.”

They stayed quiet, waiting.

“I hear trucks,” Katie said. “Two vehicles.”

They heard the vehicle doors slam and then voices. Staying just high enough to see over the pool deck they watched for the men. Seconds later two men came from the side of the house, then another two came from the other side. Riker nodded to the others. Together the three of them rose from the water, rifles at their eyes, and fired. Two men dropped instantly. Then Riker hit another one before he could shoot back. The final man tried to run behind a wall. Katie put two bullets into him before he could make it.

They held their rifles ready, waiting for anyone else. No one came. Getting out of the pool, they confirmed the kills. Riker examined one of the bodies.

"Look at the tats. These guys are Mexican special forces."

"They weren't that special," Katie said.

"Put on some dry clothes. We need to get out of here," Riker said as he began changing. The others did the same.

"We have to get to Mexico City to help Danni and Blake," Katie said.

"The Director could track us to their location," Riker said. "We could be putting them in danger."

"What do you think we should do?

"I have an idea," Eve said. She called Cole. "Could you put William on the line?"

"I'll call him."

"Put it on speaker," Eve said.

"How can I help?" William said.

Eve explained what happened.

"You've worked with Directors at Control for years, William. Why would this one lie to us and nearly get us killed?"

"I don't believe she would. I would suggest her contact in Mexico lied to her. Maybe they didn't want you alive to tell anyone about the president."

"Are you sure about that?"

"I can't confirm it."

"Thanks, William. We'll see you soon."

"What do we do?"

"We're going back to Control. I want to sit the Director down and have a long chat with her."

Chapter 75

Danni and Blake drove into the mountains and turned onto what seemed to be a seldom-used road. After three miles they stopped.

Pulling the president out of the trunk they slapped him awake. After dumping him on the ground they gave him water to drink.

"You're the hookers," he said, his voice still hoarse.

"Escorts," Danni said. "Not hookers."

"You will die for this. I'm the president of Mexico. I will kill you myself."

Blake retrieved a knife from her bag and stood over him, staring down.

"You're a short fat man with no fighting skills. I don't consider you a threat. You're an idiot."

"We'll see," he said, trying to act defiant.

"What I'm about to do to you I'm sure you've done to others."

He tried to get up and she kicked him back down.

"I have questions."

"What questions?"

"First, I need to cut you up. I want to know you're taking me seriously."

He looked up at her, then lowered his head. He knew she would do it.

Blake grabbed his hand and pressed it on the ground. She raised her hand to slam her knife through it.

"Wait!" he yelled. "I'll tell you."

She froze with her knife still in the air.

"None of this was me. The vice president is in charge." They heard the pleading in his voice. "I'm a figure head. I don't make any decisions. It was him."

"Why would I believe that?"

"Why would I be in a resort with two hookers if everything I did was going wrong? I'd be in the capital finding someone to blame."

"You were hiding," Danni said.

"No. He sent me there. The guards were not there to protect me. They were there to make sure I didn't escape. He's going to blame me for everything, and then kill me."

"Blake," Danni said. "Can we talk?" They moved out of earshot. "I believe him."

Blake looked back at him whimpering on the ground. "I agree. He's going to piss himself if we keep this up. He doesn't have the balls to deal with the Russians and the cartels."

"Maybe the Director was lied to."

"Doesn't matter now. What do we do with him?"

They sat on the car hood staring at him. He looked up at them. They could see the fear on his face.

"Stand up," Danni said.

He stood and stared at them. His fear increasing.

"Do you have any proof you're an idiot?"

"Yes."

"What?"

"I loved President Richard Nixon. I did what he did."

"What did he do?" Blake asked.

Danni smiled. "You taped everything in your office?"

"Yes."

"You have tapes of the VP telling you what to do. Are they enough to convict him?"

"Yes. The meetings with the Russians and the Cartels were also in my home. I recorded everything, even the bribes."

"Brilliant," Blake said. "How do we get the footage?"

"I'm betting he sent the recordings to the cloud," Danni said.

"Yes," he said. "My niece set it up for me."

"Where does she live?" Blake asked.

"Mexico City."

"We can release the footage to the press and social media," Danni said. "The Russians will have to leave, the Cartels will lose their advantages, and the politicians involved will be taking communal showers in jail. I love it."

****

When they arrived in the city the President took them to a condominium. A rotund girl in her late teens answered the door. She looked at Blake and Danni.

"Let me in," he said. "I need your help."

She hesitated, then slowly opened the door. "Where are your guards?" she asked as they sat in the living room.

"These are my guards now."

"Do you know what's happening?" she said.

"What?"

"The Vice President accused you of taking bribes from the cartels. He says you are destroying Mexico and many other bad things. It's on the news."

"It was not me. It was him. You need to believe me."

"I do. I listened to some of the recordings."

"I need the password and the name of the cloud where you stored the video."

She looked at Danni and Blake, then back at him. "Are they forcing you to do this?"

"No. Things have changed. Please give them to me."

"I can't. Remember when I installed it? You told me the recordings could destroy Mexico and had to be extremely secure, so they are automatically stored on the cloud in an encrypted file. I made the password too complex to remember so I put it on a USB with the cloud address."

"Where's the USB?" Danni asked.

"I hid it at your home."

"The National Palace?"

"No. Your personal home. It's in a book in your office."

"Which book?"

"The Old Man and the Sea by Hemingway. I liked that one."

"Thank you. You may have saved my life."

"We can't leave her here," Blake said. "The VP could round up your family in an attempt to find you. She could be tortured and killed."

"Ease up, Blake," Danni said. "She's a kid."

"They torture kids the same as adults," Blake said.

"You don't need to scare her."

"I know what they do," she said. "I'll come with you."

"We'll take you to the airport," Danni said. "You can fly to Chicago. A man named William will meet you and take care of you until we get back."

"What about you, uncle?"

"I have to go with them," he said. "They'll never find the book without me."

"Let's go," Blake said. "Put on a cap and don't wear your glasses. It's the best we can do for now."

They drove to the airport. The president stayed in the car while Danni got the girl on a plane and called William. The sun had set by the time they drove to his house. It had nightlights in the yard that lit the landscaping more than the residence. Oversized and passed down through the generations, it was begging to become another boutique hotel. They sat outside in the car scanning the area.

"It's too dark to see anyone," Danni said.

"They could be inside," Blake said.

"What do we do?"

"Everything depends on that USB. We have no choice but to get it."

"We can go in the back," he said. "There are trees and bushes to hide us."

They moved to the back of the house. He unlocked the door and turned off the alarm system. They moved through the entrance and climbed the stairs. At the far end of a hallway was a closed door. Inside was an office. Books of all sizes were scattered haphazardly on shelves.

"Why don't I see security cameras?"

He showed her one in a painting frame and one in the back of a book.

"My niece put them in. I'm very proud of her."

"You taught her corruption early in life," Blake said. "Good Job."

Danni scanned the room. "Where's the book?"

The President went to a shelf and removed it. A hole was cut in the pages and the USB lay inside. Blake grabbed it before the President could touch it.

"Let's get out of here," she whispered. They began moving to the door. Blake held her hand up to stop them. They heard someone opening the front door.

The President took a gun from his desk. Blake took it away from him and gave it to Danni. She told him to hide under the desk. Without hesitation he did.

Danni and Blake moved to the hallway. Blake glanced over the railing. She held up four fingers to Danni. Danni nodded.

Blake ran to the other side of the staircase. She held her gun in both hands. They waited. She glanced again. Two men were coming up the stairs side by side.

Blake kneeled. She waved for Danni to do the same. Danni felt the sweat on her hands as she held the gun. Blake leaned around the corner and saw the tops of their heads. She fired. Danni leaned around the corner. Both men were firing at Blake. She put a bullet in the one closest to her. It hit his shoulder and he turned his gun in her direction but shot too high, thinking she was standing. She fired twice more, and he fell. The other man tried backing down the stairs as he fired. Blake stood and shot twice, both hit him in the head.

They ducked behind cover. There were two more men somewhere in the house. Danni looked down the stairs. The dead men were sprawled across them halfway down.

Blake ran to Danni's side, and they moved back to the office. They heard a burst of fire, then another one. The bullets shattered the corner of the hallway where Blake was just standing. She would have been killed.

Blake saw the President peek over the desk. "Get down," she whispered. "Stay down."

They stood on either side of the door. Blake glanced out and saw the men reaching the top of the staircase. They were walking towards them. She didn't see the President peering over the desk again. Suddenly he stood, raising his hands in the air.

"Don't shoot! I am your president."

A burst of fire came before he finished speaking. Danni and Blake leaned out and fired the rest of their rounds into the men. Both dropped. They turned to the president. He was lying halfway on his desk, blood oozing onto his papers.

"Idiot," Blake said, looking at him.

"That's a bit harsh."

"If you're an idiot when you're alive you're still an idiot when you're dead."

"I won't ask you to do my eulogy."

"His death will be on the video," Blake said. "We have our proof."

"So will we," Danni said. She went around the room destroying the cameras so they would stop recording. "Now all of it is on the cloud. I can edit us out later."

They moved down the stairs, hoping there were no more attackers. Minutes later they were driving down the street.

"Now what?" Blake asked.

"I have to get to Control to download the files."

"It's 500 miles to the closest border crossing. Not to mention we go through three cartel territories and will be closer to the Russian military base."

"We need a place to hold up until we figure this out."

"They'll think we'll go north to get back to the States. I say we go south to Acapulco. It's filled with Americans, and we can hide in the crowds until we can figure out how to get home."

"You want to go deeper into Mexico?"

"They won't expect us to do the unexpected."

Chapter 76

Riker, Eve, and Katie flew a commercial flight to O'Hare airport. It was early morning, and no one was expecting them. They wanted it that way.

Arriving at the museum they went to the apartment. Cole was on the couch. He stood when they came in and hugged each of them.

"You're looking better," Katie said.

"Boredom is a great healer. I want the details on what happened."

William arrived and welcomed them back. He made coffee and listened with Cole to the story.

"Where's the President's niece?" Katie asked.

"She got a hotel downtown," William said. "Seems the president gave her a substantial amount of money each month. He used her to hide his bribes. He never knew she transferred it to the States in her name. Now she plans to spend it."

"I see morality runs in their family," Riker said.

"Does anyone know where Blake and Danni are right now?" Katie asked.

"No," Cole said. "I'm sure they're worried about their phones being compromised. They'll cut off all communications until they're safe."

"Perhaps we should discuss the situation with the Director," William said. "Would you like me to ask her to come here?"

"Yes. Maybe she knows where Balke and Danni are."

"Where would they go?" Eve asked.

"If I know Blake she would do the opposite of what a normal person would do," Katie said. "I think she would drive south, not north."

"To where?" Eve asked.

"She'd want to fit in. The closest place with a lot of Americans is Acapulco. Then she might take the coast road to Puerto Vallarta and fly home from there."

"How sure are you?"

"It's a guess."

They looked when the elevator doors opened. The Director walked in and sat with them.

"Welcome back," she said. "I need an update."

"We blew up the hacienda and escaped," Riker said.

"Not about you. About Blake and Danni."

Cole told her what the president's niece told him, including the part about the recordings and the USB.

"Do you think they have it?"

"We don't know."

"Now we have questions for you," Katie said.

"We don't have time to waste."

"Yes, we do. Did you know the President was a fall guy and the VP was the bad guy?"

"No," she said without a pause. "That would mean my contact in Mexico got it wrong."

"You only have one source?"

"When everyone is on the take it's hard to get snitches."

"Why would you send Danni and Blake into danger knowing your intel could be wrong?" Katie said.

"We all have our jobs."

"Forget about a Christmas present this year," Riker said.

"I'll get over it. Now tell me where the USB is."

"No," Cole said. "We can't tell you anything if you're dealing with a bad informer."

"Don't forget you work for me."

"We can change that," Cole said.

"You need to tell us everything you know and where you get the information or we go rogue to get our friends out of Mexico," Katie said. "And we'll give the USB to Sofia to broadcast."

The Director glared at them, going from face to face. She could tell they meant it. She walked to the window and stared out.

"Fine," she said, not turning toward them. "I knew the President was a puppet." She returned to her chair. "He was weak and greedy and did whatever he was told. That's why they put him in power. The VP wanted to do everything without being noticed and it was working for him."

"You knew?" Katie said.

"Yes. I knew the minute I talked to the president. It's easy to recognize stupidity."

Katie looked at her. “You wanted all this to happen. You wanted the Russians in Mexico. Why?”

“When the president is dead, we’ll remove the VP as well. We have a new president we are putting in power. One that we’ll control. Same with the VP.”

“For what reason?” Cole asked.

“He’ll ask us to come to Mexico to remove the Russians. We could do it without an international incident.”

“And then you could control Mexico,” Katie said.

“Yes.”

“You’re interfering with another country.”

“Don’t be so naive. Our politicians have interfered with dozens of countries. Why do you think there are so many illegal immigrants? Washington screwed up their countries so bad the people left and came to ours. It’s a cost of doing business.”

“We’ve been helping the evil empire,” Riker said.

“The winner decides who will be called evil,” the Director said. “If you say anything about this, you’ll be considered traitors and spend your lives in jail. Do you understand that?”

Katie stood in front of her. “You need to leave.”

“This isn’t over,” the Director said.

“It won’t be until we get our friends home.”

“You have 24 hours to get me the recordings.” She turned and left.

“I wonder if that bitch ever tells the truth,” Katie said.

“If anything happens to Danni and Blake it won’t matter what she says when I kill her,” Cole said.

Chapter 77

Danni and Blake booked a suite in a resort hotel in Acapulco. They checked in and went to the room. Danni took out the USB and kept looking at it.

"I'm going to buy a laptop and see what's on this?"

"Can they trace us if we go to the cloud website?"

"I'll download security software. I'm worried about leaving it on the cloud where his niece put it. She could sell the videos to the VP."

"We don't trust anyone, do we?" Blake said.

"Not since Billy Morris in grade nine."

"Mine was Suzy Johnson. Grade eight. We all have stories."

"But we can trust each other, right?" Danni said.

"Yes. I have your back."

Danni nodded and smiled at her. "I have all your bits." She stood. "I'm going laptop shopping. And I'll buy two burner phones."

"Want me to come with you?"

"No. I'll stay in public."

"I'm going to check out the hotel. See if I can find any bad guys that might be looking for us."

Danni bought the best laptop and phones she could find and went back to the hotel room. Blake was sitting on the balcony wearing a bikini and having an umbrella drink.

"Why are you dressed like that?" Danni asked.

"To look like a tourist. Put yours on."

"Later." She went inside and loaded the protection software then inserted the USB. A password request appeared on the screen. Blake came in and saw it. "Now what?"

"I can bypass a USB password pretty easily." In a few minutes, she was in. "It has the password and the website on it. Looks like the girl didn't lie."

Danni went to the site and downloaded everything to her laptop, then deleted the files off the cloud. She entered the password for the encrypted files.

She and Blake looked at a few videos. "She had cameras in the other rooms and the backyard," Danni said. "Even the kitchen." Danni loaded another video. "Oh god." It was a video of the president and a woman having sex on his desk. Danni closed the file.

"Hey! She was hot."

"He wasn't. You can watch the porn videos later."

She kept opening them until she found the meetings. In the first one, the president and VP were talking. The VP was telling him what to say to the media about the Russians. He talked to him like he was an employee. "This confirms the president was a fall guy."

They watched two more.

"This will destroy the VP," Blake said.

"Let's watch a few more."

They saw one where the President got a call from the Director. He mentioned her name when he answered the call. They heard him saying he would have Sofia and her team killed.

"I'm such an idiot," Danni said. "I can't believe I worked for that bitch."

"That's the reason I work for money. It never lies."

"It's too dangerous to keep the files on the laptop." She went into a Control server and uploaded them.

"Won't Control see them?" Blake asked.

"I have my own server that's hidden from Control. Only I can access it. She watched the upload until it was done. "I'm going to wipe the USB and put a strong password on it."

"Why?"

"It could act as a diversion if we're caught. Maybe give us time to escape if they think I have the password."

"And then they could torture us for it?"

"You'll save me by then. We need to get back to Chicago so we can figure out what to do next. If we use the plane the Director will find us."

"You know the Director is going to try to take the files and kill us. We know too much."

"Always the optimist." Danni took a sip from Blake's drink.

"It's a 15-hour drive to the border. That's a long gauntlet to run."

“We could go to Puerto Vallarta and take a commercial flight from there. It’s a shorter drive.”

“We’ll have to travel during the day.” We’ll leave in the morning.”

“What about today?”

“We sit by the pool and fade into the crowd. The worst thing that can happen is drunk guys try to pick us up.”

“I’ll go if I can get some umbrella drinks.”

“My treat.”

“I can buy. I still have the 50 grand you gave me.”

Danni put on her bikini, and they went to the pool. Blake kept scanning the crowd for anyone suspicious. Whenever they saw guys coming to talk to them Blake would hold Danni’s hand and smile at her. One guy never gave up, so she kissed Danni, and he left.

“You can’t keep kissing me,” Danni said, holding her straw to her lips.

“You never pull away.”

“I like boys.”

“You like Cole.”

“I do. I want to have his babies.”

Blake laughed. Then Danni laughed. Without warning Blake stopped. Danni looked at her, then in the direction she was staring. There were two guys in street clothes walking out of the hotel to the pool area.

“Are they bad guys?”

“I don’t know. Let’s go to our room.”

They went into the hotel using another entrance. When they got to the room they went on the balcony and looked down at the pool area. The men were walking around, looking at the tourists.

"They're looking for us," Blake said.

"How do you know?"

"They're ignoring all the hot chicks, which means they're looking for someone."

"I'm betting all the hotels are being checked. We'll eat in the room and stay here until morning when we leave."

Danni stood and stared over the ocean.

"What's the matter?" Blake asked.

"I'm so tired of being scared."

Blake wrapped her arms around her. "I'm hugging you as a friend."

Danni hugged her back and hung on for a long time. "I needed that. Do you ever get scared?"

"There have been times."

There was a knock at the door. Blake looked out the peephole. "It's the two guys from the pool."

"What do we do?"

Blake got her gun and held it in her hand. She waved for Danni to move away from the door. "What do you want?"

"Cole sent us. We're from Control."

"Prove it."

"Danni. We've met. I'm Greg. You did some research for me when I had a mission last month."

Danni looked through the peephole. She nodded at Blake. "How do we know Cole sent you?"

"He told me to say you kissed him when you were almost caught by the Russians in the computer room."

Danni opened the door and let them in. “Did he say anything else about me?”

“Not now Danni,” Blake said. “Why are you guys here?”

“To help you get back to Chicago. They sent us because no one will recognize us.”

“How did he know where we are?”

“They thought you would go south, and we checked every hotel in town. I showed your pictures to the shop clerk, and she said you bought bikinis. We need to leave now. If we can find you so can the Mexicans.”

“We’ll change,” Blake said. They went into the bedroom and put on street clothes then grabbed their bags.

“We have a car in the parking lot,” the man said. “You’ll both have to stay in the trunk until we clear town.”

They took the stairs and went to the car. Blake got in first and then Danni. They closed the trunk. Their faces were inches from each other.

“I guess I should have got in with my back to you,” Danni said.

“That’s usually how it’s done.”

“Sorry.”

“I don’t mind.”

They felt the car pull into traffic and start driving.

“I just thought of something,” Danni said. “The Russians would know Cole and I kissed. It would have been on their security cameras.”

“Oh, hell,” Blake said. “We may have just kidnapped ourselves.”

Chapter 78

The car continued down the highway with Blake and Danni in the trunk. Blake found the safety latch inside and held the trunk as she pushed it open a crack.

"Where are we?" Danni asked.

"No idea. But we're heading north, which could mean these guys work for the Russians and we're being taken to their base."

"Which also means we're facing a torture scenario."

"They're slowing," Blake said.

The car pulled off the highway onto a dirt road. They drove for another 10 minutes before stopping. The dust seeped into the trunk, covering them and making it hard to breathe. Blake pulled it shut, keeping her hand on the latch.

"Don't open it," Danni said.

"The car has an indicator light that shows if the trunk is open. They already know."

"Oh, yeah."

Blake opened it. The men were standing behind the car.

"Cole didn't send you," Danni said.

"Finally figured it out. Good for you."

They pulled them out and took them to a treed area a short distance away. One man searched them while the other kept his hand on his gun, but kept it holstered. Blake noted that meant they didn't think they were a threat.

The man doing the search stuck his hand in Danni's front pocket.

"Hey, jerk," she said trying to step away from him.

The other man pulled his gun. Danni stopped resisting. The man found the USB. He held it up for his friend to see. He went to the car and removed a laptop, inserting it.

"It has a password."

"That's the client's problem. They can crack it at the base."

"You guys contracted for the Russians," Danni said. "I used to think the mafia was the worst for no loyalty. Now I think it's Control."

"Get back in the trunk."

"No," Blake said.

"Get in or I'll put you in."

"We can put them in the back seat. We don't want to deliver damaged goods." He got their bag from the back seat and took it to the trunk, then opened it.

"You see this?" he said. "There has to be 60 grand in here."

"Fifty," Danni said. "It's mine."

"Now it's ours."

"You guys are a lousy first date."

"It's not over yet, honey."

"Honey?" Danni said. She slapped his face, and he started laughing, then his partner did.

Blake reacted instantly. She side-kicked one in the stomach, and he doubled over. Before his friend could react, she jumped up and kicked high, hitting him under the chin. His head snapped back but he never fell. Danni took the gun she left in her bag and aimed it at the man. He was about to slug Blake.

"Don't try it," she said. The man stopped. He knew he couldn't reach her before she could shoot.

Blake grabbed the other gun from the bag. "On your knees. Hands on your heads." The man ignored her. She fired into the ground in front of him. "Next one is a ball shot."

She lowered her aim. He quickly got on his knees. The other man did the same.

Danni looked in the car. "Keys are inside."

"Do they have a bag in there?"

"Yes." Danni went through it. "Clothes, cuffs, extra gun, and a military knife." She took the plastic cuffs and secured their hands behind them. Then she took the USB back.

"What do we do with them?" Danni asked.

"They'll keep coming after us if we leave them alive," Blake said.

"You can't murder them."

Blake paused before replying. "Why can't I?" She looked into their eyes.

"Blake. Don't."

Blake paused, looking into their eyes. "No intention. I just wanted to see the fear in their eyes. The fear everyone they killed has gone through."

"This isn't over," one man said.

"You're the one on your knees, scumbag." She cuffed their ankles and kicked them over, then took their phones and guns.

"You come near us again and you'll be in a grave," Danni said. They got in the car and left.

"That wasn't a very good line," Blake said as she drove to the highway.

"I know. I couldn't think of anything else. We should write some down for next time."

"We may as well keep driving. We'll make it to Puerto Vallarta and stay there tonight. If it's safe we can fly out tomorrow."

"Should I just release the videos now?"

"No. I'd like to talk to the rest of the team first. There could be consequences we don't see. We don't get a second chance if we screw this up."

"I'm going to call Cole," Danni said.

"It could give away our position if the Director is monitoring his calls."

"We need to take the chance." She dialed. "Cole, it's Danni."

Cole put it on speaker. "Where are you? Are you safe?"

"I'd prefer being a minister or a tour guide. It seems safer than dealing with these lizards. Don't worry about us. I'll contact you when I can.

"Wait!" he said, but she disconnected.

"What the hell was she talking about?" Riker said. "What's with the minister or a tour guide and the lizard?"

"No idea," Cole said. "Katie, why are you smiling?"

"Danni and I were watching old movies one night. We both loved the one called The Night of the Iguana."

"Of course," Eve said. "I watched that movie with my dad. Richard Burton played a defrocked minister who became a tour guide, and an iguana is a lizard. It was filmed just outside of Puerto Vallarta. That's where they're headed."

"It's good having old-movie aficionados around," Cole said. "They know the clues."

"That's true," Riker said. "The 'Expendables' movies are pretty much clueless."

"I can leave a message for Danni on her control computer. She showed me how in case of an emergency."

"I'll call the pilot," Cole said. "He owes me a favor. I can get him to fly us there without going through the Director."

"Control can still track us."

"We can pick them up and be back here by the time they send someone after us."

"You can't come," Katie said. "You need to recuperate some more."

"I guess. We can use burner phones to communicate. I have the number for the pilot in my room." Cole left and came back a few minutes later. "We have a problem."

"What?"

"The Director locked down the plane. She said it was a cost-cutting measure."

"That's a lie. Control has a massive amount of cash," Riker said.

"She doesn't want us using it to get Danni and Blake," Eve said.

Katie stood. "I'm going to pay that bitch a visit."

"She's the head of a secret agency that could make you disappear," Riker said. "Choose your enemies wisely."

"Then we steal the plane."

"The pilot works for Control. He has a family to feed."

"We could use TJ. He said he flies fixed wing, and he's a contractor like us," Eve said. "I asked for his number."

They all looked at her.

"What? I asked in case we ever needed him again. Professionally."

"Sure," Katie said. "Call him. "Tell him we have to leave ASAP."

"Are we all going?" Eve asked.

"Just me," Katie said. "Control will get suspicious if we all leave. Tell TJ to post on his social media he's taking me away for a lover's weekend."

Eve held up her phone and took Katie's picture.

"Why did you do that?"

"He'll want to brag to his friends he's that he's banging a hottie. That way Control will see it."

"I'm not going to be banging anybody. Except Cole. Just you Cole."

"Good to know."

Chapter 79

As Danni drove, she stared at every driver that passed.

"You need to take a deep breath," Blake said. "It'll take some time before they find us."

"If they find us."

"There's a town a few miles ahead of us," Blake said, looking at her phone. "We'll stop and buy new clothes. Something touristy. And we need to get a new car. I have fake ID so we can rent one."

They pulled into the town and found a clothing store. It was a tourist town so there wasn't much to choose from.

"We need shorts and t-shirts with 'I Love Mexico' written on the front, and caps big enough to pull part way over our faces. We need to make it American tacky. Oh, and get sunglasses and towels."

"I wish we could buy wigs."

"I could cut your hair."

"Never happening."

"While I rent the car, you can get snacks."

"Anything else?"

"A bottle of Tequila. It'll keep me awake in case you want me to drive."

They got everything they needed and drove further up the coast. It was getting dark. Headlights became mesmerizing and a couple of times Danni crossed the center line. "We need to get some rest. Even a couple of hours."

"We could use the trunk."

"No more trunks for me. We need a motel."

"It's too dangerous. The VP could have the cops checking them. We can stay on the beach."

"You remember Mexico is a narco-state?"

"Yes, but there are a lot of places in Chicago that are worse."

"We'll find a beach and take turns sleeping."

"You're a bad tour guide."

"You're still alive. You owe me that much."

They found a secluded beach and lay on their towels. Danni was asleep in minutes. Blake had a couple of swallows of the tequila and watched the area.

Eventually, four boys in their late teens wandered down the beach with beers in their hands. They saw the girls and walked towards them, one punching the other in the arm and laughing about their great find.

When they were closer Blake stood. Her arms were at her sides, a gun in each hand. She stared at them. They stared at the guns. After looking at each other for courage they went back the way they came. Danni slept through the whole thing. Blake needed to stay awake. She stripped and ran into the ocean. It was cooling and the waves were strong. It rejuvenated her. Danni was sitting up watching her when she walked out.

"Are you perving on me?" she said, drying herself off. "Not that I mind."

"It's your turn to sleep. I'm not tired anymore."

"You should take a plunge. It works."

"I will. When you're asleep."

Blake dressed, then spread her towel out and lay on it. She rolled on her side and fell asleep until sunrise. She woke when she heard movement beside her.

She blinked and rolled over, snapping awake when saw the two men that kidnapped them standing over her. Danni was standing beside them, one of the men holding her arm.

"I should have killed both of you jackasses," Blake said.

"We underestimated you," one man said. "It won't happen again. Get up."

"Do we shoot them?"

"No. It's too hard to get rid of the bodies. We'll drown them. It'll look like American tourists were caught in a rip tide. The police won't investigate."

The man beside Danni grabbed her hair and pulled her backward toward the water. She grabbed his hand with both of hers, but he was too strong. When she fell to the ground he dragged her into the water.

Blake's mind raced for a way out of this. If she didn't act quickly Danni would be killed. The man beside her aimed his gun at her and grabbed her arm. He pulled her waist deep into the water and put his hand on her head. Blake reacted instantly. She pushed the gun hand away and drove her thumb under his armpit, immobilizing his arm.

Then she drove her fist into his throat. The man gasped and brought his other arm up to swing at her. Blake slammed the palm of her hand under his nose with as much strength as she had. It drove the cartilage up into his brain and he collapsed face down in the water.

The other man had his back to her. He was holding Danni under the water with both hands. Danni had stopped fighting. Blake moved behind him and put her hands on opposite sides of his head then jerked them toward each other. She heard the snap his neck made and pushed his body out of the way.

She grabbed Danni under her arms. She wasn't moving. Dragging her onto the shore she lay her down and began CPR. Pushing on her chest and breathing into her, she checked for signs of life. She kept at it. It was taking too long.

"Wake up!" she yelled. She kept going. Without warning Danni spit up water and began coughing. Blake turned her on her side. She kept coughing before she was able to breathe properly, then rolled on her back. She looked up at Blake.

Danni sat up and wrapped her arms around her. Blake could feel her sobbing. "It's alright. You're good."

She gently pulled her arms away and helped her up.

"I owe you my life," Danni said. "From now on you can kiss me anytime you want."

"Another time. We need to get out of here. Grab your stuff."

They ran to the car and started driving.

"Why does my chest hurt so much?" Danni said.

"From the CPR. I tried not to break any ribs."

"Next time just do mouth-to-mouth."

"It doesn't work that way."

"Do you think anyone saw us?"

"It won't matter. I doubt they'd report it to the cops."

"How did they find us?"

"There must have been a tracker on their car. It's my fault for not checking properly."

"At least that's over."

"We're not out of this yet. If the Russians sent two contract killers after us, there'll be more. Maybe they put an open hit on us."

"We'll be in Puerto Vallarta soon," Danni said. "Hopefully the plane will be waiting for us."

"Hopefully only the plane is waiting for us."

"I showed Katie how to leave a message for me on my control computer. I'll see if she did." Danni used her phone to connect. "She did. I knew she'd remember the movie. We'll meet her at the airport."

Danni kept silent for the next few miles. Blake kept looking at her, wondering if she was traumatized by nearly drowning. "What are you thinking?" she asked.

"I'm worried about the videos. Everyone seems to be one step ahead of us. Could you call Cole and put it on speaker?"

Blake called and Cole answered.

"We've been worried. How are you guys?"

"Surviving," Danni said. "Thanks to Blake. I'm worried about the videos. I put them on my secure server at Control, but now I don't trust it. Could you pull them down to my computer at the museum and delete them off the server?"

"I'll need your password."

"Hang on. I'm going to put you on mute for a minute."

"Sure."

Blake muted the call. "What's wrong?"

"The noise in the background is wrong."

"There is no noise."

"That's what's wrong. Cole always has the ceiling fan running. I don't hear it."

"Do you think the call was intercepted?"

"Control could do it easily with the AI voice-mimicking software."

"What do we do?"

"Unmute it. Cole. Sorry. I almost died today. It made me think about us. Remember the airport when you tried to kiss me, and I said no. I regret that now."

"Sure. I remember. Let's talk about it when you get back. What's the password?"

Danni reached over and disconnected the call.

"What's the matter?" Blake said.

"It's not Cole. I would never say no to him. We kissed and he got to second base. I got him there."

"Why do I feel like I'm in high school?"

"Call Eve."

Blake dialed.

"Eve. Control is intercepting calls to Cole. I need you to download some files from my server. I'll give you the location and password. You need to do it right now."

"Hang on, I'll start your computer."

While they waited Blake explained to Eve how Danni knew it was faked. Danni glared at Blake who tried to hide her smile.

"Is the system on?" Danni said.

"Yes."

"What's the background picture?"

"A selfie of you and the T-Rex. Why?"

"I had to confirm it's you and you're on my computer." Danni gave her the logon and told her how to download the files. "Make sure you wipe them off the Control server."

"Will do."

"Got to go. Keep those files safe. Everything depends on it," she said, disconnecting.

"Find out where the airport is in Puerto Vallarta."

Blake checked her phone map. "It's two miles north of the city. I can guide you in."

"We need to change into jeans and a shirt. My shorts are still damp."

Blake changed as they drove. "Your turn."

"I'm driving."

"I'll hold the steering wheel."

Danni thought about it and then decided she could do it. The top was easy. It took three miles to get the shorts off and the pants on. Blake couldn't stop laughing.

Chapter 80

Eve was watching the videos when Cole and Riker walked in to see what she was doing.

"Why are you watching Mexican porn?" Cole asked.

"Look closer," Eve said.

"I really don't want to," Cole said.

Riker leaned closer. "Jesus. That's the Mexican president."

"These are the videos Danni stole from his house. He had cameras in every room and hookers in every other room."

"Why do we care?" Cole said.

Eve opened a different file. It was from his office. The VP and a cartel leader were there. They were discussing bribes. She showed them other footage with the Russians and other cartel leaders.

"This is exactly what we want," Cole said. "It'll destroy the VP. Maybe we can help the people get a real president sworn in. Someone that will kick out the Russians and not bring in the Americans."

"There's something else. Danni called you and Control intercepted the call. Danni talked about when she turned you down the time you tried to get to second base in the airport. They didn't know she lied."

"I don't remember that."

"You don't remember kissing and fondling Danni?" Riker said. "Nice try, buddy."

"Fine. I told Katie about it. It was work-related."

"I want your job."

Eve slapped his arm. "Control is in the middle of us. We have to be careful about all our comms and what we say. And we need to run a bug sweeper in our rooms."

"I'll start that now," Riker said.

"I'll run a wireless blocker," Eve said. "We can turn it off when we need to connect.

"We have another problem," Cole said. "If they know we have the only copy of the videos we become a target."

"Should we leave the museum?" Eve said.

"Did you want to face Katie if T-Rex is shot up?"

"You're right. We should leave. I'll put the files on a USB, and we can take them with us."

"Where are we going?"

"I have an idea," Cole grabbed a burner phone and called Katie. "Are you in Puerto Vallarta?"

"Yes. At the airport waiting for Danni and Blake."

Cole explained the situation.

"If that's the case you need to get out of the museum," she said.

"You worried about us or your T-Rex getting shot?"

"Both. Don't ask me what order."

"You still own your dad's house. Can we use that?"

"Of course, but he was a Chicago mafia leader. I can't guarantee it'll be safe."

"It's our best chance of staying alive."

"The front door code is 524615. I have a service that maintains the house. I'll get them to stock the fridge."

"Thanks. Any booby traps?"

"If you try to break into the safe and enter the wrong password a 9 mm will blow your head off."

"That's no way to treat guests," Riker said.

"And there is a safe room you can access through his walk-in closet. It's fireproof, waterproof, and bulletproof. It's small, but he only wanted to protect himself. Just don't open it."

"Another gun trap?"

"A vial of acid explodes in your face."

"Wow. Think hard. Are there any others?"

"I don't remember any."

"We'll wait at the house for you."

"I'll see you soon."

****

The house was a mansion. It had a long, curved driveway with a covered entrance. Trees were in the front and in the back was a pool. On the kitchen table was a list of maintenance done for the pool, house cleaning, and food. Riker checked the fridge. Someone had already stocked it.

"I guess crime pays," Eve said, looking around the house.

"You remember someone killed him, right?" Riker said.

"Good point."

"Let's choose a bedroom and check the security systems," Cole said. "Then we can do a perimeter check."

It was afternoon by the time they settled in. Eve sat at the computer and checked the security tapes, then went to the living room.

"Let's take a walk, guys," Eve said. "The grounds are worth seeing."

Eve brought her laptop, and they went to the front and sat in the shade under a tree.

"There has to be a reason you brought us out here," Cole said. "Is the place wired?"

"Yes."

"See anything suspicious?" Cole asked.

"The maid is stealing the wine, the pool boy brought his girlfriend to go skinny dipping and then did her on the diving board, and the woman that stocked the shelves with food took half with her when she left."

"Just a day in the suburbs," Riker said.

"Anything that affects us?"

"Yes." Eve opened a laptop and loaded a video. "This is from the main security system."

They watched two men at night opening a back door. The men planted cameras in the living room and the bedrooms then relocked the doors.

"I know those guys," Riker said.

"I recognize them too. They're with Control," Cole said.

"The Director had to order them to do this. She must have thought we would move here."

“Do we dismantle the cameras?” Riker said.

“No reason to,” Eve said. “I’ll put on a wireless blocker. They can look in the windows if they want to know what we’re doing. It’s what good neighbors do.”

“Don’t activate it yet. We’ll let them see us hide a fake USB in the living room first,” Cole said. “They’ll think it’s what they’re looking for.”

“Since the others aren’t here yet they’ll wait until they get back before they try to kill us and take the files,” Riker said.

“Our mission was to remove the Russians from Mexico,” Eve said. “The videos are the only way to do that. We have to protect them at all costs.”

“That’s why I hid the real USB in the museum before we came here,” Cole said.

“Where in the museum?” Eve said.

“In a fake T-Rex bone. I carved a hole, put it in, and recovered it. They won’t find it.”

“Tricky,” Riker said. “Let’s eat and have some drinks while we wait for the kids to come home.”

“Good plan,” Eve said. “I like drinks.”

Chapter 81

It was morning when they arrived from Mexico. Everyone hugged and they sat in the living room.

"Feels weird being here," Katie said. "Despite my dad being a mafia boss, I did have the odd, good time. Some of his men were nice to me. Of course, they were just trying to nail me, but I met some interesting people. Mostly killers and drug dealers." She took a big breath and puffed out her cheeks as she exhaled. "Who am I kidding? My life pretty much sucked."

"You got a nice house of it," Blake said.

"I did. I'd sell it but I think if anyone renovates they would find a few bodies."

"Ew," Danni said.

"What matters is I like my life. I have great friends and aside from being hunted by bad guys, all is good."

"Good attitude," Eve said

Cole explained he thought they would be attacked the next night.

"Do you think it'll be Control contractors?" Katie asked.

"Could be. Or Russians. Or Cartel. Or maybe all of them."

"This isn't good."

"There are six of us," Danni said. "How many could they send."

"They won't allow any risk of failure," Riker said. "They'll maximize the number of attackers. If I was them I'd send in the first string and hold the others back for the second attack."

"So, we can say lots."

"Definitely lots."

"What defense strategy did you come up with?" Blake asked.

"We stay alive until we can shoot everyone," Riker said.

"Wow," Katie said. "Did that take all night to figure out?"

"We thought it up over dessert."

"I have some better ideas," Katie said. "My dad thought he could be attacked by a mafia gang that wanted him dead. So he set up non-lethal defensive measures. We can use them."

"Why non-lethal?" Blake asked.

"He knew if he killed most of a gang they would retaliate. The war would go on forever and the only ones that would win are the cops. If he could incapacitate them and release them as a kind gesture it might not start a gang war. He told me if it didn't work he could always kill them later."

"You must have had some great bedtime stories," Eve said.

“Some kept me up at night.”

“Did he win?” Riker asked.

“He did a catch and release. They came back the next night and he had to kill them all.”

“Then I guess we go lethal,” Cole said.

“Yeah. I guess you’re right.”

“The contractors will have orders to capture and torture us until they get the files,” Riker said. “Then they’ll kill us. Have no doubts about that.”

They looked at each other. They knew he was right, but they didn’t want anyone to say it out loud.

“What’s our plan?” Danni asked.

“I want the Director to be here. She caused the problems, so she can be part of the solution.”

“How do we get her here?”

“We tell her we’ll give her the files. I’m guessing she’ll keep her men outside. When she leaves she’ll tell them to go into the house and kill us.

“What do we do tonight?” Danni asked.

“We have a party. Life is too short not to have fun.”

“I’m not in the party mood.”

“We need to make it look like we have no idea they’re coming for us. Let’s set up a drinks table and put on some music. I’ll bring out some food. Then some of us should go in the pool and hot tub.”

“I’ll do the hot tub,” Danni said. “I don’t want to swim for a while.”

“I’ll be your hot tub lifeguard,” Blake said.

They played some music and did as they discussed. People drink more when they think they could die the next day. Riker and Eve sat by the drinks table while Katie and Cole got in the pool. Danni got in the hot tub with Blake.

"For someone as smart as you I'm surprised you're so brave," Blake said.

"Are the two things exclusive?"

"You have to be dumb to risk your life doing things for other people. A whole ton of people died being brave and I bet no one remembers their names."

"True. And the dumb ones in my school got laid the most," Danni said, having her fourth tequila. "I wanted to get laid more in school. I didn't even get to experiment with another girl in college. It seems so unfair."

"You can make up for it now."

Danni looked at her and smiled. She leaned toward her and kissed her, then sat back.

"Why are you stopping?" Blake said.

"This is not how I want to do this. Too many people in the room."

The party continued with Eve pushing Riker into the pool and jumping in after him. Cole kept looking around the area and towards the house.

"Relax," Katie said. "The alarm system will tell us if anyone is coming."

"I don't want any of my friends getting hurt."

"You can't control that."

"I know."

"How about I take your mind off it? Let's go to bed."

"That would work. You should have been a psychologist."

After they left the others partied for another two hours. None of them noticed the two men watching them from the treeline. They were there to make sure no one escaped.

****

In the morning Cole came on the deck and began cleaning up dishes and glasses. He took a bikini top out of the hot tub and put it on a chair. Danni came from her room.

“That yours?” he asked.

“It’s Blakes. I like her, but I found out only men work for me.”

“As long as a person knows what they like that’s all that matters. I’ll make a pot of coffee.”

“I’ll keep cleaning up.”

As the others wandered out they helped. After breakfast, they gathered around the deck.

“I called the Director,” Cole said. “She’s coming to visit us after dinner.”

“We have to get supplies for the fight,” Riker said. “Eve and I will go. We can get into Control’s weapons room to get what we need.”

“I’m going to go into Controls computers,” Danni said. “I can get access to the booking system and see what contractors are coming. Maybe I can get a count.”

“Won’t they know you did it?”

“I’ll delete the logs. What are you going to do, Blake?”

“I was told to report as soon as I got back. I’ll go to control and give a fake update, then come back here.”

"They might not let you go."

"I'll be okay."

"Katie and I will find defense positions for all of us," Cole said. "And we'll plan an escape route if we need it. Everyone needs to be back here by dinner." He looked around the table. "Anyone want to give a pep talk?"

No one spoke.

Chapter 82

Everyone returned for dinner that night, although no one ate much. Later in the evening, the Director showed up. She sat in the dining room with them.

"It's good to see all of you again," the Director said. "I understand you have the video files. I'd like them now. I have another appointment."

"That's not why I asked you here," Cole said. "And I don't want to play word games. We know you betrayed us."

"Don't be ridiculous."

"I don't care the reason. I do care you put my team in extreme danger."

"We can talk about this in the morning. I told you I have an appointment."

"We know you have a hit team outside. I'm sure that's the reason you're in such a hurry to leave."

"Did you forget I'm your boss? You work for me. I gave you a mission and I want the videos."

"You gave up being our boss when you lied to us."

She looked at Cole, then the others. “Fine. If you give me the videos I’ll call off the hit.”

“How many are coming?” Cole said.

She looked at him, pausing before speaking. “Six.”

“She’s lying,” Danni said. “The booking system said twelve.”

“Cuff her to the stairs,” Cole said.

Riker cuffed one of her wrists to the stair railing.

The director kept pulling on it as if it would break. “You’ll pay for this. All of you will pay.”

“If you’re lucky your men will figure out it’s you before they shoot,” Riker said.

“Three SUVs are at the front of the driveway,” Danni said, staring at the security cameras on her laptop. Four got out of each of them. “That’s our twelve attackers. All with rifles using silencers. ETA two minutes.”

“Put on your bulletproof vests,” Cole said. “And use your silencers We don’t want to wake the neighbors and have the cops show. Take your positions.”

“Uncuff me!” the Director yelled. They heard the fear in her voice.

“Screw you.” Cole went to the garage and turned off the breakers, plunging the house into darkness. His team dispersed, each moving to their locations. The only light came from the streetlamps and neighbor’s houses. The men split as they approached the house, some going to the back. One man slammed the front door lock with a battering ram, and they moved inside.

At the back, they passed the pool. It was too dark to see under the surface. They moved toward the deck doors.

Riker rose so his eyes were above the water. He hit the water gently and sank below again. One of the men heard it. He turned and walked towards the pool, his rifle raised and ready to shoot. Riker fired his crossbow from just under the water. The bolt shot through the surface and pierced the man's chin. He fell into the water.

Another man turned. He moved in a crouch toward his partner. Riker stood, the water falling off him. He fired. It hit the man in the chest. He fired again and hit his stomach. Riker sunk below the surface and moved to a different location. An attacker fired a burst at the pool, not knowing where Riker was. He ran toward the water, firing more bursts.

Eve stood on a branch using the tree trunk for support. She lined up the crosshairs on the man's temple. She squeezed the trigger. The man moving towards Riker collapsed into the water. The rest were in the house. Eve put four shots through the doors. She checked her night scope. The Director was slumped forward, holding her upper leg.

"Oops, bitch," Eve said.

A man entered the garage and found the breaker box. As he opened it to turn on the power Cole stepped behind him. He rammed his knife into the side of the man's neck, pulling it out as he fell. Cole went back into the house, entering into a hallway.

A man was walking down it. He fired a burst at Cole. He would have been hit but Katie ran at him from the bedroom and knocked him into an open laundry room door. She fired at the attacker. He ducked into a room. Katie walked down the hall and fired into the wall where she thought he was. She fired another burst. The man dropped across the doorway entrance.

Three men began going up the stairs. Blake waited until the first one reached the top. She fired from a bedroom door and ran at him, kicking him backward. The man fired as he fell back, knocking the others down the stairs. Danni ran out and fired burst after burst into the tangled bodies.

She grabbed Blake by the arm and dragged her back into the bedroom. Blake was holding her shoulder, blood seeping through her fingers. The bullet hit near the top of it. Danni wrapped a bandage over the wound to stop the bleeding.

"I'm good," Blake said. "Go."

Danni entered the hallway. She saw rifle flashes near the deck doorway. On the other side of the room, she saw Katie and Cole returning fire. Katie stepped out too far and Cole moved in front of her to protect her. He kept firing. The attackers fired a burst. Cole jerked backward and he and Katie hit the ground.

"No!" Danni screamed. She leaned over the railing and pointed her rifle down at the men. She held the trigger down until it clicked. Return fire shattered the railing. Before she could step back she felt a sharp pain in her hand. She fell with her back to the wall, cursing herself for doing something so stupid, but she knew she got one.

Blake crawled out to her and looked at her hand. She took a bandage from her pocket and wrapped it around the wound.

"It didn't go through," Blake whispered. "It grazed the side. You'll be okay."

The last three men backed out through the deck doors, still firing inside. Riker rose from the water and fired a bolt into the back of one of them. Eve shot the man beside him in the head. The last man turned. He couldn't find her in the trees. She fired twice into his chest.

The noise was replaced with silence and the smell of gunpowder. No one moved. No one knew if there were wounded waiting for a final kill.

Blake and Danni eased down the stairs, stepping over the bodies. None of the attackers showed signs of life. Katie was kneeling over Cole. He was gasping for breath. She helped him take off his body armor and opened his shirt.

"Jesus," Katie said.

Riker examined Cole's chest. "You have some cracked ribs. Maybe one is broken. Who else is hit?"

"Blake took one in the shoulder," Danni said.

"I'm good," Blake said.

Riker looked at Danni's hand.

"It's not serious," Danni said.

Riker helped Cole up and took him to the car. Katie was phoning the doctor to meet them at the museum apartment.

Danni looked at Blake's wound, then they followed Riker. She helped Blake into the car, watching as they sped off. She turned and walked back to the house. Eve was checking for signs of life. They heard someone groan. It was the Director.

"You did all this," Danni said.

“Grow up, Danni,” she said, her head facing down as she held her leg where she was shot. “Uncuff me and maybe I won’t send all of you to a black site for the rest of your goddamn lives.”

Danni stood over her. She took Eve’s gun in her good hand, aimed at the Director’s head, and fired. After pausing she gave the gun back to Eve and sat on the stairs next to the Director’s body, exhaustion overcoming her.

“I never liked her,” Danni said.

“Come on, sweety,” Eve said. “Let’s go to the museum. We have friends there.”

“She was so mean.”

“I know. Pretty sure she regrets it now.”

Chapter 83

Danni and Eve stood in the elevator. When Eve reached for the top floor button Danni touched her hand to stop her.

"When I first did field work I was terrified I would be killed," she said. "Now I'm terrified one of you will be killed."

Without speaking Eve wrapped her arms around Danni for a moment. "We all feel the same way." She kissed Danni's cheek, then pressed the button. When the elevator doors opened they saw Katie in the living room with Riker.

"How's Cole?" Danni asked.

"The doc's working on him," Katie said.

"What about Blake?"

"She's in the bedroom. Doc fixed her and she's resting. Are you guys hurt?"

"Nothing serious," Danni said getting two glasses and filling them. She handed one to Eve.

They sat in silence for a long time until the doctor came out.

"Blake's going to be okay. She needs a couple of weeks of recovery. Cole has three cracked ribs. I'll have to get him to X-ray in the morning, but as far as I can tell none are broken."

"He'll be okay?" Katie asked.

"He'll be good as new."

Katie nodded and gulped her drink. The doctor rebandaged Danni's hand.

"You guys need to stop getting shot at for a while," the doctor said.

"Tell the shooters," Riker said.

The doctor nodded and took the elevator.

"What happened in the house after we left?" Riker said.

"Danni put a bullet into the Director's head," Eve said.

"Thank you," Katie said.

Danni nodded but said nothing.

"We should get some sleep," Riker said. "Tomorrow is going to be a busy day."

"What about the bodies in my house?" Katie said.

"Control will already have a cleanup crew there," Danni said. "They'll send in a construction crew in the morning. No one will know it happened."

"I'll stay with Blake in case she wakes up and needs anything," Danni said, filling her glass.

"We'll see you guys in the morning," Eve said.

When Danni walked into the bedroom Blake was awake and sitting up.

"How are you?" Danni asked.

"The painkillers kicked in. What about your hand?"

"I can still type. I'll stay with you tonight."

"That's nice of you. Want some of my painkillers? They're really good."

"I don't want anything with the word killers in it. I'll stick to drinking."

****

The next morning Riker and Eve were up first. They were explaining to William what happened.

"That's the second director that was evil," William said. "I'm seeing a trend."

"What happens now?" Eve asked.

"They appoint a new Director, and we start again."

Katie came in and sat with a cup of coffee.

"How's Cole?" Eve asked.

"He slept last night. I didn't. I woke up every time he moved."

They waited until Blake and Danni came in.

"How are you guys?" Katie asked.

"Danni babysat me, which was nice," Blake said.

Katie stood when she saw Cole coming in. "Shouldn't you stay in bed?"

"I'm hungry. What are you guys talking about?"

"I'm wondering what happens next," Katie said.

"I'll talk to Sofia. Then we broadcast the videos of the ex-president and VP talking to the cartels and the Russians."

"The Mexican people aren't going to be happy," Danni said. "The VP will be kicked out of office."

"I think they'll torture him to give up the names of his partners," Riker said.

"I'm hoping Sofia will do some news interviews to ask the people to help them fight the cartels."

"It'll make her a bigger target," Katie said.

"That's why I'm going to ask her. If she says no we'll find another way."

"She's got a lot of guts," Riker said. "I doubt she'll say no."

"The Mexicans are going to want the Russians to get out of their country once they find out there could be a war with the States."

"I agree," Eve said. "The new president will run on making that happen."

"What do we do now?" Riker asked.

"We take a break," Danni said. "Cole and Blake need to recover."

"I meant after that."

"I'd like to leave Control," Cole said.

"Quit?" Riker said. "I can't. This is what I do."

"Quit Control, not each other. We have a great team. We can accept our own contracts."

They looked at each other, wondering what the others would think before they said anything.

"I don't trust Control anymore," Eve said. "I like the idea."

"If we keep the team together I'm in," Riker said.

"I'll talk to T-Rex later, but I'm sure he'll join us," Katie said. "We could concentrate on the American cartels. We can only fix Mexican problems if we fix ours."

"Danni?" Cole said.

Danni looked at Cole, then around the table. “You guys are the best friends I’ve ever had. I’m in.”

“Blake?”

“It feels good to be part of a team. Plus I have more work to do on Danni. I’m in.”

“William,” Cole said. “Will you stay with us?”

“Before I say yes I need to apologize.”

“What for?” Katie said.

“I seem to be very bad at hiring directors.”

“What are you talking about?” Cole said.

“I started Control to honor my daughter, but I didn’t want to run it.”

“You’re the big boss?” Cole said. “Why didn’t you tell us?”

“More than anything else in my life, I want peace. At the same time, I want to do some good in the world. Without your team, I don’t think I can do that. Will you stay and help me?”

Katie stood and hugged him, then patted his back. “I’m not sucking up to the boss. I just love what you’re doing.”

Cole shook his hand. “You’re a good man, William. If you stay in charge I’ll stay with you.

“Me too,” Riker said.

“And me,” Eve said.

Blake looked at him. “Okay. I’ll give it a chance.”

“Danni?” William said.

“These guys would be going back to typewriters without me. I’ll stay.”

“Thank you all. I promise to get better at hiring directors.”

"Our team needs a name," Danni said. "Something cool."

"And a logo," Eve said. "How about a T-Rex?"

"Yes! I love you so much right now," Katie said.

"On to new adventures," Danni said. She raised her coffee cup, and they all toasted the future.

Made in the USA
Columbia, SC
27 July 2024

ce4e656a-af4a-43eb-86e5-c5dbc05aeebcR03